A Bibliographical and Critical Account of the Rarest Books in the English Language

Collier, John Payne

Contents

A BIBLIOGRAPHICAL AND CRITICAL

ACCOUNT OF THE RAREST BOOKS IN

THE ENGLISH LANGUAGE

BY

Collier, John Payne

Bibliographical Account

OF

EARLY ENGLISH LITERATURE.

SABIE, FRANCIS.—Adam's Complaint. The Olde Worldes Tragedie. David and Bathsheba. *A Jove Musa.*—Imprinted at London by Richard Johnes, at the Rose and Crowne next above Saint Andrewes Church in Holborne. 1596. 4to.

This production is by an author who ambitiously attempted all kinds of verse,—Francis Sabie. He began with blank-verse in 1595, when he reproduced Robert Greene's "Pandosto, the Triumph of Time" (afterwards called "Dorastus and Fawnia") under the title of "The Fisherman's Tale." In the same year came out "Pan his Pipe," consisting chiefly of English hexameters; and in 1596 he published the work in our hands in rhyming stanzas. He had no great success in any department. He rendered Greene's pretty novel almost wearisome. He displayed no skill in classical measures, which he fancied were especially adapted to pastorals, because they had been used by Virgil; and his rhymes are only tolerable. He seems to have taken up the sacred subject of "Adam's Complaint," &c., because he had failed in his profane experiments.

The dedication, signed Francis Sabie, is in twelve lines to the Bishop of Peterborough, Dr. Howland, though what claim he had upon that prelate does not appear. [Note 1: From the Registers of the Stationers' Company, in an entry that has never been noticed, we find that Francis Sable was a schoolmaster at] We will give a few quotations, not for any great merit they possess, but because no specimens have hitherto been anywhere printed. Sabie's blank-verse and his hexameters, on the other hand, have received more attention than they deserve. [Note 1: See **Brit. Bibl.** I. 459, 497. **Poet. Decam.** I. 187, &c.] "Adam's Complaint" opens thus:—

"New formed Adam of the reddish earth,
Exilde from Eden, Paradice of pleasure,
By Gods decree cast down to woes from mirth,
From lasting joyes to sorrowes out of measure,
Fetch'd many a sigh, comparing his estate
With happie blisse, which he forewent of late."

It may be too nice to object to the tautology of "happy bliss," especially in Sabie's case, with whom it is a not unfrequent ornament; and after calling upon his Muse "to rowse herself," as if in fear that her aid might not be sufficient, he implores "great Jehovah, heaven's great architect," to direct his "fainting Muse," while she essays "the horrors to rehearse" of the task he has un¬dertaken. Adam then narrates his fall and its consequences, not very charitably, or gallantly, laying the blame upon his wife:—

"O wretched Evah! mankinds deadly foe,
Accursed Grandame, most ungentle mother,
Sin-causing woman, bringer of mans woe,
Woe to thy selfe, and woe unto all other!
Thy mighty maker, in his just displeasure,
Hath multiplied thy sorrowes out of measure."

In the end Adam foresees the redemption of man through a vista of thousands of years, and is rapturously grateful for it.

The "Old World's Tragedy" is the story of the Flood; and after some pieces of exaggerated description we arrive at this bathos:—

Lichfield, and in 1587 bound his son Edmond apprentice to Robert Cullen, Stationer:—

"12 Junij Edmond Sable, sonn of Francis Sabie of Lichefield in the countie of Stafford, Scholmaister, hath putt himself apprentise to Robert Cullen, citizen and stationer of London, for the terme of seven yeres from the date hereof."

The usual fee of 2*s.* 6*d.* was paid to the Company on the occasion. It is not stated whether the father was a clergyman as well as a schoolmaster. It seems probable that he was so, although we do not meet with Sabie's name in the records of either University.

"Some upon roofes and turrets high did clime:
One takes the highest mountain he can see;
Another sits a fishing in a tree."

We are also told that,—

"Twise twenty dayes, as blacke as any cole,
The murthering raine distilled from the Pole;"

and when the earth was covered with waters, that

"The Dolphins woonder under watrie floods
To see faire turrets and thicke growing woods:
In steed of sacrifice on Altars faire,
Sit seemly Marmaydes combing of their haire;
In Churches eke, their Organists now wanting,
Melodious Odes and ditties now recanting."

This etymological use of the verb to "recant" is not usual, though we have it in Spenser in a sort of double sense,—"Till he recanted had his wicked rhymes."

Sabie's compound epithets are now and then amusing; "bristle-bearing boar" is not bad, but we have also the following:—

"The silly Lambe was, with the ravening Wolfe,
Drown'd in the vast no-pitie-taking gulfe."

"Stark" is well applied in describing the beasts leaving the ark; but perhaps Sabie was helped to it, as Dryden admits that sometimes he had been, by the rhyme. The huge creatures

"Alive on earth came forthwith from the arke,
There stretcht their limmes, unweldy yet, and starke."

In the third portion of the work, which relates to David and Bathsheba, (here, though not on the title-page, called Beersheba,) the author is not very sparing of "the man after God's own heart." He first describes David's vain conflict with himself:—

"And now begins the combatant assault
Betweene the willing flesh and nilling spirit;
The flesh alluring him unto the fault,
The spirit tells him of a dreadful merit;
And, in the end, flesh conquered the spirit.
He sends, she came, he woos, she gave consent,
And did the deed, not fearing to be shent."

Just afterwards Sabie thus reproaches David:—

"Oblivious Prophet, call to minde thine oth:
Thou vowdst to keepe the covenant of the Lord,
More sweet, thou saydst, then combe or honey both,
More deare then Gems which Tagus doth afford:

Thou brag'dst thou joyedst only in his word.
Chose he not thee his tender lambes to keepe,
And, like a Wolfe, wilt thou devoure the sheep?"

Ultimately David, having "warbled out an ode," repents, and the last stanza
is,—

"Thus did the Psalmist warble out his plaints,
And ceaseth not from day to day to mone:
His heart with anguish of his sorrowe faints,
And still he kneels before his maker's throne;
At midnight sends he manie a grievous grone.
So did his God in mercie on him looke,
And all his sinnes did race out of his booke.

Finis F. S."

SACK-FULL OF NEWS.—The Sackfull of News—Some Lyes and some
Truths.—Printed at London by T. Cotes for F. Grove and are to be sold at his Shop
on Snow Hill, neare the Saracins head. 1640. 8vo. B. L.

This is a reimpression of an old jest-book, certainly in existence anterior to the
year 1575, when we find it mentioned by Langham in his "Letter from Kenilworth,"
as part of the library of Captain Cox,—"the Churl and the Burd, the seaven wise
Masters, the wife lapt in a Morels skin, *the sak full of nuez,* the Seargeaunt that
became a Fryar," &c.; (see Vol. II. p. 228.) It had been entered in the Stationers'
Registers, and no doubt printed, almost at the commencement of the existence of
the Company, in the following terms, the date being 1557-58:—

"To John Kynge these bokes folowynge, called a nose gaye; the scole bowse of
women; and also *a sacket full of newes* . . . . xijd."

Again, in the year 1581-82, on the 15th January, we find John Charlwood pay-ing for the registration of a number of works, including "A pennyworth of witte; A hundred merry tales; Adam Bell; The banishment of Cupid; Crowley's Epigrams; A Fox Talc; Kinge Pontus; Robin Conscience; A proude wyves p[ate]rn[oste]r; *A Sackefull of newes;* Sr. Eglamore," &c. There was, it is true, an early drama so named, which a company of players was prevented from acting on the 5th of September, 1557, (Hist. Engl. Dram. Poetry and the Stage, I. 162,) but it is quite clear, from the company in which the "Sack-full of News" was placed by Kynge, as well as Charlwood, that they entered the Jest-book and not the Drama. Five years afterwards, 5th September, 1587, it was entered to Edward White in this form:—

"Edward White. Rd of him for *a sackfull of newes,* being an old copie, which the said Eward is ordered to have printed by Abell Jeffes vjd."

It was, in all probability, called "an old copy," because it was to be a reimpression of the work that had been licensed to Kynge in 1558, and to Charlwood in 1582. How many reimpressions it went through between 1557 and 1673 it is vain to speculate; but at the latter date it still bore the title of "The Sack-full of Newes," although the second part of the title, as we find it in 1640, in the edition under consideration, was dropped. It was probably meant, in the poetical license of popular literature of the reign of Charles I., that "news" and "truths" should be taken as rhymes; and whether such was the title it anciently bore must remain uncertain, until, by some chance, a copy of an earlier date than the one we have used be discovered.

We take it for granted that the number and character of the jests were the same in all editions. We are sure that they are the same in the only two known impressions of 1640 and 1673, without even a verbal variation. Differences of spelling were of course to be expected, but even these are few, and in no respect change the meaning of a single sentence. The main discordance is, that in the copy of 1640 the jests are numbered, while in that of 1673 they are not numbered. We quote the second as one of the shortest, and certainly one of the best. It speaks of times anterior to the Reformation, thus affording some proof of the antiquity of the collection.

"2. *Another.*

"There was a fryer in London which did use to goe often to the house of an old woman, but ever when he came to her house she hid away all the meate she had. On a time this Fryer came to her house bringing certain companie with him, and demaunded of the wife if she had any meat? And she said nay. Well, quoth the fryer, have you not a whetstone? Yea, quoth the woman, what will you do with it? Mary, qd he, I would make meate thereof. Then she brought the whetstone. He asked her likewise if she had not a frying pan? Yea, said she; but what the divell will you do therewith? Mary, said the Fryer you shall see by and by what I will doe with it. And when he had the pan, he set it on the fire, and put the whetstone therein. Cocks body, said the woman, you will burn the pan. No, no, quod the fryer; if you will give me some eggs it will not burn at all. But she would have had the pan from him when that she saw it was in danger; yet he would not let her, but still urged her to fetch him some eggs, which she did. Tush! said the Fryer, here are not enow: go fetch me ten or twelve. So the good wife was constrayned to fetch more for feare lest the pan should burn: and when he had them he put them in the pan. Now, qd he, if you have no butter the pan will burn and the eggs to[o]. So the good wife being very loth to have her pan burnt and her egges lost, she fetcht him a dish of butter, the which he put into the pan, and made good meate thereof, and brought it to the table, saying much good may it doe you, my masters; now may you say you have eaten of a buttered whetstone. Whereat all the com¬pany laughed, but the woman was exceeding angrie because the Fryer had subtilly beguiled her of her meate."

Another very ancient jest in this little volume is the 13th, which may carry us as far back as to the year 1537, when the interlude of "Thersites" was written, though it was not printed until between the years 1550 and 1563. We quote the punning jest first from "the Sack-full of News":—

"13 *Another.*

"A man there was that had a child borne in the north Countrey, and upon a time this man had certain guests, and he prepared sallets and other meate for them;

and bid his boy go into the cellar and take the sallet there (meaning the herbs) and lay them in a platter, and put vineger and oile thereto. Now the boy had never seen a Ballet eaten in his Countrey; but he went, and looking about the cellar at last he espied a rusty Ballet of steel sticking on the wall, and said to him selfe, What will my master doe with this in a platter? So downe he took it, and put it into a platter and put oile and vineger unto it, and brought it to the table. Why, thou knave (quoth his master) I bid thee bring the herbes which we call a Ballet. Now, by my sires sawle (said the boy) I did never see such in my countrey. Whereat the guests laughed heartily."

This equivoque is more humorously and pointedly put in "Thersites," in a dialogue between the hero and Mulciber, whom Thersites employs to make him a new suit of armor.

"*Thertites.* Nowe, I pray to Jupiter that thon dye a cuckolde:
I meane a sallet with which men doe fight.

Mulciber. It is a small tastinge of a marines mighte
That he shoulde, for any matter,
Fyght with a few heroes in a platter:
No great laude shoulde folowe that victorye.

Thersites. Goddes passion, Mulciber, where is thy wit and memory?
I wold have a sal let made of stele.

Mulciber. Whye, syr, in your stomacke longe you shall it fele,
For stele is harde to digest."

Thus we see how curiously, and appositely, one old book sometimes illustrates another. The whole number of jests in the edition of 1640 is twenty-two, and they were not increased in 1678. Of the drama of "The Sack-full of News," which the players at the Boar's Head in Aldgate were anxious to represent in the reign of Queen Mary, we can give no account, as it is not now in existence: the copy used by the actors was seized by the Lord Mayor of that day, and forwarded immediately to the Privy Council. As there is nothing dramatic in the Jest-book, we may presume that the similarity was only in the popular name.

SAKER, AUSTEN.—Narbonus. The Laberynth of Libertie. Very pleasant for young Gentlemen to peruse, and passing profitable for them to prosecute. Wherein is contained the discommodities that insue by following the lust of a mans will in youth: and the good-nesse he after gayneth, being beaten with his owne rod, and pricked with the peevishnesse of his owne conscience in age. Written by Austen Saker of New Inne.—Imprinted at London by Richard Jhones, and are to be solde at his shop overagainst S. Sepulchres Church without Newgate. 1580. 4to. B. L. 135 *leaves.*

We never saw or heard of more than a single copy of this unrecorded romance. It was entered at Stationers' Hall on the 8th March, 1579-80, in a peculiar manner, and the clerk obviously could not read or understand the hard word with which the title commences. The form was this:—

"viij die Marcij.

"Richard Jones. Lycenced unto him a booke intituled the—of libertye, written by Augustine Saker, gent. upon the said Richard Jones his promise to bring the wholle impression thereof into the hall, in case it be disliked when it is printed. By me Richarde Jones.

xijd and a copy."

In the margin a note is added stating that "this book is intituled the Labirinth of Libertye," and hitherto all that has been known of it was derived merely from the entry; (Herbert, *Typ. Ant.* p. 1053.) It is in two parts, each, perhaps for the sake of speed, by a different printer. We have given the general title-page above, and the title-page of Part II. runs in these explanatory terms: "Narbonus. The seconde parte of the Lust of Libertie. Wherin is conteyned the hap of Narbonus, beeing a

Souldioure: his retume out of Spayne, and the successe of his love betweene him and Fidelia. And listly his life at the Emperoures Court, with other actions which happenned to his friend Phemocles. By the same Authour. A. S.—Imprinted at London by Willyam How for Richard Johnes. 1580." The probability therefore is, that Jones, wishing to publish the work in a hurry, would not wait until his own types were disengaged from the first part, and employed How to print the second part for him.

In the dedication of four pages to Sir Thomas Parrat, Knight, the author speaks of himself as a young man, or at all events as a young author, but we know no more of him:—"Expect not, then, I beseech you, of this plant, but of two yeares grafting, so much fruite as from the tree of twentie yeares growing; for the apprentice must cast any bill before he keepe his maisters booke; and the shoemaker must learne to fashion a latchet before he sowe on a laste. So this simple author must lie in Diogenes tub before his writing like his owne fantasye, and put on Socrates gowne before his dooings please all favours." Afterwards he terms him¬self "a rusticall writer," perhaps living in the country, and is not sparing of alliteration, which he clearly considered a valuable ornament of style. "No marveile," ho observes, "if amongst many readers some prove riders; but let them laugh to see if I will lowre."

In an address of two pages "to the gentlemen Readers," he tells them that he bad long paused to consider whether he should give his "troublesome trashe" to a printer; but at last, he adds, "I thought my booke might as well lie in a shop, as other ballads which stand at sale," and he therefore handed over the MS. of his first production to a stationer. In the commencement the scene is laid in Vienna, but the author obviously means London, and describes its manners; especially touching upon the public theatres, which at that date (1580) had recently been constructed. In one place he remarks, "the Theatres could not stand except Narbonus were there, nor the plaies goe forwarde unless he trimmed the stage:" this we take to be an early authority for the feet, that young gallants delighted to display themselves and their gay apparel by sitting on stools upon the stage. Elsewhere Saker warns young people of all things to shun plays and players. "Thou mayst for recreation use the Tennis Courtes, and the dauncing schole to refresh thy weary spirits; but the

Theatres in any wise refraine, and all such mischevous motions." This was just the period when the Curtain and the Theatre, as it was called in Shoreditch, and the private playhouse in the Black-friars, (built about 1576 or 1577,) to say nothing of the temporary stages in inn-yards, were absolutely proscribed by the Puritans.

Saker also cautions his readers against gaming and sharpers, and gives an account of the various kinds of false dice then in use, some of which were afterwards enumerated by more popular writers. He says: "Here walked another mannerly mate with a paire of blanckes, and a paire of flattes, a pair of langrets, and a paire of stopt dice, a paire of barde quater treis, and other dice of vauntage."

The first part of Narbonus concludes with a promise of the second part, as if it had been originally intended to publish them separately.

The story, from the beginning to the end, is excessively tedious, ill conducted, and barren of incidents, while no interest is felt for either hero or heroine. The events are supposed to take place soon after the abdication of Charles V., for one of the persons in the narrative remarks: "I commend our noble Emperour, Charles, for his prowesse, but I blame his wisedome in this respect; in youth so noble a servitour, and now to take in age the courtesie of a cloyster." There is not a scrap of verse of any kind throughout the 269 pages to which the first and second parts extend: the prose is stiff and stilted, and alliteration comes in, now and then, as a sort of relief and lightening of the burden of the narrative.

At the end Saker seems to have felt that he must have wearied his reader, and in "the Authors conclusion," which winds up the work, he deprecates severity of criticism, and promises something better if Narbonus be received with favor. He signs it "Finis. A. S.," but we never hear of him afterwards: even his name does not occur in our bibliography.

SALTER, THOMAS.—A Mirrhor mete for all Mothers, Matrones and Maidens, intituled the Mirrhor of Modestie, no lesse profitable and pleasant, then necessarie to bee read and practised. A pretie and pithie Dialogue betweene Mercurie and

Vertue.—Imprinted at London for Edward White, at the little Northdore of Paules at the Signe of the Gun. 8vo. B. L. 34 *leaves.*

"We never inspected more than a solitary copy of this prose puritanical production, but in the new edition of Lowndes (***Bibl. Man.*** p. 2180) we are informed, we think erroneously, that two are in existence. It is on many accounts highly curious and amusing, giving us much information regarding the education and habits of young ladies at the date of its publication, probably 1579-80, when it was entered by White at Stationers' Hall. E. W. (probably Edward White) dedicated it to Lady Anne Lodge, the wife of Sir Thomas, at one period Lord Mayor of London, and whose son, Thomas Lodge, figures so conspicuously in our second volume, as dramatist, novelist, and lyric poet The name of the author of the "Mirrhor of Modestie" does not appear until near the conclusion, when it intervenes thus,—

"***Finis*** qd Thomas Salter
Ne ça ne la,"

between the principal subject and a short dialogue, of which we shall say more presently, held by Mercury and Virtue: at the close of that colloquy Salter only places his initials, T. S. An introductory "Epistle to all Mothers, Matrones, and Maidens of England" is not subscribed, and the main purpose of it is to impress upon them "the greate abuse that, by the default of good bringing up, many of our Englishe Maidens doe daiely runne into, to the great reproche of their Parentes, hartes grief of their kinsfolke, infamie of their persones, and (whiche is moste to be lamented) losse of their soules." This theme Salter follows up with great zeal and edification in the body of his work, and ere long we arrive at the following censure of the mode in which "unwise fathers" educated their daughters.

"Before I passe farther, I will stave to shew the use of many unwise Fathers, who beyng more daintye and effeminate in following their pleasures, then wise and diligent in seeking the profite of their Daughters, doe give them, so sone as they have any understandyng in reading or spelling, to cone, and learne by hart bookes, ballades, songes, sonettes and ditties of daliance, excityng their memories thereby, beyng then moste apt to retayne for ever that whiche is taught them, &c. therefore I would wish our good Matrone to eschew such use as a pestilent infection."

He quotes, as might be expected, the examples of Claudia, Portia, and Lucretia; and addressing himself especially to mothers, he exhorts them "to remove detestable dangers from yong maidens," and on no account to "permit them to have acquaintaunce with kitchine servauntes, or such idle housewives as commonly, and of custome, doe thrust them selves into the familiarities of those of good callyng." He inveighs against such parents even as allow their daughters to read "Prudentio, Prospero, Juvenco, Pawlino, and Nazianzeno," because in that case they will be sure to deviate into "the lascivious bookes of Ovide, Catullus, Propertius, Tibullus, and in Virgill of Eneas and Dido, and amonge the Greeke poettes of the filthie love (if I maie terme it love) of the Goddes themselves, and their wicked adul¬teries and abhominable fornications, as in Homer and suche like."

It is to be hoped that his own work would not fall in their way, for if it did, it would at least show young ladies where impurities were to be found. He adds here:—

"For such as compare the small profit of learnyng with the greate hurt and domage that commeth to them by the same, shall sone perceive (although that they remaine obstinate therein) how far more convenient the Distaffe and Spindle, Nedle and Thimble were for them, with good and honest reputation, then the skill of well using a penne, or wrightyng a loftie vearce with diffame and dishonour."

Elsewhere he shows that he has not much admiration for what he, nevertheless, well calls "lofty verse" (and Milton, long after him, "lofty rhyme"), but does not omit to inform us, in the following brief paragraph, the sort of reading to which he would limit the fair sex. "And yet, notwithstandyng al this, I would not have a maiden altogether forbidden or restrained from reading, for so muche as the same is not onely profitable to wise and vertuous women, but also a riche and precious jewell; but I would have her, if she reade, to reade no other bookes but suche as bee written by godlie Fathers to our instruction and soules healthe, and not suche lascivious Songes, filthie Ballades and undecent bookes as be moste commonly, now a daies, sette to sale." He does not exclude Plutarch, nor even "Boccas," from their studies; but he, of course, means Boccaccio's De prœclaris Mulieribus, not his variegated "Decameron." He would especially have girls taught household duties, to see that "the chambers are kept cleanly," and even to note how the servants "laye leven" for baking the bread of the family.

All this is enforced with considerable enlargement and redu¬plication, after which we arrive at "A pretic pithie Dialogue betwene Mercurie and Vertue,"— made by T. S., which occupies the last nine pages, and betrays considerable cleverness, both satirical and ironical. He supposes Virtue "poorely apparrelled," and "evill intreated both of Gods and men, and in this wise disdained and abandoned" to petition Jupiter for redress of grievances; and it seems odd that, even in an invention of the kind, so severe a Puritan should allow himself to treat the heathen gods and goddesses as really existing beings, and capable of influencing and regulating the affairs of mankind. Mercury is sent down by Jupiter to hear the complaint of Virtue, who especially directs her attack against Fortune, who, besides other offences, had called Virtue "a presumptuous callot." Mercury can give the unfortunate lady no hope of better usage in the world, particularly since she was at enmity with Fortune; on which Virtue remarks,—

"*Vertue.* Ah! then I see how it will ensue. I must nodes retourne and hide my self for ever, as one disdained and rejected of all.

"*Mercurie.* Vertue, adiew."

And so the discussion closes.

A few years after the appearance of Salter's work, the famous Robert Greene published, as one of his first experiments in authorship, an octavo tract, of a very different character but under the same name, "The Myrrour of Modestie." It relates solely to the story of Susanna and the Elders, and the whole title-page is this:—

"The Myrrour of Modestie, wherein appeareth, as in a perfect Glasse, howe the Lorde delivereth the innocent from all imminent perils, and plagueth the bloud thirstie hypocrites with deserved punishments. Shewing that the graie heades of dooting adulterers shall not go with grace to the grave, neither shall the righteous be forsaken in the daie of trouble. By R. G. Maister of Artes.—Imprinted at London by Roger Warde, dwelling at the signe of the Talbot neere unto Holburne Conduit. 1584."

Greene only put his initials to his address to the Readers, but signed his name at length to the dedication to "Ladie Margaret, Countesse of Darbie"; and therein seems to refer to Salter's "Mirror of Modestie," observing, "I excuse my selfe with the answere that Varro made when he offred Ennius workes to the Emperour: I give you, quoth he, another mans picture, but fresh-lie flourished with mine owne coulours." Here, too, he calls his own production the "Mirrour of Chastitie," as if at that time he meant to avoid the title Salter had previously chosen; and he afterwards varies it again, calling his performance "A princelie Mirrour of peerelesse Modestie." We are not about here to enter into a particular examination of Greene's little volume, but as it was one of his earliest productions, we will quote a sentence or two from it, in order to show that, even at that date, his style was in a manner fixed, and such as he afterwards very much adhered to.

"Nowe, Susanna seeking oftentimes to be solitarie, whither to muse upon hir worldlie businesse, or to meditate upon some heavenlie motions, I know not, but it was hir custome coutinunllie about noone to walke into hir husbandes garden, which was heard adjoining to the house, and most pleasantlie scituate, seeming a second paradise, for the most fruite-full trees and flagrant flowers that there passing curiouslie were planted. These two elders, seeing hir dailie to passe awaie the time with walking in that pleasant plot, noting the exquisite perfection of hir bodie, and how she was adorned with most singular gifts of nature, began to fixe their eies uppon the forme of hir feature, and to be snared within the fetters of lust: lascivious concupiscence had alreadie charmed their thoughts, and they were droonken sodenlie with the dregs of filthie desire: they were scorched with the beames of hir beautie, and were inflamed towardes hir with inordinate affection: fond fancie had alreadie given them the foyle, and their aged haire yeelded unto vanitie, so that they tourned awaie their minds from God, and durst not lift uppe their eies to heaven, least it should be a witnesse of their wickednesse, or a corasive to their guiltie conscience; for the remembraunce of God is a terrour to the unrighteous, and the sight of his creatures a stinge to the minde of the reprobate."

In this strain he goes through the incidents of the story, never pausing to check the luxuriance of his expressions, or the indelicacy of his descriptions, adapting his story to the approbation of the more severe, and his style to the gratification of his younger readers.

Mr. Dyce, in his account of Robert Greene prefixed to his Works, p. xxxiv., tells us (as before noticed, Vol. II. p. 87,) that "the date of the earliest of his publications yet discovered is 1584." It is not easy to reconcile this statement with the date of Greene's "Mamillia," which was printed in 1583, 4to. At that time he called himself only "graduate in Cambridge," so that he had not then become, as be did soon afterwards, also a graduate of Oxford. According to the excellent authority of Messrs. Cooper (***Ath. Cantabr.*** II. 127), Greene took his degree of M. A. at Clare Hall in 1583, having been matriculated on 26th November, 1575, at St. John's. As early as 20th March, 1581, he had written a ballad entitled, "Youth seeing all his ways so troublesome, abandoning virtue and leaning to vice, recalleth his former follies with an inward repentance." In the entry of it at Stationers' Hall his Christian name was not inserted, and "By Greene" was interlined; as if the fact had been subsequently ascertained. This information also will be new to Mr. Dyce, who, as he mentions Greene's "Mamillia," 1583, committed a mere oversight when he asserted that the earliest of Greene's known publications was in 1584.

SAMPSON, THOMAS.—Fortunes Fashion, Pourtrayed in the troubles of the Ladie Elizabeth Gray, wife to Edward the fourth. Written by Tho. Sampson.—London, Printed for William Jones, and are to be sold at his shop at Whitecrosse streete end by the Church. 1613. 4to. 24 *leaves.*

The worst thing about this poem is its title, for it is by no means a contemptible piece of versification, in six-line stanzas. More than three copies of it have not survived, and though the facts are mainly derived from Stow and other chroniclers, they are not unpoetically narrated, and it was expedient that some facts should be historically stated. That Sampson did not slavishly follow authorities is evident, when we find that he makes the Queen entirely acquit her husband of infidelity as regards Jane Shore and others. Of the author nothing is known, but he dedicates his work to his "many waies indeered friend Mr. Henry Pilkington of Gadsby in the county of Leicester, gentleman," and expresses his conviction that the name of that friend will shield his work "against the many find-faults that this age is pestered with." To this is added a historical "Argument," and the poem opens with these stanzas:—

"Sometime I was, unhappie was the time
Wherein I livd, and never tasted joyes
That did not wither ere they were in prime;
Honors are such uncertaine fading toyes.
I was king Edwards wife, a wofull Queene,
As in this history may plaine be seene.

"O, had my love in my first choice remaind,
How happie had I bene, from griefe how free!
Of wofull haps I never had complaind,
But that must needs be that the fates decree.
The Cottage seated in the dale below
Stands safe, when highest towers do overthrow."

The Queen afterwards bitterly laments the loss of her first husband "slain on Henry's part," but observes that Cupid having another dart for her, she became the wife of Edward IV. Of king-maker Warwick she says, that he was

"A valiant Knight and fortunate in warre,
Ulysses-like for prudent policie;
Yet this did all his other vertues marre,

And was a blot to his posteritie,
That right or wrong, he car'd not how it was,
But as he would so things should come to passe."

To the birth of Edward V., under circumstances of much sorrow and deprivation, she thus adverts:—

"Where was my cloth of state, my canopie,
Ladies of honor to attend ray will?
Where my rich hangings of rare tapestrie,
The stateliest banquets that device or skill
Could set before us? where the songs of mirth
To tell the world we joy'd a Princes birth?"

Although he touches upon many points that had found their way to the stage in the most popular drama of the day, Sampson never alludes to Shakspeare and to the applauses he was obtaining; in this respect pursuing a very contrary course to that which Christopher Brooke had taken in his very able poem, "The Ghost of Richard the Third," (see Vol. I. p. 114.) Thomas Hey wood also had produced an excellent play upon the same incidents treated in Sampson's performance, but that also he passes over without notice. Of Richard the Third and his usurpation he thus speaks:—

"When thus the Boare had seiz'd into his hand
Them whom he thought were objects in his way,
He did not long in doubtfull censure stand,
But fell to action without all delay;
Foreknowing well that he that acts an evill
Must neither thinke on God, nor feare the Devill. * * *

"Then did usurping Richard claime the Crowne;
And by the help of Buckingham he gain'd
The regall Seate, not caring who went downe

So he might hit the marke whereat he aim'd.
The Crowne by bloud and tyrannie he won,
To friend or foe regardlesse what was done."

In spite of the marriage of her daughter with Richmond, after the battle of Bosworth, the Queen complains that in the second year of the reign of Henry VII. she was deprived of most of her lands and revenues, and was dismissed to end her days in the Abbey of Bermondsey. It does not appear, until very near the conclusion of the poem, that Sampson was prompted in its contents by a vision with which he was favored by the dead Queen; and then we learn, on her own authority, that she had reserved wealth sufficient for the foundation of Queen's College, Cambridge. Just before the close the writer introduces some well-worded, but not very novel, reflections upon the decline of greatness, among which is the following, referring to a remarkable saying by the predecessor of James I.:—

"If such the world in former times hath beene,
That highest states most subject were to fall,
How true said she that late was Englands Queene,
When she her selfe at that time was in thrall,
Loe! yonder milk-maid lives mare merrily
Then I that am of noble progenie."

Opposite the above Sampson put the subsequent note in his margin: "It was the saying of Queene Elizabeth, when she was prisoner in the time of Queen Mary." [Note: 1: She seems to have been fond of the allusion to milkmaids, for, after the trial of Mary Queen of Scots, she wrote to her victim, that, "if they had been two milkmaids with pails upon their arms," she would never have thought of depriving her of life. See Nicolas's "Life of Davison," p. 52.] The chief fault of his production is, that it is too prosaic; but our notion is, that the author was an old man at the time he wrote, and that he bore too much in mind similar heavy narrations in "The Mirror for Magistrates," which had been reprinted, with important additions by Richard Niccols, (see Vol. III. p. 45, &c.,) only three years before.

SAVILE, HENRY.—A Libell of Spanish Lies: Found at the Sacke of Cales, discoursing the fight in the West Indies twixt the English Navie, being fourteene Ships and Pinasses, and the fleete of twentie saile of the king of Spaines, and of the death of Sir Francis Drake. With an answere briefely confuting the Spanish lies, and a short relation of the fight according to truth, written by Henry Savile Esquire, employed Captaine in one of her Majesties Shippes, in the same service against the Spaniard. And also an Approbation of this discourse by Sir Thomas Baskervile, then Generall of the English fleete in that service: Avowing the maintenance thereof, personally in Armes against Don Bernaldino, if hee shall take exceptions to that which is heere set downe, touching the fight twixt both Navies, or justifie that which he hath most falsely reported in his vaine printed letter, proverb. 19. ver. 9. A false witnes shall not bee unpunished, and he that speaketh lies shall perish.—London Printed by John Windet, dwelling by Pauls Wharfe at the signe of the Crosse Keyes, and are there to be solde. 1596. 4to. 26 *leaves.*

There are two copies of this very rare historical tract in the British Museum, both imperfect, one of them wanting the four last pages, the other having lost half a leaf, while the marginal notes are cut into. There is also a copy in the Bodleian Library: that from which the above title is transcribed is therefore the fourth. It has a woodcut of a sphere at the back of the title-page, and of a ship in full sail on the last leaf.

The most interesting portion of it relates to the acts and ends of those two great naval heroes, Sir Francis Drake and Sir John Hawkins, both of whom died in the course of the voyage to which the tract applies. The origin of the publication appears to have been this:—At the siege and sack of Cadiz, under the Earl of Essex and others, a Spanish printed letter, from Don Bernaldino Delgadillo de Avellanado to Dr. Peter Flores, "President of the Contraction House for the Indies," fell into the hands of the English; and it was found to give a most false account of an engagement, or engagements, with the English fleet in the West Indies commanded by Drake and Hawkins. Capt. Savile undertook to answer it, denying or refuting the "lies" *seriatim,* and stating what he asserted and knew to be the truth. These "Spanish lies" appear to have been six in number, all separately stated and exposed in the

tract, followed by an account of "the meeting of our English Navie and the Spanish fleete, and the order of our encounter"; and this again by "Thomas Baskervile,
Knight, his approbation to this Booke,"—where he maintains the truth of all that
Savile had written, and challenges the Spaniard to single combat, if he persevered
in his falsehood.

The Spaniard in his printed letter had stated, among other things, that Sir Francis Drake had died "for grief that he had lost so many barks and men." Savile denies
that he had lost more than one small pinnace, and thus proceeds: "This, I think, in
wise men's judgements, will seeme a seely cause to moove a man [to] sorrowe to
death. For true it is, Sir Fraunces Drake dyed of the Flixe, which hee had growne
uppon him eight daies before his death, and yeelded up his spirite, like a Christian,
to his creatour quietly in his Cabbin. And when the Generall shall survey his losses,
he shall finde it more then the losse of the English, and the most of his destroyed
by the bullet: But the death of Sir Fraunces Drake was of so great comfort unto the
Spaniard, that it was thought to be a sufficient amendes, although their whole fleete
had been utterly lost"

As to the place where Drake expired, Savile says, just before the above, in an-
swering the first lie: "For it had been sufficient to have said that Fraunces Drake was
certainly dead, without publishing the lye in print by naming Nombre de Dios: for
it is most certaine Sir Fraunces Drake dyed twixt the Island of Scouda and Porte-
bella. But the Generall being ravished with the saddaine joy of this report, as a man
that bad escaped a great daunger of the enemie, doeth breake out into an insolent
kind of bragging of his valour at Sea, and heaping one lye upon another, doth not
cease untill he hath drawne them into sequences, and so doth commende them
unto Peter, the Doctor, as censour of his learned worke."

The pamphlet does not seem a very successful answer; and Savile commits the
error of magnifying the Spanish misstatements into needless importance. The letter
of Don Bernaldino, which is given in Spanish and English, seems, in our day, hardly
worth the notice that is taken of it; but at that date the death of Drake, and the real
cause of it, were attracting unusual interest and attention. Sir John Hawkins had

been treasurer of the Navy, and several of his official letters are extant; one of them, dated 1583, is before us.

SAVIOLO, VINCENTIO.—Vincentio Saviolo his Practise. In two Bookes. The first intreating the use of the Rapier and Dagger. The second, of Honor and honorable Quarrels. Both interlaced with sundrie pleasant Discourses, not unfit for all Gentlemen and Captaines that professe Amies. At London, Printed for William Mattes, &c. 1595. 4to. 152 *leaves.*

This is the work to which Touchstone, in "As you like it," Act V. sc. 4, makes such obvious allusion, his reference being to that division which is headed, "Of the manner and diversitie of Lies." These are, "Lies certaine," "conditional lies," "lies in general," "lies in particular," and "foolish lies."

It appears that Saviolo was an Italian fencing-master, born at Padua, patronized and employed by Lord Essex. In the address "to the Reader," which succeeds the dedication, he speaks of his foreign birth and travels. "The first book," which is conducted in dialogue, is furnished with a number of woodcuts, perhaps from Italian designs, to illustrate the employment of the rapier and dagger.

The whole is dedicated to the Earl of Essex, the author pro¬fessing to have been "bound by the bounty" of "the English Achilles." He laments that he had not "copie [*i. e.* plenty] of English to have expressed his meaning as he would."

"The second book" has a separate preface, in which the author apologizes for his insufficiency, and it bears the date of 1594, the year, perhaps, in which it was originally intended to bring out the whole work. The last chapter relates to "the nobility of Women," which no doubt was introduced for the sake of the panegyric upon Queen Elizabeth, with which it enabled Saviolo to conclude.

SAXONY, THE DUKE OF.—A Defiance to Fortune. Proclaimed by Andrugio, noble Duke of Saxony, declaring his miseries, and continually crossed with unconstant Fortune, the banishment of himselfe, his wife and children. Whereunto is adjoyned the honorable Warres of Galastino, Duke of Millaine, in revenge of his wrongs, upon the trayterous Saxons. Wherin is noted a myrrour of noble patience &c. Written by H. R.—Printed at London for John Proctor, and are to be sold at his shop upon Holborne bridge. 1590. 4to. B. L. 16 *leaves.*

What is most remarkable about this romance, is, that the narrative is very continuous, regular, and not uninteresting. The adventures of the hero are not extravagant, nor improbable, and the story has no connection with celestial or diabolical agency. In fact, it is a mere prose novel, not ill calculated to give entertainment to the readers of such incidents. At the same time the style offers nothing noticeable, and we have no suggestion to make as to the ownership of the initials H. R. upon the title-page, and at the end of the dedication "to the worshipful William Borough, Esquire, comptroller of her Majesties Navy." He had been an officer of distinction in the Queen's Fleet, and in 1583 had been very successful against the pirates who at that date infested the English seas. Stow's *Ann.,* edit. 1605, p. 1175.

H. R. tells the "courteous Reader" that he had published his work, most unwillingly, at the instance of friends, who made him item as bold as the craven, in one of the battles of Edward III., whose courageous horse, against the will of the rider, carried him into the thickest of the encounter. Here H. R., nevertheless, promises to finish the subject he had thus commenced; but we never hear more of Andrugio, Duke of Saxony, the hero, or of his wife Susania, the daughter of a miller, who had tended him when wounded and left for dead by banditti. The writer is an imitator of Greene, especially in the extemporal invention of stones, birds, fishes, &c, that would answer his purpose in a simile. Thus we have "the stone quacious that freeseth within when it fryeth without," and "the hawke that will never be called to that lure, wherein the pennes of a Camelion are pricked." It is the first and only time we hear that a chameleon was then clothed with feathers.

It is useless to pursue in any detail the progress of the story; but after Andrugio has fallen in love with Susania, he is sent by his father to the University of Sienna, where he forms a friendship with the heir to the Duke of Milan. And here we may remark upon the utter disregard of geographical correctness, for Saxony, to the Dukedom of which Andrugio soon succeeds, is represented as contiguous to the Dukedom of Milan; and when the hero is expelled from his territory by two usurpers, those usurpers are overthrown and suppressed by Galastino of Milan, Andrugio's faithful friend. Galastino also preserves the lives of Andrugio's wife and children, and after various adventures conquers the Dukedom of Saxony for Alphonsus, the son of Andrugio and Susania. The author hardly supports the dignity of his hero, for he makes him fly from his enemies, and hide from them in a wood for the space of thirteen years, while his wife is lamenting his loss, and while his son Alphonsus is making rapid progress to manhood. This part of the narrative ends with the restoration of Susania and Alphonsus, before anything has been heard of the retreat of Andrugio, who has taken upon himself the life, if not the habit, of a hermit. The following passage, where the Duchess Susania is watching and waiting for the preparations of Galastino for the re¬covery of Saxony, may be taken as a fair specimen of the writer's style as a novelist:—

"The Duchesse, for whose sake those preparations were made, conceived such joy at the same, that she thought every moneth a yeare and every day a moneth, until she saw to what happy end the Dukes pretended jorney would happen unto, often commending in her heart the faithfulnesse of the Duke of Millaine to his friend. In recounting whereof she shed many bitter teares for Andrugio, her beloved lord and husband, somtime exclaiming against the Gods and men for his losse who so dearely she loved. The remembrance of whom was likely divers times to bereave her of life; yet in the midst of her sorrowes, when she beheld the yoong Prince, a lively picture of the exiled Duke, how often with sweet imbracings woulde she kisse the tender youth, bathing his tender cheeks with teares, distilling in aboundance thorow extreame griefe of heart from her eies, hoping yet, before death should shut those eyes of hers, to see him and once again to injoy his companie."

The story, as far as it goes, may be said to be divided into two portions: 1. that part of it which relates to the early life of Andrugio and the usurpation of his dukedom; 2. that which belongs to the wars of Galastino, entirely undertaken to revenge his friend upon his triumphant enemies. In the latter the hero has nothing to do; but we may more than guess that in the sequel of the narrative (which has not reached us, if it were ever printed) Andrugio came forth from his solitude, and, while disguised and unknown, importantly contributed to the victory which restored him, in the end, to his dukedom. The great fault of the piece is the tedious length of some of the speeches, but this was a defect belonging to all romance-writers of the period. They caught it chiefly from the old "Amadis de Gaule"; but it is no¬where more apparent than in some of Robert Greene's pieces, where the characters patiently argue every question, *pro* and *con,* and, even then, sometimes arrive at no conclusion.

SCHOOL OP SLOVENRY.—The Schoole of Slovenrie: or Cato turnd wrong side outward. Translated out of Latine into English verse, to the use of all English Christendome, except Court and Cittie. By R. F. Gent—London Printed by Valentine Simmes &c. 1605. 4to. 79 *leaves.*

Very few copies of this translation exist; but one, we are informed, bears the date of 1604. Of the translator nothing is known but what he himself tells us in his Epistle "To all that can write and reade and cast accompt," which follows the title-page. "In the minority of my grammar-schollership," he states, "I was induced by those, whom dutie might not withstand, to unmaske these Roman manners, and put them on an English face . . . . The truth is, this translation was halfe printed ere I knew who had it: so that, *quo fata trahunt,* without prevention or correction, the fooles bolt must needes be shot." Afterwards he excuses himself further by stating, that "it is a punies translation only"; and soliciting indulgence for the species of verse he chose, namely, lines of fourteen syllables each, and supporting himself by the authority of Golding, and Phaer, and Twyne, who had rendered Ovid and Virgil "into as indigest and breathlesse a kind of verse." This epistle is subscribed "R. F. Gent, and no more," as if the author might have been more had he wished it. The initials are not those of any known author of the period, excepting Francis Rous, provost of Eton, who published "Thule, or Vertues Historie," in 1598, and is not very likely to have had anything to do with this translation. [Note 1: We have accidentally omitted to observe, what will naturally occur to everybody, that R. F. cannot be taken as the initials of Francis Rous, unless, as was not very unusual at that date, he reversed them on the title-page for the sake of better concealment.]

All the rest of the production is translation, and in verse, commencing with "the Preface of Frederike Dedekind, to maister Simon Bing, Secretaire of Hassia," which fills thirteen widely printed pages. When Swift wrote his "Directions to Servants," as well as his "Polite Conversation," he evidently had the original of this book in his mind. It was printed in London, 12mo, 1661, under the title of "*Grobianus et Grobiana, de Morum Simplicitote Libri tres.*" It is not at all likely that R. F.'s translation had ever been met with by Swift, but another, printed at London in 1739, was expressly dedicated to him. The original was published in a complete shape at Frankfort in 1584, but parts of it had previously appeared in 1549, 1552, and 1558.

Dr. Nott does not seem to have been aware, when he wrote the note on a passage in his reprint of Dekker's "Gull's Hornbook," 1609, p. 4, that an English version of "Grobianus et Grobiana" had appeared in print only four years earlier. Dekker's obligation to it is pointed out in Vol. I. p. 253. The work before us consists of three books, divided into thirty chapters.

What follows will show the general style in which R F. executed his task, although a good deal of grossness is here and there to be complained of, fully warranted, however, by his original. It is from Book II. Chapter 2, entitled, "What manners and gestures the guest ought to observe in eating:"—

"As soone as ere thou spi'st some dishes on the table stand,
Be sure that thou, before the rest, thrust in thy greedie hand.
Snatch that you like; I told you so before—you know it well:

It is but labour lost that I againe the same should tell.
That which I once have told to you you never should refuse,
But in each place and companie you boldly must it use.

"And whatsoever meate your hoste unto the boorde doth send,
Although you cannot choose but very much the taste commend,
Yet finde therein something or other that mislikes your minde,

And, though it can deserve no blame, be sure some fault to finde.
'This is too salt, and this too fresh, and this is too much rost;
This is too sowre, and this too sweete: your cooke's to blame, mine host.'
And speake so lowde that all may heare thee which are then in place,
For by this meanes thou maist in jeast the carefull cooke disgrace.
And by this tricke thou wilt deserve a civill yonker's name,
And happy is he nowadayes which can attaine such fame. * * *

"When thou art set, devoure as much as thou with health canst eate;
Thou therefore wert to dinner bid, to helpe away his meate.
Thrust in as much into thy throate as thou canst snatch or catch,
And with the gobbets which thou eatst thy jaws and belly stretch.
If with thy meate thou burne thy mouth, then cloake it craftely,
That others may, as well as thou, partake that miserie.

"To throw thy meate from out thy mouth into the dish againe
I dare not bid thee, for it is too clownish and too plaine."

Such, however, was not Dr. Johnson's advice, nor his practice. Dedekind's hero came within the Doctor's class of "fools who would have swallowed it"

We make another extract from Chapter 7 of the same Book, where the author describes what ought to be the conduct of a man of spirit and promise, who, with his companions, has freely partaken of any intoxicating beverage:—

"And if you heare that any man is gone unto his bed,
Because the wine had long before (poore man!) possest his head,
Then have a care that from his bed you strait way call him backe,
And make him come perforce, although his garments he do lacke:
And then beginne afreshe great store of strongest wine to take,
And drinke it off, therewith thy selfe more pleasant for to make.
Then break the pots and windows all: this cannot much offend,
For this next day the glazier shall have something for to mend. * * *

Upon the benches and the tables boldly thou maiest go;
Nay, which is more, I give thee leave all these to overthrow:
In briefs with formes throwne up and downe thou oughtst the harth to breake,
Before one word of thy departure thou beginst to speake."

The work ends on sign. S 4 b, with "the Author's Conclusion to Master Simon Bing, wherein he showeth all the intent and practise of this present worke."

SCOTT, THOMAS.—Philomythie or Philomythologie, wherin outlandish Birds, Beasts and Fishes are taught to speake true English plainely. By Tho. Scott, Gent &c.—London for Francis Constable &c 1616. 8vo. 89 *leaves.*

This is the first edition of a curious, but not very intelligible book. The author seems to have been so fearful lest his satire should be considered personal and individual, that ambiguity often renders him incomprehensible. The present copy differs from some others in the circumstance that the second title-page, on sign. F 2, "Certaine Pieces of this Age paraboliz'd," is dated 1615, and not 1616. The first title-page is engraved by R. Elstracke; and in an address "to the Reader" (which follows "Sarcasmos Mundo" and other preliminary poems) we meet with the following mention of Spenser:—

"If Spencer were now living to report
His Mother Hubberts tale, there would be sport
To see him in a blanket tost, and mounted
Up to the starrs, and yet no starre accounted."

This shows clearly that Spenser by his "Mother Hubberd's Tale" had given such offence, that, had he been living in 1616, he would have run the risk of being "tossed in a blanket." It seems probable that it was "called in" on account of the severity of its satire and personal allusions; but a question has arisen whether a notice of the "Tale of Mother Hubburd" in "The Ant and the Nightingale," 1604, which unquestionably was highly disapproved, applies to Spenser's satirical apologue, or to some tract published under nearly the same title. The reason for the latter opinion is, that, as "Mother Hubberd's Tale" has come down to us, it contains nothing about "rugged bears," or "the lamentable downfall of the old wife's platters." This is true; but that may have been the very part of the poem which most offended, and was therefore afterwards erased by Spenser. Still, we are of opinion that the writer of "The Ant and the Nightingale" did not refer to Spenser, but to some imitator; and we are confirmed in this belief by a second allusion to "Mother Hubburd "in another tract which the same author, T. M., also printed in 1604, called "The Black Book," which contains the following words: "And to confirm this resolution the more, each slipped downe his stocking, baring his right knee, and so began to drinke a health halfe as deepe as Mother Hubburds cellar, that *she was called in for selling her working bottle-ale to bookbinders, and spurting the froth upon Courtier's noses."* Here again there is nothing of the kind in Spenser's "Mother Hubberd's Tale"; and we may conclude, with tolerable certainty, that some lost publication, with a title similar to that of Spenser, and purposely adopted for the sake of his popularity, was intended by T. M.

Scott professes himself afraid to follow the example of Spenser. The second portion of his work contains four emblematical engravings, which may also doubtless be assigned to Elstracke. The most remarkable poem is entitled "*Regalis Justitia Jacobi,"* in which Scott celebrates the impartial justice of King James, in refusing to pardon Lord Sanquhar, or Sanquier, for the deliberate murder of Turner, the celebrated fencer, in 1612, as may be seen in Wilson's History of that reign. Turner had himself killed an adversary named Dunn in 1602, by piercing him to the brain through the eye, (see Hist. Engl. Dram. Poetry, I. 326,) and the animosity of Lord Sanquhar was occasioned by the loss of an eye while fencing with Turner. Scott alludes as follows to these incidents:—

"This silly Fencer, in his ignorance bold,
Thinks his submissive sorrow will suffice
For that unhappy thrust at Sanquier's eyes;
And, begging pardon, seemes to have it then.
What foole dares trust the unseal'd words of men?

Yet Turner will: a reconciled foe
Seemes a true friend to him would have him so.
He thinks (now Dunne is dead) to die in peace,
But blood cries out for blood," &c.

On p. 126 is a blank for some part of the copy which the printer had lost, "the Author being far from London," but it is promised that the defect shall be supplied in the next impression. The second edition did not make its appearance until 1622, and there was a third in 1640. The author's style is diffuse and wordy, and his satire, where it is intelligible, far from pungent.

SENECA, L. A.—L. A. Seneca the Philosopher, his Booke of Consolation to Marcia. Translated into an English Poem.—London. Printed by E. P. for Henry Seile &c. 1635. 4to. 24 *leaves.*

This production has been attributed to Sir R. Freeman, but erroneously, for an existing copy has a special dedication to the Earl of Bridgewater, subscribed "Most devoted to your Vertues, R. C.," the letters R. C. being MS., and the whole leaf containing the dedication being specially prefixed to the book, and of a larger size. The initials are added in MS., probably because the writer originally meant his work to be entirely anonymous, and not even thus far to subscribe the dedication. The following is a part of this unpublished address:—

"How well your life doth hit the triple white,
Whose goodnesse, gravenesse, greatnesse all delight.
May that bright name shine uneclipsed here,
Whom all his Country justly holds most deere!"

At the back of the title-page the translator requests the reader not to mar his verses in the reading; and whoever R. C. might be, he writes with considerable facility. He thus commences his tenth chapter:—

"These goods of fortune that about us shine,

As children, honours, riches and a fine
And noble wife, fair palaces, and store
Of suitors, that attend us at our doore,
With all things else that are from fortune sent,
Are ornaments, not given us but lent.
Our scene therewith is for the time adorn'd,
Then to the owners backe they are return'd:
Some stay a day, some more, few to the end.
We cannot boast them ours what others lend.
The use is ours during the owners will:
What's borrow'd for uncertaine time must still
Be ready without strife to be repay'd:
No debtor should his creditor upbray'd."

Thomas Lodge translated the whole of Seneca, 1614, folio, and the copy he presented to his friend Dekker is now before us.

SERVINGMEN.—A Health to the Gentlemanly profession of Servingmen: or the Servingmans Comfort: with other thinges not impertinent to the Premisses, as well pleasant as profitable to the courteous Reader.

Felix qui socii navim periisse procellis
Cum vidit in tutum flectit sua carbasa portum.

—Imprinted at London by W. W. 1598. 4to. B. L. 37 *leaves.*

This is an important Shakspearean tract, of which we only know of one or two copies. Its connection with our great dramatist's works was pointed out by Dr. Farmer many years ago, and there can be no doubt that the same joke, and in nearly the same terms, is found both in the tract under consideration, and in "Love's Labours Lost," Act III. sc. 1. The coincidence has been mentioned in every annotated edition of the comedy.

The initials at the end of "The Epistle to the gentle Reader, of what estate or calling soever," would point to either Jervis Mark ham or John Marston; but to the first they cannot belong, because he had commenced author in 1595, and J. M. tells us that this "Health to the gentlemanly profession of Servingmen," 1598, was his earliest production, "being *primogeniti*—the first batch of my baking." Marston may indeed have been the writer of it, but it is very unlikely, even supposing the character of a Serving-man, in which it is written, to have been merely assumed: his "Pygmalion's Image and Certain Satires," however, came out with the same date of 1598. [Note 1: The late Mr. Miller informed us that he had in his possession two distinct editions of Mars ton's Satires in 1599, a fact which shows their popularity. We never saw more than one impression of 1599, but Mr. Miller was too accurate to be mistaken. The Satires certainly created n sen¬sation when first published.] We do not believe that it was by either Markham or Marston, but by some clever author with the same initials, who was not what he pretends to be, when be assures us that he received "five marks and a livery" annually, as the ordinary wages of a man-servant.

His style is a little rambling and diffuse, but lively and unpretending; and in the outset he undertakes a threefold task: first, "to what end it [*i. e.* servingmanship] was ordained;" secondly, "how flourishing was the prime of this profession;" and thirdly, "the ruin and decay of this ancient building." He does not do much towards the performance of the second part of his title-page, "the Servingmans Comfort," because throughout, and especially at the close, he shows his unhappy state of dependence, and his final neglect and misery. He mentions the gentlemanlike qualifications for a worthy attendant upon a man of wealth and rank, and insists that "the Clowne, the Sloven, and Tom Althummes are as farrc unfit for this profession, as Tarletons Toys for Paules Pulpit." In one place J. M. thus describes the duties of a servingman:—

"The gentleman receaved even a gentleman into his service, and therefore did limit him to no other labour then belonged to him selfe, as to helpe him readie in the morning, tọ brush his aparrel, Cloake, Hatte, Girdle on other garment, trusse his poyntes, fetch him water to wash and other such like necessaries. His Maister thus made ready, yf it pleased him to walke abrode, then to take his liverie and weapon to attende him, being himselfe ready, handsome and well appoynted: at his returne, yf it pleased him to eate, then with all diligence decently and comely to bring his meate to the table, and thereon in seemely sort being placed, with a reverend regarde to attende him, placing and displacing dysshes at the first or seconde course according as occasion shall serve, tyll time commaunde to take away: which done, grace sayd, and the table taken up, the plate presently conveyed into the pantrie, the Haul summons this consort of companions (upon pnyue to dine with Duke Ilumfrie, or kisse the Hares foote) to appeare at the first call, where a song is to be sung, the undersong or holding whereof is, *It it merrie in Haul when Beardes wagge all.*"

One point he presses strongly is the ruin of the servingman's profession in consequence of the death of Liberality, whom he personifies; [Note 1: This poem on the death of Liberality cannot fail to remind us of Richard Barnfield's more serious and lengthened effusion on the same subject—" The Complaint of Poetrie for the death of Liberalitie,"] and he introduces a clever poem upon the subject, from which some stanzas might perhaps be advantageously omitted, but which we prefer to give entire, as we are not aware that it has ever been extracted, or even mentioned:—

"Cease, Sunne, to lende thy glorious shine,
Moone, darkned be as cloudy night;
Starres, stay your streaming lights divine,
That wonted were to shine so bright:
Weepe, woofull wightes, and wayle with me
For dead is Liberalitie!

"You, Fire, Water, Earth and Ayre,
And what remaynes at your commaunde
Foules, Fysh or els be fyld with care,
And marke the summe of my demaund:
Weepe, weepe, I say, and wayle with me
For dead is Liberalitie.

"You silver streames that wont to flow
Upon the bankes of Helicon;
You sacred Nimphes, whose stately show

which came out in the same year; (see Vol. I. p. 69.) We make a brief quotation from it in proof of the general similarity:—

"Bat Liberalitie is dead and gone,
And Avarice usurps true Bounties seat.
For her it is I make this endlesse mone,
Whose praises worth no pen can well repeat.
Sweet Liberalitie, adiew for erer,
For Poetrie againe shall see thee never!

"Never againe shall I thy presence see,
Never againe shall I thy bountie tast;
Never againe shall I accepted bee,
Never againe shall I be so embract:
Never againe shall I the bad recall;
Never againe shall I be lov'd of all.

"Thou wast the Nurse whose bountie gare me sucke;
Thou wast the Sunne whose beames did lend me light;
Thou wast the Tree whose fruit I still did plucke;
Thou wast the Patron to maintain my right.
Through thee I liv'd, on thee I did relie;
In thee I joy'd, and now for thee I die!"

We are to bear in mind that the whole of this, and much more, is put into the mouth of Poetry. In, point of mere sprightly cleverness it seems to us that J. M. has the advantage, ills effusion is much shorter and lighter, and it wants Barnfield's serious variety.

Bedimd the bright of Phaeton;
Weepe, weepe, I say, and wayle with me
For dead is Liberalitie.

"If Due-desert to Court resort,
Expecting largely for his payne,
The Prince he findes then alamort,
No love, his labour is spent in vayne:
May he not then come wayle with me?
Yes; dead is Liberalitie.

"The paringea from the Priucea fruite,
That sillie groomes were wont to feede,
Now Potentates for them make suite,
True Gascoine sayth, the Lord hath neede.
Weepe, therefore, weepe, and wayle with me,
For dead is Liberalitie.

"The Courtly crew of noble mindes
Would give rewarde for every legge:
To crouch and kneele now dnetie bindes,
Though Suitor nought but right doth begge,
Weepe, therefore, weepe, and wayle with me,
For dead is Liberalitie.

"When Countroys causes did require
Each Nobleman to keepe his house,
Then Blewcontes had what they desyre,
Good cheare and many a full carouse:
But now, not as it wont to be,
For dead is Liberalitie.

"The Haul boordes-ende is taken up,
No dogges do differ for the bones;
Blacke Jacke is left, now glasse or cup:
It makes me sigh with many grones,
To thinke what was now thus to be
By death of Liberalitie.

"Where are the Farmes that wont to flye
Rent-free by service well deserved?
Where is that kinde Annuitie,
That men in age from want preserved?
What, do you looke for wont to be?
No, dead is Liberalitie.

"What Squire now but rackes his rentes,
And what he hath who will give more?

The giffe gaffe promise he repentes:
The Lord bath neede, surceasse therefore.
Weepe, weepe, for now you well may see
That dead is Liberalitie.

"The golden worlde is past and gone,
The Iron age hath runne his race:
The lumpe of Lead is left alone
To presse the poore in every place:
Nought els is left bat miserie,
Since death of Liberalitie.

"Weepe, weepe, for so the case requires;
The worlde hath lost her second Sunne:
This is the summe of my desires,
To ende where earst I have begunne.

Even still I say, Come wayle with me
The death of Liberalitie.

J. M. gives us another and much shorter song on a favorite subject, the decay of hospitality, from which we extract only the concluding stanza:—

"And where the Porters lodge did yeelde beefe bread and beere,
The Kitchen, Haul and Parlor to[o] now wantes it twice a yeere:
Now Servingmen may sing, adue you golden dayes!
Meere miserie hath taken place where plentie purchast prayse."

He then subjoins the anecdote about "guerdon" and "remuneration," which we need not repeat, seeing that it has been so often printed; and towards the conclusion he despondingly asks what a Servingman is to do in his extremity?

"What shall he then do? Shall he make his appearance at Gaddes Hill, Shooters Hill, Salisbury playne or Newmarket heath, to sit in commission and examine passengers? Not so, for then yf he mistake but a worde, "Stande" for "Goodmorow," he shall straight, whereas he did attende, be attended with more men then his Maister kept, and preferred to a better house then ever his father buylded for him, though not so holsome."

Finally, he prints as prose the old saying which in fact is verse:—

"A Bakers wyfe may byte of a bunne,
A Brewers wyfe may drinke of a tunne,
And a Fishmongers wyfe may feede of a Cunger,
But a Servingmans wyfe may starve for hunger."

In close connection with this subject we may here refer to a very scarce poem by a person who subscribes himself William Bas, and who was perhaps the father of the William Basse whose "Great Brittaine's Sunnes-set," 1613, we have reviewed in our first vol¬ume, p. 70. The two were clearly not the same person, nor is the style of the one at all like that of the other. William Bas, as he spells his name, published in 1602, 4to, "Sword and Buckler or the Serving-mans Defence," in six-line stanzas, easily as well as pointedly written, and with much the same purpose as the prose tract of J. M. which preceded the poem by four years. Bas, too, like J. M., professes to be in service; and to show the similarity of some of the ideas in the one and in the other, we will quote only a couple of stanzas. William Bas says:—

"But in these times (alas, poore serving-men)
How cheape a credit are we growne into!
With what enforcing taxes, now and then,
This envious world doth our estates pursue!
How poore, alas! are we ordained to be,
How ill regarded in our povertie!

"What duty, what obedience daily now
Our hard commanders looke for at our hands!
And yet how deadly cold their bounties grow,
And how unconstant all their favour stands!
How much we hazard for how little gaine,
How fraile our state, how meane our entertaine!"

There are seventy-five such stanzas in the whole, and they are not dedicated to any great man of the day, but "to the honest and faithful Brotherhood of True-hearts, all the old and young Serving-men of England." This address is in five stanzas, signed William Bas, and there are two others "to the Reader."

SHAKESPEARE, WILLIAM.—Lucrece.—At London, Printed by N. O. for John Harison. 1607. 8vo. 32 *leaves.*

This is the fourth known edition of Shakspeare's "Tarquin and Lucrece"; the first appeared in 1594, the second in 1598, the third in 1600. [Note 1: We ought to have called it "Lucrece" only, and so it continued to be entitled until 1616, when it was republished as "The Rape of Lucrece, by Mr. William Shakespeare, newly re-

vised." It was then printed at London by T. S. for Roger Jackson, in 8vo, 82 leaves.]
Malone mentions that he had also "heard of editions in 1596 and 1602," but their existence is more than doubtful, for no copies with such dates have ever been brought
to light. He tells us that all the copies, after that of 1594, were in sextodecimo, (Ritson, **Bibl. Poet.** 329, asserts that the edition of 1598 is in 4 to,) but in fact the size is
8m Mistakes of the kind have been made, with respect to other productions, by not
attending to the circumstance that the old folio, quarto, and octavo were of the size
of foolscap, or, as Thomas Nash calls it in his "Have with you to Saffron-Walden,"
of "pot-paper," folded more or less frequently. The signatures of the edition in our
hands show the error.

It is also stated by Malone (Shaksp. by Boswell, XX. p. 100), that the edition of
1607 is "the most correct of all those that preceded"; but he should have remarked,
nevertheless, that it and "those that preceded" were printed for the same stationer
or bookseller as the earliest copy of 1594, to whom it was entered on the Stationers'
Books on the 9th of May of that year, under the tide of "The Ravishment of Lucrece." The edition of 1607 was also the last published during the life of the author,
unless we suppose one of 1616 (printed by T. S. for Roger Jackson) to have come out
before the 23d of April in that year. Malone adds, that the "more modern editions"
"appear manifestly to have been printed from that of 1607"; but in his notes to the
poem he has failed in establishing this position, and a correct examination shows
some important variations. Thus, on sign. A 5 b, we have these lines in die edition
of 1607 before us:—

"Till sable night, ***mother*** of dread and feare,
Uppon the world dim darknesse doth display,
And in her vanity prison ***stowes*** the day;"

which precisely accords with the copy of 1594; while in those of 1616, 1624,
&c. the passage stands thus:—

"Till sable night, ***sad source*** of dread and feare,
Uppon the world dim darkness doth display,

And in her vanity prison *shuts* the day."

Malone must have collated very carelessly; for, in reference to the last line of the fifth stanza of the poem, he tells us that all the "modern editions," varying from the "old copy," read,—

"From thievish *cares,* because it is his own,"

when in the edition before us, as well as in that of 1624, it stands as in the "old copy":—

"From theevish *eares,* because it is his owne."

Again, Malone asserts that the modern editions close the twenty-third stanza thus:—

"To slanderous tongues and wretched hateful *lays;*"

whereas, in fact, in the copies of 1607 and 1624, the line stands,—

"To sclanderous tongues & wretched hatefull *daies.*"

The edition of 1607 sometimes restores the old reading of 1594, which had been corrupted in the two intermediate impressions; and the following is an instance. The line,—

"O, that *prone* lust should stain so pure a bed,"
is changed in the copy of 1600 to,—

"O, that *proud* lust should stain so pure a bed,"

and restored in the edition of 1607 to the true text of the author. In some subsequent impressions the epithet *prone* is changed to *fowl.* On sign. C 7, edit 1607, is this passage:—

"No man *inveighe* against the withered flower,
But *chide* rough winter," &c.

Malone maintains that all the editions, excepting the first, have *inveighs* and *chides,* but this corruption is not introduced even into the impression of 1624. Again, farther on, he states that "all the modern editions" read the line—

"As lagging souls before the northern blast,"

instead of "As lagging *fowls,*" &c. The edition of 1607 has, "As lagging *fowls.*"

It would be easy to point out other proofs of the same hastiness of condemnation. Sometimes the edition of 1607 may be of use in another respect. Malone would mend the last line of the eighth stanza of the poem thus:—

"Virtue would stain that *or* with silver white;"

introducing a poor conceit on the difference between or (gold), and silver. Now the oldest copy has it *ore,* which was then the common mode of spelling the abbreviation of over, i. e. *o'er,* the meaning of Shakspeare being clearly,—

"Virtue would stein that *o'er* with silver white;"

and in the copy of 1607, followed by that of 1624, this plain meaning is enforced by an apostrophe:—

"Vertue would stein that *o're* with silver white."

Later in the poem, where Lucrece is lamenting her fate, and that her compelled offence was the destruction of the honor of her husband, she exclaims,—

"Yet I am *guilty* of thy honour's wreck;"

an obvious reading, and supported by every authority, ancient or modern; yet Malone has altered the text to,—

"Yet I am *guitless* of thy honour's wreck,"

entirely mistaking Shakspeare's meaning, and attempting afterwards to vindicate his blunder.

What has been advanced tends to the conviction that the copy of 1607 is of much value, sometimes restoring the old and true reading which had been abandoned in 1600, and at others illustrating the real sense of disputed passages. It is more true to assert that the editions of 1616, 1624, &c. followed the text of that of 1600, than that furnished by the edition of 1607. Every old impression deserves to be most minutely and critically examined.

SHAKESPEARE, WILLIAM.—A Banquet of Jeasts or Change of Cheare. Being a collection of Moderne Jests. Witty Jeeres. Pleasant Taunts. Merry Tales. Never before Imprinted.—London, Printed for Richard Royston, and are to be sold at his shop in Ivie-Lane next the Exchequer-Office. 1630. 8vo. 107 *leaves.*

This volume of Jests has sometimes, in later impressions, had the name of Archee, i. e. Archibald Armstrong, Charles the First's Jester, prefixed to it; [Note 1: We have not seen any such edition, but Lowndes (Bibl. Man.) points out two so called in 1689 and 1657. Such was not the case in 1684, (an edition not noticed by bibliographers,) when it was still entitled "A Banquet of Jests," and the number was increased from 195 to 261. A peculiar feature in the edition of 1634 is, that the following lines, mentioning various preceding popular collections, and terming it" the fourth impression," face the title-page:—

"*The Printer to the Reader.*"
"Since, Reader, I before hare found thee kinde,
Expect this fourth impression more refinde;
The coorser cates that might the feast disgrace
Left out: And better serv'd in in their place.
Pasquels conceits are poore, and Scoggins dry,
Skeltons meere rime, once read, but now laid by:
Peeles Jests are old, and Tarletons are growne stale.
These neither bark nor bite, nor scratch, nor raile.
Banquets were made for laughter, not for teares:
Such are our sportive Taunts, Tales, Jests and Jeeres."] but we have given as our heading, the name of Shakspeare, not only because he is mentioned with peculiar honor in one of them, but because so many of the jests or anecdotes are theatrical. Another of them relates to William Kempe, the great comedian, who figured in Dogberry, Peter, &c; a third, to William Rowley, the dramatic author and actor; and several more to various matters connected with plays, players, and playhouses. We are to recollect that, when the book was printed, Shakspeare had been dead fourteen years; and the principal, if not the only value of the anecdote is, not that he was himself personally concerned in it, but that it shows the height, breadth, and strength of the reputation that had survived him. In the interval between his death and the publication of the "Banquet of Jests" in 1630, the first folio of his works had appeared, and in 1632 it was reprinted. The "jest" is placed under the heading of "Stratford upon Avon," in 1630, and is inserted upon p. 157. It is, moreover, the first time Shakspeare has been spoken of in print in connection with his native town:—

"One travelling through Stratford upon Avon, *Towne most remarkable for the birth of famous William Shakespeare,* and walking in the Church to doe his devotion, espyed a thing there worthy observation, which was a tombestone, laid more then three hundred years agoe, on which was ingraven an Epitaph to this purpose, "I, Thomas such a one, and Elizabeth my wife here under lye buried; and know, Reader, I, R. C. and I, Chrystoph Q, are alive at this houre to witnesse it."

We do not recollect to have seen the above anywhere alluded to, and its sole value obviously is what we have pointed out, with reference to the extent and permanence of the reputation of our great dramatist at an early date after his demise. Another "jest," so to call it, shows the sort of disrepute in which players in general were then held. Here again the anecdote is in itself of no value.

"*Of an Oatemeale-man.*

"An Oatemeale-man, a rich fellow, fell at some difference with a Comedian about the towne, and began to upbraid him with his profession, and according to the small talent of wit hee had, came hotly upon him with the common objection: "If, saith he, all men were of my mind, you should keepe your doores shut, and find your galleries empty, and then you would bee more poore and lesse proud." "I believe it, said the other; so, if every man would, as I could find in my heart to doe, that is, to forswears the eating of Puddings and Pottage, who would be more poore and lease proud then the Oatemeale man?"

We next give a passage which relates to the celebrated William Kempe, and records a fact in his life with which we were not previously acquainted. The accident, we may imagine, happened on the stage, when the comedian was interposing between two combatants. It is headed "a cleanly lie," meaning, probably, a most obvious and self-contradicting falsehood.

" ***Will Kempe,*** by a mischance, was with a sword run quite through the leg: a Country Gentleman, comming to visit him, asked him how he came by that mischance? He told him, and withal, "troth, saith he, I received the hurt just eight weekes since, and I have line of it this quarter of a yeare, and never stirr'd out of my chamber."

Kempe was jeering the "country gentleman," to see how much and how fast he would swallow. The next quotation we shall make is of a more elaborate character, and comes properly under the denomination of "a jest." It is headed:—

"71. *Of Rapessed.*

"A handsome young fellow, having seene a play at the **Curtaine,** comes to **William Rowley,** after the Play was done, and entreated him, if his leisure served, that hee might give him a pottle of wine to bee better acquainted with him. He thankt him and told him, if hee pleased, to goe as farre as the Kings Head at Spittlegate, hee would, as soone as he had made himselfe ready, follow him and accept of his kindnesse. He did so, but the wine seeming tedious betwixt two, and the rather because the yong fellow could entertaine no discourse, Rowly beckoned to an honest fellow over the way to come and keepe them company; who promised to be with them instantly. But not comming at the second or third calling, at last he appeares in the roome, where William Rowly begins to chide him because he had staid so long. Hee presently craved pardon, and begins to excuse himselfe, that hee had been abroad to buy Rapeseed, and that he staid to feede his birds. At every word of Rapeseed the man rose from the table with a changed countenance, being very much discontented, and said, Mr. Rowly, I came in curtesie to desire your acquaintance, and to bestow the wine upon you, not thinking you would have called this fellow up to taunt mee so bitterly. They wondering what he meant, hee proceeded: Tis true indeed the last session I was arraigned at Newgate for a Rape, but, I thank God, I came off like an honest man, little thinking to bee twitted of it here. Both began to excuse themselves, as not knowing any such thing, as well they might. But he that gave the offence, thinking the better to express his innocence—Young Gentleman, saith he, to expresse how farre I was from wronging you, looke you here, as I have Rapeseed in one pocket for one bird, so here is Hempe seed on this side for another. At which word **Hempseed,** saith the young man, Why, Villaine, doest thou thinke I have deserved hanging? and tooke up the pot to fling at his head, but his hand was stayed; and as errour and mistake begun the quarrell, so wine ended it."

Thus it appears that the young gull had made W. Rowley's acquaintance by seeing him perform at the Curtain Theatre, which had been in the occupation of various companies of players since about the year 1575, when it was constructed. It may be doubted whether Rowley was living at the time theatres were silenced in 1647, but we know that he was residing in Cripple-gate in 1637, and that he had previously belonged to the Companies of the Prince and of the Duke of York. In the work before us we first meet with the epigram upon old Philemon Holland and his translation of Suetonius; but as he was still a busy man with his pen in 1630, (not having died till 1636,) his name is not given.

"One that had translated many books and volumes, at length publishing the history of Suetonius Tranquillus in English, a pleasant Gentleman writ this distick—

Philemon with Translations doth so fill us,
He will not let Suetonius bee Tranquillus."

It is most likely that this joke is considerably older than 1630, because Holland's translation of Suetonius came out as early as 1606. We extract the following merely because it relates to the old tapestry of the House of Lords, which was unfortunately consumed in 1884.

"Two ancient Captaines, looking upon the rich hangings of Eighty Eight, observing in the border thereof the faces of the prime Commanders and Gentlemen of note that had beene in the service, "Well, saith the one to the other, if every one had his right, my face might have had the honor to have bin placed before some that I see; for, I am sure, I was engaged in the hottest incounter." To whom the other replied "Content thy selfe, Captains; tis well knowne thou art an old souldier, and reserved for another hanging."

There were two or three later editions of this "Banquet of Jests," (we have seen them in 1636 and 1642,) but we know of no earlier impression than that of 1630. The editor subscribes himself "Anonimos," and only professes to have "gathered them from the mouths of others." The table of contents shows them to be 195 in number, and it is followed by some rather clever verses, in which the writer promises that no such good cheer shall be found in Bartholomew Fair, adding, in a farewell address to his little volume,—

"I wish it may not be your lots

(Poore Pupes) to be rent by sots,
Or such as will stop mustard pots."

Here "poore ***Pupes***" must be an error of the press for "poore Paper"; but in general the book is better printed than might be expected.

SHARPE, ROGER.—More Fooles yet Writtenby R. S. At London Printed by Thomas Castleton and are to be sold at his shop without Cripplegate. ***An.*** 1610. 4to. 18 ***leaves.***

Had not Roger Sharpe subscribed the address "to the Reader," in thirty-six lines, with his names at length, we might have been inclined, until we read the collection of Epigrams, to have supposed that it was by Samuel Rowlands, with his initials reversed. The truth, however, is, that there is not one production upon the thirty-six pages that is good enough for the author of "Tis merry when Gossips meet," "Humour's Ordinary," &c. There was a dramatist of the name of Lewis Sharpe, who wrote one play published in 1640; and whether Roger Sharpe was any relation to him, we have no means of knowing. Only two copies of "More Fooles yet" have been recorded, and the production requires notice rather for its extreme rarity than for any merit it possesses. In his preliminary lines the author refers to incorrigible rogues who cannot be controlled by religion nor the law, and, Dogberry-like, wisely lets them alone. He observes,—

"Therefore since milde perswasion cannot moove them,
Nor reprehension, whosoere reproove them,
Nor Lawes severity nor Justice sword,
I will not to reclaime them wast a word:
Nor will I taxe their vice, because I see
They will persist in spight of you or mee;
And so I leave them to their damned rules.
I will not deale with villaines, but with fooles."

A new page is headed, "More Fooles yet, Love's Metamorphosis"; but there seems to be no connection between the two; and we take it that "Love's Meta-morphosis" was only added, because in 1601 a play with that title, attributed to the celebrated John Lily, had been printed. The earliest epigram by Sharpe that deserves any notice is the following, called "A confident Cuckold," meaning a con-fiding one:—

"You wrong Zelopio to repute him so:
Tell me that he is jealous? faith, Sir, no.
He will permit his wife to see a Play,
And let her drinke with Captaines by the way;
Will give her leave to walke to Westminster
To see the Tombes and monuments are there;
Will suffer her to drinke and stay out late,
To be led home by each associate.
This proves him confident; and which is more,
When his wife knocks, himselfe will looke to the doore.
And wot you why Zelopio seems content?
She keepes the house, keepes him, and paies the rent."

Sharpe makes various other attacks upon complying and submissive husbands, and in the last of the ensuing couplets mentions a most popular tune, which has been used in the old interlude of "Tom Tiler and his Wife," in T. Hey wood's "Woman killed with Kindness," 1607, in Brathwaite's "Shepherds Tales," 1623, and in Henry Bold's Poems, 1685,—so that it continued a favorite for considerably more than a century:—

"When John *Cornutus* doth his wife reproove
For being false and faithles to her love,
His wife, to smooth the wrinckles on his brow,
Doth stop his month with *John come kisse me now.*"

Houses yisited by the plague, and so pointed out by public inscriptions, are thus mentioned under the heading "A charitable Clowne":—

"***Rusticus,*** an honest country swayne,
Whose education simple was and plaine,
Having surveyd the Citie round about,
Emptyed his purse, and so went trudging out:
But by the way he saw, and much respected,
A doore belonging to a house infected,
Whereon was plac't (as 'tis the custome still)
Lord, have mercie upon us! This sad bill
The sot perusde; and having read, he swore
All London was ungodly but that doore.
Here dwells some vertue yet, saves he, for this
A most devout religious saying is:
And thus he wisht, with putting off his hatte,
That every doore had such a bill as that"

"Fortune favours Fooles" is a new sort of half-title to the few later pages, and from them we copy the succeeding stanza, only because it is an early allusion to the corpulency of Falstaff:—

"How Falstafe like doth sweld ***Virosus*** looke,
As though his paunch did foster every sinne,
And sweares [that] he is injured by this booke:
His worth is taxt, he hath abused byn.
Swell still, ***Virosus;*** burst with emulation:
I neither taxe thy vice, nor reputation."

Four lines, called "Conclusion," dismiss, with great contempt, "the idle Zanies of this age," the author having no sort of suspicion that by his itch for scribbling verses he had, in a manner, entitled himself to a place among them.

SHAVING.—The treatyse answerynge the boke of Berdes. Compyled by Col-lyn clowte, dedycatyd to Barnarde barber dwellynge in Banbery.—[Colophon] R.

W. *ad imprimendum solum.* 8vo. 8 *leaves.*

Only a single copy of this curious and droll tract is extant, and that, unluckily, is imperfect. It wants a leaf, that is to say two pages, so that how the poetical portion of the work commences we cannot ascertain. Still, it ought not to be passed over without notice, in order that, if a second copy should ever be discovered, it may be identified, and prized according to its value.

R W. in the colophon are the initials of Robert Wyer, the printer, who put forth many singular works with and without dates, but who exercised his art between the years 1531 and 1542, so that the "noble king," prayed for near the end of this "Treatise," was Henry VIII. As for the subject, it appears that Dr. Andrew Borde, the physician, philosopher, and humorist, had advocated the fitness of shaving, and had made an attack upon the wearers of beards, which the latter resented. A person of the name of Barnes (whose name occurs on the last page of this tract) undertook the defence of beards, and executed his task in a number of comic stanzas, the point of many of which is now, of course, lost They are illustrated by a couple of woodcuts, on the title-page, being the figures of Collyn Clowte, Andrew Borde, and a lady; while the next page contains a representation of Cock Lorell and his boat, with these lines:—

"To drynke with me be not a ferde,
For here, ye se, groweth never a berde.
I am a Foole of Cocke lorellys bote.
Calling al knaves to pull therin a rope."

They have reference to one of Dr. Borde's arguments against beards, viz., that they were kept so filthy, that he objected to drink after any man who wore one. To this point the vindication by Barnes (if indeed he were the author) is mainly directed, but it also includes other matters connected with "valours excrement," and the wearers of it. Barnes explains how it happened that Borde became an enemy to beards, asserting that when the latter was at Montpelier, (where the writer also happened to be at the same time,) the Doctor got so drunk that he was put to bed, and then, wearing a large beard, he was sick over it, and next morning had it shaved off by a barber, in order to get rid of the nuisance. This feet is narrated in "the preface or the pystle" which follows the title-page, and in a preliminary "treatyse made answerynge the treatyse of doctor Borde upon Berdes."

The beginning of the poem, as already stated, is lost, owing to the imperfectness of the book; but what remains commences with a reference to Borde's resolution "not to drink with bearded men," and afterwards it proceeds thus:—

"Of berdes he sayth ther com no gaynes,
And berdes quycknyth not the braynes.
Lo! how in Physyke he taketh paynes:
He merytes a busshel of brewers graynes.
He warneth also every estate
To avoyde berdes for fere of debate:
If men lyke hym shnld use to prate,
His warnyng then shnld come to late.
I fere not."

Every stanza is in this form, and each ends with "I fere not," or nearly equivalent words. Some portion of the poem is too coarse and dirty for extraction. It is divided into two parts, and the second stanza of "the seconde parte of that Songe" contains a mention of Cock Lorell and his boat.

"A berde upon his over lyppe,
Ye saye, wyll be a proper tryppe,
Wherby ye shall the better skyppe.
Go your wayes; I dare let you slyppe,
Where as be many more,
I thynke by XX score
In cocke lorelles bote before,
Ye may take a nore.
I fere it not."

The humorous satire called "Cock Lorell's Boat," we need hardly say, was originally printed by Wynkyn de Worde, and has been four times reprinted in our day. The last page of the tract in hand is headed "Barnes in the defence of the Berde," and as it consists of only seven lines, we extract it

"Barnes, I say, yf thou be shent
Bycause thou wantyst eloquence,
Desyre them that thyne entent
May stonde all tymes for thy defence:
Consyderynge that thy hole pretence
Was more desyrous of unyte,
Then to envent curyosyte."

The whole was composed merely as a piece of pleasantry, and, although we may not relish some of the coarse humor, it no doubt answered the purpose for which it was written. Skelton died in 1629, or we might fancy he had a hand in it.

SHEPHERDS TALES.—Shepherds Tales, Containing Satyres, Eglogues and Odes. By R. B. Esquire.—London Printed for Richard Whitakers. 1623. 8vo.

This work is in fact the same as "Natures Embassie or the Wilde mans Measures," which Brathwayte published with the date of 1621; but as the work does not appear to have sold well under that title, Whitaker, the Stationer, (or Whitakers, as the name is here given,) had a new title-page printed, dating it 1623. The four other title-pages in the course of the volume remain unaltered, and severally bear date in 1621. The pagination continues as far as p. 26, then begins afresh, and continues as far as 264, with new signatures.

This is a circumstance we have not seen noticed by bibliographers, nor the fact, which is here apparent, that Brathwayte was in some way "kinsman" to Sir Richard Hutton, one of the puisne judges of the Court of Common Pleas. The book is dedicated, not to "Sir T. H. the elder Knight," as is the case with the impression of 1621, but to the son of Sir Richard Hutton.

The volume displays much talent, and possesses much variety, and various songs and tunes are mentioned in different parts of it Among them are, "Peggie Ramsie," "Spaniletto," "the Venetto," "John, come Kisse me," "Wilson's Fancy," and "Touch me gently." The most lively and attractive performance is thus entitled:— "The Shepheards Holy day, reduced in apt measures to Hobbinolls Galliard, or John to the May-pole." It is a musical dialogue between a Shepherd and Shepherdess, Mopso and Marina, and opens thus spiritedly:—

> *Mopso.* "Come, Marina, let's away,
> For both Bride and Bridegroome stay.
> Fie for shame! Are swaines so long
> Pinning of their head-geare on?
> Praythee, see
> None but wee
> Mongst the Swaines are left unreadie.
> Fie! make hast,
> Bride is past:
> Follow me, and I will lead thee.
>
> *Mar,* "On, my lovely Mopsus, on.
> I am readie all is done:
> From my head unto my foote
> I am fitted each way to't.
> Buskins gay,
> Gowne of gray,
> Best that all our flocks do render:
> Hat of stroe,
> Platted through;
> Cherrie lip, and middle slender."

And so they proceed through many more stanzas than we have room to insert, though all very animated, and pleasantly descriptive of country life. In one of her replies the Shepherdess is rather bold in her invitation, and free in her talk. This is the last poem in the division properly called "Shepherd's Tales."

SHERLEY, SIR ANTHONY.—Sir Antony Sherley his Relation of his Travels into Persia. The dangers, and distresses, which befell him in his passage, both by sea and land, and his strange and unexpected deliverances. His magnificent Entertainement in Persia, his honourable imployment there-hence as Embassadour to the Princes of Christendonie, the cause of his disappointment therein, with his advice to his brother, Sir Robert Sherley &c. Penned by Sr. Antony Sherley, and recommended to his brother, Sr. Robert Sherley &c.—London Printed for Nathaniell Butter, and Joseph Bagfet 1613. 4to. 74 *leaves.*

This narrative relates to the same expedition as that regarding which William Parry wrote a tract in 1601, (see Vol III. p. 140,) which was published in some haste in order that the parties might avail themselves of the interest excited by the return of Sir Anthony Sherley to Europe. The latter part of Parry's account may be said to make up for the meagreness of the conclusion of this "Relation," as we have it from the pen of Sir Anthony Sherley, supposing, as there is every reason to believe, that he was the author of the tract the tide of which is above given.

In an address "To the Reader," not subscribed with name or initials, we are informed that the work was drawn up at the instance of a gentleman who had had many interrupted conferences with Sir Anthony.—"On the entreaty of the said Gentleman, for the better satisfying of himselfe and such others of his friends as might be desirous, out of their curiosity, to understand the whole progresse, dependance, and prosecution of the said voyage into Persia, hee obtained of the Persian Embassadour a copy of this discourse, penned by his Brother Sir Anthony Sherley (as it seemeth) since his returne out of Persia into Europe, for the better satisfaction of his friends, and preserving the memory of so memorable an action."

What is headed "The true History of Sir Anthony Sherleys Travels into Persia, penned by himselfe," commences with a statement of his employment in Italy in the first instance, by the Earl of Essex, whom, according to Sherley, he made the especial object of his imitation. He says of the unfortunate nobleman:—

"Amongst which, as there was not a subject of more worthinesse and vertue for such examples to grow from, then the ever-living honour and condigne estimation, the Earle of Essex, as my reverence and regard to his rare qualities was exceeding, so I desired (as much as my humility might answere with such an eminency) to make him the patterne of my civill life, and from him to draw a worthy modell of all my actions. And as my true love to him did trantforme me from my many imperfections, to bee, as it were, an imitator of his vertues, so his affection was such to mee, that hee was not onely contented I should do so, but in the true noblenesse of his minde gave me liberally the best treasure of his minde in counselling mee, his fortune to helpe mee forward, and his very card to beare mee up in all those courses which might give honour to my selfe, and indeed worthy the name of his friend."

The mission from the Earl of Essex to Italy not succeeding as was desired, the Earl dispatched Sherley and his younger brother into Persia; but it does not at all distinctly appear for what purpose, until we get far into the tract, when we find that the object was to stir the Persian government up against that ancient enemy, the Turk.

They set sail from Venice for Aleppo on 24th May, 1599; and Sir Anthony dismisses briefly the affair regarding which Parry goes into some descriptive detail, namely, the beating of an Italian on board the ship for abusing Queen Elizabeth, which incident brought Sir Anthony and his followers into various troubles, from which they narrowly escaped.

Afterwards Sir Anthony goes at great length into his journey and proceedings; but few things are more remarkable in the narrative than the precision with which he gives the various tedious speeches, not only his own, but those of Abas, the King of Persia, his Vizier, and other Ministers. They are all in the first person, as if every word had been written down at the time; and yet Sir Anthony repeatedly states that in his conferences he was obliged to resort to the aid of an interpreter. According to his own story he was received in Persia, rather as if he had been a monarch than an envoy; and the Persian King treated him to the lull with as much respect and ceremony as Sherley displayed towards the King. Nevertheless, it is admitted that Sir Anthony failed here also in his object; for Abas, though at first willing to adopt the advice for making war against the Turk, seems afterwards to have been dissuaded by his ministers from so hazardous and unprovoked an undertaking, in opposition to existing treaties.

In the end Abas was content to employ Sir Anthony as his own ambassador to the Christian Princes of Europe, and for this purpose commanded two of his own nobility to accompany him; but, for some cause not very clearly explained, this matter was not brought to bear satisfactorily, and Sir Anthony quitted Persia, leaving his brother Robert behind him, as he intimates, in conse¬quence of the affection borne to him by Abas, and as a sort of surety for the stipulated return of the self-important Sir Anthony.

The later portion of the tract is mainly devoted to the instructions given by Sir Anthony to his brother, who remained behind him, and it is very evident that Sir Anthony thought very well of his own sagacity in these directions. Throughout there is a considerable display of conceit and vanity on the part of the writer: he uses many grandiloquent and affected terms, and all that be says and does is very patiently recorded, whiletype is not unfrequently used to enforce and emphasize his axioms of prudence and policy, as well as his moral reflections. Towards the close of his residence in Persia he was much annoyed by a friar, who obtruded himself upon him, but he does not quite support the bad character Parry had given of the same ecclesiastic. The whole may not unfitly be called a glorification of the Sherleys.

SIDNEY, SIR PHILIP.—The Covntesse of Pembrokes Arcadia, written by Sir Philippe Sidnei.—London Printed for William Ponsonbie. ***Anno Domini,*** 1590. 4to. 363 ***leaves.***

There are few books of greater rarity than this first edition of Sidney's "Arcadia" in 4to. We never saw more than one perfect and two imperfect copies of it.

The crest, arms, and supporters of the Sidneys occupy the centre of the title-page, the shield surrounded by the garter of St. George, and the motto of the family, **Quo fata vocant,** underneath.

It may reasonably be doubted whether this romance was not actually in print before Puttenham's "Art of English Poesie," which came out with the date of 1589, ("At London Printed by Richard Field," &c.,) because on p. 204 of that elaborate work we read as follows: "Sir Philip Sidney in the description of his mistresse excellently well handled this figure of resemblaunce by imagerie, as ye may see in his booke of Archadia." We have nowhere seen this point adverted to, but Puttenham's readers could hardly have "seen" the illustration he alludes to in the "Arcadia," if it had not then been published. It is, however, to be borne in mind that manuscript copies of it were in circulation, from one of which, indeed, Ponsonby procured to be printed the 4to impression, the title of which stands at the head of the present article. There certainly had been an intention to put it to press late in 1586, soon after Sidney's death, as is proved by the subsequent letter from Fulke Greville to Sir Francis Walsingham (the father of Sidney's widow) indorsed by Walsingham's secretary "November 1586." The handwriting is very difficult, and some of the expressions rather obscure, but it is very curious with reference to the work before us, and is well worth deciphering: it is addressed "To the Right honorable Sr. francis Walsingham," and we give it exactly as it stands in the original:—

Sr, this day one ponsonby, a bookebynder in poles church yard, came to me, and told me, that ther was one in hand to print Sr. Philip Sydneys old arcadia, asking me yf it were done with your honors cons[ent] or any other of his frendes? I told him, to my knowledge, no: then he advysed me to give w[ar]ninge of it, ether to the archbishope or doctor Cosen, who have, as he says, a copy of it to peruse to that end.

"Sr, I am loth to renew his memory unto you, but yeat in this I must presume, for I have sent my Lady, your daughter, at her request, a correction of that old one, done 4 or 5 years since, which he left in trust with me, wherof ther is no more copies, and fitter to be printed then that first which is so common: notwithstanding even that to be amended by a direction sett down undre his own hand, how and why; so as in many respects, espetially the care of printing of it is to be don with more deliberation. Besydes, he hathe most excellently translated, among div[ors] other notable workes monsieur du Plessis book againste Atheisme, which is sinse don by an other; so as both in respect of lov betwen Plessis and him, besydes other affinities in ther courses, but espetially Sr. Philips un-comparable judgement, I think fit ther be made a stey of that mercenary book, so that Sr. Philip might have all thos religious wor[ks] which ar worthily dew to his lyfe and death.

"Many other works, as Bartas his Spanyard, 40 of the spalm[s] translated into myter &c., which requyre the care of his frends; not to amend, for I think it falls within the reach of no man living, but only to see to the paper and other common errors of mercenary printing. Gayn ther wilbe, no doubt to be disposed by you, let it be to the poorest of his servants: I desyre only care to be had of his honor, who, I fear, hath caried the honor of that latter ages with him.

"Sr. perdon me, I make this the busines of my lofe, and desyre God to shew that he is your God. From my Lodge, not well, this day in hast,

"Your honors
"FOULK GERVILL.

"Sr. I had wayted on you my selfe for answer,
because I am jelous of tyme in it, but in trothe
I am nothing well. Good Sr. think of it."

The above letter (which we copied some years ago from the original, then in the State Paper Office) shows that what was called the "old Arcadia" was in 1586 a common manuscript, and that Sidney's friend, Fulk Greville, was apprehensive that it would be printed for the mercenary profit of a stationer; whereas, if it were to be published, he naturally wished it to have its author's last corrections, and that the "gain" should be divided by Sir Francis Walsingham among the poorest of Sidney's servants. It appears also that Sidney, before he went to Flanders, had placed in Greville's hands a corrected copy of the "old Arcadia," which copy he had forwarded to Lady Sidney. A year and three quarters after the date of Greville's letter, Ponsonby had obtained the authority of the Archbishop of Canterbury for the publication of the work; so that we are to presume that the manuscript from which he printed was then considered a good one, although in the 4 to of 1590 it differs very materially from the "Arcadia," as it subsequently appeared in the folio of 1593: the terms of the Ponsouby's entry of it at Stationers' Hall, in 1588, were these:—

"28 Augusti. [1588]

"Wm. Ponsonby. Rd. of him for a booke of Sr. Php. Sidneys makinge, intitled Arcadia: authorised under the Archb. Cante hand. . . . vjd."

When printed, it bore the date of 1590; so that again about a year and a half elapsed before what had been licensed appeared in type, and was purchasable by general readers. It does not seem at all likely that the "Arcadia" should have come out previously in any printed form, however imperfect; and when Put-tenham re-ferred to it in 1589, as a source of illustration on the point he was advancing, he must either have spoken of a manuscript then in ordinary circulation, (for Greville says that they were common,) or of the printed copy as it had been entered by Pon-sonby in August, 1588, and as it was published by him with the date of 1590.

There is no name of printer on the title-page of 1590. Ponsonby was not a ty-pographer but a stationer, and when he published a work, he employed somebody else to put it in type. He availed himself of the services of John Wolfe when he put forth the first three books of Spenser's "Fairy Queen," in the same year that he put forth Sidney's "Arcadia"; and it is not likely that Wolfe, in his small office, would have been able to set up two such important and long works at the same time. Our belief, therefore, is, after a close inspection of the type used, that, al¬though he is not named, Richard Field, who had been apprentice to Vautrollier, and had married his master's daughter, was the printer of the first 4to edition of the "Arcadia." Field, as we have pointed out, was also the printer of Puttenham's "Arte of English Po-esie," and in this way it is not impossible that Puttenham may have obtained a sight of the sheets of the "Arcadia" some time before they were published in the volume of 1590. This speculation, if well founded, would put an end to the difficulty arising out of the fact that Puttenham, in 1589, referred his readers to a book which bears the date of 1590. The entry of Puttenham's book at Stationers' Hall was three months later than that of the "Arcadia." There would of course be a great demand for Sidney's "Arcadia," and its appearance may therefore have been hastened, while the work of Puttenham may have been postponed in its favor, though actually bearing date a year earlier.

Sidney's "Arcadia" and Spenser's "Fairy Queen" were in the press at the same moment, and for the same publisher: it is very possible, therefore, that our great romantic poet may have looked over the sheets of our great romantic prose-writer; and by whom the "Arcadia" was really edited, before it was published in 1590, is not at all known. We can hardly suppose that Spenser would have had time, even if he had the inclination, to perform this duty, while busied with his own great work; but whoever did it added the following information on the page immediately succeeding the dedication of the "Arcadia" by Sidney to his sister, Lady Pembroke.

"The division and summing up of the Chapters was not of Sir Philip Sidneis dooing, but adventured by the over-seer of the print, for the more ease of the Readers. He therfore submits himselfe to their judgement, and [if] his labour answere not the worthines of the booke, desireth pardon for it. As also if any defect be found in the Eclogues, which although they were of Sir Phillip Sidneis writing, yet were not perused by him, but left till the worke had bene finished, that then choise should have bene made, which should have bene taken, and in what manner brought in. At this time they have bene chosen and disposed as the over-seer thought best."

It is quite certain that the family and friends of Sidney were little satisfied with the work as it appeared in 1590, and the scarcity of copies of the 4to may in part be owing to the calling in and suppressing of them. The very paragraph, above quoted, was probably an after-thought to excuse the imperfection of the "Arcadia" in that shape. The only complete copy we ever saw certainly has it; but in another, wanting the printed dedication, which was supplied in manuscript, it was not found.

It is possible that the copyist omitted it for the sake of brevity; but as in itself it is short, that does not seem likely. Our notion is, that some of the quarto impressions were without it, and that it was not added until the family and friends of the author interposed, and thus very conveniently occupied a page that would otherwise have been blank.

We have given the exact title-page of the 4to (1590) at the head of our article, and the brief dedication that comes upon the next leaf was repeated (with only trifling literal variations) in the folio impressions of 1593 and 1598, both published by Ponsonby. The copy of 1598 professes to have been "now the third time published"; but in the next year Waldegrave of Edinburgh put forth an impression, which he called the ***third,*** and which, find¬ing its way to London, occasioned a dispute between Ponsonby and John Harrison: regarding it, we find the following memorandum in the Registers at Stationers' Hall, which has never, we think, been quoted:—

"21 July 1601. John Harrison the younger, in a cause betweene him and Ponsonby, confessed be had VH of the bookes of Arcadia, printed in Scotland or elsewhere by Waldegrave."

What was the consequence of this confession, whether John Harrison the younger was fined, or whether he was ordered to give up the five pounds' worth of copies to Ponsonby, is not stated in the same record. By an indorsement on the letter of Thomas Nash to Sir Robert Cotton (MSS. Jul. C III) it appears that the price of a copy of the "Arcadia" was then six shillings and sixpence; but in all probability, judging from the date, the writer was speaking of the folio of 1593, and not of the 4to of 1590.

It is a mistake to say that "not a few original poems are found in the 4to, which were not reprinted when the Countess of Pembroke revised the whole," as they appear in the folios of 1593 and 1598. The main difference is, that their places are changed,—not that there are more in the 4toe than in the folios, for while some are omitted, as many are added. In one of his notes to his translation of Ariosto in

1590, Sir John Harington complains that a sonnet written by Sidney, had, "by what mishap he knew not," been omitted in the 4 to "Arcadia "of the same year. He gives it thus:—

> "Who doth desire that chast his wife should be,
> First be he true, for truth doth truth deserve:
> Then be he such as she his worth may see,
> And always one credit with her preserve:
> Not toying kind, nor causlesly unkind,
> Not stirring thoughts nor yet denying right:
> Not spying faults, nor in plaine errors blind;
> Never hard hand, nor ever reins too light
> As far from want, as far from vain expence;
> Tone doth enforce, the tother doth entice.
> Allow good company, but drive from thence,
> All filthy mouths that glory in their vice,
> This done, thou hast no more; but leave the rest
> To nature, fortune, time and womans brest"

This excellent poem is certainly not in the 4to "Arcadia" of 1590, but the Countess of Pembroke had the good taste and good sense to insert it in the folio of 1598, p. 380, the only material difference being that there, in the last line, "virtue" is substituted for ***nature*** as Harington gives it.

In the 4to before us, the whole work is divided into three Books, and those Books into chapters. The first Book has nineteen chapters, the second twenty-nine chapters, and the third nineteen chapters. There is no ***Finis,*** or words equivalent to it, at the end of the volume, but three asterisks to indicate that the work was incomplete.

What Lady Pembroke did towards finishing her brother's work may be seen only by a comparison of the 4to, 1590, with the second edition in folio, 1593, where, after Sidney's dedication, comes an address "To the Reader," subscribed H. S., avowing the manner in which her Ladyship had perfected what had been left incomplete. Among the additions, we may presume on the authority of manuscripts left in her hands and in those of Sidney's friends, is the Epitaph upon Argalus and Parthenia. In the 4to, 1590, a blank space was left for it on folio 311 b, and in some copies it has been partly supplied in writing of the time; but the whole of it, consisting of only eight lines, may be seen in Book 3 of the later impressions: it occurs on p. 294 of the folio of 1598. Lady Pembroke, instead of including the whole "Arcadia" in three Books, as in 1590, divided it, rather unequally, into five Books in 1593.

SIDNEY, SIR PHILIP.—An Apologie for Poetrie. Written by the right noble, vertuous, and learned, Sir Phillip Sidney, Knight *Odi prqfanum vulgus, et arceo.*—At London, Printed for Henry Olney &c. Anno 1595. 4to. 42 *leaves.*

This is the first edition of Sir Philip Sidney's "Apologie for Poetry," which in 1598 was appended to his "Arcadia," under the title of the "Defence of Poesie." The Edward Wotton, spoken of in the commencement, is there merely designated by his initials, and the "foure Sonnets written by Henrie Constable to Sir Phillip Sidney's soule," which follow the title-page, were omitted, and never reprinted. The last is the happiest, and may be taken as a happy specimen of Constable's powers. (For a review of Constable's "Diana," 1592, see Vol. I. p. 187.)

"Great Alexander then did well declare
How great was his united Kingdomes might,
When ev'ry Captaine of his Army might,
After his death, with mighty Kings compare:
So now we see, after thy death, how far
Thou dost in worth surpasse each other Knight,
When we admire him as no mortall wight,
In whom the least of all thy vertues are.
One did of *Macedon* the King become,
Another sat in the *Egiptian* throne,
Bat onely *Alexander* selfe had all:
So eurteous some, and some be liberall,

Some witty, wise, valiaunt, and learned some,
But King of all the vertues thou alone.

"HENRY CONSTABLE."

The third of the sonnets prefixed to the work before us has the peculiarity of being in the measure of twelve syllables, although the form of a sonnet is still preserved. Constable had an extraordinary reputation, but what he has left behind him hardly warrants the praise bestowed upon him in the old play, "The Return from Parnassus," 1606, in a couplet, which will remind the reader of a beautiful passage in Milton's "Comus":—

"Sweet Constable doth take the wond'ring ear,
And lays it up in willing prisonment."

Anthony Wood says that Constable had been "not unfitly ranked with Sir Edward Dyer," by whom no separate poetical work in verse is known, [Note 1: On p. 75 of Vol. III. we have reviewed Dyer's prose paradox, "The Praise of Nothing," printed in 1585.] excepting "Sixe Idillia," translated from Theocritus, and printed by Joseph Barnes at Oxford in 8vo, 1588; for which see Vol I. p. 292.

SLANDER.—A plaine description of the Auncient Petigree of Dame Slaunder, togither with her Coheires and fellowe members, Lying, Flattering, Backebyting, (being the Divels deare darlinges), Playnly and Pithely described and set forth in their colours from their first descent, of what linage and kinred they came off. Eyther of them severally in his place set forth, as thou mayest reade hereafter.

I wil not be ashamed to defend a freend, neither will I hide my selfe from him, though he should do me harme. Eccle. 22.

—Imprinted at London by John Harrison. 1573. 8vo. B. L. 64 *leaves.*

No criticism of this singular production is anywhere to be found. In opposition to the words of the author's motto, he does "hide himself," for it is anonymous, though dedicated "To the right worshipfull and my especiall deare freend and Vallentine, Mistresse F. S. in all humblenes of dutie your accepted partner and allotted Vallentine wisheth all grace," &c. Moreover, an address from "The Printer to the Reader" warns him not to apply initials to individuals.

The whole is divided into five parts, and is rather more of a religious and moral treatise than the title promises. However, the writer has no objection to draw illustrations from the Stage, and recognizes "comedies and interludes." Thus in the beginning of "the second part" he says:—

"First selaunder is an accusation made for hatred, unknowen to him that is accused, wherein the accuser is not called to give answer, or to denye anything; and this definition standeth on three persons, even like as matters of Comedie doe. * * * And first of all, if you list, let us bring the Capten of the Interlude, and ring leader, which is the maker of this selaunder."

Afterwards we read as follows:—

"It is not possible to expresse how readie Dame Selaunder is, and how much she prevaileth, if she meete with one that is desirous to heare her; for if evil report and light of credence never meet, there could never so much harme be done by Dame Selaunder; but when these two compan¬ions meete, then beginneth the mischief, and at their departure then there is—*I heare say so, but say nothing that I told you to; for I tel it you for meere good wil and therefore would be loth to hear of it again; for I know my tale and tales maisler, but I like not to come to fending and proving:* and with this persuasion departeth the backbiting selaunderer."

The subject would easily have enabled a clever writer to be amusing; but towards the close the author becomes more script¬ural, though not without allusions also to profane history. He urges a diligent perusal of the Bible as a remedy for slander, and winds up with a text from 2 Maccabees xv. 88: "If I have done well, and as is fitting the story," &c.

SLATYER, WILLIAM.—The Psalmes of David in 4 Languages and in 4 Parts. Set to the Tunes of our Church: with Corrections. By W. S.—London Printed by P. Stent at the white horse in Guiltspur streete &c. n. d. 12mo. 35 *leaves.*

Opposite an engraved architectural title is "the true Portraiture of the learned Mr. William Slater, D. D.," but his real name, and that which he himself signed in existing MSS., was Slatyer. The Epistle to the Reader is also subscribed Wil. Slatyer: this is a long rambling introduction, in which the author refers to the translations of the Psalms by Sandys and by James L, to whose Queen Slatyer had been chaplain; and he states that with some alteration, as far as English was concerned, he had adopted the "vulgarly received and publickly authorized translation." The four languages in which he gives the Psalms, are Hebrew, Greek, Latin, and English. After the Epistle there is another engraved title-page, by which this volume should appear to be only "Pars prima" of the intended work. Opposite to it are forty-two English lines, headed Frontispicii Enarracö. This undated impression seems to have escaped notice, but there were reimpressions of it in 1643 and 1652.

SMITH, JOHN.—A Description of New England: or the Observations and Discoveries of Captain John Smith, (Admirall of that Country) in the North of America, in the year of our Lord 1614: with the successe of six Ships that went the next yeare 1615 &c.—At London Printed by Humfrey Lownes for Robert Clerke &c. 1616. 4to. 40 *leaves.*

The copy of this work preserved at Bridgewater House was obviously a presentation to Lord Chancellor Ellesmere, and on the inside of the cover is written, "My L. Chanseler," no doubt in Captain Smith's hand: at the top of the title-page is printed, "For the Right Honourable the Lord Elesmere, Lord High Chancelor of England." We know of no other exemplar with the same peculiarity; but it is not unlikely that the author had a certain number of copies struck off for persons of rank about the Court, with similar and separate printed directions, and the title-page thus distinguished is pasted in, and the ordinary title-page removed.

The dedication is to Prince Charles, followed by addresses to the King's Council, and to the New-England Adventurers: to these succeed verses in praise of the author, by John Davies of Hereford, J. Codrinton, N. Smith, R. Gunnell, George Wither, and Rawly Croshaw. Michael and William Phettiplace, and Richard Whiting, who had served under Captain Smith, also prefix verses; and others (which perhaps came too late) are added at the conclusion, signed Ed. Robinson, and Thomas Carlton, who call the author their "honest captain." We need not enter into it, but the general object of the tract is to show the advantages likely to arise to adventurers in New England. We have noticed another tract upon the same subject, the authorship of which is disputed between Captain Smith and Thomas Watson, under the heading VIRGINIA.

SMITH, SIR THOMAS.—Sir Thomas Smithes Voiage and Entertainment in Rushia. With the tragicall ends of two Emperors, and one Empresse, within one Moneth during his being there: And the miraculous preserva¬tion of the now raigning Emperor, esteemed dead for 18 yeares.

Si quid novisti rectius istis
Candidus impertie si non. His utere mecum.

—Printed at London for Nathanyell Butter, 1605. 4to. 47 *leaves.*

This account reads as if it had been drawn up by one of the persons who attended Sir Thomas Smith in his embassy; but, in an address "to the Reader," the writer speaks of the scattered and contradictory information that had got into circulation on the subject, and adds: "But I, taking the truth from the mouths of divers gentlemen that went in the Journey, and having some good notes bestowed upon me in writing, wrought them into this body, because neither thou shouldst be abused with false reports, nor the Voyage receive slaunder." Farther on he tells us, that he had done so without the consent of Sir T. Smith, or of anybody else. Nevertheless, the details are often very particular, and no doubt in most cases authentic, but obviously put together and printed in great haste. The writer was some person, not ill acquainted with the literature of the time, whom Butter, the publisher, employed.

He often makes excursions a little out of his way, in order to allude to persons and publications of the time, in this style mentioning Sidney, Fulk Greville, and Ben Jonson by their names.

"Oh, for some excellent pen-man to deplore their state: but he which would lively, naturally, or indeed poetically, delyneate or enumerate these occurrents, shall either lead you thereunto by a poeticall spirit, as could well, if well he might, the dead-living, life-giving Sydney, Prince of Poesie; or deifle you with the Lord Salustius devinity, or in the earth-deploring sententious high rapt Tragedie with the noble Foulk Grevill, not onely give you the Idea, but the soule of the acting Idea; as well could, if so he would, the elaborate English Horace, that gives number, weight and measure to every word, to teach the reader by his industries, even our Lawreat, worthy Benjamen, whose Muze approves him with (our mother) the Ebrew signification to bee the elder Sonne, and happely to have been the childe of Sorrow. It were worthy so excellent rare witt: for my selfe I am neither Apollo nor Apelles, no nor any heire to the Muses; yet happely a younger brother, though I have as little bequeathed me as many elder brothers and right borne heires gain by them: but *Hic labor, Hoc opus est.*"

In the following passage, in an earlier part of the tract, the author or compiler, among other matters, speaks of Prince Plangus in Sidney's "Arcadia," and of the Earl of Essex.

"It might be fitting for me to speake somewhat of this famous river [Volga] as is, I think, for length and bredth any (one) excepted in the world; but so many excellent writers, as in the worthy labors of Master Richard Hacklyute, have made particular mention therof, as it induseth me to leave the description of this river and towne to those that have largely and painfully wrote of such things; especially M. Doct. Fletchers true relation, sometime Ambas. to this Emperor. The 21 of September we went from Yeri-slane, being well accompanied from the Citty, passing through Shefetscoy (where wee lay) and dwels an English gentleman named Georg Garland, sometime servant to that noble but unfortunate E. of Essex, of whom many through the world do make in divers kinds, but (as that learned and heroycall Poet Sir Phil

Sidney speaks of Prince Plangus) never any can make but honorable mention."

The whole of this is evidently confused and corrupt, though a meaning can be made out of it Many other sentences in the tract are in the same predicament, and the abbreviations may show with what speed the materials were put together.

On the second page is an anecdote of Henry Howard, Earl of Northampton, which is not much in his favor.

"But the king wondering that the detention there would be so long (for Sir Thomas said it would be full xv moneths by reason of the winters cruelty, whose frosts were so extream, that the seas were not at those times navigable) pleasantly said—It seemes then that Sir Thomas goes from the Sun:—upon which the Earle of Northampton, standing by, replyed—He must needes go from the Sunne, departing from his resplendant Ma.—At which the King smiled, giving Sir Thomas his hand to kisse, and bestowing the like grace upon all the gentlem. that were for the voyage."

The author refers afterwards to the "Quadrones of the Lord of Pibrac," and thus inserts four lines of translated quotation from them: ***"Petit source ont les grosses Rivieres,"*** &c.

"Even as from smallest springs the greatest rivers rise,
So those that rore aloud, and proud at first,
Runne seldom farre; for soon their glorie dies
In some neere Bogg, by their self-furie burst."

Subsequently we have another highly laudatory, but strangely jumbled, allusion to the Earl of Essex, in these terms:—

"For our being at Colmigro, it was not much unlike (for the strangenea of reports, troublesomnes of the State, and mutable events of time) to that one and the only unhappie day of the unfortunate (too sudden rysing) Earle of Essex; wherein most mens mindes, for as many dayes as wee weekes, weare bewondered as much with the not well directed beginning, as the unhallowed successe or the bemoaned (oh be it ever lamentable, such conclusions, but as farre different in the rarenes as the goodnes between them) ill-advised, well-intended, ever good resolutions in the one, ill-intended work enacted, never-good-conclusions in the other: One as the unhappie time-falling of a great Noble, with some others: but by the goodnes of God and the gratiousnes of our renowned King, within short and memorable time restored in his posteritie and theires. The other the fatall and finall overthrow of a mightie Emperour and his posteritie and familie, never till the Resurrection to be raysed: and then, oh then! it is to be feared to a terrible Judgement for their high-offending, Heaven-crying sinnes."

There is a good deal of this rhapsodical matter interspersed, but the personal allusions, as in the above instance, as far as the sense can be made out, are interesting. In one place we have the fol¬lowing not very apposite mention of "Hamlet."

"That his fathers Empire and Government was but as the poeticall furie in a Stage-action, compleat, yet with horrid and wofull tragedies; a first, but no second to any *Hamlet;* and that now *Revenge,* just revenge, was comming with his sworde drawne against him, his royall Mother, and dearest Sister, to fill up those murdering sceanes; the embryon whereof was long since modeld, yea digested (but unlawfully and too-too vively) by his dead selfe-murdering Father."

Shakspeare's "Hamlet" had been brought out two or three years before this tract was published; but it may be doubted whether the reference be not to the older play on the same story, which Lodge had noticed in 1596 in his "Wits Misery and the Worlds Madness," when he spoke of "the ghost who cried so miserably at the Theatre, Hamlet, revenge!" That tragedy of "Hamlet" had been acted at Henslowe's Theatre on 9th June, 1594, and was not then a new play; (Diary, p. 35.) We see, by the reference above quoted from the tract in our hands, that it had not gone out of recollection in 1605, in spite of the superior attraction and greater novelty of Shakspeare's drama. It it possible, too, that there had been a second part to the old tragedy.

SMITH, WALTER.—XII mery Jests of the wyddow Edyth.

This lying widow, false and craftie,
Late i Englad hath decevied many,
Both man and woman of every degree,
As well of the spirituall, as temporaltie,
Lordes, Knights and Gentlemen also,
Yemen, Groomes, and that not long ago;
For in the time of King Henry the eight
She hath used many a suttle sleight,
What with lieng, weepyng and laughyng,
Dissemblyng, boastypg and flatteryng,
As by this Booke hereafter doth appere,
Who so list the matter now for to here:
No fayned stories, but matter in deed,
Of xii of her Jestes here may ye reede.
Now newly printed this present yeare
For such as delite mery Jests for to here.

1573. 4to. B. L. 32 *leaves.*

The above is the whole of the title-page of a tract, of which no older copy is now known, although Ames records (and Herbert and Dibdin refer to no other authority) that it was originally printed by John Rastell in 1525. (Dibd. *Typ. Ant.* III. 87.) It does not seem as if Ames had copied the lines on the title-page correctly, for, independently of the two last lines, which may have been added in 1573, he omitted the tenth line, so that "laughyng" has no corresponding rhyme. There are also other variations, besides the differences of spelling; and as a copy of Rastell's edition (once in the Harleian Library, and included in the Catalogue) is not now forthcoming, we are compelled to take the whole matter upon the representation of Richard Johnes, who printed the edition of 1573: at the end of it we read as follows:—

"FINIS. by Walter Smith
Imprinted at London, in Fleetlane
by Richard Johnes."

On the leaf next to the title-page we meet with "The Contentes of these xii mery Jestes folowyng"; and as the work has only been mentioned, never quoted, by bibliographers and antiquaries, we subjoin the list exactly as it stands:—

"The first mery Jest declareth how this faire and merye Mayden was maryed to one Thomas Ellys, and how she ran away with another, by whom she had a bastard Doughter; and how she deceived a Gentleman, bearynge him in hand, how her Doughter was heire to faire Landes and great Richesse.

"The second merye Jest: how this lying Edyth made a poore man to unthatch his house, bearyng him in hand that she would cover it with Lead; and how she deceived a Barbour, makyng him beleeve she was a widow, and had great aboundance of Gooddes.

"The thyrd mery Jest: how this wydow Edyth deceived her Hoste at Hormynger, and her Hoste at Brandonfery, and borowed money of them both; and also one mayster Guy, of whome she borowed iiii Marke.

"The fourth mery Jest: how this wydow Edyth deceived a Doctor of divinitie, at S. Thomas of Akers in London, of v Nobles he layd out for her, and how she gave hym the slyp.

"The fifth merye Jest: how this wydow Edyth deceived a man and his wife that were ryding on Pylgremage, of iiii Nobles yt they laid out for her; and how she deceived a Scrivener in Lodon, whose name was M. Rowse.

"The sixt merye Jest: how this wydow Edyth deceived a Draper in Lodon of a new Gowne, and a new Kyrtell; and how she sent him for a nest of Gobblets and other Plate to that Scrivener whome she had deceived afore.

"The vii mery Jest: how she deceived a servat of Sir Thomas Nevells who, in hope to have her in Manage, wt. all her great Richesse, kepte her company tyl al his money was spent, and then she tooke her flight and forsooke him.

"The eight mery Jest: how this wydow Edyth deceyved a Servant of the Byshop of Rochesters, with her coggynge and boastynge of her great Richesse, who like wise thought to have had her in Maryage.

"The ix mery Jest: how she deceived a Lord, sotyme Earle of Arudell; and how he sent v of his men servantes and a handmaid to beare her company and fetch her Doughter, who, as she boasted, was an he ire to great Landes.

"The tenth merye Jest: how she deceived three yong men of Chelsey, that were servantes to Syr Thomas More, and were all three suters unto her for Maryage; and what mischaunce happened unto her.

"The xi mery Jest: how she deceived three yong men of the Lord Legates servants with her great lying, crakyng, and boastyng of her great Treasure and Juelles.

"The xii merye Jest: how this wydow Edyth deceyved the good man of the three Cuppes in Holburne, and one John Cotes; and how they both ryd with her to S. Albons to oversee her houses and landes, and how they were rewarded."

"The Preface," following the above list, is in verse, and relates how Edyth's father, John Hankyn, had three wives, and then died, leaving a daughter by the last. The mother brought up the girl in all kinds of artifice and roguery, and she afterwards took a husband herself:—

"Thomas Ellys she maryed for a yeare or two,
And then left him, and away dyd go
With a servant of the Erle of Wyltshyre,
The which payd her well her hyre.

By hym in advoutry a childe she had,
Which dyed when it was but a lad:
Than her Lemman cast her up,
Go where she wold, gup, queaue, gup!"

There is no doubt that she was a real personage; and Walter Smith, the author of these tales, admits that he had suffered by her. The "Jests," or stories of her iniquities, vary in length from one to thirteen pages. They have little humor, but a good deal of coarseness and indecency. The following, No. 3, is one of the least exceptionable:—

"This wydowe she walked withoaten fere,
Till that she came to Hormynger,
Within two myles of S. Edmunds bery,
And there she abode, full jocunde and mery,
For the space fully of vj weekes day,
And borrowed money there as she lay.
Her old lyes she occupied still;
The people gave credence her untyll:
At Thetford she sayd her stuffe lay,
Which false was proved upon a day.
Than one master Lee committed her to ward,
And little or naught she dyd it regard.
On the vj day after delivered she was,
And at her owne lyberty to passe and repasse.

Then straight way she tooke to Brandonfery,
In all her lyfe was she never so mery;
And there she borrowed of her Hoste
Thirteene shillings, with mickle boste
Of her great substance which she sayd she had.
To Bradefolde straight her Hoste she lad,
Where she sayde that she dwelled as than;

And when she came thyther, she fild him a can
Full with good Ale, and sayd he was welcome
For his thirteene shillings: she bad him bum.
And laughed tygbe; no more could he have.
An oth he sware, so God hym save,
The Justice should know of her deceyt,
A, whore! (quod he) heyt, whore, heyt!
The Justice name was master Lee:
He sent her to Saint Edmonds berye,
And there in the Jayle halfe a yeare
She continued without good cheare;
But after she was delivered out
Upon a day withouten doubt.
My Lorde Abbot commaunded it should so bee,
When he was remembred of his charitye.

From thence she departed, and to Coulme she come,
Wherwith her lyes all and some
She sudjorned, and was at borde
In a house of my Lorde Oxenforde,
Wherin a servant of his owne did dwell,
Which brewed bere, but none to sell.
The Brewer was called John Douchmon,
With whom vj dayes she dyd won:
Then after to Stretford at the Bow
She repayred right as I trow,
And vij dayes there she abode.
Spreding her lyes all abrode.

In which tyme one maister Gye,
Supposing nought that she did lye,
And trustyng of her to have some good
Fowre Marks, by the swete roode,

He lent her out of his purs anon,
And asked ay when she wold gon
To the place where her goods were layd,
Which was at Barking (as she sayd).
Master Guy and his sister both
To ride with her they were not loth,
Ne grudged nothing, till they perceived
That she had them falsly deceived.
Then master Guy, with egre moode,
In the place there as they stoode,
Raft her both Kyrtle and gowne,
And in her Peticote to the Towne
He sent her forth. Mahound her save!
For his iiij Marks no more could he have."

Such incidents are common in these tales, and they are not narrated with much spirit or vivacity. The eighth, respecting the trick she played the Bishop of Rochester's servant, is shorter than the rest, and we quote it as a further specimen of a highly curious book that has hitherto had little attention paid to it:—

"The Wydow northward tooke her way,
And came to Rochester the next day;
And there within a little space
To a yongman, that servant was
Unto the Byshop in the Towne,
She promised him date and downe
On that condition he would wed,
And keepe her company at boord and in bed.

This yongman was glad and light:
Now, thought he, I shal be made a knight
By the meanes of this gentlewomans store:
Gramercy Fortune! I can no more.

He permytted in hast to be assembled
With her at the church, and there resembled,
Or joyned in one flesh, that is dying,
And two soules evermore livyng.

Good cheare he made her in her Inne,
And eke he would not never blinne,
Tyl he had brought her to his Lorde,
Before whom they were at accorde,
Upon a condition maryed to be;
Which condition was, if that she
Could performe all that she had sayd,
He wolde then marry her: it should not be delayd.
Here upon they departed and forth went.

On the morrow my Lorde for her sent
To dyne with him, and to commen further.
Then was she gone: but when and whether
No wyght any worde of her could tell;
But yet she walked to my Lorde of Arundell."

It is beyond question that the original edition by John Rastell was formerly in the Harleian Collection, where it must have been seen and used by Ames, who gives the following as its colophon: "Emprinted at London at the sygne of the meremayde at Pollis gate next chepesyde by J. Rastell. 23 March MvCxxv." According to Rastell, the widow was "still living "when he printed her adventures.

SMITH, WILLIAM.—Chloris, or the Complaint of the passionate despised Shepheard. By William Smith.—Imprinted at London, by Edm. Bollifant. [Note 1: He was not a typographer who was much employed at the close of the seventeenth century.] 1596. 4to. 15 *leaves.*

The most remarkable circumstance about this very rare book (only three copies of it have ever been mentioned) is, that it is, not indeed dedicated to, but addressed to Spenser, who roust have given encouragement to the author to print his creditable sonnets to an unknown mistress, whom he calls Chloris. Regarding Smith we have no information excepting that he was not the writer of the play printed in 1615 under the title of "Hector of Germany," although it has been assigned to William Smith in all lists,—last in Lowndes' ***Bibl. Man.*** edit. 1863, p. 2431. This mistake arose out of the initial of the Christian name of both; but "Chloris," as we see above, was by William, and "Hector of Germany" was by ***Wentworih*** Smith. They were, however, contemporaries, but the talent of William Smith appears to have been entirely undramatic, while Wentworth Smith was the author of several plays imputed of old to Shakspeare. William Smith could write verse, but it hardly ascended to the rank of poetry, while Spenser seems to have been anxious to promote the success of a juvenile aspirant, who more than once speaks of his "maiden Muse," and of "the young-hatched" offspring of his brain. Two sonnets, addressed "To the most excellent and learned Shepheard Collin Cloute," immediately follow the title-page, and we quote them:—

> "Collin, my deere and most entire beloved,
> My muse audatious stoupes hir pitch to thee,
> Desiring that thy patience be not moved
> By these rude lines, [that] written heere you see.
> Faine would my muse, whom cruell love hath wronged,
> Shroud hir love labors under thy protection,
> And I my selfe with ardent zeale have longed,
> That thou mightst knowe to thee my true affection.
> Therefore, good Collin, graciously accept
> A few sad sonnets which my muse hath framed:
> Though they but newly from the shell are crept,
> Suffer them not by envie to be blamed;
> But underneath the shadow of thy wings
> Give warmth to these yong-hatched orphan things.

> "Give warmth to these yoong-hatched orphan things,

Which chill with cold to thee for succour creepe:
They of my studie are the budding springs,
Longer I cannot them in silence keepe.
They will be gadding, sore against my minde;
But, curteous shepheard, if they run astray
Conduct them, that they may the path way finde,
And teach them how the meane observe they may.
Thou shalt them ken by their discording notes:
Their weedes are plaine, snob as poore shepheards weare,
Unshapen, torne and ragged are their ootes;
Yet foorth they wandring are devoid of feare.
They wich have tasted of the muses spring
I hope will smile upon the tunes they sing.

Finis. W. SMITH."

These are followed by forty-nine love-effusions of the same measure, (with one exception, which found its way into "England's Helicon," edit. 1600, sign. M 2 b,) but before we quote a specimen from them, we will extract a third sonnet to Spenser, (the last in the volume, and numbered 50,) which, however, merits attention chiefly on account of the poet (here called Colin, and not Collin) spoken of in it. It runs thus, not unmusically:—

"Colin, I know that in thy loftie wit
Thou wilt but laugh at these my youthfull lines:
Content I am they should in silence sit,
Obscurd from light, to sing their sad designes;
But that it pleased thy grave shepheardhood
The Patron of my maiden verse to bee,
When I in doubt of raging Envie stood,
And now I waigh not who shall Chloris see:
For fruit before it comes to full perfection
But blossome is, as every man doth know:

So these being bloomes, and under thy protection,
In time, I hope, to ripenes more will grow.
And so I leave thee to thy woorthy muse,
Desiring thee all faults heere to excuse."

Spenser was, no doubt, at this date in a forbearing and approving mood, for he had published his own *Amoretti* in the year preceding. Of course the two works will not bear an instant's comparison, and Smith endeavors to make up for the absence of real inspiration and genuine feeling (in which Spenser abounds) by artificial ornaments, and by the frequency of classical allusions. As an example of a sonnet with fewer of these impeding aids, we extract that numbered 39:—

"The stately Lion and the furious Beare
The skill of man doth alter from their kinde,
For where before they wilde and savage were
By art both tame and meeke yon shall them finde.
The Elephant, although a mighty beast,
A man may rule according to his skill;
The lustie horse obaieth our beheast
For with the curbe you may him guide at will:
Although the flint most hard containes the fire,
By force we do his vertue soone obtaine,
For with a Steele you shall have your desire.
Thus man may all things by industry gaine;
Onely a woman, if she list not love,
No art nor force can unto pitie move."

Certainly Smith's "art" was not of a kind and degree to move much pity in any lady who was a judge of the real excellence of poetry, its fire and its fervor; and he owns that his complexion, "which was black," did not suit the taste of Chloris. We are inclined to think that Smith's best production is the six-and-twenty lines called "Corins Dreame of his faire Chloris," which obtained for him a place in both editions of "England's Helicon," 1600 and 1614. [Note: 1: It is only subscribed W.

S., and is found on the reverse of sign. M 2 of the edition of "England's Helicon," in 1600. There are several variations between the printed copies of 1596 and 1600, but they are not worth pointing out, as they do not affect the meaning of the poet.] Most of the sonnet-writers of that day, with the great exceptions of Shakspeare and Spenser, were more or less imitators of each other—the main difference being the degree of imitation.

SONGS AND AIRS.—Two Bookes of Ayres. The first conteyning Divine and Morall Songs: The second, light Conceits of Lovers. To be sung to the Lute or Viols, in two three and foure Parts: or by one Voyce to an Instrument Composed by Thomas Campion.—London: Printed by Tho. Snodham, for Mathew Lownes, and J. Browne. ***Cum Privilegio.*** Folio. 25 ***leaves.***

Both the words and music of this work were the production of Thomas Campion, who in 1602 had printed "Observations in the Art of English Poesie, wherein it is demonstratively prooved, and by example confirmed, that the English toong will receive eight severall kinds of numbers, proper to it selfe." This production was the occasion of Samuel Daniel's "Defence of Ryme," which was not first printed in 1603 (as would seem from the reprint in "Ancient Critical Essays," 4to, 1815), but in 1602, showing that Daniel lost no time in preparing his reply, which is a very elegant piece of prose composition. We notice the two editions of 1602 and 1603, because they vary, a circumstance not noted by the editor of the reprint of 1815, who was only acquainted with the impression of 1603. Our business here is with Campion's original poems in the "Two Bookes of Ayres" now before us, which are not included in any enumeration of his productions that we have been able to examine.

Very soon after 1590 Campion's talents as a versifier were appreciated, and in 1593 he was by name applauded by Peele in the "Prologus" to his poem, "The Honour of the Garter." We may here note that one copy of this piece, which we have met with, had no date at the bottom of the title-page.

The "Two Bookes of Ayres" are separately dedicated, one to the Earl of Cumberland, and the other to his son and heir. To the former Campion says:—

"What patron could I chuse, great Lord, but you?
Grave words your years may challenge as their owne,
And every note of music is your due,
Whose house the Muses pallace I have knowne."

To the son he apologizes both for "his notes and rime"; and in an address to the Reader he observes: "In these English Ayres I have chiefely aymed to couple my words and notes lovingly together, which will be much for him to do that hath not power over both." All we can undertake here is to give a few specimens of Campion's "words," and the following is, perhaps, as graceful lyric as can easily be found in our language:—

"Give Beauty all her right;
Shees not to one forme tyed:
Each shape yeelds faire delight,
Where her perfections bide;
Helen, I grant, might pleasing be,
And Bosomond was as sweet as shee.
"Some the quicke eye commends,
Some swelling lips and red:
Pale looks have many friends,
Through sacred sweetnesse bred.
Medowes have flowers that pleasure move,
Though Roses are the flowers of love.

"Free Beauty is not bound
To one unmoved clime;
She visits every ground,
And favours every time.
Let the old loves with mine compare,
My soveraigne is as sweet and fayre."

Here we plead guilty to making an emendation in the second stanza, where "swelling" has been misprinted *smelling.* In "Antony and Cleopatra," Act II. sc. 2, the reverse error has been committed by patting *swell* for "smell." The subsequent song is of a different character, but very charming, and the close felicitous:—

"There is none, O! none but you
That from me estrange your sight,
Whom mine eyes affect to view,
Or chained eares heare with delight.

"Other beauties others move
In you I all graces finde:
Such is the effect of love
To make them happy that are kinde.

"Women in fraile beauty trust:
Onely seeme you faire to mee,
Yet prove truely kinde and just,
For that may not dissembled be.

"Sweet, afford mee then your sight,
That surveying all your lookes,
Endlesse volumes I may write,
And fill the world with envyed bookes:

"Which when after ages view,
All shall wonder and despaire,
Woman to finde a man so true,
Or man a woman halfe so faire."

Besides more serious pieces, on which we need not dwell, there is a very lively rustic song, which concludes thus:—

"Now, you courtly Dames and Knights
That study onely strange delights,
Though you scorne the home-spun gray,
And revell in your rich array;
Though your tongues dissemble deepe,
And can your heads from danger keepe,
Yet for all your pompe and traine,
Securer lives the silly swaine."

Such easy and cheerful words seem, in reading, to inspire their own music. No date can be assigned to the work in hand, but we may presume that it was written while the author was young and his spirits buoyant. [Note 1: George Clifford Earl of Cumberland, to whom Campion dedicates the first of the two books, died in 1605, but his son did not succeed him: he must have died before his father, whose brother inherited the title.] He afterwards became more constrained, and sometimes harsh, as may be seen in the songs for several Masques of his composition. At the end of the "Two Books of Ayres" is a very curious and interesting list, thus entitled: "A Catalogue of all the Musicke Bookes that have been printed in England, eyther for the Lute, Base Violl, Voyces, or other Musicall Instruments." It is upon a large separate folded sheet in three columns, and comprises nearly 150 distinct publications, beginning with those in folio and proceeding to the quartos, each alphabetically arranged. We can only specify a few, but among them are these: Alfonso's Ayres, Bartlet's Ayres, Coperario's Ayres, Corkine's Ayres, Cavendish's Ayres, Campion's first, second, third, and fourth bookes, Dowland's four bookes, Daniel's Ayres, Ford's Ayres, Jones's Musical Dreame, Jones's Muses Garden, Morley's Consort, Bathe's Introduction, Bird's set of Gradualia, East's four Sets, Gibbons' Madrigals, Farmer's Madrigals, Holborne's Gitterne Booke, Ravenscroft's four bookes of Catches, Wilbie's six Sets, Kirbie's six Parts, Bennet's Madrigals, Watson's six Parts, Wilkes' Fantastickes, Carlton's five Parts, Youle's Canzonets, Sir William Leighton's Songs and Sonnets, Sr. Edwin Sand's Psalmes, &c.

One of Campion's rarest works, of a middle period, (only two copies of it have come down to us,) was his "Songs of Mourn¬ing: bewailing the untimely death of Prince Henry," the music to which was not his own, but by John Cooper, who Italianized his name as Coperario. They were printed together, in 1613, "for John Browne;" and we quote only a single specimen, since, in every respect, the grief and words" are too artificial, as if un¬prompted by genuine grief and sensibility. The following is headed—

"*To the most disconsolate Great Britaine.*

"When pale famine fed on thee
With her insatiate jawes,
When civill broyle set murder free,
Contemning all thy lawes;
When heaven enrag'd consam'd thee so
With plagues, that none thy face could know,
Yet in thy lookes affliction shewed lesse
Than now for one's fall all thy parts expresse.

"Now thy highest States lament
A Sonne and Brother's losse;
Thy Nobles mourne in discontent,
And rue this fatall crosse.
Thy Commons are with passion sad
To thinke how brave a Prince they had.
If all thy rockes from white to black should turne,
Yet couldst thou not in shew more amply mourne."

This is in a very different style and strain to that which Campion could produce when unfettered by his subject, and allowed free range to his fancy and imagination. He was an excellent scholar, as well as a fine poet and an accomplished musician, and be prefixes to his "Songs of Mourning" some good hexameter and pentameter lines. They are followed by an English Elegy, in which the author was evidently not less anxious to propitiate the living Prince, than to lament the dead one. It requires no further notice.

SOOWTHERN, JOHN.—Pandora. The Musyque of the beautie of his mistresse Diana. Composed by John Soowthern, Gentleman, and dedicated to the right Honorable, Edward Dever, Earle of Oxenford &c. 1584 June 20. ***Non careo patria, me caret Illa magis.***—Imprinted at London for Thomas Hackette, and are to be solde at his shoppe in Lumbert streete under the Popes head. 1584. 4to. B. L. 40 ***leaves.***

The title of this volume has never before been given, and the only copy known to Ritson was deficient in this respect One or two other exemplars, more or less complete, are mentioned by bibliographers; but the contents are so worthless that we shall dismiss the work comparatively briefly. We believe that the only perfect copy was that belonging to Heber, which we have used. Steevens conjectured that Soowthern, Soothern, or Southern, was a native of France; but we apprehend that he was English, and had been educated abroad before he came to this country to follow his profession as a musician. It has been supposed that Drayton referred to this rhymster (who scarcely deserves even to be so called) when, in the first ode of his "Poemes Lyrick and Pastorall" (n. d., but printed soon after the death of Elizabeth) he thus addressed a person, whose name he spelt—

> "Southerne, I long thee spare,
> Yet wish thee well to fare,
> Who pleased'st greatly,
> As first, therefore more rare,
> Handling thy harpe neatly."

Here we have no Christian name, and it is impossible to believe that Drayton would mean to praise anything in Soowthern (if the same man were intended) but his neat handling of the harp. Whatever may be the value of the lines as a kindly tribute, they have not hitherto been cited. Puttenham, in his "Arte of English Poesie," 1589, does not name Soowthern, but ridicules the affectation, self-conceit, and plagiarism of his productions. His words, of easy application by those who were acquainted with Soowthern's style, are the following:—"Another, of reasonable good facilitie in translation, finding certaine of the hymnes of Pyndarus and of Anacre-on's Odes, and other Lirickes among the Greekes, very well translated by Rounsard, the French Poet, and applied to the honour of a great Prince in France, comes our minion, and translates the same out of French into English, and applies them to the honour of a great nobleman in England; wherein I commend his reverent minde and duetie, but [he] doth so impudently robbe the French Poet, both of his prayse and also of his French termes, that I cannot so much pitie him, as be angry wilh him for his injurious dealing; our sayd maker not being ashamed to use these French wordes, ***freddon, egar, superbous, filanding, celest, calabrois, thebanois*** and a number of others for English wordes, which have no maner of conformitie with our language, either by custome, or derivation" (p. 211).

By the "great nobleman" Puttenham means the Earl of Oxford, to whom, upon his title-page, and in an unusual manner, Soowthern dedicates his volume. In some verses "to the Reader," he tells him to expect only amorous effusions, and not "furi-ous alarms," from France, Spain, Germany, or Italy; and the following, numbered 5, is a sonnet "to his Diana," so far anticipating Constable (see Vol. I. p. 187) in the name given to his mistress:—

"Of stars and of forrests Dian is the honor,
And to the seas to the Goddesse is the guide:
And she hath Luna, Charon and Eumenide
To make brightnes, to give death, and to cause horror.
And, my warrier, my light shines in thy fayre eyes;
My dread is of thee, the to great excellence:
Thy wordes kyll mee, and thus thou hast the puissance
Of her that rules the flodes, and lightens the skies.
And as sylver Pheb is the aster most clare,
So is thy beauty the beauty the most rare:
Wherefore I call thee Dian for thy beau tee,
For thy wisedome and for thy puissance celest.
And yet thou must be but a Goddesse terest,
And onely because of thy great crueltee."

It is just possible to make sense out of this "mingle mangle," (as Puttenham afterwards terms Soowthern's barbarous mixture of languages,) but when the sense is made out, it is not worth the trouble. Not a little, and certainly the best part of the collection, is stolen from Ronsard, without acknowledgment or reference; but when the author trusts solely to himself he is merely inane, and yet ridiculously and despicably self-satisfied. The following is the opening of one of his "Elegies," and is addressed

"To THE GODS.

"When the eye of the world doth washe
His golden shining haire
In the large Occean seas; and that
They have coverd the lyght,
A murmuring repose and a
Restfull and sleepy night
Is spreded both over the earth
The waters and the ayre.
But I chaunge nature then. For than
Dooth my brightest Aurôr,
In a sweete dreame present her selfe.
O dreamw, no dreame! but well,
The Ambrozie, the Nectar, and
The manna Eternell:
And to be breefe, a vision that
I lyke a God adore.
Wherefore farewell, day of night, and
Welcome night waking daye;
And farewell waking of my sleepe,
Welcome sleepe, lyving joye.
But what say I? my wealth is false,
And my evill veritable;

And I plaine of them both, for I
Have in neither delight:
Except ye Gods will short these dayes,
And eternish this night;
And that God that will doo it, shall
Be a God charitable."

We feel confident that no further sample from such a miserable, self-deluded dabbler can be required; but the latter part of his volume professes to contain "four Epitaphs by the Countes of Oxenford, after the death of her young sonne, the Lord Bul-becke"; and an "Epitaph made by the Queenes Majestie at the death of the Princesse Espinoye," together with "Verses, Stanzas, Hymnes, and Elegies, all dedicated or sent to his Mistresse Diana." Soowthern was resolved to furnish sufficient variety, and added to all these what he calls "Odellets," as well as some French rhymes, which purport to be original; and from which we judge, that, although an Englishman by birth and name, he, probably, had had a foreign education. His productions do no credit to either country.

SOUTHWELL, ROBERT.—Mary Magdalens Funerall Teares. Jeremiæ Cap. VI. verse 26. ***Luctum unigeniti fac tibi planctum Amarum.***—London, Printed by A. I. G. C. 1594. 8vo. 47 ***leaves.***

We are the more desirous to notice this, as far as we know, unique edition of Robert Southwell's earliest printed work, because, although the title of it has been mentioned, (Lowndes, Bibl Man. p. 2461, edit 1863,) it has been incorrectly given, and the body of the work, as it here exists, has never been examined. It was several times reprinted, in 1607, 1609, 1620, and 1626; the later impressions are very inaccurate, often substituting one word for another, and otherwise perverting the meaning of the author. Thus, on the very first page of the edition of 1620, we are told that the blessed Mary Magdalen loved our Lord more than "her selfe," when the edition of 1594 shows that ***selfe*** was a misprint for "life"; and just afterwards "***owne*** death" is substituted for "one death," and ***turnedst*** for returnedst. Without pursuing this point further, we may add, that in all the accounts regarding Southwell, even in that by the late Mr. Turnbull, ("Poetical Works of Southwell," 8vo, 1856,) an introductory address to the Sackville family, which was written by Trussell, and printed with his name at length in 1596 and several times afterwards, is assigned to Southwell, under the initials S. W., which were assumed in 1594 in the production before us. This was a blunder into which Mr. Turnbull fell because it had previously been committed by Haslewood, in ***Censura Literaria,*** II. 7, edit. 1815.

The name or initials of Southwell were not upon the title-page, nor annexed to the preliminary matter of the work in our hands; and we see that even the printer and stationer did not give their names. A. I., reversed, we may suppose to have been John Allde, and G. C. Gabriel Cawood. The dedication "To the worshipfull and ver-tuous Gentlewoman Mistresse D. A.," and the address "to the Reader," are both sub-scribed "Your loving friend S. W.," though changed to R. S. in subsequent impres-sions. In the dedication, the author (who, after all, may not have been Southwell, but some other nameless and zealous Roman Catholic) thus adverts to the loose and idle character of the prevailing poetry of his day; and we may almost fancy that he had in his mind (though, of course, he does not name it, nor any other performance of the kind) Shakspeare's "Venus and Adonis," which had come out in the previous year, and had been reprinted at the very time when the following attack was di-rected against such productions. S. W. expresses his hope that his "pleasing theme" will be welcome to "Mistresse D. A.," and then adds:—

"For as passion, and especially this of love, is in these daies the chiefe com-maunder of moste mens actions, and the Idol to which both tongues and pennes doe sacrifice their ill-bestowed labours; so is there nothing nowe more needefall to bee intreated than how to direct these humours unto their due courses, and to drawe this floude of affections into the right chanel. Passions I allowe and loves I approove; only I woulde wishe that men would alter their object, and better their intent."

He then calls upon worthier pens to take up the subject, observing: "And therefore sith the finest wits are now given to write passionate discourses, I would wish them to make choise of such passions, as it neither should be shame to utter, nor sinne to feele." Possibly, to this admonition we may owe such pieces as Nash's "Christ's Tears," [Note 1: Of course we refer here only to the "reissue," because the original edition, without the author's tendered amends to Gabriel Harvey, came out in 1593, as we have sufficiently explained on p. 16 of Vol. III.] in prose, which was reissued in 1594, or such poems as Mark ham's "Syon's Muse," which came out in 1595. Again, in his address "to the Reader," S. W. (for so he subscribes it) complains of the poets of his day for taking up profane fables of love, "wisely telling a foolish tale, and carrying a long lie very smoothly to the end." On these he laments that "exquisite labours" have been bestowed; and of his own work he says, using a word we do not recollect to have met with elsewhere, "This commoditie, at the least, it will carrie with it, that the reader may learne to love without improofe of puritie, and teach his thoughtes either to temper passion in the meane, or to give the bridle onelie where the excesso cannot be faultie."

He opens his "Mary Magdalen's Funeral Tears" with these labored sentences:—

"Amongest other mournefull accidents of the Passion of Christ, that love preseuteth it selfe unto my memorie, with which the blessed Mary Magdalen, loving our Lord more then her life, followed him in his journey to his death, attending uppon him when his Disciples fled, and being more willing to die with him then they to live without him. But not finding the favour to accompanie hym in death, and loathing after him to remaine in life, the fire of her true affection enflamed her heart, and her enflamed heart resolved into uncessant teares, so that burning and bathing betweene love and griefe, she led a life ever dying, and felt a death never ending. And when he by whom shee lived was dead, and she for whom hee died enforcedly left alive, shee praised the dead more than the living; and having lost that light of her life, she desired to dwelle in darknesse and in the shadow of death, choosing Christes Tombe for her best home, and his corse for her chiefe comfort. For Mary (as the Evangelist saith) *stoode without at the Tombe weeping.*"

The above will afford a notion of the artificial, antithetical, and somewhat inflated style of the whole work: it is in many respects like a long sermon upon the text from Jeremiah on the title-page, and as we proceed, we wonder how so much eloquence can be wound upon so small a foundation. There is not a scrap of poetry, strictly so called, from the beginning to the end, but the writer warms as he proceeds, and in some places works himself up to a high pitch of religious enthusiasm. [Note 1: Gabriel Harvey, in 1598, ("Pierces Supererogation,") says, "Who can deny but the Resolution and Mary Magdalens Funerall Teares are penned elegantly and pathetically?" This praise, judging by the dates, preceded the publication of the works to which they apply. It appears from the accounts of the Lieutenant of the Tower, which we have inspected, that Robert Southwell was a prisoner there in 1592, as well as afterwards.] In one place he apostrophizes Mary Magdalen, and in another, near the end, he appeals thus earnestly, on her behalf, to the Saviour:—

"O good Jesu! what hath thus estranged thee from her? Thou hast heretofore so pitied her tears that, seeing them, thou couldest not refraine thine. In one of her greatest agonies, for love of her that so much loved thee, thou didst recall hir ded brother to life, turning her complaint into unexpected contentment. And we know that thou doest not use to alter course without cause, nor to chastise without desert. Thou art the first that invitest and the last that forsakest, never leaving but first left, and ever offering till thou art refused. How then hath she forfaited thy favor? or with what trespasse hath she earned thy ill will? That she never left to love thee, her heart will depose, her hand will subscribe, her toonge will protest, her teares will testifie, and her seeking doth assure. And, alas! is her particular case so farre from example, that thou shonldest rather alter thy nature, than shee better her fortime, and be to her as thou art to no other?"

The fault of Southwell's style, both in prose and verse, is a want of simplicity, and the defect is well illustrated in our last quotation, where he enumerates so elaborately the claims of his heroine (if we may so consider her) to the especial favor of our Lord. Southwell was executed as a concealed Jesuit in 1595; and it is singular to find his biographers citing, as his, a poem which, in 1596, alludes to his own sufferings and decease:—

"But now, by Death's none-sparing cruelty

Is turn'd an orphan to the open air," &c.

This poem was composed by, and signed by, John Trussell, the author of "The first Rape of Faire Helen," published in the year when Southwell was executed.

SOUTHWELL, ROBERT.—Saint Peters Complainte. Marie Magdalens Teares, with other workes of the author R. S.—London Printed for W. Barrett 1620. 12mo. 288 *leaves.*

The above title is in a small compartment in the centre of an engraving representing four passages in the history of the Saviour at the corners, with the figures of Mary Magdalen and St. Peter at the sides. The whole volume is dedicated by the stationer to the Earl of Dorset. It is divided into five parts by separate printed title-pages:—1. St. Peter's Complaint. 2. Mæoniæ. 3. Mary Mag¬dalen's Funeral Teares (in prose). 4. The Triumphs over Death (in prose). 5. Short Rules of good Life (in prose). Most of these were often printed separately at earlier dates, beginning with "Mary Magdalen's Funeral Tears" in 1594, and "St. Peter's Complaint" and "Mæoniæ" in 1595. In the edition before us, the poems, &c. purport to have been written by R. S.; but an impression of several of them was made abroad in the same year, where they are stated to be "by the R. Father Robert Southwell, Priest of the Society of Jesus." To the present copy is added a poem called "The Christian's Manna," not found elsewhere, but which, though not reprinted by Mr. Turnbull, there is no sufficient reason for doubting to be by Southwell. He was a writer whose thoughts often possess striking novelty. He was violently bigoted to his religion, but such stanzas as the following, from the "Christian's Manna," belong to no peculiar body of believers. The author is arguing against the presumptuous folly of those who refuse faith merely because they cannot understand:—

"The Angels eyes, whom veiles cannot deceave,
Might best disclose what best they do discerne:
Men must with sound and silent faith receave
More than they can by sense of reason learne.
Gods power our proofe—his workes our wits exceed:

The doers might is reason for the deed."

It should be mentioned that "St Peter's Complaint" is dedicated by the author to his "loving Cousin"; "Mary Magdalen's Funeral Tears," as we have seen, "to the worshipful and vertuous Gentlewoman Mistresse D. A.;" "The Triumph over Death" to Richard Sackville (who became Earl of Dorset in 1609); and "The short Rules of good Life" to his "dear affected friend M. D. S." "Mæoniæ" has no dedication, and it was originally printed as a supplement to "St. Peter's Complaint." The Christian's Manna" is so scarce that Mr. Turnbull could not obtain the sight of it, but we have a copy now before us.

SPENSER, EDMUND.—Complaints. Containing sundrie small Poemes of the Worlds Vanitie. Whereof the next Page maketh mention. By Ed. Sp.—London. Imprinted for William Ponsonbie &c. 1591. 4to. 91 *leaves.*

The poems enumerated at the back of the title-page are these: 1. The Ruines of Time. 2. The Teares of the Muses. 3. Virgil's Gnat 4. Prosopopoia, or Mother Hubberds Tale. 5. The Ruines of Rome by Bellay. 6. Muiopotmos, or the Tale of the Butterflie. 7. Visions of the World's Vanitie. 8. Bellayes Visions. 9. Petrarches Visions. Of these, "The Teares of the Muses" and "Prosopopoia, or Mother Hubberds Tale," have distinct title-pages, dated 1591. "Muiopotmos, or the Fate of the Butterflie," has also a distinct title-page, but it is dated 1590.

It is in the address of "The Printer to the gentle Reader" that mention is made of certain other poems and "pamphlets" by Spenser, then no doubt existing, although Ponsonby could not procure copies of them, but now irrecoverably lost. These are, "Ecclesiastes et Canticum Canticorum translated—A senights slumber—The hell of Lovers—his Purgatorie;" together with "The dying Pellican—The howers of the Lord—The sacrifice of a sinner—The seven Psalmes, &c." In the same address, Ponsonby notices his publication of "the Faerie Queene," meaning, of course, only the first part, the three books which appeared in 1590.

The poems before us were printed probably while their author was in Ireland, but he seems to have prepared them for publication, and they are severally dedicated to the Countess of Pembroke, Lady Strange, Lady Compton and Mounteagle, and Lady Carey.

The Visions of Bellay and Petrarch in this volume had been printed, with variations, more than twenty years before they appeared here. They were unquestionably the very earliest extant work of Spenser, having been inserted by Vandernoodt in his "Theatre, &c. for Voluptuous Worldlings," which came out in 1569, when Spenser was not more than sixteen years old. "Petrarch's Visions" are there called "Epigrams," and Vandernoodt professed to have rendered them himself from the Brabant language into English. In the same way he asserts that he had translated the "Visions of Bellay" "out of Dutch into English." The most plausible solution seems to be, that Spenser translated them for him, while Vandernoodt took the credit of it. The "Visions of Bellay" Vandernoodt calls "Sonnets," and it is remarkable that they are in blank-verse, as he printed them, although, when republished by Spenser in the volume before us, he changed them from blank-verse into the ordinary form of the rhyming sonnet. The "Visions of Petrarch" were originally printed in rhyme, but some of them were then only of twelve lines. Spenser subsequently added an additional couplet to such as were deficient. See "The Life of Spenser," 1862, pp. xxii, xlii.

SPENSER, EDMUND.—Foure Hymnes, made by Edm. Spenser.—London, Printed for William Ponsonby. 1596. 4to. 23 *leaves.*

These hymns "Of Love," "Of Beauty," "Of heavenly Love," and "Of heavenly Beauty," are dedicated to the Countesses of Cumberland and Warwick, the dedication being dated, "Greenwich, this first of September, 1596." Respecting them, see "The Life of Spenser," 1862, p. cxxiv. "Daphnaida," an elegy on the death of "the noble and vertuous Douglas Howard, daughter and heire of Henry Lord Howard, Viscount Byndon, and wife of Arthur Gorges Esquire," is appended to most copies of this volume.

SPENSER, EDMUND.—The Shepheards Calendar. Conteining twelve Aeglogues proportionable to the twelve Monethes. Entituled to the noble and vertuous Gentleman most worthie of all titles, both of learning and chivalry, Maister Philip Sidney.—London Printed by John Windet for John Harrison the yonger &c. 1591. B. L. 4to. 56 *leaves.*

This is the fourth, or perhaps the fifth, edition of "The Shepherd's Calendar," which originally appeared in 1579, dedicated, as above, to "Maister Philip Sidney." The favorable acceptance of it perhaps encouraged Stephen Gosson, in the same year, to dedicate to Sidney a work of a very different kind, "The School of Abuse," which was scornfully repudiated by Sir Philip. See "The Life of Spenser," 1862, pp. xxxi, lxxvi.

SPENSER, EDMUND.—Certaine worthye Manuscript Poems of great Antiquitie Reserved long in the Studie of a Northfolke Gentleman. And now first published by J. S. The statly tragedy of Guistard and Sismond. The Northren Mothers Blessing. The way to Thrifte.—Imprinted at London for R. D. 1597. 8vo. 38 *leaves.*

This little volume has been reprinted within the present century, but we notice it under the heading of our great romantic poet, because it is dedicated to him,— "To the worthiest Poet Maister Ed. Spenser,"—and because there is a circumstance connected with one of the three pieces it contains that has not hitherto attracted attention. It may be that the scarcity of the book has led to the non-detection of the fact, that "The Northren Mothers Blessing," which comes second on the title-page, is the very poem which Sir F. Madden printed in 1838, as from a manuscript once belonging to Dr. Adam Clarke, and afterwards the property of Mr. Loscombe of Corsham, Wiltshire. Sir F. Madden mentions one other MS. of the same production, in the library of Trin. Coll. Cambridge; but besides the printed copy of 1597 now before us, there is a third and well-known MS. of it in the Lambeth Library, No. 853, where it bears the title "How the Good wife taught her Daughter." Considering that the reprint was made as long since as 1812, it is singular that it should have been unknown in 1838; and in his Introduction to his "Sir Gawayne," in the next year, Sir F. Madden still only speaks of it as a MS., as if not aware that it had been in print in our language for more than two centuries. "The Northren Mothers

Blessing" is a didactic poem of thirty-three stanzas, in which a Goodwife instructs her daughter in the ways of the world, and in the manner in which she ought to carry herself. We are not about to criticise or to make extracts from it, further than is necessary for the purpose of showing the identity between the MS. used by Sir F. Madden and the printed copy of 1597. The MS. used by Sir F. Madden must have wanted the introductory stanza, which stands thus in the old printed copy in our hands:—

"God wold that every wife that wonnyth in this land
Wold teach her doughter as ye shal understand,
As a good wife did of the North countré,
How her doughter should lere a good wife to bee:
For lacke of the moders teaching
Makes the doughter of evill living,
My leve dere child."

If Sir F. Madden had seen this stanza, or the name of the poem as reprinted in 1812, or as printed in 1597, he could not have said, "the locality of its composition it is not easy to determine; it contains some traces of a northern dialect," because the Mother is expressly called "northren," with the addition that she was "of the north countré." He was quite right in assigning the original MS. to about the reign of Henry VI., but in the impression of 1597 the language (and especially the spelling) is somewhat modernized. The first stanza in Mr. Loscombe's MS., Sir F. Madden tells us, runs as follows:—

"Doughter zif thou wilt ben a wif, & wiseliche werche
Loke yt thou love welle god, & holy cherche:
Go to cherche when thou mygthe, lette for no reyne
Alle the day thou farest the bette that thou hast god yseyne.
Wele thryvethe that god lovethe, my dere childe."

The second stanza in the printed copy of 1597 is this, showing that the poems are identical:—

"My doughter gif thou be a wife, wisely thou werke,
Looke ever thou love God and the holy Kirke:
Go to Kirke when thou may, and let for no rayne,
And then shall thou fare the bet, when thou God has sayn.
Full well may they thrive
That serven God in their live,
My leve dere child."

Here "leve dere" is merely pleonastic, the Saxon word "leve" signifying ***dear;*** and here we may remark that there is a misprint in the heading of Sir F. Madden's printed copy of 1838, where "fele tyme & ofte" (unless our exemplar differ from others) is misprinted "***sele*** tyme & ofte": "fele tyme & ofte" of course is ***many*** a time and oft, A. S. ***fela;*** a fact of which we cannot suppose Sir F. Madden to have been ignorant, though it is possible that his printer mistook the *f* for the long *s.* However, in an important point, relating to the life of Sir Thomas Gresham, he certainly mistook the letter T for G, and thus confounded Sir Thomas Gresham with Sir Thomas Gresham;—"Sir Frederick Madden has cited a manuscript which states that Queen Mary was proclaimed at Northampton by Sir Thomas Gresham, with the ayd and helpe of the towne, being borne amongst them." Here for Sir Thomas Gresham (who was born in London) we ought to read Sir Thomas Tresham, who was born at Northampton, (Cooper's ***Ath. Cantabr.*** II. 415.) Sir F. Madden misread the MS. and strangely confounded the two old capital letters which begin the names of Tresham and Gresham. It would indeed have been a curious and novel incident in Sir Thomas Gresham's life, if it could have been shown that he assisted at the proclamation of Queen Mary when she came to the throne. [Note 1: And, moreover, that Sir Thomas Gresham was born at Northampton and not in London. We have quoted the ***Athena Cantabrigienses*** for this correction of Sir F. Madden, not being ourselves aware of the particular publication where the strange error was committed,—so strange indeed that we cannot help thinking that the printer, as in the case of "sele" for ***fele*** must have been in fault. Our reference to the ***Ath. Cantabr*** ought to have been to the ***first*** instead of to the ***second*** volume of that valuable work.]

We need not doubt that the author of "The Northren Mothers Blessing" was in the Church, if only for the emphasis with which he makes the matron enjoin her daughter to pay her tithes cheerfully:—

"Gladly give thou thy tithes and thine offrings both;"

which in Mr. Loscombe's MS. stands thus, the word "blethely" (i. e. ***blithely***) being used for "gladly":—

"Blethely zeve thi tythys & thin offerynges bothe."

It was clearly an original old English poem, which J. S. here and there modernized; and the same may be said of "The Way to Thrift," while it seems equally certain that "The statelie Tragedie of Guistard and Sismond" was not from the Italian of Boccaccio (Day IV. Nov. 1). ***Tancredi Prence di Salerno uccide l'amante della figliuola, & mandale il cuore in una coppa d'oro, laquale messa sopr' esso acqua acelenata, quella si bee, & cosi muore.*** It first appeared in our language through the medium of a French version. [Note 2: This was not the only poem that William Walter translated from the Italian, "through the medium of a French version." He also rendered into English the story of Titus and Gesyppus: they were printed by Wynkyn de Worde, the first in 1532, and the last without date. Dr. Dibdin, (***Typ. Ant.*** II. 338,) making a quotation from Walter's "Spectacle of Lovers," misprints "Endever thy selfe" "***And*** ever thy selfe," making the passage nonsense.]

We ought to add that the poem called "The Northren Mothers Blessing" has a separate title-page, (wanting in a copy of the volume of 1597, which was formerly in our hands,) and that it is in these terms: "The Northren Mothers Blessing. The way of Thrift. Written nine yeares before the death of G. Chaucer.—London, Printed by Robert Robinson for Robert Dexter. 1597." The dedication to Spenser, at the back of the first general title-page, which has no printer's name at the bottom of it, is in this form:—

"To the worthiest Poet
Mauler Ed. Spenser."

Who J. S., the dedicator, may have been, is unknown.

STAFFORD, W.—A compendious or briefe examination of certayne ordinary complaints, of divers of our country men in these our dayes: which although they are in some part unjust and frivolous, yet are they all by way of dialogues thoroughly debated & discussed. By W. S. Gentleman.—Imprinted at London &c. by Tho. Marshe. 1581. B. L. 4to. 59 *leaves.*

This tract was reprinted in 1751, accompanied by a preface to prove that it was written by Shakspeare,—a position which the date alone ought to have refuted. Shakspeare did not come to London until 1586 or 1587; but a passage in the dedication to the Queen, wherein W. S. (*i. e.* W. Stafford, as has since been ascertained) expresses his gratitude to her Majesty "in pardoning certayne my undutifull misdemeanour," was easily perverted (supposing time of no consequence) into an allusion to Shakspeare's offence as a deer-stealer, and the mere mention of a "venison pasty," in the first dialogue, would have been enough to afford a confirmation.

The work is divided into three parts or dialogues between a Knight, a Doctor, a Merchant, and a Capper: the first adverts to the complaints and "griefs" of the country; the second to the causes of them, and the third to the remedies for them. It shows that the writer was a man of considerable learning, much knowledge of the state of affairs, and of great judgment and acuteness of observation. Regarding him, nothing has reached our day, but possibly he was father to the author of the next article.

STAFFORD, ANTHONY.—Staffords Heavenly Dogge: or the life and death of the Cynicke Diogenes, whom Laertius stiles Canem Cœlestem, the Heavenly Dogge, by reason of the Heavenly precepts he gave. Taken out of the best Authors &c.—London, Printed by George Purslowe for John Budge, and are to be sold at the great South-doore of Paules, and at Brittaines Burse. 1615. 12mo. 67 *leaves.*

This zealous and eloquent author's earliest work was called after himself, "Stafford's Niobe, or his Age of Teares," which came out in 1611, although the writer was then an extremely young man, for in 1608 he was only seventeen, and a commoner of Oriel College. It has been noticed by bibliographers that "Stafford's Niobe" arrived at a second edition in the same year in which it was originally published; and it was followed immediately by "Stafford's Niobe dissolv'd into a Nilus," also with the date of 1611: to it was appended, with fresh pagination, "An Admonition to a discontented Romanist," so little reason was there for the suspicion of the Puritans that Stafford meant to encourage popery. Of this "Admonition" no account has been given, nor has it, we believe, been anywhere mentioned, yet all through Stafford assails the Roman Catholics without reserve or moderation. In one place he remarks, "I doe not clearelie see in what the Pope doth imitate Peter, except it bee in his deniall of Christ Peter sought to convert both Jewes and Gentiles: the Pope studieth how to couzen Christians. Peter offered a piece of silver for tribute to Cæsar: the Pope sendeth a piece of Steele to Princes. Peter willeth the People to pray for their Princes: the Pope not only willeth, but hireth slaves and rascalls to raile against their Soveraignes."

Reading the two parts of Stafford's "Niobe," a general invective against vice and a laudation of virtue, it seems difficult to extract from them anything sectarian, and least of all anything papistical. Although the Puritans found fault with the work, and wrote against it, there is much in it that is favorable to their habits and tenets. The writer was an enthusiast, and did not always weigh nicely the import of his language; and among other things he gravely tells us of an interview with which he was favored by the spirit of Sir Philip Sidney. All, or nearly all, he produced was in prose, and he strongly censures poets who "disguise their lasciviousnesse under a veile of smooth running words." The only scrap of verse he has left behind him, as far as we know, is the following brief translation from that "everlasting Worthy of the French, divine du Bartas, *Peu je regretteroy la perte de leurs ans,*" &c.

"Yet would I grieve their losse of time the lesse
If, by their guilefull verse, their too much art

Made not their hearers share with them a part.
The sugred baits of those their learned writs
Doe shroude that poyson, which the younger wits
Quaffe down with breathless draughts, and love's hot wine
(Making them homage do at Bacchus shrine)
Distempreth so their stomachs, that they feed
On such ill meates as no good humours breed."

In fact, in the small work immediately under notice, devoted to the praise rather than to the biography of the Cynic Diogenes, Stafford refers, without much respect, to such persons as "read ballads and books balladical," as if there really were nothing of greater worth in poetry. His "Niobe" he dedicated to the Earl of Salisbury; but his "Heavenly Dog" to Sir John Wentworth, in terms of the warmest friendship. The greater part of the tract consists of a long speech by Diogenes, in which he enforces his own doctrines and principles, and represents himself as much more of a braggart, especially in the company of Alexander, than was becoming the real character of the philosopher. Diogenes exclaims in one place,—

"I need not blush at any one of my actions: I make the people my spectators and judges. I approve myself to God; the censures of men I regard not, nor care I if all my thoughts were registered. What is good I applaud, what is evill I reprehend in whome soever I finde it. Thus it often falls that my patients beate me, and will not attend the cure of their bad affections. My mind alters not, notwithstanding their stubbornenesse; but I still endeavour to teach those that correct me, and with the fondnesse of a father love them."

It is singular to find a scholar, like Stafford, making Diogenes talk of the two hemispheres of the globe, and of Alexander conquering the one by means of the other, about 2000 years before the western world was discovered. He says little or nothing regarding the life of the Cynic, and thus ends his tract regarding his death:—

"The sunne in the spane of twelve houres saw Diogenes die with the courage of a man, and Alexander with the pusillanimity of a pesant of Babylon. Thus did one day finish the dayes of the worlds terrour and the worlds wonder."

Stafford introduces his "Niobe" by an address "to the long-eared Reader," but his Diogenes, with more humility, "to the modest Reader." To the last tract is prefixed a very neat engraving of Diogenes in his book-furnished tub.

STAGE-PLAYERS.—The Stage-players Complaint. In a pleasant Dialogue betweene Cane of the Fortune, and Reed of the Friers. Deploring their sad and solitary condition for the want of Imployment in this heavie and contagious time of the Plague in London.—London, Printed for Tho: Bates, and are to be sold at his shop in the Old Bailey, &c. 1641. 4 to. 4 *leaves.*

Only two copies of this tract, relating to the Stage and Drama, just before the closing of theatres by the Puritans, are known. The plague was prevailing in London at the time it was written, and the enemies of Plays and Players availed themselves of the visitation, as if it were sent by heaven as a punishment for indulging in such profanations.

There are woodcuts of two male figures on the title-page, one much larger than the other; and which was intended for Andrew Cane (or Kane), and which for Immanuel Reed, does not appear: the first, in 1641, was a famous comedian at the Fortune Theatre in Golden Lane, Cripplegate, and the second quite as celebrated a performer at the Blackfriars Theatre. The reputation of Cane long survived him; and in a tract by Henry Chapman, printed in 1673, on the virtues of the Bath waters, we read as follows:—"Without which a pamphlet now a days finds as small acceptance, as a Comedy did formerly at the Fortune Play-house without a Jig of Andrew Keins into the bargain." Regarding Reed, we may quote the following lines from "The Careless Shepherdess," printed fifteen years after the date of the tract before us:—

"There is ne'er a part
About him but breaks jests.—
I never saw Reade peeping through the curtain,

But ravishing joy entered my heart."

In our "Stage-Players Complaint" they are brought together conversing in the street about their misfortunes, and the dialogue commences thus:—

"*Cane.* Stay Reed! Whither away so speedily? What! you goe as if you meant to leape over the moone. Now, what's the matter?

"*Reede.* The matter is plaine enough: You incuse me of my nimble feet; but I thinke your tongue runnes a little faster, and you contend as much to out-strip facetious Mercury in your tongue, as [I do] lame Vulcan in my feete."

The piece is wretchedly printed, and even at the very commencement we find "incuse" put for *accuse,* and the words *I do,* absolutely necessary to the sense, entirely omitted. In the next speeches, and for the rest of the dialogue, Cane is called *Quick* in the prefixes, and Reed *Light,* which probably gives us the appellations by which they were then popularly known. They continue:—

"*Quick.* Me thinks you're very eloquent. Prithee tell me, don't Suada, and the Jove-begotten braine Minerva lodge in your facundious tongue? You have, without doubt, some great cause of alacrity, that you produce such eloquent speeches now. Prithee, what is it?

"*ight.* How! Cause of alacrity? S'foot I had never more cause of sorrow in my life. And dost thou tell me of that? Fie, fie!

"*Quick.* Prithee why? I did but conjecture out of your sweet words.

"*Light.* Well; I see you'le never be hanged for a Conjurer. Is this a world to be merry in? Is this an age to rejoyce in? Where one may as soone find honesty in a Lawyer's house as the least cause of mirth in the world. Nea; you know this well enough, but onely you love to be inquisitive, and to search the nature of men."

Hence they proceed to advert to their individual sufferings and disappoint-ments, owing to the prevalence of the infection, and the disposition of the Puritans to terminate, and exterminate, all theatrical exhibitions and performances:—

"*Quick.* But, i'le assure you, tis to be feared; for Monopolies are downe, Projec-tors are downe, the High Commission Court is downe, the Starre Chamber is down and (some think) Bishops will downe: and why should we, then, that are farre infe-rior to any of those, not justly feare least we should be downe too?

"*Light.* Pish! I can show thee many infallible reasons to the contrary. We are very necessary and commodious to the people: first for strangers, who can desire no better recreation then to come to a Play: then, for Citizens to feast their wits: then, for Gallants, who otherwise, perhaps, would spend their money in drunkennesse and lasciviousnesse, doe find a great delight and delectation to see a Play: then, for the learned, it does increase and add wit constructively to wit: then, for Gentle-women, it teacheth them how to deceive idlenesse: then, for the ignorant, it does augment their knowledge. Pish! a thousand more arguments I could add, but that I should weary your patience too much. Well, in a word, we are so needfull for the Common good, that, in some respect, it were almost a sinne to put us downe: there-fore, let not these frivolous things perplex your vexatious thoughts."

Cane (*alias* Quick) was, however, a true prophet, and the blow fell, perhaps sooner than even he expected, for an Ordinance of the Lords and Commons for the suppression of Stageplays and the closing of theatres throughout the kingdom was issued on the 2d September, 1642, although it was evaded, and was not finally put into operation until about five years afterwards. Everything about this tract—its authorship, its typography, and its purpose, show that it was brought out with ex-treme celerity.

STAGE-PLAYS.—A shorte Treatise against Stage-playes. Prov. 10. 23 &c. Prov. 21. 17 &c. Ephes. 5. 11 &c.—Printed in the yeere of our Lord 1625. 4to. 14 **leaves.**

The dulness of this anonymous attack is somewhat compensated by its brevity. It has no place nor printer's name, and the type has some appearance of foreign manufacture. We never met with more than one other exemplar of it.

The title-page is followed by "An humble supplication tendered to the High and Honourable House of Parliament, assembled May xviij, 1625"; and we may perhaps suppose that by one "house of Parliament" both were intended. It contains an untrue assertion that stage-plays "have been justly censured and worthily prohibited by statutes made in the late raigne of famouse Queene Elizabeth, and of our noble and learned King James." No statutes were passed in either of those reigns doing more, in effect, than regulating and limiting such performances. They were never prohibited excepting on account of the prevalence of the plague.

On the 18th May, 1625, Charles I. had not been two months on the throne, and the object perhaps was to induce him to interpose his authority for the entire suppression of the stage.

The tract, short as it is, is divided into four parts: "1 The original beginning of Stage-plays is shewed. 2 The end is pointed out for which they were devised. 3 The generall matter or argument acted in them is opened in a few words. 4 The reasons to prove them unlawfull are rendred." The old grounds of attack are slightly touched upon without a single syllable of novelty.

STALBRIDGE, HENRY.—The Epistel Exhortatorye of an Inglyshe Chrystian unto his derely beloved countrey of Ingland, agaynst the pompouse popysh Bishops therof, as yet the true membres of theyre fylthye Father the great Antychryst of Rome. Made by Henry Stalbrydge. Hieremie L. Deale with babylon as she hath deserved, &c. 8vo. B. L. 36 *leaves.*

It has been usual to assign this tract to Bishop Bale, and it is certainly as coarse and abusive as his style was wont to be; but there is no other reason for attributing it to him, and strong ones for concluding that it was written by Henry Stalbrydge, whose name it bears on the title-page. He distinctly claims it, and Bale disclaims it; for he does not insert it in his own list of his works, as he probably would have done had it really come from his pen. The impression in our hands has not been noticed by bibliographers, and at the back of the title is the following preface:—

"As I have compyled thys treatise in the zeale of God and my prince against the tyraunt of Rome and hys secret mainteyners, so it is my desyre that hys grace may have it as the frute of my Christen obedience. And I doubte not but somme godly man, lovinge hys grace better then that wycked pope, wyll faythfully delyver it unto him, the sleyghtes of their false generation considered. Pray (gentyl reader) that it maye fynde grace in his syght."

At the end of "the Epystel," and before the word *Finis,* we read thus: "Written from Basyle a citie of the Helvecyans by me Henry Stalbrydge;" so that he again asserts it to have been his work. Then follows "An Appendyee" addressed to Gardiner on his answer to "the Hunting of the Romish Fox," and to it is added "A brefe Table," containing all the principal points discussed; but there is no date from beginning to end: it belongs, however, to about the year 1544, and thus refers to the statute that had been passed a year or two earlier against Players and Minstrels who endeavored to promote the Reformation: Stalbrydge is addressing Roman Catholic Priests:—

"And you like tiraunts, more cruell then the Turke, constrayne men to professe your false faith by divers kindes of death: none leave ye un-vexed and untroubled— no, ***not so much as the poore minstrels and players of interludes,*** but ye are doing with them. So long as they played lyes, and sange baudy songes, blasphemed God, and corrupting mens consciences, ye never blamed them, but weere very well contented. But sens they persuaded the people to worship theyr Lord God aryght, accordyng to hys holic lawes and not yours, and to acknoledge Jesus Chryst for their onlye redemer and saviour, without your lowsie legerdemaines, ye never were pleased with them."

This passage, referring to the manner in which Protestant dramas had been at that date substituted for Roman Catholic miracle-plays, is interesting; and a little farther on, Stalbrydge tells us that "players and syngers," as well as godly ministers, writers, and preachers, had been burned as heretics. Elsewhere he mentions the name of one of the most popular dramas of the period, "Hick Scorner," printed by Wynkyn de Worde, and his tract is full of temporary allusions. We will only make another brief quotation, where he applauds the Reformers of Germany:—

"The noble Germaynes have gracyouslye done before him, [Henry VIII.] makynge theyr monasteryes, nonnes coventes, and fryers bowses, scoles of Chrysten learninge, hospy talles for sycke people, and convenyente dwellynge places for the impotente poore and aged, reservenge the reste of the landes and goodes to the mayntenaunce of theyr cyttes and con trees; whych godly distribucyon is much commended all Christendome over, where as it is throughlye knowen. Not unknowen is it to these pom-pouse Prelates, that whan those landes and goodes were fyrst delyvered unto their predecessours, it was not to the intent that they should become possessours or lordes of them, but faythfull disposers to the use of the weake and nedye, that Chryst might so be harboured, noryshed, covered, fedde and visited in his diseased membres, as wilbe required at the latter day."

We do not feel called upon to supply any specimen of the strong epithets abundantly showered upon the Pope, the Priests, and Roman Catholics generally, the use of which ornaments of speech led to the belief, in which we do not accord, that the Epistle was the work of Bale. We look upon it as a successful imitation of Bale's style of treatment, and argument There were two distinct impressions of it, but they only differ literally.

STANTHURST, RICHARD.—The first foure Bookes of Virgils Æneis Translated into English Heroicall Verse by Richard Stanyhurst: With other Poeticall devises thereto annexed.—At London, Imprinted by Henrie Bynneman dwelling in Thames streate neare unto Bay-nardes Castell. Anno Domini 1583. 4to. B. L. 54 *leaves.*

This very rare work, the copy of which in the Bodleian Library is imperfect at the end, was reprinted in 1839; and we should not here notice it, were it not that we wished to introduce a carious passage, not known to the editor, relating to Stanyhurst, which we find in one of Barnabe Rich's tracts called "The Irish Hubbub, or the English Hue and Cry," dated from Dublin, 24th June, 1618. Here Stanyhurst is spoken of as living, although in the prefatory notice to the reprint it is stated that "he died at Antwerp in the year 1618": if so, perhaps it occurred late in the year, or Rich had not heard of it when he wrote as follows:—

"And as the Irish are thus pleasantly conceited, to jest and to scoffe when they find occasion, so they have as great facilitie in weeping, as Stanhurst, a famous man amongst them for his excellent learning [states]; for he was a Chronicler, then a poet, and after that he professed Alchymie, and now hee is become a massing Priest. This Stanhurst in his History of Ireland maketh this report of his countrey-men:— they follow the dead corps to the ground with howling and barbarous outcries, pittifull in appearance, whereof (as he supposeth) grew this Proverbe—*to weepe Irish.*"

This in most respects agrees with the account given by the editor of the reprint of Stanyhurst's translation of the first four books of Virgil; and to it we may add what Thomas Nash says of Stanyhurst's method of versification; for that able pamphleteer and satirist was in no way tolerant of hexameters, or of any other classical forms in English: 1—[Note 1: We do not know that it has been observed upon, bnt it is a fact, that no less a poet than Chaucer was the earliest introducer of classical measures into our language. He commences his prose version of Boethius with these two hexameter lines, which are as correct as many of those which Stanyhurst inserted in his Virgil:—

"Alas, I wepyng am constrayned to begin verse of sorowful mater,
That whilom in flourisshyng studye made delytable verses."

They are the rendering of the following couplet:—

"Carmina qui quondam studio florente peregi, Flebilis, heu, mæsios coger in ire modos."] "Master Stanyhurst (though otherwise learned) trod a foule lumbring, boystrous, wallowing measure in his translation of Virgil. He had never been praised by Gabriel for his labour, if therein he had not bin so famously absurd."

We transcribe the above from Nash's "Strange Newes," 4 to, 1592, sign. G 3, which (see Vol. III. p. 11) came out with a new title-page in 1593 as "the Apologie of Pierce Pennilesse." Of this circumstance the editor of the reprint under consideration was possibly not aware, and it may have led him into the mistakes in his quotation, where he printed "though" *the,* and "wallowing" *walloping,* besides inserting "Gabriel Harvey" at length, when, as we see, Nash gives Harvey only his Christian name, in order to treat him more contemptuously. In the same way, probably from not consulting the original, he makes Bishop Hall speak of "*chaunted* feet" instead of "changéd feet"; and in the long quotation from Phaer's Virgil he has printed *worke* for *"wroke,"* (the past tense of the verb *to wreak,*) and *same* for "fame,"—the last error arising, as usual, out of the confusion between the long *s* and the letter *f*. *The text in general is correct, excepting that in the dedication a marginal note is omitted, and that in Book I. we are told that "Ganymed by* love *too skytop is hoysed," when, as we know, and as Stanyhurst wrote, the feat was performed by "Jove" and not by* love. *In the brief introductory prose to the "Certaine Psalmes of David" the word* first *is accidentally inserted, when it has no place in the original; and "played" is misprinted* payed *in the description of Liparen.*

We believe that the reprint of 1839 was confined to fify copies; and Stanyhurst's experiment in English hexameters has been so often mentioned, and ridiculed, that we are unwilling not to add a brief specimen. [Note 1: A very singular experiment in English hexameters was made in 1599, by an anonymous author, in a small unique volume, entitled, "The first Booke of the Preservation of King Henry the vij. when he was but Earle of Richmond." What is most curious in it perhaps is, that the author, whoever he may have been, introduced his work by an explanation of the "Prosody" he had observed. At the back of the title-page he tells the Printer, R.B.:—

"Print with a good letter, this booke, and carefully Printer:
Print each word legibill, not a word nor a sillabil alter:

Keepe points, and commas, periodes, the parenthesis observe;
My credit and thy reporte to defend, bothe safely to conserve."]

In the third line he commits his first blunder, as regards our language, for we never pronounced the word "observe," as he requires it for his measure, with the emphasis on the first syllable. His introductory matter is superabundant, and an address to the Queen occupies many pages; it ends with these so-called hexameters:—] We will part of the speech of Dido before her death, and follow it by the same passage as rendered by Lord Surrey, more than forty years earlier, in blank-verse:—

"O my sweet old leavings, whilst mee good destinie suffred,
And god of his goodnesse you mee too pleasure alowed,
Take ye my faint spirit, mee from these troubles abandon:
I liv'de, and the travail graunted by fortun I traced;
Also my goast shortly too pits of Limbo shal hobble.
A citty I founded stately, thee wals did I see rais'd,
And the death of my husband on freendleesse broother I venged.
Blessed had I rested, yee, thrice most blessed, if only
In theese my regions no Troian vessel had anchor' d."

It seems strange that the mere beauty of Virgil's versification did not save us from the infliction of Stanyhurst's "hobbling" hexameters. The Earl of Surrey (we quote from Tottell's first

"Here I wil end, O Queen. O Lord our only creator,
(Our Lord Emmanuel, our Christ and sole mediator)
Adde to thy life many yeares, as he did to the King Ezechias,
Safely defend thee from harme, as he safely preserved Elias:
And that he graunt to thy Grace, after this life (as a chosen
Vessel of his, purify'd) joyes in celestiall heaven;
Joyfully there to remaine with Jesus Christ the Redeemer,
Imparadix'd as a Saint, with Saints in glory for ever.
As two Greeke letters in Grecian Alphabet, Alpha

First letter plaste is; but placed last is Omega:
So will I continuall, first and last, praise thee for ever;
If that I could poetise, as I would, thy glory to further."

It is the more singular that the writer did not give his name, because it is clear that he was in no way dissatisfied with his "poetizing." The body of the work hardly occupies 60 much space as the introductory matter, and we never hear of a second book, to be added as a continuation of the "first." It is printed in oblong 8vo. The author especially mentions Stanyhurst with applause, but advises him, if still living, to correct some of his misshapen lines. He likewise praises Spenser, not for his "Fairy Queen," but for his endeavors to introduce classical measures into English. For the rhymers of his day, though he mentions several, be seems to have had as little admiration as they must have felt for him. This circumstance alone is sufficient to convince us that "The Preservation of Henry VII." was not by Sir Edward Dyer. Besides, the style of the whole production is unlike what would have proceeded from his elegant and accomplished mind. Dyer, however, lived till the spring of 1607. edition of 1557) gives the same passage more tersely and harmoniously:—

"Swete spoiles, whiles God and destenies it wold,
Receive this sprite, and rid me of these cares.
I lived and ranne the course fortune did graunt,
And under earth my great gost now shall wende.
A goodly town I built, and saw my walles:
Happy, alas, too happy, if these costes
The Troyan shippes had never touched aye."

It is quite clear that Stanyhurst was not encouraged to continue his labor, although he lived more than thirty years after he printed his "First foure Bookes of Virgils Æneis."

STATUTES, &C. OF WAR.—Hereafter Ensue certayne Statutes and Ordenauces of warre made ordeyned enacted & establysshed by the most noble victoryous, and moste Christen Prynce our moste drade Soueraygne lorde Kynge Henry the viij. B.

L. 4to. 16 *leaves.*

This publication, from the press of Pynson, was wholly unknown to Ames, Herbert, and Dr. Dibdin. The colophon is, "Emprynted at the hyghe Comaundement of our Soueraygne lorde the Kynge Henry the viij. By Rycharde Pynson, prynter vnto his noble grace. The yere of oure lorde M.CCCCC. and xiij."

Under the title are the king's arms, supported by two winged angels, and below them the crowned rose, and a square including three castles. The back of the title is filled by Wynkyn de Worde's largest device, as given in Dibdin's *Typogr. Ant.* II. 38. At the back of the last leaf is Pynson's device, number five, as also given by Dr. Dibdin. The last signature is C iiij. The subsequent extract from the preamble shows upon what occasion these statutes and ordinances were published:—

"Semblably oure soueraygne lorde Henry of this name the viij, by the grace of god kynge of Englande and of Fraunce, & lorde of Irlande entendynge by the same grace with all goodly spede to passe ouer the see in his awne persone with an Armye and hoste Royall for yᵒ repressynge the great tyrannye of the Frensche kynge now lately comytted and doon aswell in vsurpynge vpon cristes Churche and the Patrymonie of the same and in rayaynge noryssynge and maynteygnynge a detestable Scisme in the sayd Churche to the great inquyetacion of all xpendome, as also in deteignynge by vyolence Reames, Landes, Senyoryes and dominions of dyuerse and many xpen Prynces distourbynge and inqnyetynge by suche sedicious ambicious and contencions meanes the states tranquylyties and restfulnes of all xpen regyons, to the manyfest danger of his hyghnes & this his Realme of Englande and subgiettes of the same, vnlesse the inordynate appetyte of ye sayd Frensche kynge be spedely with myght and power repressed and resysted," &c.

The following are among the "Statutes and Ordinances n:—

"*For dysynge, cardynge, and all maner of games.*

"Also that no man play at dyse, cardes, tables, close, handout, nor at none other game, wherby they shall waste theyr money or cause debates to aryse by ye same. And if any so be foude playinge at any of thyes games, that for ye firste tyme he or they shalbe comytted to warde, there to remayne viij dayes, and to lose all suche money as they or any of them playe for, the one halfe to the prouoste of the marshall, and ye other halfe to hym that so fyndeth them playinge. And if any of the sayd armye be foude twyes playinge he shalbe comytted to the prouostes warde there to remayne a moneth and to forfayte a moneth wages, the one halfe to ye kynge and the other halfe to the fynder. Prouyded alwaye yt he that so fyndeth any of them warne the tresourer of the warres, incontynent after he hath so foude them or as soone as he maye, or els to take no profyt of that parte of the sayd wages. And if any so be founde the thrydde tyme playinge he to be comytted to warde there to abyde ye kynges pleasure, and to have suche further punycion as shall please the kynge.

"*For theym that crye hauoke.*

"Also that noo man be so handy to crye hauoke, vpon payne of hym that so is founde begynner to dye therfore and the remenaunt to be emprysoned, and theyr bodyes to be punysshed at the kynges wyll.

"*For women that lye in childbedde.*

"Also that no man be so hardy to go into no chambre or logynge where that any woman lyeth in childbedde her to robbe ne pyll of no goodes the whiche longcth vnto her refresshyng, ne for to make none affraye where thorugh she & her childe myght be in any disease or dispayre, vpon payne he that in suche wyse offendeth shall lose al his goodes, halfe to hym that accuseth and halfe to the marshall, and hym selfe to be dede, but if the kynge gyue hym grace and pardone."

STEVENSON, MATHEW.—Occasions Off-spring, or Poems upon severall Occasions. By Mathew Stevenson &c.—London, Printed for John Place &c. 1645. 12mo. 72 *leaves.*

The author produced the contents of this volume at various periods, and here collected them into a volume, probably the first time he had seen his poems in print. They are dedicated to his cousin, Mr. Benjamin Cooke, and are ushered into the world by numerous commendatory lines, all signed with initials. The following, with the initials F. B. at the foot, speak of a very distinguished poet of that day:—

"Tell me no more of Withers wilde abuses;
Thy booke a thousand times more wit produces.
Withers shall wither, whilst thy bays are seen,
Like Daphnes chapplet, of immortall green."

In one of his poems, which are generally of a temporary and trashy description, Stevenson mentions a circumstance relating to Thomas May of some curiosity. He is writing ***In honorem Poetarum.***

"Yea, do not all men say
Poets dare any thing?
Pray, was not noble May,
Call'd brother by a King?"

This must of course refer to a period anterior to the date when May became Historiographer to the Parliament, and produced his History of it from the year 1640. All parties, Clarendon, Fuller, Phillips, Winstanley, &c., agree that he quitted the royal side because "his bays were not so richly gilded" as he had hoped: some assert that he took umbrage at the royal preference of Davenant for the office of the Queen's poet.

STRAFFORD, THO. WENTWORTH, EARL OF.—Great Straffords Farewell To the World: Or his ***Ultimum Vale*** To all earthly Glory. Written by his owne Hand in the Tower, and left behinde him for his friends or foes to peruse and consider.— Printed in the yeare 1641. 4to 4 ***leaves.***

A poem apparently divided into twenty-seven six-line stanzas, but, in fact, entirely in couplets. On the title-page is a coarse woodcut of the Earl, and under it, "Thomas Earle of Strafford L. Leutenant of Ireland &c."

The whole is written in a strain of self-accusation and reproof, and it thus concludes:—

"I doe confesse I have deserved death,
And willingly submit to lose my breath:
The world I freely with my heart forgive;
Since all must die, why should I wish to live?
I justly die by th' Law: fame ring my knell;
Earths fading pompe adieu; vaine world farewell!"

These lines, like some others, run easily enough, and whoever might be the author of them, he was neither an unpractised versifier, nor an impartial judge. We never met with any other copy of this temporary tract, but there exist various pieces of the same character. One of an entirely different complexion is in the shape of a broadside, and bears for title "The Earle of Strafford his Ellegiack Poem, as it was pen'd by his owne hand a little before his Death," and at the bottom is "*Finis.* Printed in the Yeare 1641." It is a very poor production, in which Strafford is made to vindicate himself, especially his conduct in Ireland, and it closes thus:—

"For all the service I have done the State,
My early risings and my sleeping late;
For all those cares kept sad my charge, my long
Zeale to my Prince, which you misconster'd wrong;
For all my labours, and in that pursuit
My slaughtered honours, and my life to boote,
Doe this, and you shall by my counsaile prove
Happy on earth, as I in Heaven above;
And though (for this shall your most comfort bring)
You lov'd not me, yet love my Lord your King."

The logic and sense of this passage are not very apparent, but we are not for a moment to suppose that either the above or what precedes it really came from the pen of the unhappy Earl. His friends could do him little service after his enemies had cut off his head.

STRIPPING, Whipping, and Pumping. Or The five mad Shavers of Drury-Lane; Strangely Acted and truely Related. Done in the Period, latter end, Tayle, or Rumpe of the Dogged Dogge-dayes, last past, August, 1638.—Together with the names of the severall parties which were Actors in this foule businesse.—London: Printed by J. O. for T. Lambert 1638 8vo. 12 *leaves.*

This is a rare humorous tract, though not perhaps rarely humorous; and facing the title-page is a woodcut, representing one woman in the midst of four others, (all with labels and inscriptions from their mouths,) two of whom have rods in their hands, and all of them engaged in tormenting her in various ways. One of the four persecutors is cutting off the victim's hair, and a second appears to be inflicting a wound upon her with a knife. Below, and as if coming out of the ground at one corner, is a man's or boy's head and arms, holding a barber's basin. The woodcut and the letter-press seem calculated for the meridian of Drury Lane, where in fact the scene is laid. The narrative was no doubt founded upon some incident that had made a disturbance, and had attracted attention in that populous neighborhood. After a brief introduction, the main narrative begins thus:—

"About the latter end of August last, 1638, this hellish fire of Jealousie did most strangely inflame five women, whom my pen should not name, nor should they be knowne by any writing of mine, but that they and their mad and barbarous proceedings are too much true, and too many wayes scattred and spread abroad by sundry Pens and Tongues, some of them making the matter, that was (and is) bad enough already, worse."

The story relates to the jealousy of Mrs. Evans, the wife of a barber in Drury Lane, occasioned by the suspected intimacy of her husband with Joan Isley. Mrs. Evans and four or five friends treacherously invite Joan Isley to supper to partake of pig, and then set upon her in the most pitiless manner with birchen twigs, razors, &c, and finally drive her naked into the street at eleven at night, and there pump upon her. In the end Joan is rescued by a coachman of the name of Finch, who prosecutes her persecutors.

What is most curious in the tract are the local allusions. Thus Evans, the barber, invites Joan Isley to take a pint of wine with him at "a Taverne (the signe of the Phœnix) neare the lower end of Drury-lane, behind, or on the back-side of the Bell, which is an Inne and a Taverne in the Easterne part of the Strand." This Phœnix was, no doubt, a public house close to the theatre of the same name, and deriving the sign from it. Further on we have a mention of "Reine-Deere Court" in Drury Lane, whither Mrs. Evans was carried, with only an apron before her, to be pumped upon. Helmet Court is still known in the Strand, and we are here informed that Mrs. Evans was, at the time of the affray, nursing "a sicke Gentleman, (a Captaine) at the signe of the Helmet in the Strand"; so that the court was named, as was very usual, from a public house in or close to it.

The tract ends with some grave reflections upon the subject, a sort of improvement, or moral deduction from the incidents. The tract is, we think, unique, and it deserves to be so.

STUBBES, PHILIP.—The Anatomie of Abuses: Contayning a Discoverie, or briefe Summarie of such Notable Vices and Imperfections, as now raigne in many Christian Countreyes of the Worlde: but (especiallie) in a verie famous Ilande called Ailgna: Together with most fearefull Examples of Gods Judgementes, executed upon the wicked for the same, aswell in Ailgna of late, as in other places, elsewhere.— Verie Godly to be read of all true Christians, euerie where: but most needefull to be regarded in Englande.—Made dialogue-wise, by Phillip Stubbes.—Seene and allowed, according to order.—Math. 3 ver. 2. Repent, for the kingdome of God is at hande.—Lvc. 13 ver. 5. I say unto you (saith Christ) except you repent, you shall all perish.—Printed at London, by Richard Jones. 1 Maij. 1583. 8vo. 125 *leaves.*

We believe that the only existing perfect copy of the first edition of "The Anatomy of Abuses" by Philip Stubbes is that now before us. One or two other exemplars are known, but we apprehend that they are more or less defective.

It is dated at the bottom of the title-page "1 Maij 1583," and it was published, as we may infer, in consequence of the following entry of it at Stationers' Hall (Extracts II. 178):—

"Primo Die Martij.—Rich. Jones. Licenced unto him, under thandes of the Bishop of London, and both the Wardens, The Anatomye of abuses by Phillipe Stubbes vjd."

We may conclude that it was then in its passage through the press, and it was completed in the next two months. An important part of its contents was an unmeasured attack upon May-games, and the appearance of the volume on the first day of May was perhaps designed. As some doubt and confusion prevail regarding the number and periods of publication of later editions, occasioned in part by misstatements on the title-pages of one or two of the old impressions, we subjoin an accurate account of them.

The second edition is dated 16th August, 1583, and we have given the exact terms of the title-page at the head of the next article. Thus, whatever number of the first edition was struck off, the copies were exhausted in rather more than three months. The third edition came out in the autumn of the following year, for it bears date 12th October, 1584; but the fourth edition, also dated 1584, is without any specification of the month, and the same observation will apply to the fifth edition in 1585. This last is remarkable, because, although for the same printer and stationer, Richard Jones, it is by clear error called the third edition;—"And now newly revised, recognised and augmented *the third time* by the same author." We have examined all anterior impressions of the book and their dates, so that we are in a condition to speak positively on the subject. It had been printed four times before it was reprinted in 1585; and in every instance it had been separately composed, and was not a mere reissue of copies left on hand. It was on the title-page of the edition of 12th October, 1584, that it was first said that the work had been "newly revised, recognised and augmented." In later impressions, of which there were several, none but accidental variations occur; and the main differences are to be found in the second edition of 16th August, 1583, as compared with the first edition of 1st May, 1583.

In the very outset we encounter an important variation, because "A Preface to the Reader," which follows a long dedication to Philip Earl of Arundel, was never inserted after the first impression. Among other points it contains the following remonstrance against the performance of plays on Sunday:—

"So that when honest and chast playes, tragedies and enterluds are used to these ends, for the Godly recreation of the mind, for the good example of life, for the avoyding of that which is evill, and learning of that which is good, than are they very tolerable exercyses. But being used (as now commonly they be) to the prophanation of the Lord his sabaoth, to the alluring and invegling of the People from the blessed word of God preached, to Theaters and unclean assemblies, to ydlenes, unthriftynes, whordome, wantonnes, drunkennes, and what not; and which is more, when they are used to this end, to maintaine a great sort of ydle Persons doing nothing but playing and loytring, having their lyvings of the sweat of other Mens browes, much like unto dronets devouring the sweete honie of the pore labouring bees, than are they exercyses (at no hand) sufferable."

Now, it so happened that in the interval between 1st May, 1583, when the above censure appeared, and 16th August, 1583, when it was suppressed, the evil against which the passage was directed had been, at least in part, remedied; for a public order had been issued forbidding the profanation of Sunday by the representation of plays and interludes. We know that the order was afterwards more or less disobeyed, and that the complaint was therefore renewed; but when Stubbes put forth his second edition, the experiment of Sunday-suppression had hardly been tried, and it was not known what effect the directions of the Privy Council might produce. On this account Stubbes cut away his "Preface to the Reader," and he took care not to leave even his cautious approbation of dramas, which contained "matter both of doctrine, erudition, good example and wholesome instruction." We can readily believe that, considering the offence it had given at Court and elsewhere, he was glad also to omit what he had said, in the first instance, on the subject of indecency and extravagance in dress. Proclamations, or sumptuary laws, had rendered his observations somewhat superfluous. (Egerton Papers, pp. 247-489.)

Stubbes considered himself a poet both in Latin and English, and he prefixed to his "Anatomy of Abuses" four Epigrams in the former language, and a dialogue between himself and his book in the latter: we subjoin it, as a specimen. "The Author" thus commences:—

"Now, having made thee, seelie booke,
and brought thee to this frame,
Full loth I am to publish thee,
lest thou impaire my name.

"*The Booke.* Why so? good Maister, what's the cause,
why you so loth should be
To send mee foorth into the World
my fortune for to trye?

"*The Author.* This is the cause; for that I know
the wicked thou wilt move;
And eke because thy ignoraunce
is such as none can love.

"*The Booke.* I doubt not but all Godly Men
will love and like mee well,
And for the other I care not,
in pride although they swell.

"*The Author.* Thou art also no lesse in thrall,
and subject every way
To Momus and to Zoilus crew,

who'le dayly at thee bay.

"*The Booke.* Though Momus rage and Zoilus carpe,
I feare them not at all:
The Lord my God, in whom I trust,
shall soone cause them to fall.

"*The Author.* Well, sith thou wouldst so faine be gone,
I can thee not withhold:
Adieu therfore; God be thy speade,
And blesse thee a hundred fold.

"*The Booke,* And you also, good Maister mine,
God blesse thee with his grace;
Preserve you still, and graunt to you
In Heaven a dwelling place."

The author's fixed determination to publish, in spite of pretended coyness, must have been strong, or such poor arguments as his Book uses would hardly have prevailed. The whole work is in the form of a colloquy between two persons called Spudeus and Philoponus, the latter pretending that he had been long a traveller "in Ainabla, after Ainatirb, but nowe presently called Ailgna," (merely reversing the letters of different names of our island;) and he proceeds to give an account of all he had seen. The first portion is merely introductory, after which we come to the following sixteen separate headings:—

"A perticuler Description of apparell in Ailgna by degrees.
"A particulare Discription of the Abuses of Womens apparell in Ailgna.
"The horryble vice of Whordome in Ailgna.
"The gluttonie and drunkennesse in Ailgna.
"Great Usurie in Ailgna.
"The Maner of sanctiflyng the Sabaoth in Ailgna.
"Of Stage-playes and Enterluds, with their wickedues.

"Lords of Mis-rule in Ailgna.

"The Manner of Church-ales in Ailgna.

"The maner of keeping of Wakeses and feasts in Ailgna.

"The horrible Vice of pestiferous dauncing used in Ailgna,

"Of Musick in Ailgna, and how it allureth to vanitie.

"Cards, Dice, Tables, Tennisse, Bowles, and other exercyses, used un lawfully in Ailgna.

"Beare baiting and other exercyses used unlawfully in Ailgna.

"A Fearfull Example of God his Judgement upon the prophaners of his Sabaoth.

"A fearfull Judgement of God shewed at the Theaters."

Such are the various divisions Stubbes makes of his subject, but he has many digressions, some of them more interesting and informing than if he had closely adhered to the particular topic in hand. Thus, under the last heading, without more than a few words of introduction, he breaks out into an attack upon the sort of books then usually read, and upon the facility with which a license could be obtained for them.

"And as for the reading of wicked Bookes, they are utterly unlawfull.* * * And yet notwithstanding, whosoever wil set pen to paper now a dayes, how unhonest so ever, or unseemly of Christian eares his argument be, is permitted to goe forward, and his work plausibly admitted, and freendly licensed, and gladly imprinted without any prohibition or contradiction at all: wherby it is growen to this issue, that bookes and pamphlets of scurrilitie and baudrie are better esteemed, and more vendible then the godlyest and sagest bookes that be: for if it be a godly treatise, reprooving vice and teaching vertue, away with it! for no man (almost) though they make a floorish of vertue and godlynes, will buy it, nor (which is lesse) so much as once touch it. This maketh the Bible, the blessed Book of God, to be so little esteemed. That worthie Booke of Martyrs, made by that famous Father and excellent Instrument in God his Church, Maister John Fox, so little to be accepted, and all other good books little or nothing to be reverenced; whilst other toyes, fantasies, and bableries, wherof the world is ful, are suffered to be printed."

Recollecting that Fox's "Martyrs" is so bulky a work, and that the publications complained of by Stubbes were chiefly mere tracts, it is not wonderful that they should have sold more rapidly. The author of "the Anatomy of Abuses" had contributed eight Latin lines introductory of the work of Fox, to which on every account his partialities would be strong, and he entitled them, in the true puritanical spirit,—***In sanguisugas Papistas Phil. Stubbes.***

At the conclusion of their conference, Spudeus heartily thanks Philoponus for the novel information and excellent advice he has given him, and the friends separate after a sort of prayer.

The number of editions, and the rapidity with which they followed each other, (the work was republished between 1585 and 1595, the latest of the old editions we have seen,) bear witness to the reception of "the Anatomy of Abuses" by the Puritans; and encouraged by his success, Stubbes immediately set about a second part, which came out in 1583, but which is extremely dull, and which, though reprinted in the same year, was seldom afterwards heard of. It was expressly called, "The second Part of the Anatomie of Abuses."

STUBBES, PHILIP.—The Anatomie of Abuses: Containing a Discoverie, or briefe Summarie of such Notable Vices and Imperfections as now raigne in many Countreyes of the World: but (especiallye) in a famous Hande called Ailgna: Together with most fearefull Examples of Gods Judgements executed uppon the wicked for the same, aswel in Ailgna of late, as in other places elsewhere. Very Godly to be reade of all true Christians: but most needefull to be regarded in Englande. Made Dialogue-wise by Phillip Stubbes. Seene and allowed according to order. [Math. 3. Vers. 2. Luc. 13. Vers. 5.]—Printed at London by Richard Jones. 16 August 1583. 8vo. 133 ***leaves.***

The chief differences on the title-pages of the first and second editions of this work, besides the date, are, that the word "Christian" is here omitted before "Countreyes of the World," and "verie" before "famous Ilande." There is also a colophon to the second edition, in order, perhaps, to enforce the assertion that the work was not surreptitiously published: it runs thus: "Perused, aucthorised, and allowed, accordyng to the order appoincted in the Queenes Majesties Injunctions. At London Printed by Richard Jones: dwellyng at the Signe of the Rose and the Croune, neere unto Holborne Bridge. 1583." At the back of the above, which is on a separate page, is Day's original woodcut of an old man walking, in a long cloak, with flat cap and a pair of gloves in his left hand.

The internal differences are of much more importance than the external, besides the total omission of the "Preface to the Reader," as noticed in the last article. In the first place comes an additional copy of commendatory verses by C. B. of no merit, but entreating persons of all ranks to buy his friend's book. Considerable additions are then made to the author's text, and among them a whole section is devoted to "Greate sweareyng in Ailgna," which occupies nearly twelve pages, and is the more curious because in it Philoponus (*i. e.* Stubbes) thus adverts to a previous publication of his own:—

"There was a certaine yong man dwellyng in Enlocnilshire in Ailgna (whose tragicall discourse I my self penned about two yeares agoe, referring you to the said booke for the further declaration therof) who was alwaies a filthie Swearer: his common othe was Gods bloud. The Lorde willyng his conversion, chastised him with sicknesse many times to leave the same, and moved others ever to admonish him of his wickednesse: but all chastisementes and lovyngs corrections of the Lorde, al freendly admonitions and exhortations of others he utterly contemned, stil persevering in his bloudie kinde of swearing. Then the Lord, seeing that nothing would prevaile to winne him, arested hym with his Sargeant Death," &c.

Passing by the coincidence of Shakspeare and Stubbes both using the terms "Sargeant Death" and the figure of the "arest," (Hamlet, Act V. sc. 2,) we may notice that the tract here referred to has been discovered of late years, accompanied by a second relation of a similar character about an old woman to whom the devil appeared. It is dated 1581, and the title-page runs as follows:—

"Two wunderfull and rare Examples of undeferred and present approching judgement of the Lord our God: the one upon a wicked and pernitious blasphemer of the name of God, and servaunt to one Maister Fraunces Pennell, Gentleman, dwelling at Boothbie in Lincolnshire, three myles from Grantham. The other upon a woman named Joane Bowser, dwelling at Donnington in Leicestershire, to whome the Devill verie straungely appeared, as in the discourse following you may reade. In June last. 1681. Written by Phillip Stubbes.—Imprinted at London for William Wright, and are to be solde at his shoppe in the Poultrie: the middle shoppe in the rowe, adjoyning to Saint Mildreds Church."

We need not enter into the particulars; but after a prose introduction we arrive at Stubbes's versified narrative of the facts, most wretchedly and prosaically carried on; but as specimens of verse by this author are very rare, we quote some lines which, though consisting only of fourteen-syllable couplets, are divided in the original into four-line stanzas. Little can be expected from such a commencement as this:—

"O mortall men, which in this world for time have your repast,
Approch the fearfulst thing to heare that ever happened erst;
Yea, such a thing as dooth importe the Lord our God on hye,
Through swearing by his blessed name offended for to be."

He goes on to tell us how the young man expired swearing "by Gods blood," and how his own blood gushed out at his toes and finger-ends. Stubbes then asks:—

"Whose heart is now so obdurate that, hearing of this thing,
Will not permit out of the same great floods of tears to spring?
Or whose minde is so fascinate, or eke so lulde on sleepe,
That for to heare heereof will not constrained be to weepe?
And that for feare he should his God through swearing thus offend,
And thereby purchase to him selfe like dyre and rufull end.
O! you that sweare at everie word, repleate with devilries,
For to abstain from swearing vile let this a caveat be."

The interview of Joan Bowser with Satan is narrated in the same lively and poetical style; but she took warning and reformed:—

"It pleased God that she should be to health againe restorde,
By whom all sinne and wickednes, God graunt, may be abhord:
And now she liveth honestly, and ready is to showe
Unto the world the workes of God perfected heare belowe."

The above and other temporary publications sufficiently explain the reason why Gabriel Harvey, in 1593, termed Stubbes (joining him with Deloney and Armin) "one of the common pamphleters of London." There is no doubt that his name was very popular; and for this reason, when Dr. Parry conspired with others to take away the life of Queen Elizabeth, Stubbes prepared a very small pamphlet, of only four leaves, containing particulars regarding the plot and its discovery. As it is not mentioned in any extant list of the productions of Stubbes, we quote the title at length.

"The intended Treason of Doctor Parrie, and his Complices, against the Queenes moste excellent Majestie. With a Letter sent from the Pope to the same effect.— Imprinted at London for Henry Car, and are to be solde in Paules Church-yard at the Signe of the Blazing Starre."

Having noticed these particulars connected with the biography and productions of Stubbes, we return to the second edition of his "Anatomy of Abuses," observing that, besides the whole division on Swearing, in the later copy of that work, (it is not in the first impression,) we meet with the singular relation regarding the young bride, who, not being able to set her ruffs to her mind, after "cursing and banning and casting the ruffes under her feet," wished that the Devil might take her; upon which invitation Satan made his appearance, and "writhe her necke in sonder, so that she died miserably." Some of Stubbes's principal additions are in a division of his work containing "a particular description of the Abuses of women's apparell in Ailgna"; and he there gives the very date of the young lady's death as the 27th May, 1582. We may infer that the account had reached him in the interval between the first and second editions of his work.

Here and there he changes his phraseology, in order, perhaps, to render it more intelligible: thus, for the old expression "it forceth not," as it stands in the first edition, he substituted "it is not material" in the second: in another place in the first edition, when exclaiming against" caterpillars "and "locusts" who "massacre the poor," he ends with a prayer "the Lord remove them!" but seeing that this was calling upon the Creator to destroy the rich and powerful, he altered it in the second edition from "the Lord remove them" to "God amend them."

STUBBES, PHILIP.—A Motive to good Workes. Or rather, to true Christianitie indeede. Wherein by the waie is shewed, how farre wee are behinde, not onely our forefathers in good workes, but also many other creatures in the endes of our creation: with the difference betwixt the pretenced good workes of the Antichristian Papist, and the good workes of the Christian Protestant.—By Phillip Stubbes, Gentleman.—Matthew. 5. verse 16. Let your light so shine, &c.—London, Printed for Thomas Man, dwelling in Pater Noster rowe, at the signe of the Talbot 1593. 8vo. 114 *leaves.*

In quoting the sacred text, which the author chose as the motto of his book, it is singular that he, or his printer, should have left out so important a word as "good" before "workes."

This is the only copy of the book that we ever met with. Lowndes originally mentioned it, and the short title is given in the new edition, p. 2539; but in both it is erroneously dated 1592. It is entirely prose.

Stubbes, in his dedication, tells Cuthbert Buckle, Lord Mayor of London for the year, that "he took his gelding about the Annunciation of S. Mary last past," and made a journey, which lasted about three months, into various parts of the kingdom, partly for pleasure, and partly to avoid the infection of the then raging plague. As he subscribes it "from my lodging by Cheapside, 8 of November, 1593," we may conclude that by that date the virulence of the disorder had considerably abated. He complains that he everywhere found the country fertile and beautiful, but the people utterly unworthy of it,—a deplorable deficiency of good works, and a lamentable decay of hospitals, almshouses, churches, schools, &c. His object in writing his book is therefore evident; and in a brief address "to the courteous Reader" he apologizes for the unadorned plainness of his style:—"I have not desired to be curious, neither to affect filed phrases, culled or picked sentences, nor yet loftie, haughtie or farre fetched epithetes."

Considering the purpose for which the author travelled, we might reasonably expect some minute and interesting details of what he saw in the country nearly three centuries ago; but we have little beyond general invective and pious lamentation over the prevailing vices, until we arrive at page 184, where remarks are made upon the facility with which a license was obtained for a worthless or immoral book, while permission to publish a religious or meritorious work was long delayed. As this is a point which he had touched upon in his "Anatomy of Abuses," we transcribe only a few sentences. He says:—

"I cannot a lyttle mervayle that our grave and reverend Bishops, and other inferiour magistrates and officers, to whom the oversight and charge of such things are committed, will either license (which I trust they do not, for I wyll hope better of them) or in anie sorte tollerate such railing libels and slanderous pamphlets as have beene of late published in print, one man against another, to the great dishonour of God, corruption of good manners, breach of charitie, and, in a worde, to the just offence and scandall of all good christians. And truely, to speake my conscience freely, I thinke there cannot a greater mischiefe be suffered in a common wealth, than for one man to write against another, and to publish it in print to the. viewe of the world."

In this passage we can scarcely fail to observe an allusion to the very personal controversy about this date so vigorously carried on, through the medium of the press, between Nash and Harvey. The Martin-marprelate feud was also then at its height, and Stubbes, as a zealous Puritan, sincerely sympathized with his pen-persecuted brethren. He proceeds:—

"I wis, the noble science of printing was not given us to that end, being indeede one of the chiefest blessings that God hath given to the sons of men heere uppon earth. For is not this the next way to broach rancor, hatred, malice, emulacion, envie and the like amongst men? Nay, is not this the next way to make bloudshed and murther, to rayse up mutenies, insurrections, commotions and rebellions in a christian commonwealth? and therefore I would wish both the bookes and the authors of them to be utterly suppressed for ever, the one by fire, and the other by the halter or gallowes, if nothing else will serve. But what should I say? I cannot but lament the corruption of our time, for (alas) now adayes it is, growen to be a hard matter to get a good booke licensed without staying, peradventure, a quarter of a yeare for it; yea, sometimes two or three yeares before he can have it allowed, and in the end happly rejected too: so that that which many a good man hath studyed sore for, and traveyled long in, perchance all the dayes of his life, shall be buryed in silence, and smothered up in forgetfulnes, and never see the light; whitest in the meane tyme other bookes, full of all filthines, scurrilitie, baudry, dissolutenes, cosonage, conycatching and the lyke (which all call for vengeance from heaven) are either quickely licensed, or at least easily tollerate, without all denyall or contradiction whatsoever."

At all events Stubbes had not much reason to complain of delay. He collected his materials in the summer of 1593, wrote his book on his return in November, and published it, duly registered and licensed, before the end of the year.

He is especially vehement on the neglected and ruinous state of the churches in the country; and does not spare the Roman Catholics and Jesuits for their many attempts on the Queen's life, enumerating Parry, (about whom he had himself written,) Somerville, Arden, Throckmorton, and Babington as among the principal offenders.

This seems to have been the latest work of its author, and it is very possible that he died of the plague in the year it was published. He may have returned from his country expedition too soon. When he took up his abode in Cheapside, in November, 1593, the infection proved to be by no means at an end, and he placed himself in the midst of it It is rather singular that in the work in our hands he says nothing of the death of his wife, which had occurred on the 14th December preceding, at Burton upon Trent Perhaps his journey, for the three months during which he was absent, might in part be caused by it; but if so, it is still more singular that he should not have alluded to his loss. How highly he valued her, and what an admirable pious woman she was, he himself bore ample testimony in a tract which came out in 1592, and went through almost innumerable editions, the last we have seen bearing a date considerably subsequent to the Restoration: he called it "A christall Glasse for Christian Women; containing a most excellent discourse of the godlie life and christian death of Mistresse Katherine Stubbes &c. by Phillip Stubbes, Gent." It was printed in the first instance by Richard Jones, who had published "The Anatomy of Abuses"; but in 1600 the copyright was in the hands of Edward White, the stationer at the north door of St. Paul's. It is entirely prose, with many details of the dying speeches and godly end of the lady, who had made an exemplary wife.

SURREY, THE EARL OF.—Songs and Sonettes written by the ryght honorable Lorde Henry Haward late Earle of Surrey, and other.—Apud Richardum Tottel. 1557. *Cum priuilegio.* 8vo. B. L. 107 *leaves.*

Such is the exact title-page of the earliest edition of what has generally been called "Tottell'ss Miscellany." The poems it contains have many times been reprinted, but invariably, as we apprehend, not from the first, but from the second edition. Bibliographers have mistaken the second for the first edition; and Lowndes (Bibl. Man. 1863, p. 2547) gives the title partly from the first, and partly from the second edition. At the bottom of the title-page of the first edition we read precisely as follows:—

"Apud Richardum Tottel.
1557
Cum privilegio."

Whereas at the bottom of the title-page of the second edition (also called the *first* in the Brit. Mus. Catalogue) it stands thus:

"Apud Richardum Tottel.
Cam priuilegio ad imprimendum
solum. 1557."

Of other differences in the body of the work we shall speak presently. The colophon of the first edition is in these words: "Imprinted at London in flete strete within Temple barre, at the sygne of the hand and starre, by Richard Tottel the fift day of June. An. 1557. *Cum priuilegio ad imprimendum solum.*" By the colophon of another edition of the same year, which we take to be the second, it appears that it came out on 31st July,—"the xxxi of July, anno 1557." We do not believe that Tottell published more than two impressions bearing date in 1557. Dr. Nott (Surrey and Wyatt, Vol. I. p. cclxxvii.) asserts, loosely, that in the course of June and July, 1557, the poems "went through no less than *four* distinct impressions." There may possibly have been three impressions in 1557, but we are convinced that there were not four. Of the first edition we have never seen more than a single copy, and of the second only three copies; one of which, under the notion that it was the first, was reprinted by Bishop Percy. Dr. Dibdin never saw more than a copy of the second edition, which he also miscalled the first, (*Typ. Ant.* IV. 431.) Besides the differences of the title-pages, we are now about to point out an infallible, and hitherto unnoticed, mode of distinguishing the two.

The fact is, that when Tottell began to print his first edition, dated 5th June, 1557, he had not all his materials before him. He had collected a certain number of Surrey's and Wyat's poems, but not all that, before he had completed the work, fell in his way. He had set up in type as far as signature Cc iii, when other poems by Surrey fortunately came to his hands, and these he added to the rest with the subsequent heading:—

"Other Songes and Sonettes written by the earle of Surrey."

And the titles they bear are these:—

"The constant lover lamenteth.
A prayse of Sir Thomas wyate thelder for his excellent learning.

A song written by the earle of Surrey by (*sic*) a lady that refused to daunce with him.

The faithfull lover declareth his paines and his uncertain ioies, and with only hope recomforteth somwhats his wofull heart."

These are followed immediately by the word ***Finis,*** and on another page we read thus:—

"Other Songes and sonettes written by Sir Thomas wiat the elder."

These supplemental productions have the subsequent titles:—

"Of his love called Anna.
That pleasure is mixed with every paine.
A riddle of a gift geven by a Ladie.
That speaking or profering bringes alway speding.
He ruleth not though he raigne over realmes that is subject to his owne lustes.
Whether libertie by losse of life, or life in prison and thraldome be to be preferred."

Then, after a repetition of ***Finis,*** we have on the reverse of the page Tottell's colophon as given above. This impression consists, in the whole, of 271 separate productions; but there is no "Table" as it exists in the second impression, which, instead of 107, (as in the first impression,) consists of 120 leaves. In the second impression, also, the supplemental poems both by Surrey and Wyat are incorporated in what were considered their right places. Those belonging to Surrey come after his poem entitled, "A carelesse man scorning and describing the suttle usage of women towarde their lovers." As we have stated, in Tottell's first impression, of 5th June, 1557, both Surrey's and Wyat's additional pieces, obtained by Tottell while the work was going through his press, form a sort of supplement; and this is the circumstance that mainly distinguishes the earliest from later impressions. Of course we shall not think it necessary to make any quotations from productions so well known and so often reprinted; but in order more completely to show the minute differences, we shall subjoin Tottell's address, not "To the Reader," as in the second impression, but as it stands in the first impression:—

"*The Printer to the Reader.*

"That to have wel written in verse, yea, and in small parcelles, deserveth great prayse, the workes of divers Latinos, Italians and other doe prove sufficiently. That our tong is able in that kynde to doe as prayse-worthely as the rest, the honorable stile of the noble earle of Surrey, and the weightinesse of the depe witted sir Thomas Wyat the elders verse, with several graces in sondry good Englishe writers, doe show abundantly. It resteth nowe (gentle reader) that thou thinke it not evill doon to publish, to the honor of the Englishe tong, and for profite of the studious of Englishe eloquence, those workes which the ungentle horders up of such treasure have heretofore envied thee. And for this point (good reder) thine own profit and pleasure in these presently, and in moe hereafter, shal answere for my defence. If perhappes some mislike the statelynesse of stile removed from the rude skill of common eares, I aske helpe of the learned to defend theyr learned frendes, the authors of this work: And I exhort the unlearned, by reding to learne to be more skilful!, and to purge that swinelike grossenesse, that maketh the swete majerom not to smell to their delight."

In this brief preface Tottell's first edition differs in more than twenty places from the repetition of it in the second edition. In the same way, the first poem, "Descripcion of the restlesse state of a lover, with sute to his ladie to rue on his dying hart," contains nearly as many variations as lines, including in the fourth line the word "new" instead of ones, as in all later impressions. Upon this point we are not disposed to enlarge; but we may mention that in the fifth poem, "expressed," in the last line but seven, ought certainly to be *impressed,* and so it stands in the first edition.

As little notice has at any time been taken of Tottell's re impression of 1565, we may here insert the full title of it, remarking that the date, standing by itself at the very top of the page, seems to have been specially meant to direct attention to it:—

"1565. Songes and Sonettes written by the right honorable Lord Henry Hawarde late Earle of Surrey and other.—*Apud Richardum Tottell. Cum priuilegio.*"

"The Table," which fills two leaves, was first added to the second impression of 1557, and on a separate leaf of the edition of 1565 is this colophon: "Imprinted at London in Fletestrete within Temple barre at the signe of the hand and starre, by Richard Tottell. Anno. 1565. *Cum priuilegio.*" Like the second edition, it consists of 120 leaves. Tottell continued to print to as late a date as 1594, but we do not hear of any copies of the "Songes and Sonettes" by him after 1574. In 1585 John Windet put forth an impression, and two years afterwards it came from the press of Robert Robinson, disfigured by many gross misprints. Thus, in the third line of the first poem, "despoiled," as it is given in 1557, became *displayed* in 1587, and in a subsequent piece, entitled "Complaint of a lover rebuked," "taketh his flight" is misprinted "taketh *delight.*" One of the most noticeable blunders serves to show that the ordinary old prefix of y to verbs was not well understood in 1587, for there Surrey's "swift ybreathed horse" is converted into "*swifties* breathed horse": this is in the famous poem headed, "Prisoned in Windsor, he recounted his pleasure there passed" This error began with Tottell in 1559.

There is no entry of any edition of Tottell's "Songes and Sonettes" at Stationers' Hall; but we find memorandums of two pieces in the Miscellany, which seem to have come out separately, having been registered by "John Wallye and Mrs. Toye," in 1557-58, and there called "Yf Care may cause men crye," and "When ragyng Love." Surrey's claim to various effusions may be doubted; and Puttenham, in his "Arte of English Poesie," 1589, p. 200, tells us that the poem beginning "When Cupid scaled first the fort," was not by Surrey, but by Lord Vaux.

As "Tottell's Miscellany" (the most valuable, as well as the earliest collection of the kind) has never been reprinted from the first authentic impression, we are glad to learn that the Bodleian copy, the only one at present extant, is about to be reproduced in, as nearly as possible, its original form.

SURREY, HENRY EARL OF.—Certain Bokes of Virgiles Aenæis turned into English meter by the right honorable lorde Henry Earle of Surrey.—Apud Ricardum Tottel. ***Cum priuilegio ad imprimendum solum.*** 1557. 8vo. B. L. 26 ***leaves.***

We never have been able to obtain the use of a copy of John Day's undated edition of "The fourth Boke of Virgill, &c. drawn into a straunge metre by Henry Earle of Surrey," but Tottell's impression of the second and fourth books of the Æneid (though strangely omitted by Dibdin) is not very uncommon. It was printed with the following colophon: "Imprinted at London in flete strete within Temple barre, at the sygne of the hand and starre, by Richard Tottell the xxi day of June, An. 1557." We notice it for the sake of showing that the modern reprint (2 vols. 8vo, 1831) is very inaccurate. Thus, near the commencement, and within the compass of a dozen lines, we have three variations from the original text, namely, ***stuck*** for "stack," ***stood*** for "stand," and ***this*** for "his". A little farther on, the line

"Yea and either Atride would bye it dere,"

does not mean ***buy*** it dear, but ***abide,*** or ***suffer*** for it, dear. Dr. Nott fell into this mistake, (Vol. I. p. 253.) The reprint of the fourth book almost begins with an error, for in the second line the word "nourisheth" is misprinted ***nourished,*** while Dr. Nott transformed the word into ***nourised,*** and even Percy let it stand ***norished,***—the past for the present tense. On the next page, both in Percy and in the modern reprint, "Iarbas set so light," meaning made to be esteemed so lightly, is altered to "Iarbas set ***to*** light," which is nonsense. We know not whether the copy used by Percy was or was not complete, but although he gave the colophon, he prefixed no title-page. On the whole, however, his reprint is by far the best, especially because he did not venture, like Nott, to modernize the spelling. We may add that the title-page, as it is inserted in Lowndes (Bibl. Man. 1864, p. 2782), is incorrect, for "London" does not appear upon it, and the Christian name of Tottel, or Tottell, is not spelt **Richardum,** but **Ricardum.** These are minute matters, and perhaps hardly worth notice, but for the sake of extreme accuracy.

The second and fourth books of the Æneid, as reprinted by Bishop Percy, are contained in a volume which has accidentally become of great rarity, because, according to **Restituia,** III. 451, and Lowndes, Bibl Man. 1861, p. 1830, only four copies were saved out of the fire which destroyed the premises of Mr. Nichols, the printer, in 1808. The primary purpose of the editor was to make an assemblage of the works of all poets who, anterior to Milton, had written blank-verse. Some of the copies preserved contain more or less of the productions intended to be included: one or two have not above half the matter included in the volume now before us, and we never heard of any other which has more. We will therefore give an analysis of its contents, for the information of those who may fortunately possess other portions, not one of which, we can venture to state, is complete according to the original intention of Bishop Percy:—

I. Songes and Sonnettes of Surrey and other. These are consecutively paged as far as page 272, the folios of the original edition (extending to 117) being noted in the margin: that original contains 120 leaves, including title, &c.

II. "The second boke of Virgiles Acnæis," and "The fowrth boke of Virgiles Acnæis," extending to p. [57], when we come to this colophon:—"Imprinted at London in flete strete within Temple barre, at the sygne of the hand and starre, by Richard Tottell, the xxi day of June. An. 1557."

III. Eeelesiastes, and Certain Psalms; &c. by Henry Earl of Surrey.—From ancient MSS. never before printed.—Continuing regularly to p. [76].

IV. Additional Poems by the Earl of Surrey. Continuing to p. [81].

V. Certayne Psalmes chosen out of the Psalter of David commonlye called thee vii penytentiall Psalmes, drawen into englyshe meter by Sir Thomas Wyat, knyght, &c.—Imprinted at London in Paules Church yarde at the sygne of the Starre, By Thomas Raynald. And John Harrington.—Continuing to p. [109], where occurs this colophon.—Cum preuilegio ad imprimendum Solum, M.D.XLIX. The last day of December."

VI. Additional Poems by Sir Thomas Wyat.—Continuing as far as p. [112].

VII. An Oration By Sir Thomas Wyat, Being his Defence after Indictment and Evidence.—First published in 4to. Strawberry-hill. Printed by Thomas Kirgate, M.DCC.LXXII.—Continuing to p. [141], where we read "The End of Wyat's Works."

VIII. (A new title-page) Poems in Blank Verse, (not Dramatique) prior to Milton's Paradise Lost—Subsequent to Lord Surrey's in this Volume, and to N. G.'s in the preceding.—Continuing to p. [342], and including the following productions.

1. George Turbervile's translation of Ovid's 11th, 12th, 13th, 14th, 20th, and 21st Epistles.—From p. [145] to p. [195].

2. The Steele Glas A Satyre. By George Gascoigne, Esquire. From p. [197] to p. [237].

3. Precepts for a State. By Barnabie Riche.—From p. [239] to p. [245]. (Printed in 1584.)

4. Blank Verses by George Peele.—The Moores Address to the Lord Mayor of London, 1585. By George Peele.—From p. [247] to p. [249].

5. The Epistle of Pontius Pilate. By J. Higgins.—From p. [250] to p. [251]. (From the "Mirror for Magistrates.")

6. Elizabetha Triumphans By James Aske.—From p. [253] to p. [291]. (Printed in 1588.)

7. A Tale of Two Swannes. By William Vallans.—From p. [293] to p. [802]. (Printed in 1590.)

8. Poetical Speeches at Elvetham. By Nicholas Breton.—From p. [303] to p. [312], (Printed in 1591.)

9. A Poem on Guiana. By George Chapman.—From p. [313] to p. [319], (Printed in 1596.)

10. The First Book of Lucans Pharsalia. By Christopher Marlow.—From p. [321] to p. [342]. (Printed in 1600.)

At the end of the last production in this reprint we meet with the word FINIS.

It should seem as if it had been intended that Vol. I. should end on p. [141], and that a new volume should commence on P. [143].

SWEARERS, CUSTOMABLE.—"A Christian exhortation unto customable swearers. What a ryghte and law-full othe is: whan, and before whome, it oughte to be. Item. The maner of sayinge grace, or gevyng thankes unto God. Who so ever heareth Goddes worde, beleve it and do therafter shall be saved." 8vo. B. L. 36 *leaves.*

This book has neither name of author, printer, nor publisher. It is without imprint or colophon, but the type seems to be English, and Nicholas Hyll certainly printed one or more editions of it. (Dibdin's Typ. Ant. IV. 233, 234.) As to the date, the King mentioned in the address "Unto the reader" must have been Edward VI., who we are told "hath restored agayn the pure word of God, and hath graunted us all fre passage unto it." The main purpose of the writer (perhaps M. Coverdale, whose name is given in the reprint of 1575) was to reprove the vice of swearing, but in the course of his invectives he violently attacks the bishops, especially where he says,—"No where shall you fynde more othes, nor of more dyverse kyndes, tha in bysshoppes houses. And as for common whores, you shall have so manye, not farre from some of ther houses, as are able to serve the fylthye flocke of an whole countre."

This seems especially directed against the Bishop of Winchester, who, as is well known, had the stews in Southwark under his special surveillance. Much the same thing is stated further on: "No faute fyndeth our prelates in thys, nor breake of Christen religion, no more than they do in the daylye huntynge of the stewes, and other shamefull abhomynations."

From the following we might almost infer that the writer was not himself a clergyman.:—"Who hath so largely bene perjured as prelates, priestes and religious? whych at the receyvyng of ther popishe degrees hath forsworne the verite of God, who in baptisme they faythfully promised to städe by against all the devels in hell."

"The maner of sayeng grace after the doctrine of holy scrypture" forms a separate part of the work, which concludes with a seven-line stanza; and twelve more are added at the end under the heading of "A short instruetiä to the worlde": they are separately addressed "To Kynges and Princes," "To Judges," "To Councelours," "To Chamberlaynes," &c, and as a specimen we may quote that

" *To Controllers.*

"Go thorow the court for Christes sake,
And where ye spye any thynge abused
Do your office, and some payne take
That ydelnesse may be refused.
Great mens houses are accused
To be infecte wyth unclennesse,

Wyth pryde, with othes, and with excesse."

Another stanza (one out of five), addressed "To preestes," may also be extracted.

"Wher any vyce now is occupyed
Wythin thys world, as there is muche,
It shuld rygh[t] well be amended,
If all rulers wold rebuke such;
And yf prechers the quycke wold touch,
Where men now ar in synne so ryfe
They shuld right gladly mçde their lyfe."

It is very clear that the severity with which the author attacked all parties, rendered it dangerous for him to put his name to the tract. It seems likely that Nicholas Hyll was also the printer of this nameless and dateless edition. If Coverdale wrote the verses, they did not obtain for him a place in Ritson's **Bibl. Poetica.**

SYLVESTER, JOSHUA.—A Canticle of the victorie obteined by the French King, Henrie the fourth. At Yvry. Written in French by the noble learned and devine Poet, William Salustius, Lord of Bartas, and Counsailor of estate unto his Majestie. Translated by Josuah Silvester Marchant-adventurer.—At London, Printed by Richard Yardley, on Bredstreete hill, at the signe of the Starre. 1591. 4to. 10 *leaves.*

Sylvester, though starting, as we see, as a Merchant-adventurer, became in time so mere a literary adventurer and translating drudge, that we cannot feel much interest about him or his unoriginal works. The above, which we believe to be his first production, is dated by Ritson in 1590, but this seems to be a mistake; and as the title has nowhere been given at all accurately, we have transcribed it at length. The work is dedicated in "a quatorzaine" to "Maister James Parkinson, and Maister John Caplin Esquires, his welbeloved friendes."

SYLVESTER, JOSHUA.—The Triumph of Faith The Sacrifice of Isaac. The Ship-wracke of Jonas. With a song of the victorie obtained by the French King, At Yvry. Written in French by W. Salustius, lord of Bartas, and translated by Josuah Silvester Marchant Adventurer.—Printed by Richard Yardley and Peter Short, and are to be sold at the Starre on Bredstreet hill. 1592. 4to. 30 *leaves.*

In the dedication to the translator's "Uncle Maister William Plumbe Esquire," he calls these "the first fruites of my little labours," but, as we have seen, he had in fact printed his "first fruits" in 1591. He makes no profession of any great skill or fitness for the work, admitting that he had "never been in France, whereby I might become so absolute"; adding, "If thou finde me poore in Poetrie, remember that it is not my profession." The work ends with these lines:—

"Now, readers, if your gentle doome shall daigne
With good aspect to grace my lowly muse;
If you vouchsafe a frendly entertaine
To these first fruites shee offers to your viewes:
If you accept these patterns of her paine,
And helpe her faultes with favour to excuse,
If this first messe doe not your mouthes misleeke,
Your second course shalbe the SECOND WEEKE.
Yours,
JOSUAH SILVESTER."

It does not seem that "the Second Weeke" came out until 1598, and the whole of "Du Bartas his divine Weekes and Workes" first appeared, we believe, in 1605, and was often reprinted—last in 1641. In 1620 was published a poem by Sylvester, called "The Woodmans Bear," a sort of allegory, not very intelligible nor very complimentary to his wife, for while he is the Woodman, he describes her as the Bear. In 1615 had come out "St. Lewis; the King or the Lamp of Grace," and "A Hymn of Alms, or the Beggers Bill," with several other productions of little merit. Heber had a copy with a MS. dedicatory sonnet to Sir Edward Lewis, signed Josuah Sylvester.

When he died is not precisely known, but he seems to have subsisted mainly by his pen, especially late in his career. He lived in 1614 in the parish of Saint Bartholomew the less, where several of his children were baptized. In 1625 his wife Mary was a widow, and on 31st August buried a posthumous child named Bonaventura. These are new, though small, points in his insignificant history.

TARLTON, RICHARD.—Tarlton's Newes out of Purgatorie. Onelye such a jest as his Jigge, fit for Gentlemen to laugh at an houre &c. Published by an old companion of his, Robin Goodfellow.—At London Printed for Edward White, n. d. B. L. 4to. 28 *leaves.*

Two circumstances fix the date of this production prior to 1590: one is the death of Tarlton, (who is supposed to communicate the "News out of Purgatory,") who was buried on 3d September, 1588; and the other, which is quite as decisive, that an answer to it was published in 1590, under the title of "The Cobler of Caunterbury, or an Invective against Tarlton's Newes out of Purgatorie." This tract was again printed in 1608, at the time when, perhaps, a new edition of "Tarlton's News" made its appearance, although none is now known between the first, the title of which is given above, and a reprint of it in 1630. In 1680 also came out a new edition of "The Cobler of Caunterbury," then called "The Tinker of Turvey," the main difference being the title, the introductory matter, and the conclusion. The allusions to Tarlton, and to his "News out of Purgatory," are the same in all editions.

The "News out of Purgatory" is introduced by two pages "to the Gentlemen Readers," in which the anonymous author states that it is his first appearance in print. The work then commences by lamenting the loss of Tarlton, who had been so great a favorite at the theatre, and was so famous for that species of humorous performance then and afterwards called "Jigs," consisting of singing and recitation, accompanied by the sound of the pipe and tabor. The writer feigns a dream, in which he saw the ghost of Tarlton, dressed, as he usually was upon the stage, "in russet, with a buttonn cap on his head, a great bag by his side, and a strong bat in his hand; so artificially attired for a Clowne, as I began to call Tarlton's woonted shape to remembrance." Harleian MS. 3885, contains a rather elaborately and carefully executed likeness of Tarlton, accompanied by some explanatory lines, in which the reader is informed that the celebrated actor is represented as,

"When he in pleasaunt wise
The counterfet expreste
Of Clowne, with cote of russet hew,
And startups with the reste."

These verses were, it seems, by a person of the name of John Howe, and the likeness to which they are appended was (according to a note in one of Bagford's MSS., as we are kindly informed by Mr. Halliwell) in the possession of the Bishop of Norwich.

It appears from a scene in the old play of "The Three Lords and Three Ladies of London," 1590, 4to, that an engraving of Tarlton, doubtless on wood, was then current. Tarlton was famous for his "flat nose," as well as for "the squint of his eye."

In the work before us, Tarlton gives a description of Purgatory, and introduces many tales, among them that of Friar Onion, the Crane with one Leg, &c, from Boccaceio, although he does not state the source from which he derived them. To these succeed a translation of "Ronsard's Description of his Mistress," in lyric verse, and some more novels, the whole work being intended as a vehicle for merry stories. It appears, at the end, that Tarlton had been appointed "to sit and play Jigs all day on his taber to the ghosts," as a punishment for his sins on earth; and beginning one of them, to show how much better he performed after death than when he was alive, the shrill sound of the pipe awoke the author, and his dream was over.

"Tarltons Jests, drawn into three Parts" must have come out soon after his death, but the earliest known impression of them bears date in 1611: it included "his Court witty Jests; his sound City Jests and his Country pretty Jests," and they were perhaps originally published separately. On 4th August, 1600, Thomas Pavier entered at Stationers' Hall "the second part of Tarleton's Jests," and on 21st February, 1608-9, John Budge assigned "Tarleton's Jests "to Knight, the stationer. They were reprinted by the Shakspeare Society in 1844, but with some omissions, because one or two of the jests were considered unfit for eyes and ears polite. This defect was remedied as far as possible, in a few copies, by the insertion of printed slips, containing what ought originally to have found its place in the reprint How long the jests maintained their popularity, though not altogether well deserved, may be seen from the following lines inserted in a volume called "Wit and Drollery," printed in 1682, and perhaps before and afterwards:—

"Wit that shall make thy name to last,
when Tarletons Jests are rotten,
And George a Greene and Mother Bunch
shall all be quite forgotten."

"Tarlton's Jests" were reprinted in 1638; and we have a fragment before us of a third impression, which, judging from the type, must have been later than either of the others.

No bibliographer (Mr. Halliwell excepted, in the Introduction to his reprint of "Tarlton's Jests") has noticed that Tarlton began authorship as early as 1570, when a ballad, with his name appended, was published on the "Fierce Fluds which lately flowed in Bedfordshire." His "Toyes" were licensed in 1576, and his "Tragical Treatises" in 1578. These have not come down to our day; but his ballad on the Floods in Bedfordshire was reprinted by the Percy Society in 1840. Tarlton was, doubtless, a popular actor in 1570, and his name may have been used in order to give greater circulation to the ballad, which, in truth, has no merit, although great curiosity. It is a unique broadside.

TATHAM, JOHN.—The Mirrour of Fancies. With a Tragi-comedy intitled Love crowns the End. Acted by die Schollars of Bingham in the County of Nottingham. By Jo. Tatham Gent—London Printed for W. Burden &c. 1657. 12mo. 81 *leaves.*

The author calls this volume his "first sacrifice," and "the maiden blossoms of his Muse," and it was originally printed under the title of "The Fancies Theatre," in 1640. This in truth is the identical impression, and the old title-page is pasted under the new one. The drama, forming the second part of the volume, has two separate title-pages, one dated 1640, and the other 1657. The fact no doubt was, that the new title-page was prefixed in 1657, to get rid of some copies remaining unsold. The dedication is to Sir John Winter, Secretary of State, and Master of the Requests to the Queen; and the volume is ostentatiously ushered by commendatory verses, signed R. Broome, Tho. Nabbes, C. G., Geo. Lynn, Robert Chamberlaine, H. Davison, James Jones, William Barnes, Tho. Rawlins, An. Newport, R. Pyndar, and W. Ling. Tatham's poems in general are trifling and conceited, but the most curious is a prologue on the removal of the players at the Fortune Theatre to the Red Bull Theatre, where these lines occur:—

"Onely we would request you to forbeare
Your wonted custome, banding tyle or peare
Against our ***customes,*** to allure us forth," &c.

For "customes" we should probably read "curtains," and so Malone (Shakesp. by Boswell, III. 79) has printed it, but without stating that he had altered the text. It seems, on the same authority, that the curtains at the Bull were of silk, while those at the Fortune were worsted. Malone does not seem to have been aware that "The Fancies Theatre" of 1640 was the same as "The Mirrour of Fancies" of 1657.

TATHAM, JOHN.—Ostella: or the Faction of Love and Beauty reconcil'd. By J. T. Gent.—London: Printed for John Tey &c. 1650. 4to. 62 ***leaves.***

In point of date, this was John Tatham's second known work, but, as there had been an interval of ten years between it and "The Fancies Theatre," printed in 1640, it is very likely that he wrote some production which was either published anonymously, or has not been discovered. His "Distracted State," which came out in 1652, is said on the title-page to have been written in 1641. It has been disputed whether Tatham was at any time City Poet, but he certainly was the author of the Lord Mayor's Pageants for 1657, 1658, 1659, 1660, 1661, 1662, 1663, and 1664, besides three other occasional pieces of a similar kind in honor of the King and Queen.

His claims as a poet do not place him much above the mercenary position of rhymer to the Lord Mayor and Court of Aldermen, although the volume before us contains some pretty songs which he seems to have contributed to a Masque. One of them, in praise of a country life, opens with this stanza:—

"Who can boast of happiness
More completely sure than we,
Since our harmless thoughts we dress,
In a pure simplicity;
And chaste nature doth dispense
Here her beauty's innocence?"

If Tatham had himself "dressed his thoughts in a pure simplicity ," he would have deserved greater praise than that of a poor imitator of Cowley. On p. 111 is inserted a prologue to a play called "The Whisperer, or What you please," the existence of which we know on no other authority: it was probably acted before the closing of the theatres: it is included by Mr. Halliwell in his "Dictionary of English Plays to the close of the seventeenth Century," 8vo, 1860.

TAYLOR, JOHN.—The Eighth Wonder of the World, or Coriats Escape from his supposed drowning. With his safe Arrivall and entertainment at the famous Citty of Constantinople &c. By John Taylor.—Printed at Pancridge neere Coleman-hedge, and are to bee sold at the signe of the nimble Traveller. 1613. 12mo. 14 *leaves.*

This is one of the many pieces of ridicule levelled at Thomas Coryat, author of the "Crudities," published in 1611. It is dedicated to a person whom John Taylor calls "Sir Thomas Parsons, (*alias*) Pheander, (*alias*) Knight of the Sunne," &c, whom he puts upon a par with the King's Fool, and who was possibly Fool to the Lord Mayor. It seems by the commencement, that Taylor had an especial grudge against Coryat, for having had influence enough to procure his "Laugh and be Fat" (also directed against the traveller) to be burned. No printer's name is appended to "The Eighth Wonder of the World," lest probably it might lead to unpleasant consequences. In one of his later pieces Taylor assails Coryat, although he had then long been dead.

John Taylor was originally a waterman, and hence obtained from his contemporaries the appellation of "the Water-poet": he afterwards kept a public house. He was a man of some education and talent, and appears from his works to have been on familiar terms with many of the distinguished poets of his day. He began as an author in 1612, with some verses on the death of Prince Henry, and he continued to write and publish short pieces in prose and verse for more than forty years. He was a steady royalist, and just before the breaking out of the Civil Wars he wrote his "Plea for Prerogative," (printed for T. Bankes, 1642,) which is directed not less against the Papists than in favor of the King. He had a knack of rapid versification, but no claim to the rank of a true poet, and Ben Jonson contrasts him with Spenser. He often wrote to supply temporary necessity.

TAYLOR, JOHN.—Taylors Urania or his Heavenly Muse. With a briefe Narration of the thirteene Sieges, and sixe Sackings of the famous Cittie of Jerusalem. Their miseries of Warre, Plague, and Famine (during the last siege by Vespasian and his son Titus.) In Heroicall Verse compendiously described.—London Printed by Edward Griffin for Nathaniel Butter. 1615. 8vo. 44 *leaves.*

It is dedicated in a sonnet to Sir George More, Knight, Lieuetenant of the Tower, followed by addresses "to the Reader" and "the Author to the Printer," with commendatory poems by John Davis, William Branthwaite, Robert Branthwaite, Henry Sherlye, Richard Leigh, Thomas Brewer, and Thomas Dekker. After eight lines "to the Understander," signed John Taylor, the main body of the poem begins, and occupies eighty-five octave stanzas, entirely of a religious character. On sign. D 4 commences another title: "The severall Sieges, Assaults, Sackings, and finall Destruction of the famous, ancient, and memorable Citie of Jerusalem. Devided into two parts. By John Taylor," &c. This portion of the work is dedicated to John Moray, Esq., one of the Gentlemen of the King's Chamber, upon whom Taylor lived to write a funeral elegy. It is in couplets, the second part relating to the Siege and Destruction of Jerusalem under Titus. Taylor's style is very unequal, sometimes poor and mean, and at others turgid and inflated. See a review of a piece of the same character, and upon the same subject, in Vol. II. p. 166.

TAYLOR, JOHN.—The Praise of Hempseed, with the Voyage of Mr. Roger Bird and the Writer hereof, in a Boat of brown-paper, from London to Quinborough in Kent. As also a Farewell to the matchlesse deceased Mr. Thomas Coriat Concluding with the commendations of the famous River of Thames. By John Taylor &c. Printed at London for H. Gosson &c. 1620. 4to. 24 *leaves.*

This poetical tract is dedicated to Sir Thomas Howet, Sir Robert Wiseman, and Mr. John Wiseman, who it seems had pecuniarily aided the author and his companion (a Vintner) to undertake their "dangerous voyage," which was literally performed for a wager in a paper boat supported by bladders. [Note 1: The danger to Taylor and Bird was merely because they wagered to go the distance in a boat made of brown paper; but an earlier enterprise of a similar kind, and for a similar purpose, that of winning money, was undertaken by Richard Ferris, and two other men named Hill and Thomas, to go from Tower Wharf to Bristol, "in a small wherry," although the precise size is not stated. They accomplished their task, and published an account of it in 1590, 4to, followed by some stanzas, headed "a new Sonnet," by James Sargent, of whom no more is know, or, for any merit in his verses, need be known.] In a humorous "Preamble," the author vindicates the adoption of so trifling a subject, by reference to the works of some of his predecessors, in Greek, Latin, Italian, French, Scotch, and English. Among the latter he cites Michael Drayton, who composed a poem called "The Owl"; Richard Niccols, author of "The Cuckoo"; Sir John Davys, ho wrote "Orchestra"; Sir John Harington, who published "The Metamorphosis of Ajax"; Thomas Middle ton, author of "The Ant and the Nightingale"; Thomas Nash, who wrote a tract in praise of the Herring, &c.

The body of the tract does not require, nor merit, any very especial notice. It was produced for sale, and Taylor forced into it the description of a storm, which he states he had written three years before, but could never find a fit place for its insertion till then. In speaking of paper and its uses, he gives the subsequent enumeration of English poets who had died before 1620:—

"Old Chaucer, Gower, Sir Thomas More,
Sir Philip Sidney, who the lawrell wore;
Spenser, and Shakespeare did in art excell,
Sir Edward Dyer, Greene, Nash, Daniell,
Silvester, Beumont, Sir John Harrington."

The following, he states, were still living:—

"As Davis, Drayton, and the learned Dun,
Jonson, and Chapman, Marston, Middleton,
With Rowlye, Fletcher, Withers, Messenger,
Heywood, and all the rest where e're they are."

In "Drunken Barnaby's Journal," printed not earlier than 1640, there is a passage, accompanied by a plate, for which great credit has been given to the author. It relates to the execution of a cat by a Puritan, because it had killed a mouse on Sunday. The humorous thought came from, or was used by, Taylor twenty years earlier. He is speaking of a Brownist:—

"The Spirit still directs him how to pray,
Nor will he dress his meat the Sabbath day,

Which doth a mighty mystery unfold;
His zeale is hot, although his meat be cold.
Suppose his Cat on Sunday kill'd a rat,
She on the Monday must be hang'd for that," &c.

It is very likely to have been a sort of proverb against the Puritans before the time when Taylor employed it On the title-page is a woodcut representing the different uses to which hemp was applied.

TAYLOR, JOHN.—The Praise and Vertue of a Jayle and Jaylers. With the most excellent Mysterie and necessary use of all sorts of Hanging &c. By John Taylor.— London 1623. 8vo. 18 *leaves.*

This very amusing trifle is dedicated in verse to Mr. Robert Rugge, who had sent Taylor from Holy Island a barrel of the eggs of sea-fowl. The most curious part of the tract is an account of seventeen prisons then existing in and near London, viz.: the Tower, the Gatehouse, the Fleet, Newgate, Ludgate, Poultry Counter, Wood Street Counter, Bridewell, Southwark Counter, the Marshalsea, the King's Bench, the White Lion, the Hole of St. Katherine's, East Smithfield Prison, Three Cranes Jail, Lord Wentworth's Jail, and Finsbury Prison. This enumeration is contained in the first part of the work; the second is directed to prove "the necessity of hanging"; and the third is "the description of Tyburne." The last thus opens:—

"I have heard sundry men oft times dispute
Of trees that in one yeere will twice beare fruit;
But if a man note Tyburne, 'twill appeare,
That that's a tree that beares twelve times a yeere."

The author, with some humor and a good deal of ingenuity, enlarges upon this figure, and evinces a very extensive, and no doubt accurate personal acquaintance with his whole subject.

TAYLOR, JOHN.—The Praise of Cleane Linnen. With the Commendable use of the Laundresse. By John Taylor.—London Printed by E: All-de for Hen. Gosson. 1624. 12mo. 14 *leaves.*

This piece of drollery is dedicated to "Martha Legge Esquiresse, transparent, unspotted, snow-lilly-white Laundresse;" and the body of the tract is entertaining as well as ingenious, the author going through the various parts of dress and other purposes to which linen is applicable. As a specimen, what he says of the Ruff may be quoted:—

"Now up aloft I mount unto the Ruffe,
Which into foolish mortals pride doth puffe;
Yet Ruffes antiquity is here but small,
Within this eighty yeares not one at all;
For the eighth Henry (as I understand)
Was the first King that ever wore a band,
And but a falling band—plaine with a hem.
All other people knew no use of them,
Yet imitation in small time began
To growe, that it the Kingdome over-ran.
The little Falling-bands increased to Ruffes:
Ruffes (growing great) were waited on by Cuffes;
And though our frailties should awake our care,
We make our Ruffes as careles as we are.
Our Ruffes unto our faults compare I may,
Both careles and growne greater every day."

In the prose conclusion, "the principal occasions why this merry Poem was written," Taylor, as was not unusual, mistook coarseness for humor.

TAYLOR, JOHN.—The Scourge of Basenesse, or the old Lerry with a new Kicksey, and new cum twang with the old Winsye. Wherein John Taylor hath curried or clapperclawed neere a thousand of his bad Debters &c.—London, Printed by N. O. for Mathew Walbancke &c. 1624. 12mo. 24 *leaves.*

Taylor was in the habit of making extraordinary journeys at home and abroad, and laying wagers with persons that he would perform the undertaking. To this practice he alludes in some lines "to the Reader":—

"To Germany I twice the Seas did crosse,
To Scotland, all on foot, and backe from thence,
Not any coyne about me for expence:

And with a rotten, weake, browne paper boate
To Quinborough from London I did floate.
Next to Bohemia," &o.

A number of persons, who had wagered odds against the execution of any of these journeys, when Taylor won, had refused or neglected to pay him; and the object of this abusive, satirical, and humorous work was to revenge himself upon them. The dedication is to Andrew Hilton, an innkeeper of Daventry, whom Taylor found that he had unjustly attacked in the account he wrote of his journey to Scotland. On the title-page is an emblematical woodcut of a hand holding or letting escape a number of vipers.

TAYLOR, JOHN.—An Armado or Navye of 103 Ships, and other Vessels; who have the Art to sayle by Land as well as by Sea. Morally rigd, mand, munitiond, appointed, set forth, and victualed with 32 sortes of Ling: with other provisions of Fish and Flesh. By John Taylor &c.—London, Printed by E. A. for H. Gosson. 1627. 8vo. 27 *leaves.*

Opposite the title-page is a woodcut of a ship under sail, but the ships intended by the merry author are given in a list at the back of the titlo-page, viz.: Lordship, Scholarship, Ladyship, Good-fellowship, Apprenticeship, Courtship, Friendship, Fellowship, Footmanship, Horsemanship, Suretyship, Worship, and Woodmanship. The Ling with which they are victualled consists of words ending with that syllable, as Tipling, Fond-ling, &c. The dedication is to Sir John Fearne, Knight There are some laudatory lines by F. Mason; and on sign. C 5 is a species of mock-pageant in blank-verse, but the rest of the tract is prose.

TAYLOR, JOHN.—All the Workes of John Taylor, the Water-poet Beeing Sixty and three in Number. Collected into one Volume by the Author: With sundry new Additions, corrected, revised, and newly imprinted. 1630.—At London, Printed by J. B. for James Boler &c. 1630. folio. 326 *leaves.*

An engraved title by Cookson, with a portrait of the author at the bottom of it, precedes the printed title-page as above. The collection is inscribed to the Marquess of Hamilton, the Earl of Pembroke, and the Earl of Montgomery, followed by an address to the World, and some lines by Taylor upon the *errata;* in which he states that the volume came from the presses of four different printers, which accounts for three distinct paginations. Commendatory verses in English and Latin by Abraham Viell, Thomas Brewer, T. G., R. H., Robert Branthwaite, Richard Leigh, William Branthwaite, and Thomas Dekker, precede "a Catalogue of all the several bookes contained in this Volume," but it is by no means complete. The pieces are reprints of the scattered tracts Taylor had published prior to the year 1630.

TAYLOR, JOHN.—Wit and Mirth, chargeably collected out of Tavernes, Ordinaries, Innes, Bowling Greenes, and Allyes, Alehouses, Tobacco shops, High wayes and Water-passages. Made up and fashioned into Clinches, Bulls, Quirkes, Yerkes, Quips, and Jerkes &c. By John Taylor, Water-Poet—Printed at London by T. C. for James Boler. 1629. B. L. 12mo. 40 *leaves*

This is a collection of one hundred and thirteen jests; and Taylor tells the person to whom he dedicates them, Mr. Archibald Rankin, that, although some of them might have appeared in print before, he was not aware of it, but had gathered them in the course of his experience. The fact is, that not a few of them were current jokes derived from several published sources, and one (numbered 21) is part of a tale told in "Pasquil's Jests," of which a reprint with additions had come out in 1629. (See Vol. III. p. 149.) Others are personal, relating to Richard Tarlton; to William Barkstead, the player (to whom Marston's "Insatiate Countess" has been attributed); to Field, the author and actor; to Sir Edward Dyer, the poet; and to Taylor himself:—

"I my selfe (says he) gave a booke to King James once in the great Chamber at Whitehall, as his Majesty came from the Chappell: the Duke of Richmond said merrily to me, 'Taylor, where did you learne the manner to give the King a book, and not kneel? 'My Lord, (said I) if it please your grace, I doe give now, but when I beg any thing, then I will kneele.'"

To some of the jests verses are appended by way of application, but they generally have little merit In this instance they run as follows:—

"Be it to all men by these presents knowne
Men need not kneele to give away their own:
He stand upon my feet when as I give,
And kneele when as I beg more meanes to live;
But some by this may understand
That Courtiers oftner kneele than stand."

Taylor feigns in the commencement, in four pages of verse, that he made this collection at the command of the ghost of old John Garret, who, it seems, had been a well-known jester, and a boon companion, who had served in Ireland under Sir John Norris, and lived until Charles I. came to the throne.

This edition is not mentioned by bibliographers, the reprint of 1635 being apparently the only one known. As, however, "Wit and Mirth" was included, with some additions, in the folio of Taylor's Works in 1630, it must have appeared separately earlier.

TAYLOR, JOHN.—Taylor's Travels and circular Perambulation through and by more than thirty times twelve Signes of the Zodiack of the famous Cities of London and Westminster. With the Honour and Worthinesse of the Vine, the Vintage and the Vintoner: with an Alphabeticall Description of all the Taverne Signes in the Cities, Suburbs and Liberties aforesaid, and significant Epigrams upon the said severall Signes. Written by John Taylor.—London, Printed by A. M. 1636. 8vo. 31 *leaves.*

The contents of this production cannot fail to remind us of another work, of later date, but of a somewhat similar character, reviewed in Vol. 11. p. 300, under the heading of "Malt-worms." "Taylor's Travels" is in substance an account of all the principal inns and public-houses in London and Westminster; and it therefore comprises a good deal of local information relating to the two cities more than two centuries ago. We cannot enter at length into the subject, but it is amusing to read here of the number of old signs of places of recreation, eating, and drinking, which to this day are extant in the metropolis. Taylor introduces Epigrams, often not very pointed, upon some of them. Thus, after enumerating no fewer than ten Mermaids in Cornhill, Cheapside, Bread Street, Paternoster Row, Charing Cross, &c, he adds the following lines:—

"This Mayd is strange (in shape): to mans appearing
Shee's neither fish or flesh, nor good red-hearing:
What is shee then? A Signe to represent
Fish, flesh, good Wine, with welcome and content."

It was at the Mermaid in Bread Street that the famous club met, celebrated by Ben Jonson, Beaumont, and others; and it was a tavern as early as 1464, when Sir John Howard, afterwards Duke of Norfolk, took wine there. (P. Cunningham's "London," 1850, p. 332.)

It is somewhat singular that when Taylor enumerates the Red Bull, the Fortune, and the Globe, he should say nothing about the playhouses called after the same names, and established in the same neighborhoods: they were at that date (1636) in full activity, for there was no serious attempt to suppress them until about six years afterwards. In the preliminary matter Taylor states that he had previously written above eighty books, "some of them printed ten or twelve times over, 1500 or 2000 every time." Two of the public-houses he names had no signs, but merely, as Taylor tells us, "a bush," to indicate that wine was sold there: hence the proverb.

With the same date (and announced in the above) Taylor published a second part of his undertaking, referring to the inns and taverns in ten counties, viz., Kent, Sussex, Hampshire, Surrey, Berkshire, Essex, Middlesex, Hertfordshire, Buckinghamshire, and Oxford. In the whole he says that there were at least 686 of them, but he does not dwell upon them, and supplies no epigrams, which in the first part he found rather wearisome. He summarily settles the disputed question of the place of Chaucer's birth, observing of Woodstock: "The towne is a pretty market-towne, chiefly famous for the breeding of the famous Jeffrey Chaucer, the most ancient Archpoet of England." Leland asserts that Chaucer was born in Oxfordshire or Berkshire; but how are we to reconcile this statement with that of the poet himself, who, in his "Testament of Love," tells us that he was "a Londoner"? This agrees with Stow, Speght's Chaucer, 1598, sign, bii, who says that Chaucer's father Richard was a vintner in St. Mary Aldermary. We do not, of course, take Taylor to be any authority on the point.

He speaks in his title-page of "the honorable and memorable Foundations, Erections, Raisings and Ruines of divers Cities, Townes, Castles, and other pieces of Antiquity," of which he was to give an account; but he seems afterwards to have forgotten them, excepting in as far as they were commemorated in the signs of hostelries, taverns, and inns.

TAYLOR, JOHN.—Crop-eare Curried, or Tom Nash his Ghost, declaring the pruining of Prinnes two last Parricidicall Pamphlets &c. With a strange Prophecy, reported to be Merlin's, or Nimshag's the Gymnosophist &c. By John Taylor.— Printed in the yeare 1644. 4to. 21 *leaves.*

In this tract Taylor endeavors to imitate the satirical and objurgatory style of Tom Nash: he wishes to use against the Puritans of the reign of Charles I. the weapons employed by Nash against the Mar-prelates of the reign of Elizabeth. However, Taylor's arrows were blunt and unbarbed, and his hand was comparatively slow and feeble: his tract is therefore a failure.

On sign. E 3, Taylor enumerates the following popular romances and novels: "Lazarillo de Tormes," "Don Quixote," "Gusman of Alfarache," "Bevis of Hampton," "The Mirror of Knighthood," and "John Dory." As "John Dory" has come down to us, (*vide* Ritson's Anc. Songs, II. 57, edit. 1829,) it is merely a ballad, but Taylor places it among works of much greater length, some of them filling several volumes. At the end Taylor informs us, that while the book was printing he had been "extremely stroken lame."

TAYLOR, JOHN.—A Famous Fight at Sea. Where foure English Ships under the command of Captaine John Weddell, and foure Dutch Ships fought three dayes in the Gulfe of Persia neere Ormus, against 8 Portugall Gallions and 3 Friggots. As also the memorable fight and losse of the good Ship called the Lion &c. With a Farewell and hearty well-wishing to our English Sea and Land Forces.—London Printed by John Haviland for Henry Gosson. n. d. 4to. 16 *leaves.*

This is a temporary tract by Taylor, (who signs the dedication to Captain Weddell,) which is included in the folio of his works printed in 1630. It has one woodcut of a ship on the title-page, and another of larger size on a separate leaf following it. The "Farewell" is in verse, but of little merit.

TAYLOR, JOHN.—Aqua-Musæ: or Cacafogo, Cacadæmon, Captain George Wither wrung in the Withers &c for his late railing Pamphlet against the King and State called Campo-Musæ &c. By John Taylor.—Printed in the fourth Yeare of the Grand Rebellion, n. d. 4to. 8 *leaves.*

The tract by Wither, against which this grossly abusive production, which the author dignifies by the name of "a Satire," is directed, was printed in 1643. Taylor tells us that he had loved and respected Wither for thirty-five years, until he joined the Parliament against the King; but it is to be recollected that Wither, in his "Fragmenta Poetica," 1669, vindicated himself by asserting that his object was to reunite the two contending parties. Taylor goes the length of charging his antagonist with positive dishonesty:—

"Thou precious most pernicious Prelate hater,
To Durhams reverend Bishop thou wast cater,
Or Steward, where to make thy 'compts seeme cleare,
Thou mad'st two monthes of July in one yeare;
And in the total reck'ning it was found
Thou cheat'st the Bishop of five hundred pound."

TAYLOR, JOHN.—Bull, Beare and Horse, Cut, Curtaile and Longtaile. With

Tales, and Tales of Buls, Clenches and Flashes. As also here and there a touch of our Beare-Garden-sport; with the second part of the Merry conceits of Wit and Mirth. Together with the Names of all the Bulls and Beares.—London, Printed by M. Parsons, for Henry Gosson, and are to be sold at his shop on London Bridge. 1638. 8vo. 35 *leaves.*

The main, though not avowed purpose of this tract was to encourage what was then called "the game of Bulls and Bears," which, it seems, had been of late neglected at Paris Garden; and it is dedicated by John Taylor to his "often approved and truly beloved Mr. Thomas Godfrey, Keeper of the Game of Beares, Bulls and Dogges" there. This was an office held by Edward Alleyn (the famous actor and founder of Dulwich College) early in the reign of James I. He had been succeeded by Dorrington, and Dorrington by Godfrey; under which last, owing in part to the non-patronage by the Court, the sport had not been productive of much profit Taylor put his puff, lor such it is, into verse and prose, and no doubt was paid for it. In the opening he refers to all kinds of Bulls, including such as Milton, at a later date, alluded to when he defined "a bull" "a taking away the essence of what it calls itself." The following are some of the Water-poet's lines:—

"There are Bulbeggers which fright children much,
There are Ball Taverns that mens Wits will tutch;
And farther (for the Buls renowne and fame)
We had an ex'lent Hangman of that name * * *
And now of late a Ball's a common creature
For men (with nonsense) do speak Bulls by nature:
From East to West, from North unto the South,
Balls are produc'd each houre by word of mouth;
Which every day are brought unto the Printer
Faster than Mother Puddings made her Winter,
To the decay of many a tallow taper
And the consuming many a reame of paper."

Some of the jokes are far from new; and Taylor had little remorse in repeating himself, if he were in haste, and had a certain quantity of paper which must be filled. What he means by a "bull" may be seen from this specimen:—

"A gentleman riding in the countrey attended with one servingman, they met a fellow that was astride upon a Cowe: the servingman said, Master, behold! yonder is a strange sight. What is it? said the gentleman. Why, sir (said his man), looke you, sir; there is one rides on horseback upon a Cowe. Thats a great Bull, said the gentleman. Nay sir, said his man, it is no Bull; I know it is a Cowe by his teats."

Besides bulls and bears, baited by dogs, sport was afforded at Paris Garden by a pony which carried an ape upon its back; and the names of all the bulls, bears, &c. are inserted by the author of the tract before us. We do not think, however, that the modern reader would gain much by the repetition of them. Before the end the vein of Taylor's humor was quite exhausted.

THYNNE, FRANCIS.—The Debate betweene Pride and Lowlines, pleaded in an issue in Assize: And how a June with great indiflerencie being impannelled, and redy to have geven their verdict, were straungely intercepted, no lesse pleasant then profitable. F. T. &c. Seene and allowed.—Imprinted at London by John "Charlwood, for Rafe Newbery dwelling in Fleetestrete a litle above the Condite. n. d. B. L. 8vo. 54 *leaves.*

On the title-page of this unique and excellent poem, besides the printed F. T., are the initials F. Th. in the handwriting of Francis Thynne, the antiquary and herald; and there is no doubt that the volume was his property, and little doubt that it was his authorship. We may presume that it was presented by him to Sir Thomas Egerton, to whom Thynne dedicated a MS. collection of "Emblemes and Epigrames," and to whom he also addressed "Observations upon Speght's Chaucer." both of which are preserved in the library at Bridgewater House.[Note 1: These "Emblemes and Epigrames" by Francis Thynne, although imprinted, were clearly intended for publication, and they are dedicated in due form with the following date, "From my house in Clerkenwell Grene, the 20th of December, 1600." He here gives his reason for especially selecting the Lord Keeper as the dedicatee:—"And the rather," he observes, "because some of them are composed of thinges doun and sayed by such as were well knowne to your Lordshipp and to my self in those yonger yeares, when Lincolns Inn Societie did linke us all in one chayne of amitie; and some of them are of other persons yet living, which of your Lordship are both loved and liked." The Emblems occupy about half the MS., and among the earliest and best is what succeeds, on the famous subject, well known in most languages, the exchange of arrows by Cupid and Death. Shirley wrote a drama upon it in 1653.

"The hatefull Death joynd to the God of Love
In one cabine settled themselves to sleepe:
Both had their bowes and shaft ea their might to prove;
The one gave mirth, the other foret to weepe:
Thus blinded Love and Death, at this time blinde,
By chance doe meete, by chance doe harbor finde.

"But starting forth of this their former rest,
Beedlesee, the one the other's weapons caught:
The goulden shaftes from Cupid Death berefte,
The dartes of Death dame Venue sonne had raughte.
Thus contrarie to kinde and their nature,
Cupid doth slea and Death doth lore procure.

"Ould doating fooles, more fit for Carons shipp,
That feele the goute, to grave web take their waye,
Doe fall in love and youthfull like doe skippe,
deckinge their heads with garlands fresh and gaye.
Their years and daies they easelle doe forgett,
And from their harte colde sottishe sighes do fett.

"But striplinges and yonge boyes the wounds receive
By yonge Cupid, then nestor yet more ouide,
Aginst their kinde their wished life doe leave,
And unto Acheron the waye do houlde.

But Cupid cease, and Death thine owne stroke give;
Let yonge men love, let ould men oease to live."

Among the Epigrams is one headed "Spencers fayrie Queene," but it is disappointing in all respects, for it does not contain a syllable distinctive of the great poet. For them, see Spenser's Life, 1862, p. cxlvi.] The epistle preceding the latter is subscribed in this form, and the signature accords very exactly with the written initials upon the title-page of "The Debate betweene Pride and Low lines":—

"Yor Lordshippes wholye to
dyspose
FRANCIS THYNN."

We need not, therefore, have much hesitation in considering Thynne the author of the remarkable production before us. It is evident, whoever wrote it, that he was a lawyer, or, at all events, that he had a good deal of acquaintance with law terms and phrases, and Thynne himself states in his MS. "Emblemes and Epigrames," that he was a member of Lincoln's Inn at the same time as Sir Thomas Egerton.

Another preliminary point deserving notice is, that throughout the "Debate" there is almost an affectation of the use of antiquated, not to say obsolete, words and phrases; and how well Thynne was versed in our old language is evident from his "Observations upon Speght's Chaucer," which the Rev. H. J. Todd printed at length in his "Illustrations" of that author. Among Thynne's "Emblemes and Epigrames" is one addressed to Spenser, who, like Thynne, was fond of expressive terms not commonly employed.

Thynne was fifty-seven in the year 1602, consequently he was born in 1545, a circumstance of importance with reference to the time of publication of the work before us, which has no date in

"Towards the lawe these long xv yeeres space,
And thereof sworne to be an attorney;"

and, considering the jocose subject of the poem, and the manner in which it is handled, we may perhaps conclude that he was not more than five-and-thirty when it appeared: this would bring us to the year 1580, and the type and general appearance of the book warrant a belief that it did not come out later. Until it was noticed in the "History of English Dramatic Poetry," III. 151, the existence of such a publication had escaped the research of literary antiquaries.

There is a very peculiar circumstance connected with this publication. It shows that Robert Greene, in one of his most celebrated and amusing tracts, was a mere plagiary, having borrowed the whole design, much of the execution, and some of the very words of Thynne. Had Greene's enemy, Gabriel Harvey, been acquainted with the fact, he would have made ample use of it as a means of annoyance; and that he did not, shows how scarce Thynne's poem must have been even in 1592. Greene, however, had obtained a copy of it, and in that year founded upon it his "Quip for an Upstart Courtier, or a quaint dispute between Velvet-breeches and Cloth-breeches." On the mere inspection of the two productions, it could not be disputed for an instant that Greene's tract must have made its appearance at least ten years later than Thynne's poem. In both a dispute is carried on between the personifications of a pair of Velvet-breeches and a pair of Cloth-breeches; in both a jury is impanelled to try the comparative merits of the plaintiff and defendant; and in both the expressions are often identical.

Thynne makes an address in verse "to the godly and gentle Reader" after the title-page, in which he vindicates the whimsical notion of giving speech to two pairs of breeches, and concludes in these stanzas:—

"Have therefore (gentle Reader) in good part
This little volume, wherein thou maiest finde
Some matters (though not pullished with art)
To make thee laugh, and recreate thy minde.

"If other matter it may yeelden thee,

As morall counsel, whereby thou may lerne
What thinges are good to folowe, what to flee,
Then thanke me when we meeten at the terme."

"And pray God blesse our Queene and Countrey,
And graunt her long to raigne and prosperous;
And to us all after this journey
In heaven with him selfe a dwelling house."

The poem begins on sign. A iii, with an account of the author's dream, in which he imagined he saw a pair of Velvet-breeches (by which he designates Pride) and a pair of Cloth-breeches (by which he means Lowliness) meet in a valley, and commence a violent dispute. In his Italic: ***sweven*** (as he calls it), he fancied that he stepped between them to prevent a fray, and proposed a trial by jury, but Velvet-breeches doubted whether he should have a fair chance:—

"For I am here a straunger in this land,
And, save of late yeeres, of small acquayntaunce.
The common people dooth not understand
My woorthynesse, estate, ne countenance."

At this point Greene's words (we quote from the earliest edition of 1592) are these:—"Because I am a stranger in this land, and but heere lately arived, they will hold me as an upstart, and so lightly esteeme of my worthinesse." However, Velvet-breeches ultimately consents, on condition that his right of challenge, as well as that of Cloth-breeches, is allowed; and accordingly they proceed to select a jury from persons who accidentally arrive at the scene of action. The following is the description of a Tailor, the first juryman, after we have been told that "piked he was, and handsome in his weede":—

"A faire blacke coate of cloth, withouten sleve,
And buttoned the shoulder round about;
Of xx. s. a yard, as I beleeve,

And layd upon with parchment lace without.

"His dublet was of Sattin very fine,
And it was cut and stitched very thick;
Of silke it had a costly enterlyne:
His shirt had bands, and ruffe of pure Cambrick.

"His upper stockes of sylken Grogerane,
And to his hyppes they sate fall close and trym,
And laced very costly every pane:
Their lyning was of Satten, as I wyn.

"His neather stockes of silke accordingly:
A velvet gyrdle rounde about his wast.
This knight or squyre, what so he be, (quoth I)
We wyll empannell: let him not goe past.

"He condiscended soone to our request
Then I, beholding him advisedly,
Sawe where a needle sticked on his brest,
And at the same a blacke threed hanging by."

"Coming more neere, indeed," says Greene, "I spied a Tailor's morice pike on his brest—a Spanish needle." Cloth-breeches, according to Thynne, gives the first challenge, observing,—

"In making mee there is no gaine but one,
Which is for labour and for woorkmanship;
Except some time a peece of cloth come home,
As yf that by mischaunce the shere did slip."

In Greene's tract Cloth-breeches takes exactly the same objection in nearly the same words:—"Alas, by me he getteth small, onely be is paid for his workemanship, unlesse by misfortune bis sbieres slyppe awrye." Afterwards Thynne tells us that the Tailor will charge his customers dearly,—

"And reache them with a bill of reckoning
Shal make them scrat wheras it itcheth nought;"

and Greene adopts the humorous phrase: "and yet to overreach my yoong maister with a bill of reckonings that will make him scratch where it itcheth not" The point of plagiarism on the part of Greene may, therefore, be considered established, and need be pursued no further. A few additional quotations from Thynne will, however, be acceptable. The following is his description of a Dancing Master and a Vintner:—

"One of them had a fiddle in his hand,
And pleasaunt songes he played thereupon,
To[o] queynt and hard for me to understand:
If he were brave I make no question;

"Or if his furniture were for the daunce.
His breeches great, full of ventositie,
Devised in the castle of playsaunce;
And master of a daunsing schoole was he.

"The other was by trade a Vintener,
That had full many a hoggeshed looked in:
Travayled he had, and was a languager;
His face was redd as any Cherubyn.

"A Spanishe cloke he ware, fine with a cape;
A fine Frenche cappe on his head accordyng,
Both which upon him faire and seemely sate,
And one his finger ware a mightie ringe."

As a lively picture of the manners and habits of the times, independently of its poetical merit, this work is highly curious and interesting. Of another character the author thus speaks:—

"Yet was there one whom I had nigh forgot,
And he was master of a dysing bouse.
No woord had he but pay the boxe and pot:
So brave be was that raee thought marveylous."

This "master of a dicing-house" does not approve of that name, and remonstrates against being called by it:—

"In deede (quoth he) I keepe an ordinarye:
Eight pence a meale who there doth sup or dyne;
And dyse and cardes are but an accessarye
At aft meales, who shall pay for the wine.

"These wayten all upon our principall,
As collourable cause to bring them in;
And then from thence to sheere money they fall,
Tyll some of them be shrieven of theyr sinne.

"But of this game, and other harlotrye,
That there is used both by daye and night,
Suffiseth me to waxen riche thereby:
Thereafter yet in name I wyll not hight."

The portraits of this kind are numerous, and show that Thynne was a very close, acute, and satirical observer. Now and then he breaks away from his humor into a moral and religious strain, but there he does not seem so much at home, and his reflections are not striking nor original. In the end, just as the verdict is about to be given in favor of Cloth-breeches, some of the riotous friends of his adversary rush forward, seize Cloth-breeches, and tear him to atoms, while the jury, followed by the author, make the best of their way to a place of safety. The author wakes, finds it morning, and resolves to write his dream, thinking that it would be more profitable than "Amadis de Gaul," "The Palace of Pleasure" or any of the ballads that were then so abundant "The Palace of Pleasure" was first printed in 1566, and a portion of "Amadis de Gaul" about the same year, as nearly as can be ascertained, but it has no date upon the title-page.

The main poem is followed by "a commendation of Lowlynesse for her consolation," of which the following is part:—

"Wherefore to turne agayne to lowlines,
The matter of my woorke, and for whose sake,
To travell in so great a busines,
So hygh and woorthy, I have undertake;

"I say she hath such multiplicitie
Of favour, and of grace especiall,
That I dare call her of humanitie
The note, the proofe, and judgement principall,

"Whereby a man doth differ from a beast;
For one hath wylful inclination,
And reason none, of deede ne of beheast,
But violence of sense and passion.

"Of whom God, by his prophete David, sayeth;
Be not (sayth he) lyke unto a horse or mule,
That more his wyl, then any reason wayeth,
And must with bitte and brydle live in rule."

To this succeed two stanzas, or quatrains, "The Booke to the Reader;" one stanza called "The Epythyme," and "A Prayer to almightie God," in eleven stanzas. The same form of verse is observed in every part of the production.

Another work, in all probability by Francis Thynne, is noticed in Vol. III. p. 32, under the head of "News from the North." The "Dialogue between the Cap and the Head," Vol. I. p. 129, is also very much in Thynne's manner, and when it was printed he might be about twenty years old.

THYNNE, FRANCIS.—The Case is Altered. How? Aske Dalio and Millo.— London Imprinted by T. C. for John Smethicke, and are to be sold at his Shop in S. Dunston's Church-yard in Fleet-street 1604. 4to. 16 **leaves.**

We feel so confident from the initials F. T., and still more from the style and character of this production, that it is by the author of "News from the North," and "the Debate between Pride and Lowliness," that we have not hesitated to put it under his name: at the same time, in point of excellence, it is certainly not to be compared with either of them, and it is entirely prose. Its popularity is easily established, for it was reprinted "for Thomas Pavyer, dwelling in Cornhill," in the very next year, and other editions of 1608, 1609, 1630, and 1635 have been mentioned by bibliographers.

It is dedicated by F. T. "to his very kind and approved friende D. R.;" and F. T. are again placed at the end of an address "to the Reader." It professes, as Thynne was at one time a lawyer, to be a statement and counter-statement of various supposed cases by two old friends who humorously discuss the remedies, if any such can be pointed out, or the unfortunate condition of those who are compelled to suffer without remedy. The whole was meant as a mere piece of drollery and pleasantry, but in some places neither are quite so obvious as might be wished. The old gentlemen, Dalio and Millo, who meet under an oak, are at times rather too garrulous, and tedious in the statement of cases which have no great novelty to recommend them. Thynne (whom we fancy is meant by Millo) fairly admits that "the matters handled are of no great moment, and therefore scarce worth the reading." The public, in the reigns of James and Charles, do not seem to have been of this opinion; and there can be little doubt that, under feigned names and invented circumstances, much that was applicable to the time, and then well understood, was included in the dialogue.

Now and then cases are put with the utmost unlegal brevity, as follows:—

"*Dal.* Well then; first tell me your opinion in this. Is it not a pittifull case to see a proper man without money?

Mill. It is.
Dal. And to see a faire woman without wit?
Mill. No lesse.
Dal. And an old man leacherous?
Mill. Alas, poore man!
Dal. And a yong man vitious?
Mill. He will be sped.
Dal. And a rich man covetous?
Mill. Tis pitty that he hath so much. * * *
Dal. And a monkey kiss a woman.
Mill. Ilfavoured urchin!"

And thus they proceed through several pages, while the cases they state at length are apparently meant as a counterpoise to such smart interrogatories as the above. They relate to disputes between heirs and their fathers, husbands and their wives, widows and their suitors, &c, but of course much of the humor is lost or obscured. We will quote the commencement of one of Millo's cases, merely to show the style in which most of the book is written:—

"An old woman, a very old woman, a crooked old woman, a creeping old woman, a lame woman, a deafe woman, a miserable woman, a wicked woman, fell with halfe a sight (for shortly after she fell blind) in love with a pretty, neate, nimble, spruse, lively, handsome, and in truth lovely young man; and so faire as, after the manner of country people, she would, if she met him in a morning, bid him good morrow with how doe you sonne? I pray you come neere, if it weere neere her house; and I praie you sit downe, and I pray you drinke; and how doth your good father, and your mother, and all your house? In troth, you are welcome: I am sorie

I have no good cheer for you, but such as I have I pray you do not spare: if I have any thing in my house, it is at your commands. Indeede, I ever loved you of a child," &c.

It is needless to continue the speech of the old lady, and the result may be easily conjectured. Nearly all the personages introduced are well drawn, and the dialogues characteristically conducted; but when we arrive at the conclusion, we are disposed to wonder what object the author had in carrying on the subject to such a length. Several points of manners are rather drolly illustrated, but nothing is said of the literature or amusements of the time, and on the whole the reader is considerably disappointed. Our only doubt as to Francis Thynne's authorship arises out of the fact, that it is not good enough for him; bat in 1604 he was an old man, and, like other old men, may have fancied that what amused him in the writing would amuse others in the reading.

TILNEY, EDMUND.—A briefe and pleasant discourse of duties in Mariage, called the Flower of Friendshippe.—Imprinted at London by Henrie Denham, dwelling in Pater noster Rowe at the Signe of the Starre. Anno 1568. 8vo. 40 *leaves.*

The dedication to Queen Elizabeth is subscribed "Your Majesties most humble Subject, Edmunde Tilney," who, about ten years after the publication of this work, was appointed Master of the Revels. This fact does not appear to have struck those who have hitherto touched upon the biography of Tilney, (**Ath. Cantab.** I. 559,) and they give the date of his "Flower of Friendship," 1571, when, in fact, it first appeared and was twice printed in 1568, the copy of 1571 being merely a second reprint. Others assign it to the year 1577, but we have never seen any such impression. (Lowndes, Bibl. Man. p. 1821, edit. 1834.)

Our main object is to correct the dates; for the production itself, which the author twice over calls "this flagrant Flower of Friendship," requires no particular notice, although the topic discussed, after the Italian manner in the two divisions, was one which, at the time, attracted a good deal of attention, in consequence of reports regarding the marriage of the Queen with the Duke of Anjou. The character of his work, perhaps, recommended Tilney in 1579 to the office of Master of the Revels, which he held until his death in 1610. Charles Tilney, Gentleman-pensioner to Elizabeth, was executed with Babbington and others in 1586; but whether he was brother, or in any other way related, to Edmund, is not stated. It is, however, a fact worth observation, that in an old MS. note by Sir George Bucke, on the tide-page of a copy of the tragedy of "Loerine," 1595, Charles Tilney is asserted to have been the writer of it. If he were, the note of time in the epilogue by Ate,—

"So let us pray for that renowned maid
That eight and thirty years the scepter sway'd,"

must have been an insertion on a revival of the drama. Such additions, as well as others, were not unusual; and it was in this way (if at all) that Shakspeare's name may have become mis-associated with the tedious tragedy.

TOFTE, ROBERT.—Laura. The Toyes of a Traveller. Or the Feast of Fancie. Divided into three Parts. By R. T. Gentleman. ***Poco favilla gran fiamma seconda.***—London. Printed by Valentine Sims. 1597. 8vo. 39 *leaves.*

The initials R. T. no doubt belong to Robert Tofte, who seems to have travelled in France and Italy, if not in Spain and other countries, and thus qualified himself as a translator, which he afterwards became; but this his earliest work purports to be a collection of short original poems of ten and twelve lines each: not a few of them are dated from towns south of the Alps, or with the names of other towns added to them, as if to point out where they were composed. There is but one from "London," and that occurs on the first page, but following ten lines from "Padua." The adulatory dedication to Lady Lucy, sister to the Earl of Northumberland, states that the poems were "for the most part conceived in Italy, and some of them brought forth in England." Besides Padua and London, Venice, Sienna, Pisa, Roma, Fiorenza, Napoli, Fano, Mantua, and Pesaro, are mentioned as places where the Muse had inspired him.

It is very clear, from the dedication, that Tofte intended the work for the press, but the Printer informs the Readers that he did not know who wrote the poems, nor could he guess the lady intended to be addressed: both he and a friend, to whom the copy had been intrusted, had offended by publishing it at all. This we take to be only a literary *ruse,* as well as the most unusual address from R. B. (*forsan* Richard Barnfield) at the end of the volume, stating that he had been employed by R. T. to prevent the publication, but that he came too late, as the last sheet was then at the press. He adds, what is of greater importance, that more than thirty of the "sonnets," for so they an called, were not by R. T., but that, as they had been included by the printer, they must share the fate of the rest These, we may inspect, were by R. B.

There are forty "sonnets" in each of the three divisions, and each division has also a conclusion in verse. What makes it more certain that Robert Tofte was the author, is, that he informs *la bellissina sua Signora E. C,* that his nickname was Robin Redbreast, which we know from other sources belonged to Tofte among his familiar acquaintances. One of the best specimens we can select is the first "sonnet" of the second part:—

> "If I somewhile looke up into the skies,
> I see (faire Lady) that same cheerefull light,
> Which, like to you, doth shine in glorious wise:
> And if on th'earth I chance to cast my sight,
> The moovelesse centre firme to me doth show
> The hardnesse which within your hart doth grow.
> If seas I view, the flowing waves most plaine
> Your fickle faith doth represent to mee:
> So as I still behold you to my paine,
> When as the skies, or th'earth, or seas I see;
> For in your seemely selfe doth plaine appeare
> Like faith, like hardnesse, and like brightnes cleare."

The above is more conceited than the following, which may be deemed somewhat warm:—

"Joy of my soule, my blindfold eyes cleare light,
Cordiall of hart, right Mithridate of love,
Faire orient Pearle, bright shining Margarite,
Pure Quintessence of heavens delight above!
When shall I taste what favour grants me tuch,
And ease the rage of mine so sharpe desire?
When shall I free enjoy what I so much
Doo covet (but I doubt in vaine) to aspire?
Ah! doo not still my soule thus Tantalize,
But once (through grace) the same imparadize."

From another short piece, of the same kind, it appears that Laura, the lady he addresses, lived in Fano. In another place, while he likens her to Venus, he calls himself Adonis, and entreats her to transform him to a flower. In all this there is not one word of original thought, although the language is sufficiently harmonious. A couplet printed in the following manner makes it pretty clear that the lady whom R. T. addressed was named Caril:—

"And gainst all sense makes me of CARe and IL,
More than of good and comfoR.T. to have will."

If Tofte at all expected that his "Laura" would rival that of Petrarch, he was wofully mistaken. The work is so scarce, that we doubt if a third copy of it be in existence.

TOFTE, ROBERT.—Alba. The Months Minde of a melancholy Lover, divided into three parts. By R. T. Gentleman. Hereunto is added a most excellent patheti-call and passionate Letter sent by the Duke D'Epernoun unto the late French King, Henry the 3. of that name, when he was commanded from the Court and from his Royall Companie. Translated into English by the foresaid Author. ***Spes, Amor et Fortuna valete.***—At London. Printed by Felix Kingston for Matthew Lownes. 1598. 12mo. 40 ***leaves.***

Attention has been directed to this production, chiefly on account of its mention of "Love's Labour's Lost," by name, as "a play" which the writer had seen performed, and the title which he found consistent with his own condition as "a melancholy Lover," disappointed by the rejection of his suit:—

"Loves Labour lost I once did see, a play
Ycleped so, so called to my paine."

He goes on to complain that what seemed "jest" to others was "earnest" to him, but he praises the "cunning wise" in which "each Actor plaid his part" If he had told us also how the parts were distributed, he would have much increased our obligation, for it is not known by whom a single character was supported.

Tofte was a voluminous translator, chiefly from the Italian, and, as in the previous article, dates some of his poems from Rome, Mantua, &c., and one from Burnham, in Buckinghamshire. However, the lady to whom he was devoted lived at Warrington, and her name, he again tells us, was Carill: this is biographically interesting, but the fact has hitherto been passed over, perhaps on account of the extreme scarcity of Tofte's volumes: he says of the place:—

" **War** in that **town** Love, lord like, keepeth still,
Yet she ore him triumphs with chastest will:"

and as to the lady's name he observes,—

"Then constant Care, not comfort I do crave,
And (might I chuse) I **Care** with **L** would have."

This sort of word-play does not say much for the merit of the many separate love-poems; but, perhaps, as much as they deserve. The dedication of the volume is "to the no lesse excellent then honorablic descended Gentlewoman, Mistresse Anne Herne," to whom, in 1610, Tofle addressed his "Honour's Academie" She was the wife of Sir Edward Herne, Kt. of the Bath. Tofte's friends, R. Day, Ignoto, J. M., and

R. A., presented him with compassionate and commendatory verses to his "Alba" (the poetical appellation of Miss Carill), and from them we again learn that by his familiars he was known as "Robin Redbreast," a nickname which Queen Elizabeth had given to her spoilt favorite, Robert Earl of Essex.

TOFTE, ROBERT.—Ariosto's Satyres in seven famous Discourses, shewing the state, 1. Of the Court and Courtiers. 2. Of Libertie and the Clergie in generall. 3. Of the Romaine Clergie. 4. Of Marriage. 5. Of Soldiers Musitians and Lovers. 6. Of Schoolmasters and Scholers. 7. Of Honour and the happiest Life. In English by Gervis Markham.—London Printed by Nicholas Okes for Roger Jackson &c. 1608. 4to. 58 *leaves.*

Markham, whose name is on the title-page, was a "bookseller's hack "in the age in which he lived: bat perhaps we have no right to conclude that he was a party to the fraud here committed, by putting his name to the work of another. In his version of Varchi's "Blazon of Jealousy," 4to, 1615, Robert Tofte lays claim to this translation of Ariosto's Satires, and, as Markham did not dispute his right, we may infer that Tofte was the real translator. It was reprinted anonymously in 1611, under the title of "Seven Planets governing Italy," with the addition of three elegies.

The edition of 1608 is ushered by an address from the stationer to the reader, followed by "The Argument of the whole worke, and the reasons why Ludovico Ariosto writ these seaven Satyres." The translation, which is not deficient in spirit or fidelity, is accompanied by explanatory marginal notes.

Tofte, as we have shown, p. 157, began writing in 1597. His "Honour's Academie," 1610, gives him a claim to be mentioned among the few who endeavored to introduce classical measures into English. It is singular that when Tofte wrote in 1598 he spoke of two printed pieces by R. Greene, as if they were still unpublished.

TREATISE OF LOVE.—Here begynneth a lytell treatise cleped La conusaunce damours. [Colophon.] Thus endeth la conusaunce damours.—Imprinted by Rycharde Pynson, printer to the Kynges noble grace. ***Cum privilegio.*** 4to. 16 ***leaves.***

The original production from which this small tract was translated is known in early French literature under the title of ***La Conusance d' Amours.*** Who rendered it into English for Pynson we have no means of knowing; but it is more cleverly done, and with fewer marks of obligation, than most other pieces of the time. In the outset the writer expresses his earnest desire to compose something in praise of the female sex, whom he denominates "dames and pusels," and laments his incompetence: suddenly it occurs to him that he might be inspired, if he paid a visit to some young damsels of his acquaintance:—

"Sodaynly came in my mynde to go
Se a faire pusell, and two or three mo
Of her companions."

He met one of them at the house-door, "whose hart was on a merry pin," and entering he beheld the lady he was most anxious to see:—

"Into a goodly parler she me lad,
And caused me to sit curtesy:
Than unto us came shortly by and by
Another that me swetely dyd welcome,
Bryngyng fresshe fiowres and gave me some.

"Than we began to talke and devyse
Of one and other of olde acqueyntannce;
For comonly of maydens is the gyse
Somtyme to demaunde, for pastaunce,
If that a man be in loves daunce,
Or stande in grace of any dammusell?
Under suche maner in talkynge we fell."

They discourse of love and true lovers, and the young lady to whom the poet was attached relates the story of Pyramus and Thisbe. She also delivers her opinion upon "clandestinat maryage," and diverges to the loves of Troilus and Cressida, when she introduces what, as may be supposed, is not in the original, the praise of Chaucer for the manner in which he had related that history. She asks:—

"What shulde I herof longer processe make?
Theyr great love is wrytten all at longe,
And honce he dyed onely for her sake:
Our ornate Chaucer, other bokes amonge,
In his lyfe dayes dyd underfonge
To translate, and that most pleasantly,
Touchyng the mater of the sayd story."

This interesting notice of our great poet has escaped observation. The author rather injures the effect of his narrative by introducing two allegorical personages, one Reason, and the other Thought-and-hevynesse. What they say is not very pertinent, nor always quite intelligible; and the later portion of the tract consists of an enumeration of many classical stories of love and disappointment. In the sequel the author gives the ladies an account of what love was, according to his experience, and the poem closes with this stanza:—

"Your chere here (they sayd) is but small;
We wolde it were much better for your sake.
Our janglynge, that to us now hath fall,
Wolde suffre us no chere for to make.
And so theyr leave swetely of me they take
At the port or gate: and in they go,
And I went strayght to my home also."

This production was never seen by Herbert; and Dr. Dibdin (II. 556) in his brief account of it has given no sort of notion of the nature of its lively contents. It must have been popular, and probably would have been more so if the author, in the speeches of the symbolical impersonations, had not deviated from the sprightly to the didactic. Only two copies have ever been mentioned.

TRIAL OF FRIENDSHIP.—The Triall of true Friendship; or perfit mirror wherby to discerne a trustie friend from a flattering Parasite. Otherwise A knacke to know a knave from an honest man: By a perfit mirrour of both: Soothly to say, Trie ere you trust; Beleeve no man rashly. No lesse profitable in observing then pleasant in reading. By M. B.—Imprinted at London by Valentine Simmes dwelling on Adling Hill at the signe of the white Swanne. 1596. 4to. B. L. 18 *leaves.*

In 1594 had been printed a highly popular comedy, in which Alleyn and Kempe acted, called "A Knacke to know a Knave," and the author of the very rare tract before us adopted the name of the play, as a prominent feature on his title-page, probably in the hope that his dull treatise might thereby obtain a sale to which otherwise it was certainly not destined. Throughout sixteen closely printed pages there is not a single break, so that the performance looks most forbidding to any reader of light literature.

The writer professes that his purpose is to enforce the value of "true friendship," and he illustrates it by many allusions to ancient and modern history; but they are generally very trite, and they are not employed in a way to render them effectual The author is a violent enemy of the Pope and Papists, and he dwells with apparent satisfaction upon the manner in which the various conspirators against the life of Queen Elizabeth had been detected and punished. He now and then makes an effort to be more lively, but his humor is invariably grotesque and clumsy. He sometimes deals in Robert Greene's affected similes, and concludes with the following passage, which, bad as it is, may be taken for one of the best:—

"Therefore, to shut up al in a word, seeing the most glittering sands are found so fickle being tried, the eie-pleasing Echates so infectious being handled, and the greatest promises have so smal performance that we cannot safely beleeve friend or foe, kinsman or aliance, by his word nor his oath, let us trie ere we trust, and prove ere we put in practise: let us go as the snaile faire and softly, seeing haste makes waste, and the mault is the sweetest when the fire is softest: so shall wee the better discerne the true sterling from the counterfet coine, the preteous medicine from the perilous confection, the loyal lover from the fading flatterer; but let us not sing with Medeas song, which said I see and allow the better, but I wil follow the worse: seeing Pallas gift or Junoes proffer to be more profitable, let us not give our apple to flattering Venus, as foolish Paris did, lest she be our confusion; nor let us settle our affections on faire tongued parasites, lest like lightning they breake our bones before we can perceive our skinne to be hurt, but let us try ere we trust after good assurance: let us not trust before we trie for feare of repentance."

Valentine Simmes, the printer, dedicates the performance as "a little mite of a friend's labours" to Master Walter Flude, but to read it through must of itself have been a hard "trial of true friendship." We do not recollect to have met with any account of this very rare but wearisome production.

TROY.—The Ancient Historie of the Destruction of Troy. Divided into III Bookes &c. Translated out of French into English by W. Caxton. The sixth Edition, now newly corrected and amended.—London, Printed by B. Alsop and T. Fawcet &c 1636. B. L. 4to. 277 *leaves.*

In an address of "the Printer to the courteous Reader," after dwelling on the improvement derived from annals and histories, he says:—"And whereas before time the Translator, William Caxton, being, as seemeth, no English-man, had left very many words meere French, and sundry sentences so improperly Englished that it was hard to understand, wee have caused them to be made plainer English: and if time and leysure had served, wee would have had the same in better refined phrases." Perhaps there is not much reason to regret that "time and leisure" did not serve. As to Caxton's birth, he tells us, in his Prologue to this very work, that he was "born in the weald of Kent": in the commencement he added that it had been "translated and drawn out of French into English by William Caxton, mercer of the city of London."

TROY.—The Destruction of Troy in three Bookes &c. The Eight Edition corrected and much amended.—London, Printed by T. Passenger &c 1670. B. L. 4to.

240 *leaves.*

In this edition the passage in the preface about Caxton is omitted, and various "refined phrases" and changes are introduced into the text, so as in some degree to modernize the style, but the work is substantially the same as the impression of 1636. Everybody is aware that the French version, which Caxton adopted as his original, was not founded upon Homer, but upon the narratives of Dictys Cretensis and Guido di Colonna.

TUDOR, OWEN.—Pancharis: The first Booke. Containing the Preparation of the Love betweene Owen Tudyr and the Queene, long since intended to her Maiden Majestie: and now dedicated to The Invincible James, Second and greater Monarch of great Britaine, King of England, Scotland, France and Ireland with the Islands adjacent Mar. Valerius Martialis. ***Victurus Genium debet habere liber.***—Printed at London by V. S. for Clement Knight 1603. 8vo. 41 *leaves.*

This is a remarkable poem, whether we consider its rarity, its subject, its treatment, or its author. Only a single copy of it is believed to exist, and that is in the Bodleian Library. The main subject is Owen Tudor, the second husband of Katherine, wife of Henry V., and the author Hugh Holland, who wrote lines on Shakspeare, prefixed to the folio of 1623, and a "Cypress Garland" on the death of James I., besides a few other productions. He is mentioned with some of his works by Anthony Wood, but it is singular that Dr. Bliss, when he superintended the edition of the ***Ath. Oxon.*** in 1816, should not have noticed the unique poem in our hands.

Near the close the author informs us that his rhymes had "nigh upon two yeares layn by him," and on the title-page it is stated that they were originally "intended" for Queen Elizabeth, though now dedicated to her successor. What, however, must be looked upon as the real dedication of the poem comes at the end, "To Sir Robert Cotton, Knight, Lord of Cunnington." Here too Holland promises "a second part" of his subject, which never appeared, although the author survived the publication of the first part thirty years. Judging from that first part, there is not much reason to think the loss enormous. After the title comes an acrostic sonnet to the King; an address in verse to "the bright Queene Anne"; Latin lines to Arabella Stuart; and an address thus headed: ***Clarissimo et candidissimo ingenio Praceptori olim, semper Amico, Gulielmo Camdeno, Armorum Regi nulli secundo Poemation hoc censendum et emendandwn mitto.*** After these, we have commendatory poems, in Latin, by Andreas Downes and Nicholas Hill; Anacreontics by E. B.; and "an Ode aëëçãïñéêç" by Ben Johnson (so spelt), which was never reprinted, nor, since 1603, mentioned. [Note 1: As this Ode has never been even mentioned, much less quoted, we shall not hesitate to insert one or two extracts. It opens thus:—

"Who saith our Tunes nor hare nor can
Produce us a blacke Swan?
Behold! where one doth swim
Whole note and hue.
Besides the other Swannes admiring him,
Betray it true.
A gentler bird then this
Did nerer dint the breast of Tamesis."

The whole is in this peculiar form of stanza, and the praise is sometimes so lofty that, when we compare it with the poem it introduces, it has almost the air of irony. This is the next stanza:—

"Marke. marke, but when his wing he takes,
How faire a flight he makes!
How upward and direct;
Whilst pleas'd Apollo
Smiles in his sphere to nee the rest affect
In vaine to follow.
This Swanne is onely his,
And Phoebus lore cause of his blacknesse is."

Near the conclusion he goes beyond all he has already advanced in applause of Holland and his poem, declaring that no river of Europe, Po, Tagus, Rhine, or

Seine, can equal the glory Thames has acquired by the poem of "Pancharis." Ben Jonson perhaps praised what his own imagination conceived of the subject, rather than what Holland had made of it.] Then come five pages by Hugh Holland, "To my Mayden Muse," followed by the body of the production, headed "Pancharis: The First Booke."

We have been thus particular because the work itself has not been hitherto described. The author lays the scene at Windsor Castle, and he tells us that after the death of Henry V., Queen Katherine resided there:—

"Here the sad Queene ful many a sigh did smother,
Resolved still to leade a Widdowes life.
So chaste was she, though faire and rich and yong,
That yong and olde to praise her were at strife.
Of her high honour all Musitians sung,
And thereto each sweet Poet tun'd his pen,
That therewith England and all Europe rung.
She was the wonder of all mortal! men:
Few Queenes came neere her, and none went above
In grace and goodnesse, since, before, or then."

This is not very happy, in spite of a modest invocation to Cupid to aid the poet with a pen plucked from his own wing. Afterwards we are informed that both Diana and Venus pay a visit to the royal widow, and even drink mortal wine with her from a cup that had belonged to Edward the Confessor. Venus subsequently resolves that Katherine shall fall in love with Owen Tudor, and the goddess thus speaks of him to her son:—

"A gallant and resolved gentleman
Faire Owen Tudyr; fire thou hir in love
With him, my boy. Mother (said he) your Swanne
Shall not exceede this Eagle, nor your Dove.
Hereafter shall she stoope so to the lure

Though now a while the clowds she towre above;
For her pure bosome with a brand as pure,
I wil so kindle, yet before the sunne
Get out of Libra, that none may recure
Her heart, but only Owen."

What follows is his personal description; and we need not wonder at the sudden attachment of the Queen, when she not only sees him caper in a Masque, but when, by accident or design, he touches her "softer thigh" with his harder knee:—

"The gentle Owen was a man well set,
Broad were his shoulders, thogh his waste but smal:
Straight was his backe, and even was his breast,
Which no lesse seemely made him shew then tall.
Such as Achilles seem'd among the rest
Of all his army clad in mighty brasse;
Among them such (though all they of the best)
The man of Moue magnifique Owen was:
He seem'd an other Oake among the breers,
And ns in stature, so did he surpas
In wit and active feates his other peeres.
He nimbly could discourse, and nimbly daunce,
And ag'd he was about some thirty yeeres."

Owen Tudor's dancing was admired by all; but the Queen was quite overcome when

"therewithal
He fetch'd me such a frisk above the ground,
That O well done! cried out both great and small."

Holland docs not profess to be able to account for Katherine's love at first sight, and simply asks, almost in the very words of Shakspeare (Two Gent of Verona, Act

V. sc. 2),—

"Is it because that in faire womens eyes
Blacke men seeme pearles?"

He attributes all the merit of the conquest to Cupid:—

"This is thy power, O Love! this is thy praise,
For unto Gods it only doth belong
The mighty downe to pull, the meeke to raise."

Having carried the story thus far, Holland promises to continue it in "a second part" of his poem, which, as far as we know, never appeared; and even the first part would not have survived but for the single copy we have used. Although some of the lines run smoothly, no part of "Pancharis" does much credit to its author. Holland, being a Welshman, naturally enough chose a Welsh hero.

TUKE, THOMAS.—Concerning the Holy Eucharist, and the Popish Breaden-God to the Men of Rome, as well Laiques as Cleriques. By Thomas Take.—Anno Dni M. DC. XXXVI. 4to. 14 **leaves.**

Although, according to the statement of the author, this poem was first printed in 1625, and again, as we see, in 1636, it is extremely rare. We presume that it is by the same Thomas Tuke who in 1616 published "a Treatise against painting and tineturing of Men and Women," quoted by Prynne in his "His-triomastix," 1633. This production, against the Roman Catholic doctrine of the real presence, has no printer's nor stationer's names, and we may well believe that it was never intended for sale, and that the author was at the expense of both private impressions. After a very pious Protestant address "to the courteous Reader," on two pages, "the men of Rome, as well Laiques as Cleriques" are abused and ridiculed for their absurd belief that God was really and corporeally present in the bread and wine of the Sacrament of the Lord's Supper, and for not receiving it in both kinds. Take begins as follows:—

"Priests make their Maker Christ, yee must not doubt:
They eat, drink, box him up, and beare about.
Substance of things they turne; nor is this all,
For both the Signes must hold him severall.
Hee's whole ith' bread, whole ith' cuppe;
They eat him whole, whole they suppe;
Whole ith' Cake, and whole ith' cuppe."

Again, afterwards he asks:—

"What! Does a Temple make the Architect,
That thou of bread thy Maker should'st erect?
Or does a Servant use to make his Lord,
That Priests to theirs a beeing do afford?
O, presumptuous Undertaker!
Never Cake could make a Baker,
And shall a Priest, then, make his Maker?"

Thus the author proceeds for 639 lines, after which we meet with his name again, and the date of 2d February, 1635, as that of the new edition. A Postscript informs us that the piece had originally been printed eleven years earlier, but that a new impression had been required in order that some lines subscribed "Io. Artef" might be "subnexed," the fact being that the "subnexed lines" are only fifteen of Tuke's own, which had been already inserted. The tract is extremely ill printed, and manuscript corrections, perhaps by the author himself, are continually made in the exemplar we have employed. We cannot avoid the conviction that the writer was a very old man, indulging his fancy for rhyming controversy at the expense of his readers.

TURBERVILE, GEORGE.—Epitaphes, Epigrams, Songs and Sonets with a Discourse of the Friendly affections of Tymetes to Pyndara his Ladie. Newly corrected with additions, and set out by George Turbervile Gentleman. Anno Domini 1567.—

Imprinted at London by Henry Denham. 8vo. B. L. 145 *leaves.*

It is remarkable that at this time of day it should be a new, yet indisputable fact, that there was an impression of Turbervile's "Epitaphes, Epigrams, Songs and Sonets" anterior to that of 1567, the title of which stands at the head of the present article. And how is this fact established? Not merely by his title-page, but by a passage in the dedication of his book "To the right noble and his singular good Lady, Lady Anne Countesse of Warwick." If any bibliographer had only read the beginning of the work he was describing, he must have seen the following passage:—

"As at what time (Madame) I first published this fond and slender treatise of Sonets, I made bolde with yod in dedication of so unworthy a booke to so worthie a Ladie, so have I now also rubde my browe, and wiped away all shame in this respect, adventuring not to cease, but to increase my former follie, in adding moe Sonets to those I wrote before. So much the more abusing, in mine owne conceite, your Ladishippes patience, in that I had pardon before of my rash attempt. But see (Madame) what presumption raignes in retchlesse youth. You accepted that my first offer, of honorable and meere curtesie, and I, thereby encouraged, blush not to procede in the like trade of follie, always hoping for the lyke acceptance at your hands."

This extract unquestionably shows that Turbervile had dedicated to Lady Warwick a previous impression, which in 1567 he bad enlarged by additional poems: what they were he does not specify: it was, however, not a mere reissue, or even reprint of the former work, which we may presume he had, like that before us, called "Epitaphes, Epigrams, Songs and Sonets." We know that in 1569 Turbervile was in Russia, as Secretary to the English Ambassador: how long he remained abroad is uncertain; but a new impression of his miscellany was called for in 1570, and it was printed by the same typographer. It was then simply a repetition, without a word of novelty in the preliminary matter, or in the body of the book; and very possibly the author had not returned to England at the time it made its appearance. In it various small typographical errors are corrected, and the orthography varies, so as to show that the whole had been set up again, while the aid of the poet was in no way required. In the edition of 1567, the earliest known, Turbervile professes to have "purged his work of its former faults and scapes," and apologizes for the whole, as having been composed, not to encourage "any youthlie head to follow or pursue such fraile affections," but to "warne all tender age to flee the fonde and filthie affection of poysoned and unlawfoll love."

We may be pretty sure that Turbenrile's first edition did not contain the stanzas addressed "to the rayling route of Sycophants," because he thus refers in it to his former book, which some of his enemies had contended was composed invitâ. Minervâ.

"Though thou affirme with rath and railing jawes,
That I *invita,* have ***Minerva*** made
My other booke, I gave thee no such cause
By any deede of mine to drawe thy blade:
But since thou hast shot out that shamelesse worde,
I here gainst thee uncote my craell sworde."

He may possibly allude to hostility shown to his translation of Ovid's Epistles, also published in 1567, and which we have reviewed in Vol. III. p. 86. In consistency with what 'precedes, Turbervile calls upon the Sycophant to draw his falchion,—

"Wherewith thou hast full many a skirmish made,
And scotcht the bmines of many a learned brow;"

affording another example of the use of a Shakspearean word.

We will now speak of the contents of the body of the book, which are contained in a preliminary "Table" of 164 separate pieces. After a woodcut of the Bear and Ragged Staff, on p. 1 begins a poem "In prayse of the renowmed Ladie Anne, Ladie Cowntesse of Warwicke," of the character of which the opening stanza will afford evidence:—

"When Nature first in hand did take
The Clay to frame this Cowntesse corse,
The Earth awhile she did forsake,
And was cornpelde, of verie force,
With mowlde in hande to flie to Skies
To ende the worke she did devies."

Of course, the Gods and Goddesses all unite to make the Countess, whom Turbervile calls Pandora, perfect both in mind and form. Tymetes and Pyndara, mentioned on the title-page, are fanciful names the poet gives to himself and to the lady he had loved, but who had married somebody else: for her Turbervile professes to have written his love-poems, and he introduces them by a short song, each verse of which ends with "Helena," thus:

"By sodaine sight of unacquainted shape
Tymetes fell in love with Pyndara,
Whose beaotie faire excelde Sir Paris rape,
That Poets cleape the famous Helena."

Early in the volume we arrive at what may be considered the first of Turbervile's "Epitaphes," and it is entitled "Verse in prayse of the Lorde Henrye Howarde, Earle of Surrey," but we need not quote it, because it is to be found in Dr. Nott's "Surrey and Wyat," Vol II. p. lxxix. The "Epitaph upon the death of the worshipfull Maister Richarde Edwardes, late Maister of the Children of the Queene's Majesties Chappell" is not by Turbervile, but by Thomas Twine, the continuator of Phaer's Virgil; and as it is not mentioned by Ritson, we quote some portions. It begins thus:—

"If teares could tell my thought,
or plaints could paint my paine;
If dubled sighes could shew my smart,
if wayling were not vaine;
If gripes that gnawe my brest

coulde well my griefe expresse,
My teares, my plaints, my sighes, my wayling never should surcesse."

This is not very good nor very new; but afterwards it proceeds in a better strain:—

"His death not I, but all
good gentle harts doe mono:
O London! though thy griefe be great,
thou dost not mourn alone.
The seate of Muses nine,
where fifteene Welles doe flowe,
Whose sprinckling springs and golden streames
ere this thou well didst knowe,
Lament to loose this Plant;
for they shall see no more,
The braunch that they so long had bred,
whereby they set such store.
O happie House! O Place
of *Corpus Christi,* thou,
That plantedst first, and gavste the roote
to that so brave a bow:
And Christ Church, which enjoydste
the fruite more ripe at fill,
Plunge up a thousande sigbes; for griefe
your trickling teures destill.
Whilst Childe and Chappell dure,
whilst Court a Court shall bee
(Good Edwards) eche estate shall much
both want and wish for thee.
Thy tender Tunes and Rimes,
wherein thou woonst to play

Eche princely Dame of Court and Towne
shall beare in rainde alway."

These lines are subscribed "qd Tho. Twine," but near the end of the volume in our hands is a second Epitaph upon the same most applauded playwright and poet, which is unsigned, and which we may therefore attribute to Turbervile. Isaac Reed only spoke of it by hearsay, never having seen it; but as it has been several times reprinted, we do not think it necessary to repeat it. Other Epitaphs are upon Sir John Tregonwell, upon Dame Elizabeth Arundell, upon Maister Tufton of Kent, and upon Sir John Horsey; while the heavier matter is relieved by love-poems, and by answers to "Maister Googes Fancies," &c., which he had printed in a volume of his poems in 1563, and which we have duly noticed, Vol. II. p. 65. The "Francis Th" to whom an epistle is addressed "on his leading his lyfe in the Countrie" must have been Francis Thynne, of whom and of his works more will be said hereafter, and of whom we have already spoken in Vol. III. p. 32. One of the most interesting pieces comes very late in Turbervile's Miscellany, namely, "An Epitaph on the death of Maister Arthur Brooke, drownde in passing to New Haven." This poem gives us the lamentable end of the author of the earliest extant version of the story of "Romeo and Juliet," published by Richard Tottell in 1562: it had been acted even earlier.

As Turbervile had commenced with the praises of Lady Warwick, so he ends on the same theme, the Countess being the wife of Ambrose Dudley, who died in 1589. A brief "Epiloge to his Booke" precedes Denham, the printer's colophon, dated 1567. Malone's copy of this edition was once the property of Edward Alleyn, the rich actor and founder of Dul-wich College.

TURBERVILE, GEORGE.—Tragical Tales, translated by Turbervile in time of his troubles, out of sundry Italians, with the Argument and Lenvoye to eche Tale. ***Nocet empta dolore voluptas.***—Imprinted at London by Abell Jeffs, dwelling in the Forestreete without Crepelgate at the signe of the Bel. Anno Dom. 1587. 4to. B. L. 200 ***leaves.***

As fifty copies of this work were reprinted at Edinburgh in 1837, we do not propose to give more than a cursory notice of its contents. Turbervile had commenced his literary labors full twenty years before the date of these "Tragical Tales," and we cannot avoid thinking that there was an earlier impression of them than that of 1787, although it has not come down to our day. At all events, a small fragment with a different, and as we apprehend an earlier, type is lying before us, while we write: it is part of the "Argument" to the first tale, and of the preceding address, "The Authour to the Reader." From the last, and for the purpose of comparison, we quote the praise, well deserved, but perhaps not very disinterested, which Turbervile gives to Lord Buckhurst, so created in 1567: we have not seen it quoted elsewhere. Melpomene addresses Turbervile in a dream, and thus warns him not to continue a commenced translation of Lucan:—

> "Let loftie Lucans verse alone,
> a deede of deepe devise,
> A stately stile, a peerelesse pen,
> a worke of weighty prise;
> More meete for noble Buckhurst braine,
> where Pallas built her bowre,
> Of purpose there to lodge her selfe,
> and shew her princelie powre.
> His swelling vaine would better blase
> those royall Romane peeres,
> Than any one in Brutus land
> that livde these many yeeres.
> And yet within that little Ile
> of golden wittes is store;
> Great change and choise of learned ympes
> as ever was of yore.
> I none dislike, I fancy some,
> but yet of all the rest
> Sance envy let my verdit passe,
> ***Lord Buckhvrst is the best.***
> We all, that Ladie Moses are,

who be in number niue,
With one accord did blesse this babe;
eche said ***This ympe is mine:***
Eche one of us at time of birth
with Juno were in place,
And eche uppon this tender childe
bestowd a gift of grace.
My selfe among the moe alowde
him Poets praysed skill;
And to commend his gallant verse,
I gave him wordes at will.
Minerva held him in her lappe,
and lent him many a kisse,
As who should say, when all is done,
they all shall yeeld io this.
This matter were more meete for him,
and farre unfitte for thee:
My sister Clio with thy kinde
doth best of all agree."

Here we see various, more or less minute, differences, besides the more important substitution of ***lent*** for "let," in the line "and lent him many a kisse," which last must, we think, have been the poet's word. So in "the Argument" to the first tale we have

"Might nothing rive or pierce her marble harte,"

instead of "Might nothing ***rize,***" &c.; and in the next stanza, ***fronion*** of our fragment is "frotion" in the copy of 1587, and, of course, in the Edinburgh reprint.

These changes establish, at all events, that there was another old impression, if indeed it were not earlier than the only extant copy, among Malone's books at Oxford.

Those who have touched upon the biography of Turbervile have regretted the absence of all materials, and it seems never to have struck them that, on the very title-page of the work under consideration, he emphatically notes his "troubles,"—"translated by Turbervile in time of his troubles." He again refers to them in some preliminary lines "to his verie friend Bo. Baynes":—

"Impute it to the troubles of my minde,
Whose late mishap made this be hatcht in haste;"

and, again, he tells the Reader,—

"Yet being that my present plight
is stufte with all anoye,
And late mishaps have me bereft
my rimes of roisting joye."

This may mean that by some "mishaps" (here spoken of in the plural) he had been bereft of "roisting rimes" which he had intended to publish. Probably, however, he refers to some personal bereavement, of which we have no other account, and he does not elsewhere advert to his "troubles."

We have taken the pains to collate every line of the reprint of 1837, and we can highly praise its general accuracy. In some instances it is almost too faithful to the original, because it adopts even barefaced misprints, which ought at least to have been pointed out in notes, if it were thought necessary to include the errors in the text: thus, "Phalatis" stands for **Phalaris,** "plants" for **plaints,** "Latinus" for **Latmus,** "usage" for **visage,** &c. Here and there we regret to meet with corruptions from which the original copy is free, as **peffred** for "pestred," **bigger** for "beggar," and, worst of all, **image** for "linage," referring to the family and lineage of one of the heroines.

"Put case her byrth were base, her **image** lowe,"

is nonsense; and, as we say, it stands "linage" in the edition of 1587. On the whole, nevertheless, the work was well edited in 1837, although we might wish for some further information as to the sources to which Turbervile resorted for his stories. We are not even told that his first "tale" is the same as that which C. T. in 1569 had called the "notable Historye of Nastagio and Traversari," reviewed in Vol. 111. p. 25. In all, there are ten of these novels in verse, several of them derived from Boccaccio, but others from Bandello and Belleforest. It is in the miscellaneous poems at the end of the volume that Tarbervile addresses some epistles from Russia (where he was in 1569, as Secretary to Randolph) to a person of the name of Spenser, giving no Christian name. It is probable that his correspondent was the author of "The Shepherd's Calendar," which made its appearance in print in 1579; but it nowhere appears that Turbervile's friend was named Edmund, although Anthony Wood incautiously so gave it (***Ath. Oxon.*** I. 627, edit Bliss), and others (like the editor of the volume in our hands) have more incautiously repeated. The epistles themselves afford no internal evidence upon the interesting point; and it may seem singular that Tarbervile should say nothing about the poetical propensities of Spenser, if Edmund Spenser were the person to whom they were really transmitted. Still, we feel much confidence that Spenser and Turbervile were early friends. We may notice here, that we have before us a copy of the Works of Sir Thomas More, folio, 1557, on which, in the handwriting of a George Turbervyle, we meet with the following inscription:—

"He that feareth not God when he dothe bye his grace knowe his powre shall be shamefullye confounded.

"George Turbervyle 1584. nov. 14."

Turbervile, or Turberville, was, however, not an uncommon name in the west of England, and under date of the 17th March, 1579-80, we meet the following curious entry in the Registers of the Stationers' Company:—

"Ric. Jones.—Lycenced unto him a Dittie of Mr Turbervyle murthered, and

John Morgan that murdered him, with a letter of the said Morgan to his mother, and another to his sister Turbervyle."

This Turbervyle could neither have been our poet, who was living in 1587 (and probably long afterwards), nor the writer of the inscription of 14th November, 1584, in the copy of Sir Thomas More's Works.

TWYNE, THOMAS.—The Schoolemaster, or Teacher of Table Phylosophie. A most pleasant and merie Companion, well worthy to be welcomed (for a dayly Gheast) not onelye to all mens boorde, to guide them with moderate and holsome dyet, but also into every man's Companie at all tymes to recreat their mindes with honest mirth and delectable devises: to sundry pleasant purposes of pleasure and pastyme. Gathered out of divers the best approved Aucthors, and devided into foure pithy and pleasant Treatises, as it may appeare by the contentes.—Imprinted at London by Richarde Johnes: dwelling at the signe of the Rose and the Crown, neere Holburne Bridge. 1583. 4to. B. L. **68 *leaves.***

There was an earlier impression of this amusing work in 1576, which we have not seen: it is a translation by Thomas Twine, the versifier of the portion of the Æneid (see Vol. III. p. 189) left unfinished by Phaer, and his initials T. T. are placed after the dedication to Alex. Nowell, Dean of St Paul's. Twyne's original was mainly the ***Saturnaliorum Conviviorum Libri VII*** of Macrobius, and he tells us that much more might have been added to the volume.

As it is well known, we mention it chiefly for the sake of what has sometimes escaped notice by those who have given an account of it, namely, that Richard Jones, the notorious printer and stationer, appears in it in the capacity of a poet, if rhyme may be called poetry. He inserts what he heads "The Printer's Preamble," in six six-line stanzas, addressed to all readers. The measure, to be sure, is not very exactly observed, but the verses have meaning and merit, and we quote the last two:—

"His problemes fine wil (doubtles) please you all,

And queint demaundes, so pithie in each point:
His jestes, I knowe, will like both great and small,
And hit your reyne, and niok you on the joinet:
What so you be, or where you do sojourne,
This pleasant pithy booke wyil surely serre your turns,
"Then, bid him welcome, Gentles all, and say,
Come, merie Gheast, come neare and sit thee downe:
Undoe thy packe; show foorth, we do thee pray,
Such newes as may as mery make in Country and in Towne.
Thus him to you I leave to see what he can show,
For, doubtlesse, I to joy your mindes this charges dyd bestow."

The body of the work is divided into four parts:—1. Of the nature and quality of all meats and drinks. 2. Of manner, behaviour and usage. 3. Delectable and pleasant questions, and pretie problemes. 4. Of honest jests, delectable devises and pleasant purposes.

The fourth division is curious, inasmuch as it shows how many of the best jests, still current, were equally acceptable in the middle of the reign of Elizabeth. Even then they were far from new. We quote one which we do not recollect to have seen elsewhere:—

"A proper jest of a certen marchaunt that would never come to church, nor heare Sermons; and beeing moved oftentymes by his wife thereto, sayd alwayes unto her, Go thou for us both. On a night he dreamed that he was called into judgement, and seeing his wife, with many other holy folkes, entring in at the dore of the celestiall joy, and hee likewise would have gone in with them, the porter put him backe and sayd, ***She shall go in for you both.*** Thus he, tareing without, awaked with sorrowe and greefe, and afterward leade a godlyer lyfe."

The above reads as if it were derived from the ***Gesta Romanorum;*** and so, perhaps, it was, or from some source where the pious result would be "improved" upon. Here also we have the stories of the husband who took his wife's confession;

of the doctor and his pupil; of the Jew who fell into a jakes on his Sabbath; of the man at sea who threw his wife overboard; of the husband who was castigated for his sinful wife; of the thief who bit off his father's nose; of the Archbishop on his palfrey and the old woman; of the Prioress and the Monk's breeches, and many others of the same kind.

In both editions of Lowndes (Bibl. Man. edit 1834, p. 54, and edit. 1857, p. 57) there is a mistake in assigning to T. Twyne the translation of the novel on which Shakspeare founded "Pericles." That version was made by Lawrence Twyne, brother of Thomas, as is shown by the title-page of every impression: "The Patterne of painefull Adventures, Containing the most excellent, pleasant, and variable History &c. of Prince Apollonius, the Lady Lucina his wife, and Tharsia his daughter, &c. Gathered into English by **Laurence Twine,** Gentleman.—Imprinted at London by Valentine Simmes for the Widow Newman." This edition has no date, but the story made its appearance several times anterior to 1600, first in 1576. Malone, Steevens, and even Douce all fell into the error of imputing it to Thomas, instead of Lawrence Twyne. Shakspeare probably used an impression which came out in 1607, a little before the date of the production of "Pericles." The novel was originally printed by Wynkyn de Worde in 1510, a translation from the **Gesta Romanorum** having been made for him by Robert Copland.

This "Patterne of painefull Adventures "is not to be confounded with "The painfull Adventures of Pericles," of which we shall speak hereafter under the name of George Wilkins, and which was a narrative (the only one of its kind) founded upon Shakspeare's drama, on account of its interest and popularity, and printed in 1608.

TYRO, ROARING MEG.—Tyros Roring Megge. Planted against the walles of Melancholy. One Booke cut into two Decads. **Uno die consenui.**—At London, Printed by Valentine Simmes. 1598. 4to. 21 **leaves.**

All that is good about this work is its title, which attracts attention on account of its apparent connection with that famous virago Long Meg of Westminster, regarding whose roaring exploits a pamphlet is extant, dated 1635, but who was well known many years before that date. As early as 1594, she had furnished the subject for a play at Henslowe's theatre; and here, four years afterwards, we find her giving a title to a collection of what are called by the author "epigrams," but which are more like satires, professing to be as bold and reckless as any of that heroine's achievements. However, the anonymous author wholly miscalculated his powers, and what he meant for wit is mere coarseness, and what he hoped was severity is generally abuse. There was also a piece of artillery, which, mainly from its length, obtained the name of "Long Meg," and to the "roaring" of that gun, still in existence, the author obviously refers in his forefront We may presume from the word Tyro that he was young and inexperienced, and we doubt whether the scarce publication in our hands was ever followed by anything from the same pen. We are not aware of an allusion to "Tyro's Roaring Meg," or to its author, in any subsequent publication. They were passed over without notice.

The dedication is to a "worshipful and true gentleman," of the name of John Lucas: it is in six-line stanzas, and there the writer thus expresses his assumed diffidence;—we say "assumed," because the whole character of the tract, divided into two "decades" of epigrams, contradicts the notion that he had any doubt of his own ability and desert:—

"Naithlesse, prickt on with foolish hardiment,
I put into those gratious handes of thine
These looser numbers: fitter to be rent,
Or swept away like deft Arachnes twine
Than to be read: yet (deerest) list a while
Unto thy Tyro's democriticke stile."

What he means by "Tyro's democritic style" is not at all clear,—possibly laughing style, but we cannot compliment him on his success in any style. We quote one of his best efforts, which is "Epig. 4," of the first decad:—

"O grosse, O monstrous! fie, Tom Tyro, fie!

Give thy king Edward's shilling for a pie,
And then transport it to thy den alone,
And chop it up, and give thy fellowes none?
What! spoile a Neats-foote and a marrow bon,
And never call thy next Ucalegon?
Fie, that thy greedy-wormed tong is such!
Fie, that thy chopping knives can mince so much!
Art thou a Milo or Philoxenus,
That art so sturdie and delicious?
Th' Harpyæ would not snatch so greedily,
Whose talons were of great capacity.
How can thy noddle choose but be so dull,
When, capon-like, thy maw is cramd so full?
Right well I wot thou maist have lighter hart,
If this thou leave, and learne to ***size apart.***"

There is really nothing worth quoting in the whole disjointed performance; for sometimes Tyro seems a hero, and at others the butt of his college companions. Considerable violence is here and there done to grammar, as where, in Epig. 1, of Decad 2, "hat" is made the past tense of ***to hit,*** and we are told that Tyro threw a stone at a goose and ***hat*** it. The writer, if he were not a scholar, affected to be one, and at the end we have Tyronis Epistolœ, consisting of Latin letters, supposed to have been sent not only to his father, but to his mother, as well as to other relations, who perhaps would not be able to read the language. Besides a total want of point and pungency in the epigrams, there is a sad deficiency of humor, and almost the only attempt at it is where Tyro dates one of his pieces in the following manner:

Written in haste, the twentieth of December,
About the dinner hour of eleven,
Fifteen hundred and ninety-seven."

The Tyronis Epistolœ form part of the tract, and are not, as some bibliographers have supposed, a separate publication.

UNDERDOWNE, THOMAS.—The excellent Historye of Theseus and Ariadne. Wherin is declared her fervent love to hym, and his trayterous dealing towarde her: Written in English meeter in Commendation of all good Women, and to the Infamie of such lyght Huswyves as Phedra the sister of Ariadne was, which fled away with Theseus, her Sisters Husband, and is declared in this History. By Thomas Underdowne.—Imprinted at London by Rycharde Jones, and are to be sold at his Shop, joyning to the South west Doore of Paules Churche. 1566. 18 of Januarie. 8vo. B. L. 16 **leaves.**

We have noticed this work on page 90 of our third volume; but a complete copy having since fallen in our way, we give a specimen or two of the execution of it. What we have previously said only applies to the preliminary portion, and to the author's bitter and, we may say, unjust attacks upon the female sex. We pass over all that relates to the tale of pasiphae and the Minotaur; and after Theseus has abandoned Ariadne, she breaks out in the following strain, employing verse that would have done credit to the poetry of a period considerably more advanced:—

"I dyd repayre hit crated ahyppes,
I dyd him treatura gyve;
I dyd my selfe bequeath to hym,
Still with hym for to lyve:

"I banketted this traytoun men,
I vittayled them with store,
I shewed them sucbe pleasure as
They never had before.

"I dyd my loved countrey lothe,
My parentes I foraooke,
To go with hym unto his land
All paynes I undertooke:

"And he likewyse dyd swere to mee
By goddes and heavens hie,
That he always wolde be my man,
With me to lyve and dye."

This is considerably better than might have been looked for from the translator of Ovid's "Ibis," but the subject there was unpromising. He goes on just afterwards in these terms:—

"Amyd a forrest wyde and wyde,
For beares and wolves a pray,
He leaveth me asleepe, and he
Falsely doth goe his waye.

"His trastlesse trneth, his treason tryed,
His fayth, his falshed founde,
And I a wofull wretche in care
As any on the grounde.

"To you, ye goddes, I doe complayne,
To you this tayle I tell,
Sith that he hath your names blasphemd,
That he may hang in hell.

"Revenge my cause, sith none but you
My whole estate do knowe;
That you be goddes and wyll revenge
To Theseus do showe.

"And you that heere of mee,
That he of judgement pure,
Beware to fisshe in fancys floud,
Or els to drowne be sure.

"Beware, be wyse; example take
By Ariadnes payne,
Whiche helpyng hym who helples was,
She helples doth remayne."

In the last stanza of the poem we are informed that the Gods did take pity upon Ariadne, and translated her to the stars, "where shee shall never die." On the whole, it is a highly creditable performance, and it is remarkable, among pieces of that date, that it is without dedication. Underdowne puts the abridgment of his name, "*Finis.* Th. Un.," at the end. Of course the foundation of the story is in Ovid, but the writer did not merely translate or imitate his original.

UNDERDOWNE, THOMAS.—Æthiopian Historie: Fyrst written in Greeke by Heliodorus and translated into English by T. U. No lesse witty then pleasant: being newly corrected and augmented, with divers new additions by the same Author &c.—Printed at London for William Cotton &c 1605. B. L. 4to. 155 *leaves.*

The oldest known edition of this work is dated 1587, 4to; but it is evident from the preliminary matter that it had been printed earlier.

In his address "to the Reader," preceding his version of "Heliodorua," Underdowne places the original, in point of example at least, before "Mort Darthure, Arthur of little Britaine, yea, and Amadis of Gaule." Some scraps of verse are inserted, particularly "the song that the Thessalian Virgins song in honor of Thetis, Peleus, Achilles, and Pyrrhus."

The beginning of Heliodorus's History appears to have been translated into English hexameters by Abraham Fraunce, and printed in 1591. (*Vide* Warton, Hist. Engl. Poet. IV. 230, edit. 8vo, and Ritson's *Bibl. Poet* 212.) In 1622 a new translation of the whole of the Æthiopian History by W. Barret was published. Nahum Tate completed a version of the last four books in 1686, the first six having been attempted by another hand.

URCHARD, SIR THOMAS.—Epigrams Divine and Moral. By Sir Thomas Urchard, Knight—London, Printed by Bernard Alsop and Thomas Fawcet in the yeare 1641. 4to. 34 *leaves.*

Sir Thomas Urchard, or Urquhart, was by no means an original thinker, but he was a tolerable writer of verses upon the commonplaces of life and manners. In the dedication of the work in our hands to "the Marquis of Hamilton, Earle of Arren and Cambridge," he states that his epigrams were "flashes of wit," but they by no means deserve that character: they are rather solid than flashy, and, in the ordinary sense of the word, they have little or no pretension to be called witty. They show some knowledge of character and shrewdness of observation, but nobody, reading them in our day, would consider them worthy of much admiration on any score. This is the earliest, and indeed the only, impression of them; for, when they appeared again in 1646, they had only a new title-page "for William Leake," into whose hands some remainder copies had devolved. The epigrams are divided into three books, and after the last we read "Here end the first three Bookes of Sir Thomas Urchard's Epigrams," as if it were, at one time, intended to follow on with a fourth book, but that the stationer thought the public would not care for more. He was, like most publishers, a better judge upon such a point than the author. The pieces are much more like aphorisms, and reflections in verse, than epigrams, and they now and then approach to too near a resemblance to truisms,—sedate observations, which no one would think of disputing, if of uttering. The following is one of the happiest, and it is the first" epigram "of Book III.:—

"No kind of trouble to your selfe procure,
And shun as many crosses as you can:
Stoutly support what you must needs endure,
And with the resolution of a man
Whose spirit is affliction-proofe, possesse
A joyfull heart in all occurrences."

The concluding poor line diminishes the effect of all the rest; and of course in every epigram care should be taken to make the last line sustain and support all that precede it: it ought to be better than the rest, and should finish off the writer's full meaning. One of Sir Thomas Urchard's best is headed "Of negative and positive Good":—

"Not onely are they good, who vertuously
Employ their time, now vertue being so rare,
But likewise those whom no necessity,
Nor force can in the meanest vice insnare;
For sin's so mainly further'd by the Devill
That 'tis a sort of good to doe no evill."

We may doubt whether the last line in what succeeds is as it came from the author's pen: if it did, he allowed himself great license in the rhyme.

"External comelinesse few have obtain'd
Without their hurt: it never made one chast,
But many adulterers; and is sustain'd
By qualities which age and sicknesse waste:
But that whose lustre doth the mind adorne,
Surpasseth farre the beautie of the bodie;
For that we make our selves: to this wee're borne:
This onely comes by chance, but that by study.
It is by virtue, then, that wee enjoy
Deservedly the stile of beautifull,
Which neither time nor fortune can destroy;
And the deformed body a fairs soule
From dust to glory everlasting carries,
While vicious soules in handsome bodies perish."

According to the full-length engraving of Sir Thomas Urchard, which some-times accompanies the reissue of his Epigrams in 1646, he was a fine personable. man, and apparently not a little vain of the "handsome body" in which his soul was lodged. [Note: 1: The portrait was drawn and engraved by Glover,—"G. Glover ad vivum delineavit et sculp. 1645,"—and underneath is this couplet subscribed W. S.:—

"Of him whose shape this Picture hath deeign'd
Vertue and learning represent the Mind."

Sir Thomas Urchard is dressed in the extreme of the fashion, and a little angel is holding out to him a laurel crown, to receive which Sir Thomas, rather condescendingly, extends his right band.] Whatever he may have thought of his figure, he certainly over-estimated the powers of his mind. Each of the three books contains forty-four epigrams, and the work is very carelessly printed.

VALENTINE AND ORSON.—Valentine and Orson, the two Sons of the Emperour of Greece. Newly corrected and amended, with new Pictures lively expressing the History.—London Printed by J. R. for T. Passenger, &c. 1688. 4to. B. L. 112 *leaves.*

The "new pictures," mentioned above, are merely very old woodcuts, as is evident from wear and tear, as well as from worm-holes. On the title-page is one of them, representing Valentine leading Orson prisoner; and on a fly-leaf, preceding it, is another of the exposure of the two infants. At the end is a table of the fifty-two chapters into which the romance is divided. This is a version different from that printed by Wynkyn de Worde, as far as can be judged from the only fragment remaining, and different also from that printed by W. Copland. The present translation seems to have first appeared in 1637, but by whom it was made we have no information.

VALLANS, WILLIAM.—The Honorable Prentice: or This Taylor is a man. Shewed in the life and death of Sir John Hawkewood, sometime Prentice of London: interlaced with the famous History of the noble Fitz-walter, Lord of Woodham in Essex, and of the poisoning of his faire Daughter: Also the merry customes of Dun mow, where any one may freely have a Gammon of Bacon, that repents not marriage in a yeere and a day. Whereunto is annexed the most lamentable murther of Robert Hall at the High Altar in Westminster Abbey.—Printed at London for Henry Grosson, and are to be sold in Pannier alley. 1615. 4to. B. L. 20 **leaves.**

The only reason for assigning this very rare tract to William Vallans, the author of "A Tale of two Swannes," 4to, 1590, is, that it bears the initials W. V. at the end of the dedication. There was, however, an interval of twenty-five years between the publications. W. V. may mean anybody else, and there is not the least connection or similarity of style. William Vallans was one of our early blank-verse poets, merited high appreciation, and could never have condescended to the putting together of such a patchwork production as this narrative regarding a renowned tailor, the poisoning of the daughter of Lord Fitzwater, the flitch of Bacon at Dunmow, and the assassination of Hall in Westminster Abbey in the reign of Richard II. The tract under consideration is nearly all prose, and was clearly meant to be popular with the lower orders, while the poem of the "Two Swannes" could never have been intended for perusal by any but more refined understandings. Take, for instance, only such musical lines as these:—

"Then looke how Cynthia with her silver rayes
Exceedes the brightnesse of the lesser starres,
When ID her chiefest pompe she hasteth downe
To steale a kiss from drowsie Endymion,
So doe these princes farre excell in state
The Swannes that breede within Europas boundes."

There is nothing very novel in the simile, but there is something very graceful in the language; and the epithet "drowsie" was at that time a rather bold attempt to introduce variety of measure, by requiring the reader to pronounce two syllables in the time of one, and to carry on the last syllable of "drowsie" to the first syllable of Endymion.

The tract before us is dedicated to Robert Valens; and if W. V. had had the same, or so nearly the same, name, he would have been sure to allude to it; and perhaps to claim relationship, if Yallans and Valens had been identical as appellations. What W. V. calls "the famous History of Sir John Hawkewood," commences after a brief "Introduction," but it is nothing more than the old story avowedly derived from Paulus Jovius, upon which Richard Johnson had dwelt in 1592, when, in his "Nine Worthies of London," he represented Hawkewood as thus opening his own story:—

"Who knowes my of spring doth not know my prime;
Who knowes my birth, perhaps, will scorue my deedes:
My valour makes my vertue mure then slime,
For that survives, though I weare deaths pale weedes.
Ground doth consume the carkes unto dust,
Yet cannot make the valiants armour rust."

Into Hawkewood's adventures in the reign of Edward III. we need not enter; and the second portion of the tract, which relates to Lord Fitzwater and his fair daughter, is almost equally well known. When speaking of the death of King John, the writer inserts the following note in his margin,—"Of which matter Mr. Michael Draiton and others have written at large." The most curious and original division relates to the Gammon, or Flitch of Bacon at Dunmow, to which Chaucer refers when he makes his Wife of Bath say,—

"The bacon was not fet for hem, I trowe,
That some men have in Essexe at Donmowe."

The information in the tract in our hands professes to be derived from the records of the Priory at Dunmow, showing that the prize had been gained of old by three persons only, viz.: Stephen Samuel of Aston, in the 7th year of Edward III.; Richard Wright of Norwich, on 17th August, 23 Henry VI.; and by Thomas le Fuller of Coggeshall, in 2 Henry VIII. What follows is given as the form of the oath to be taken by the claimants before the Prior could deliver to them the flitch (forsan *.flesh* or Germ. *fleisch*) of bacon:—

"The order of the Oath

"You shall sweare by the custom of confession
If ever you made nuptiall transgression,
Be you, sythe married man or wife,
By house hoald brawles or contentious strife,
Or otherwise in bed or at board,
Offend each other in deede or word;
Or since the parish clarke said Amen,
You wisht your selves unmarried agen:
Or iu a twelvemoneths time and a day
Repented not in thought any way,
But continued true and just in desire
As when you joined hands in the holy quire.
If to these conditions, without all feare,
Of your owne accord you will freely sweare,
A whole Gammon of Bacon you shall receive,
And beare it hence with love and good leave.
For this is our custome, a[t] Dunmow well knowne:
Though the pleasure be ours, the Bacons your own."

The murder of Thomas Hall took place at the high altar of Westminster Abbey, to which sanctuary he had fled when he had refused to give up the son of the Earl of Dene. There he was slain, and on the authority of Camden's "Remains," which W. V. cites, we are told that the dead body was buried "not far from Chaucer's tombe."

There was what, at first sight, would seem to be a second edition of this tract in 1616; but it was, in fact, merely a reissue of some copies that remained on hand from the preceding year: the only difference is, that on the title-page of the impression of 1615 Henry Gosson's address in Pannier Alley is given, while in the impression of 1616 it is omitted. The rest does not vary in a single letter. It is somewhat surprising that such a catchpenny publication did not meet with a more speedy sale.

VAUGHAN, ROWLAND.—Most approved and long experienced Water-Workes. Containing the manner of Winter and Summer-drowning of Medow and Pasture, by the advantage of the least River, Brooke, Fount or Water-prill adjacent, &c. As also a demonstration of a Project for the great benefit of the Common-wealth generally, but of Herefordshire especially, &c. By Rowland Vaughan, Esquire.— Imprinted at London by George Eld. 1610. 4to. 70 *leaves.*

The author, a resident in what was called the Golden Vale of Herefordshire, and formerly a captain in the Queen's army in 1588, in this work communicates to the Earl of Pembroke, in the form of a letter, two projects; one for irrigating land, of which he claims to have been the inventor, and the other for establishing an industrious community on his estate, which was surrounded by a numerous and idle population. Both schemes appear to have met with much opposition in his own neighborhood, and he therefore prays the aid and intervention of persons in power. His singularly written work is ushered in by a long commendatory poem by John Davies, of Hereford, "your poore kinsman, and honorer of true vertue in whome so-ever," and by others of the same kind, but much shorter, by John Strangwage, Rob. Corbet, Henry Fletcher, Richard Harries, Silvanus Davies, Tho. Rant, Oliver Maynson, John Hoskins, and a sonnet by John Davies. The author also prefixed four lines of his own, and added fourteen others at the conclusion; for, in a previous part of his work, he observes, "though I am no poet, yet I can make ballads to the tune of 'Up tayls all;' for Ile lash them, i'faith, with Rimes that shall make it rancle where they fall." A person who subscribes himself Anthony Davies ends the volume by six lines "in praise of the Worke and Author."

It is to be observed that some copies of this production are without date, and have no folding plates: others have only one plate; but the copy at Bridgewater House has two, explanatory of the author's intentions, one inserted after sign. K 3, and the other after the last leaf. They are both colored, and from some manuscript corrections made by the author we may infer that it was a presentation copy to Lord Chancellor Ellesmere.

VENNAR, RICHARD.—An Apology written by Richard Vennar of Lincolnes Inne, abusively called Englands Joy. To repress the contagious Ruptures of the infected Multitude, who having diseased stomackes of their owne make the world beleeve they cast up others poyson. And dedicated to the same pur-blinde Multitude, who feede with Spectacles to make their meate seeme bigger. As hoping, not altogether unworthy the perusal of the Noblest Judgements &c.—London Printed by Nicholas Oakes. 1614. 8vo. 29 *leaves.*

This is an early and remarkable piece of autobiography, and we believe that the volume is entirely unique. Richard Vennar was the author of a dramatic entertainment chiefly consisting, as far as we can judge, of dumb show and exhibition of scenery, which was brought out at the Swan Theatre on the Bankside, in 1603, under the title of "Englands Joy": an outline of it is extant, and it appears that it was a sort of apotheosis of Queen Elizabeth. This piece procured for its author, Vennar, the nickname of "Englands Joy," as he states on his title-page; [Note 1: In all the lists of the works of Nicholas Breton this production of "England's Joy" is assigned to him, but without the slightest authority, and there can be no reason for doubting Vennar's assertion that he was the author of it An original copy of the piece, such as it has come down to us, is in the library of the Society of Antiquaries, in the shape of a broadside, and it is reprinted from that relic in Vol. X. of the last edition of the Harleian Miscellany. We cannot refuse to insert here the following extract from a gossiping letter by John Chamberlain, dated 19th November, 1602, so that the incident to which it relates occurred, not in 1603, but near the close of 1602. We copy it from the original, formerly in the S. P. O.:—

"And now we are in mirth, I must not forget to tell you of a cousening pranke of one Venner of Lincolnes Inne, that gave out bills of a famous play on Satterday was sevennight on the Bankside, to be acted only by certain gentlemen and gentle women of account. The price at comming in was two shillings or eighteen pence at least; and when he had gotten most part of the money into his hands, he wold hare shewed them a fayre payre of heeles; but he was not so nimble to get up on horsebacke, but that he was fayne to forsake that course, and betake himself to the water, where he was pursued and taken and brought before the L. Chiefe Justice, who wold make nothing of yt but a Jest and merriment, and bound him over in five pound to appear at the Sessions. In the meantime the common people, when they saw themselves deluded, revenged themselves upon the hangings, curtaines, chaires, stooles, walles and whatsoever came in they are way very outrageously, and made a great spoyle. There was great store of good companie and many noblemen."] but he is not to be confounded with a person of the name of William Fenner, or Fennor, who was a rhyming antagonist of John Taylor the water-poet.

Richard Vennar was, as he informs us, a younger son of John Vennar of Salisbury, a Justice of the Peace, and was baptized by Bishop Jewell, so that he must have been born before 1571. After travelling he became a member of Lincoln's Inn, but met with many misadventures, one of which was the loss of his patrimony by the production of a forged will in favor of his brother-in-law. It was in his distress for money that he composed "Englands Joy," of which he speaks with regret, as follows:—

"By this I may seeme, like a canning Oratour, to have produced the weakest imputations first, that this cleering might set the better glosse upon more knowne defects: for who can excuse my publique default of the Swan, where not a collier but cals his deere 12 pence to witness the disaster of the day? How should I, without blushing, deny the name of *Englands Joy,* who had so many gossips at my Christening? Surely this divill must be cast out at leasure: you must use some patience to beare, nad I rob you of a little more time to deliver the circumstance, which, with indifferency heard, I assure my selfe will prove but a Chimæra, and either appeare but a winde, or Ixions monster at most, part man, part beast."

However, he does not "deliver the circumstance" attending the performance, but goes back to his journey to Scotland in 1600, and gives us more than a hint that he was in some way concerned in the Globe Theatre on the Bankside, then carrying on most successful performances. At this period Shakspeare was in his zenith, and his plays in a course of nightly representation. Vennar, however, speaks somewhat obscurely, and there are various other parts of his memoir that require explanation. He had been imprisoned in the Counter, and obtaining his enlargement he knew not what course to pursue:—

"My minde became diversly distracted with plurality of purposes, some times carried one way, some times another: the last, that I stood not least upon in resolution, was a second intendment for Scotland; but to this purpose there wanted armes, or rather the sinewes of armes, money. I saw daily offring to the God of pleasure, resident at the Globe on the Bankside, of much more then would have supplyed my then want: I noted every man's hand ready to feede the luxury of his eye, that puld downe his hat to stop the sight of his charity: wherefore I concluded to make a friend of Mammon, and to give them sound for words, both being but aire, for which they should give double payment."

The meaning of which we take to be, that Vennar for a time became a player at the Globe Theatre, but in some inferior capacity; perhaps as a hired man, because we never find his name in any list of the Company. He also seems to have got up some species of public performance, which was not successful; and here it is that we meet with a very curious passage relating to the comedy of "The Knight of the Burning Pestle," which shows, what we already know, that it was condemned, and what we do not know, that it was only by one "writer," for only one is spoken of. Vennar's words are, "For suppose the play was hist, was I the first poet made my clients penitents? Let the ***Burning Pestle*** bee heard in my cause, which rang so dismally in your eares, and yet ***the Writer*** in state of grace."

So that whether Beaumont or Fletcher wrote it, it had done the author no harm in public estimation. However, poor Vennar's performance, whatever it may have been, was condemned, and he was arrested by bailiffs before it was well concluded.

We cannot follow the writer in all his rambling adventures, as ramblingly narrated; but the later portion of his "Apology" is rather too self-eulogistic on the benefits he had conferred upon poor prisoners, having especially interested in their behalf the Countesses of Warwick and Cumberland as well as sundry Lord Mayors and Aldermen of London. He tells us, moreover, that he had composed "a brief treatise" on the Gunpowder Plot, which has survived (see the next page); that he was the author of a known broadside on "A Papist Dormant, a Papist Couchant, a Papist Leavant, a Papist Passant, a Papist Rampant, and a Papist Pendant"; and under woodcuts of the King and Queen, on another broadside, he placed the following lines:—

"The God of all eternity
Preserve this Royall Unity,

That they may breath
An everlasting breath,
And those may pine in hell
That seeke their death.
Their States of blisse
Be Brittaines blessed story,
And give their soules
A Crowne of endlesse glory."

Vennar concludes his autobiography, rather arrogantly, by challenging any man "justly to taxe him of sclander, deceipt, fraud or cousenage"; and then leaves "this defence of his life to the able and generous protections" of the impartial. He subscribes his book,

"The wel-wisher and servant of
all vertuous mindes,
"RICHARD VENNAR."

We have only to add that from a passage in William Fenner's 'Counter's Commonwealth" 4to. 1617, p. 64, it appears that the author of "Englands Joy" (there named Vennard, as indeed he sometimes himself spelt it) had died in the utmost poverty, in what was called "the Hole" of Wood-Street prison.

VENNAR, RICHARD.—The true Testimonie of a faithfull Subject: containing severall exhortations to all estates to continue them in due obedience &c.— Imprinted at London, n. d. 8vo. 19 **leaves.**

At the back of the title is pasted an excellent woodcut of James I., to whom this loyal tract is dedicated by R. V., i. e., Richard Vennar. It has no date, but, as it contains a thanks-giving for the deliverance of the kingdom from the Gunpowder Plot, it no doubt came out very shortly after that discovery. The prose portion of the volume was in a great degree a reprint of what the author had put forth, under nearly the same title, in 1601, and dedicated it to Queen Elizabeth, then calling himself, as afterwards, "Richard Vennard of Lincolne's Inne."

The "Thanksgiving" on the Gunpowder Plot, already mentioned, is in six-line stanzas, and to it succeed a general "Thanks-giving," and a "Prayer" for the King, Queen, and Prince Henry, in the same form. As no other copy of the work is known to us, and, as it was no doubt privately printed by the author for presents, no print-er's nor bookseller's name being found in any part of it, a small portion of the first poem may be given, not at all on the score of its merit, but of its rarity:—

"Rejoyce, O Brittaine! Sing and clap thy hands,
For God himselfe doth for thee safely fight:
No foe so great but that thy force withstands,
It is so strengthened by the heavenly might.
The Popes great malice and the Papists pride
Before thy face do fall on every side.

"Now shalt thou heare of nothing but confusion
Upon the head of all thy harmefull foes:
Now shall the traitors find the full conclusion
That in the end of all rebellion growes:
And they shall fret to see their pride puld downe,
Whilst God preserves they soveraigne and his crown.

"Now shall the Pope with all his practise faile,

The hope of traitors all be overthrowne:
Nor Pope nor traitor now shall none prevaile
To do thee hurt that but defendst thine owne.
Now serve thy God and give him thanks for all,
And keepe thy faith and thou shalt never fall."

VENUS.—The Scourge of Venus: or The wanton Lady. With the rare Birth of Adonis. The second Impression, corrected and enlarged by H. A.—London, Printed by N. O. and are to bee sold by Robert Wilson, at his Shop at Graies-Inne new gate. 1614. 8vo. 22 *leaves.*

We never heard of an earlier impression of this disagreeable book, (we mean disagreeable on account of the character of its story,) although this is called on the title-page "the second impression": it professes also to have been "corrected and enlarged by H. A." whoever he may have been. It was certainly reprinted in 1620, and we are there told that it was "written" not by H. A. but "by A. H." The address "to the Reader" is the same in both impressions, one signed H. A. and the other A. H., and there they do not profess to have written it: they say of the unnamed author, "I have heard' twas done for his pleasure, without any intent of an impression, but this much I excuse him, that I know not, and commend that which deserveth well." Again, they elsewhere both tell us, that the poem "was the labour of a man well-deserving." This man was clearly neither H. A. nor A. H.; but the stationer who published the edition of 1620 thought it would answer his purpose better to put "written by A. H." on the title-page. We are not aware that either H. A. or A. H. are the initials of any poet of note in the middle of the reign of James I.

The narrative follows the tale as given by Ovid pretty exactly, and it was clearly meant as a sort of introduction to Shakspeare's "Venus and Adonis," giving an account of the birth and origin of the hero. Nothing is softened down or concealed, and the offensive parts of the fable are made prominent, and placed in the strongest light. So objectionable were some stanzas considered, that they were actually omitted in 1620, as too gross to be reprinted, a curious circumstance not hitherto noted: on the contrary, we have seen it stated that "the contents of both editions arc exactly the same." This is a mistake, which shows, either that copies of the third impression vary, or that the collation of it with the impression of 1614 was not carefully made. After the address "to the Reader," the subject of the poem is thus awkwardly and familiarly commenced:—

"Whilst that the Sunne was climing up in haste
To view the world with his ambitious eye,
Faire Myrha, yet alas, more faire then chaste,
Did set her thoughts to descant wantonly:
Nay, most inhumane, worse then bad, or ill,
As in the sequell you may reade at will.

"You that have parents, or that parents be,
Depart a space, and give not eare at all
To the foule tale that here shall uttered be:
Some filthy shame let on all other fall,
If possibly there can be any such
From nature to degenerate so much."

Here the stanza, it will be observed, is the same as that of Shakspeare, but, as may be readily believed, there is little other resemblance between the two poets. We quote also the conclusion:—

"The watry Nymphs this pretty child did take,
And on soft smelling flowers laid him downe,
Of which a curious cradle they did make:
The hearbs perfumed were for more renowne.
The Nymphs this boy affected more and more,
And with his mothers teares stil washt him ore.

As yeares encrease so beauty doth likewise,
And he's more faire to morrow then to day:
His beauty more and more did still arise,

That envy did delight in him bewray;
And Venus fell in love with him at last
Who scourg'd him for his mothers lusting past"

The edition of 1620, besides omitting stanzas, makes various verbal alterations, as in the last line, which it gives thus:—

"Who did revenge his mothers lusting past,"

which is not much more intelligible than the original. Sometimes, but not always, the changes are for the better, as where it is said in the impression of 1614,—

"This lyon seekes for her the dart did throw,
And quickly lets all the other go."

This is wrong in measure and meaning, and the edition of 1620 instructs us to read,—

"And *quietly* lets all the other go."

We might illustrate this point by many other instances, but the poem is hardly worth the trouble of correction.

There is no direct allusion to Shakspeare throughout, but in William Barksted's production of an earlier date (1607), but of a similar complexion, "Mirrha the mother of Adonis, or Lusts Prodegies," our great dramatist is mentioned by name; and we quote the short passage, chiefly because Malone, in citing it, (Shaksp. by Boswell, xx. 85,) makes more variations from the original than there are lines in the passage. What follows occurs at the very close of Barksted's performance:—

"But stay, my muse; in thine owne confines keepe
And wage not warre with so deere lov'd a neighbor,

But haying sung thy day song, rest and sleepe;
Preserve thy small fame and his greater favor:
His song was worthie merrit (Shakspeare bee)
Sung the faire blossoms, thou the withered tree:
Laurell is due to him; his art and wit
Hath purchase it: Cypres thy brow will fit."

Shakspeare in several places uses *meed* for "merit," and here we see Barksted making "merit" and *meed* synonymous. We give the title of "Mirrha the Mother of Adonis" at length, because it shows that Lewis Machin's Eclogues, which are spoken of in Lowndes (Bibl. Man. 1861, p. 1438) as a separate publication, were only a supplement to Barksted's poem, in order to swell the volume:—

"Mirrha the Mother of Adonis: or Lustes Prodegies. By William Barksted. Horace, nansicetur enim pretium, nomenque Poetœ. Where-unto are added certain Eclogs by L. M.—London printed by E. A. for John Bache, and are to be sold at his shop in the Popes-head Palace, nere the Royall Exchange. 1607."

The name of Lewis Machin is appended at length to the Eclogues; but they have little or no merit of any kind, and the allusions, personal and political, are often not intelligible. Barksted, as is well known, was an actor, and played in Ben Jonson's "Epicœne," and he may have sustained a part in Lewis Machin's comedy "The Dumb Knight," which was printed in 1608. In 1615 Barksted was one of Alleyn's Company, (Memoirs of Edw. Alleyn, 1841, p. 130.)

VICARS, JOHN.—Babels Balm or the Honey-combe of Romes Religion. With a neate draining and straining out of the rammish Honey thereof. Sung in tenne most elegant Elegies in Latine by that most worthy Christian Satyrist Master George Good-winne, and translated into tenne English Satyres by the Muses most unworthy Eccho, John Vicars.—Imprinted at London by George Purslowe &c. 1624. 4to. 65 *leaves.*

On the fly-leaf of this tract the first Earl has written in his copy,—

"J. Bridgewater ex dono Jo: Vicars;"

and to his Lordship the translation is dedicated in two pages of verse, in which the late Lord Chancellor Ellesmere is styled

"our Nestour, your Progenitour,
Englands grave Cato, prudent Senatour,
Fraught with faire Vertue, and from Vice most free."

A short address to the Reader is succeeded by Goodwin's dedication of his original work to Sir Robert Naunton, by an acrostic by Vicars upon Goodwin, and a violently abusive poem, thus headed: "To the most discourteous Momish Catholike, whose greatest grace is a graceles gracious kisse at his unholy Fathers great Toe, Greeting." Thomas Salisbury, Bach, in Divinity, subscribes some commendatory lines, to which are added, "The Argument of the Poeme, and the contents of the ten Satires." At the end of them is "a Corollarie to the Premises," and six lines "upon this Bee-hive or Honeycombe."

Vicars was married, for the second time, to Susan Martin, on 2d April, 1617, having buried his first wife, Edith, and child, in the preceding year. In the register of St Bartholomew the Less he is termed "Schoolmaster," and his son Robert was baptized there on 22d June, 1616.

VICARS, JOHN.—All the memorable and wonder-strikinge Parliamentary Mercies effected for, and afforded unto this our English Nation within this space of lesse then 2 Yeares past A⁰. 1641 and 1642.- Are to be sould by Thomas Jenner in his shop at the old Exchange. 4to. 9 *leaves.*

The above is an engraved title-page, supported by half-lengths of Time and Truth, and beneath them, in the centre, Envy eating a heart. Two texts from Isaiah are on scrolls under Time and Truth, and a third from Revelation, under Envy.

VICARS. JOHN.—Prodigies and Apparitions, or England's Warning Pieces. Being a seasonable Description by lively figures and apt illustrations of many remarkable and prodigious forerunners and apparent Predictions of God's Wrath against England, if not timely prevented by true Repentance. Written by J. V.—Are to bee sould by Tho. Bates &c 8vo. n. d. 29 *leaves.*

The title is engraved upon a drapery, supported by a child with two heads, and representing, in the background, various prodigies in the air and on the earth. There are six other plates, devoted to separate "emblems" or "warning-pieces" to England of approaching destruction for her sins. One of these (the second) represents a child with two distinct heads, two hearts, two arms, and the stump of a third growing out from the back," which had been "shewn to King Charles and the Queen, Anno. Dom: 1633." At the back are the following lines by Vicars, which show his fanatical ingenuity in applying this abortion to the circumstances of the times:—

"Behold, good Reader, here a monstrous birth
To damp thy sinnes delight, and marre such mirth:
A man-childe born in most prodigious sort,
Which for undoubted truth thou mayst report.
Two distinct heads it had, and eke two hearts,
Two arms, whence grew a stump: in other parts
Like other children. What may this portend?
Sure, monstrous plagues doe monstrous sinnes attend!
The sinnes of Heads, in government abus'd;
The sinnes of Hearts, opinions false infus'd,
And broacht abroad to raise up foes and factions,
And Arms and Armies to confound with fractions:
Disjoynted States (like stump-like Ireland)
Whiles brothers thus' gainst brothers lift their hand.
This (surely) God seemes hereby to foretell,
That having plagues must hideous Sinnes expell."

In the last line for "having" we surely ought to read *heavy.* Each plate has verses of the same description annexed to it, but the main body of the tract is prose. Near the end the author speaks of "this instant year, 1643," which was no doubt the date of publication, although none appears on the title-page.

VICARS, JOHN.—A Sight of the Transactions of these latter yeares. Emblemized with engraven plats, which men may read without spectacles.—Are to be sould by Thomas Jenner in his shop at the old Exchange. 4to. n. d. 15 *leaves.*

The engraved title to this production is from the same plate as the preceding, with the exception that the original words have been abrased, and others substituted as above. Eight of the plates are also the same, though not inserted in the same order, and three others are added, each containing two subjects, viz.: I. The pulling down of Cheapside Cross, the 2d of May, 1643. 2. The burning of the Book of Sports and Pastimes, the 10th of May, 1643. 3. Burning papistical books, crucifixes, pictures, &c, in Somerset House and St James Palace, the 23d of May, 1643. 4. The Hanging of Challener and Tomkins in May, 1643. 5. The beheading of Sir A. Carew, Sir J. Hotham, Captain Hotham, and Archbishop Land, in 1645. 6. The breaking of the Great Seal, the 11th of August, 1646.

The plates are accompanied by prose details and explanations, bringing down the events to the 11th of August, 1646, and at the conclusion are the words, "Collected by John Vicars." Vicars had the presumption, in 1632, to publish a translation of the Æneid,—a ludicrous mixture of bombast, barbarism, and bathos.

VIENNA.—Vienna. Noe Art can cure this hart Where in is storied the valorous atchievements, famous triumphs, constant love, great miseries, and finall happines of the well deserving, truly noble and most valiant Kt. Sr. Paris of Vienna, and the most admired amiable Princess the faire Vienna.—London Printed for Richard Hawkins &c. n. d. 4to. 95 *leaves.*

On some copies of this production the date of 1650 is found, but the present edition is, perhaps, earlier. Opposite to an engraved title-page, by Gifford, are some explanatory verses, and others in commendation of the author (for it is spoken of by him and his friends as an original work) are prefixed. The only writer of note who lends his praise is Thomas Heywood, the dramatist.

A translation of the original romance came from the press of Caxton in 1485, and it formed the subject of a play acted before Queen Elizabeth by the children of Westminster on Shrove Tuesday, 1371. (*Vide* Hist. Engl. Dram. Poetry, I 197.) Dr. Dibdin (Typ. Ant. I. 261) informs us that "the original is of Provencal growth, and was translated into French by Pierre de la Sippade." It is singular, as we learn on the same authority, that Caxton's impression, which purports to be "translated out of French into English," should be of an earlier date than any known foreign edition.

VINEGAR AND MUSTARD.—Vinegar and Mustard: or Wormwood-Lectures for every Day in the Week. Being exercised and delivered in severall Parishes both of Town and City, on several dayes.

A dish of tongues here's for a feast,
Sowre sawce for sweet meat is the best.

Taken Verbatim in short-writing by J. W.—London Printed for Will. Whitwood, at the Golden Bell in Duck-Lane. 1673. 8vo. 12 *leaves.*

On the title-page is a woodcut (see Roxburghe Ballads, 4to, 1847, p. 89) representing a husband returning home to his shop after a debauch, with a jug in his hand, but refused admittance by his angry wife. It is a mere chap-book, and we may reasonably believe that it was originally published considerably anterior to the date it bears. If a small tract were popular, it was sure to be reprinted, but in very many instances the ancient editions have been lost One proof of the contrary, however, is now before us, in a piece entitled "The Anatomie of Pope Ioane," which was first printed by Richard Field, in 1591,4to, and was reprinted by him in 12mo, as long afterwards as 1624, with the addition of the initials of the supposed author,—"Written by I. M.,"—possibly Jervis Markham.

"Vinegar and Mustard" consists of curtain-lectures by wives to their husbands, with such "answers" as the husbands were able to make. Neither the charges nor the replies are at all times very delicate or refined, whether as regards dirt or decency. They are calculated for every day in the week, and chiefly relate to the class of society forming the usual purchasers of such commodities. "Fridayes Lecture" is different from the others, and consists of a scolding-match between "bold Bettris" and "Welsh Guentlin," two market-women, who, after abusing each other very roundly and coarsely, agree to make up their differences over "half a dozen of ale" at the Fox public-house. This is entirely prose, but in other cases the wife's accusation is in prose, and the husband's defence in verse. There is a good deal of humor in some of the dialogues, and the following stanzas are at the back of the title-page

> ***"The Book to the Reader or Hearer.***
> "Tis no Tab Lecture which I teach,
> Bat Ile tell you what some women preach;
> then, pray come near and hear me.
> I am black ink and paper white;
> Although I bark, I will not bite:
> therefore, you need not feare me.
>
> "No modest woman I envy,
> Because I love them heartily,
> and prize them more than gold.
> None will exceptions take at me,
> Bat such as think they gauled be,
> and that's, I'm sore, a Scold."

Here we see the old use of the word. "envy" in the sense of ***hate,*** so common in the time of Shakspeare; and in the first husband's answer we meet with "warned" in the sense of ***summoned:*** (Julius Cæsar, Act V. sc. 1, &c.) In his "Tale of Melibœus," Chaucer always uses "warn" as the synonym of ***summon:***—

> "Know, I am going to the Hall,
> Where we this day Master and Wardens chose:

I, being warn'd, most not refuse."

In the second husband's answer we have an account of the attire of a smart innkeeper's wife:—

"You have good gowns unto your back,
and Wastcoats are not base;
kirtles and scarlet Petticoats,
with silk and golden lace;
Your Beaver hat, lac'd Handkerchiefs,
and yet you call me goose," &c.

The "Thursdayes Lecture" contains a droll and very characteristic speech by a wife, who was a Puritan, to her husband, "who would not be edified by her,"—where, among other things, she says: "You (forsooth) will go no where to be edified, but to your steeple-houses, upon your heathenish daies, there where they teach nothing almost but the language of the Beast," &c.

Among the local allusions, &c. we have a reference to Turnmill or Turnbull-Street, Clerkenwell, to the pond which formerly existed in Smithfield, to Billings-gate Market and its bell, to the custom of allowing women confined in Newgate to beg at the grated window, &c. We may, perhaps, conclude that the chap-book was first printed anterior to the Civil Wars, and that the initials J. W., on the title-page, were those of one of the numerous and prolific pamphleteers of that period: it is just in the style of Price, Guy, or Parker.

VIRGINIA.—A true Relation of such occurrences and accidents of noate as hath hapned in Virginia since the first planting of that Collony, which is now resident in the South part thereof, till the last returne from thence. Written by Captaine Smith one of the said Collony, to a worshipfull friend of his in England.—London Printed for John Tappe, and are to bee solde at the Greyhound in Paules-Church-yard, by W. W. 1608. 4to. B. L. 19 *leaves.*

This copy consists in fact of twenty leaves, the fly-leaf before the title-page being marked sign. A., and the first leaf after the title-page A 3. On the title-page is a woodcut of a ship in full sail.

There are differences between this copy and that in the Grenville Library: in the first place, it is avowedly on the title-page the work of Capt. Smith, and not of "Thomas Watson, Gent.": then, there is no preliminary address to the reader and no map. Yet this copy is evidently complete, and the signatures (from A to E 4) quite regular. The name of Watson nowhere appears in it, and throughout it is written in the first person, but not subscribed by anybody; there is also no date nor place at the end. In the whole it includes the incidents of about a year; for in the opening the writer of the letter speaks of 26th April, when they set sail for Dominica from the Canaries, and on sign. E he mentions the unexpected return of Capt. Nelson to the fort on 20th April: in neither instance is the year given, but it was probably 1607.

It is useless to enter into any of the events detailed, since they are very numerous and crowded into a small compass: the most important are the hanging of Capt Kendall for plotting against the Colony, and the capture and subsequent liberation of Capt. Smith by the Indians, when they had him alone and completely at their mercy. There is little interest in any part of the narrative, which is somewhat hastily and confusedly put together. Notwithstanding what is said in the address before the Grenville exemplar, we believe that Watson was the real author of the tract, though Capt Smith's more popular name was used in the copy before us.

VIRGINIA.—A Good Speed to Virginia. Esay. 42. 4. He shall not faile nor be discouraged, &c.—London Printed by Felix Kyngston for William Welbie, and are to be sold at his shop at the signe of the Greyhound in Pauls Church-yard. 1609. 4to. B. L. 15 *leaves,*

This is an able pamphlet of considerable rarity, published for the purpose of encouraging a spirit of adventure for the settlement of Virginia. Views of worldly policy and of religious duty are judiciously mixed up together, so as to secure the good opinion of various classes. The main drift is however pious, urging the duty of an expedition to North America, on the score of the advantage that would accrue to the poor savages by being brought into the Christian communion. The necessity of relieving Great Britain of surplus population, and the prospect of wealth and happiness to the undertakers are also very strongly pointed out. A new enterprise of the kind was at that time in hand.

"The Epistle Dedicatorie" to the Lords, Knights, Merchants, and Gentlemen "Adventurers for the plantation of Virginia" is subscribed R. G., and is dated "From mine house at the North-end of Sithes lane, London, April 28, *Anno* 1609."

The body of the work starts, like a sermon, with a long text from Joshua xvii. 14, and a parallel is kept up throughout between the children of Joseph, and the people of England seeking out new places of settlement Columbus and his discovery are thus mentioned early in the tract: "Christopher Columbus made proffer to the Kings of England, Portugall and Spaine, to invest them with the most precious and riches veynes of the whole earth, never known before; but this offer was not only rejected, but the man himself, who deserves ever to be renowned, was (of us English especially) scorned and accounted for an idle Novelist Some thinke it was because of his poore apparell and simple lookes, but surely it is rather to be imputed to the improvidency and imprudencie of our Nation, which hath alwayes bred such diffidence in us, that we conceit no new report, bee it never so likely, nor beleeve anything, be it never so probable, before we see the effects."

The writer, among other things, maintains the right to dispossess the savages, not only because it is for their own good, but because they have no fixed possession and residence, and because they had in fact invited a settlement on their shores.

In the course of his argument, R. G. several times refers to the book called "***Nova Britannia,*** offering most excellent Fruites by Planting in Virginia," which had just been published, like this, with the date of 1609: it seems not unlikely that it was by the same author. From his closing sentence we learn that he was not in a condition to aid the undertaking either in purse or person: "And thus far have I presumed in my love to the Adventurers, and liking to the enterprise . . . sorrowing with my selfe, that I am not able, neither in person nor purse, to be a partaker in the businesse."

The copy of the tract we have used is especially valuable, from the circumstance that it once belonged to Sir Walter Raleigh, whose autograph it bears, with the addition of "Turr. Lond.," indicating his place of confinement.

Some early owner, not knowing the interest of Sir Walter Raleigh's signature, has endeavored to erase it, and has partially succeeded; but enough is fortunately still left to ascertain the fact. It has been suggested that the production may have come from the pen of Sir Walter himself, and the last sentence it contains, coupled with the character and excellence of the arguments, may appear to support such a notion; but if it had been so, there seems no sufficient reason for withholding his name from a tract which must have been acceptable both to the King and Court.

Vox GRACULI.—Vox Graculi, or Jacke Dawes Prognostication. No lesse wittily, then wondrously rectified, for the Elevation of all Vanity, Villany, Sinne, and Surquedrie sublimate, keeping quarter in the Courts, Cities and Countries of all Christendome: For the yeere 1623. Sœpe malum hoc robis prœdixit ab œthere Cornix.—Published by Authority. 4to. 39 *leaves.*

A woodcut of a Jackdaw sitting at a desk writing, with books and instruments, occupies so much room on the title-page, that if there were (as is most probable) any printer's or stationer's name at the bottom, it has been entirely cut away.

Thomas Dekker wrote various pieces of this sort, particularly his "Raven's Almanac" in 1609, (see Vol. I. p. 253,) and he was so popular an author that ho had many imitators. One of the imitations was "The Owle's Almanacke" in 1618, and another the work before us, the dedication of which is subscribed, not T. D., but J. D., possibly intended to be mistaken for T. D., (Thomas Dekker,) and thus an additional number of purchasers secured for what in most respects is an inferior composition.

In all publications of this class we find something to illustrate the manners and peculiarities of the time, and the one before us cannot be said to be deficient, but the information is given without much point: as for instance, where J. D. speaks of the versifiers of his day, and calls them "vertues crutches, who keep life in the dying world," he enters into no particulars. Of players he remarks:—

"I should heere vnlock the casket of my knowledge (hauing well nie forgot) and lay open some rarities concerning Players; but because the Common-wealth affoords them not their due desert, and for they are men of some *parts,* and live not like lazy drones, but are still in *action,* I am content silently to referre them to three sublunary felicities, which are these: a *faire day,* a *good Play,* and a gallant *Audience,* and so let them shift for their lives."

Elsewhere the author mentions the Globe, Fortune, Phœnix, Bull, and Curtain theatres, the latter as even then in use, although it had been condemned to be pulled down many years before.

Every notice of Robin Hood is interesting, and the eye no sooner catches his name on a page than we are curious to learn to what purpose it is applied. Here it comes in illustration of the proverb "Hobson's choice—that or none," which in the tract under consideration is represented as "Robin-Hood's choice—*either this or nothing.*" Such we believe to have been the true original reading, and that in some way "Robin Hood" has been corrupted to *Hobson.* At all events, "Robin-Hood's choice" supplies an intelligible meaning, while "Hobson's choice" requires an explanation which has not yet been satisfactorily found for it. There is certainly no passage in "The pleasant Conceits of Old Hobson," 1607, that furnishes it. There probably was an earlier edition, now lost, because we find some of the "pleasant conceits" worked by Thomas Hey wood into his play, "If you know not me, you know nobody," Part II. 1606, 4to.

WALTER, WILLIAM.—The spectacle of louers. Here after foloweth a lytell contrauers dyalogue bytwene love and councell with many goodly argumentes of good women and bad, very compendyous to all estates, newly compyled by William

Walter seruaunt vnto Syr Henry Marnaye, Knyght, Chauncelour of the Duchye of Lancastre. [Colophon.]—Imprynted at London in Fletestrete at the sygne of the Sonne by me Wynkyn de Worde. 4to.

After an introduction, in which the writer professes to have overheard the discussion, on the subject of love, between a desperate ***Amator*** (so he is called) and a sage ***Consultor,*** we arrive at the speeches; and although the tract b said to have been "compyled by William Walter," we may pretty safely conclude that it was a translation. The harangues are decidedly too long, with very little spirit derived from the enlivening subject The following is a small part of one of Consultor's addresses:—

> "What is beaute but a floure vanyashynge,
> The carnall felycyte, the infeccyon of the eye,
> The deceyuynge of the mynde of men so conceytynge,
> A frayle pleasure, full of trechery?
> There as it is taken it deceyueth kyndly:
> Beaute and wysedome seldome doth agre;
> It causeth them unstable and inconstant for to be. * * *

> "Full harde it is to fynde a woman stedfast,
> For yf one eye wepe, the other dothe contrary:
> Theyr trouth and faythe but a small whyle dothe last;
> Theyr pleasure and lust is harde to satysfye.
> In wrathe and malyce they be contynually:
> Trewthe, shame, ne love can not theym refrayne,
> Theyr synguler pleasure but that they wyll optayne."

Consultor can allow no merit of any sort to the ladies, and he afterwards asserts:—

> "Women can loke on men with face double,
> For in theyr hertes they be fall varyable:

Theyr fayned loue hath put many men to trouble,
Whiche haue supposed theym to be ferme and stable,
By blandysshyuge wordes theyr bayte detestable.
Lyke the Scorpyon that sheweth the face smylynge,
And with the tayle sodeynly dothe stynge."

Amator says comparatively little, and we may well imagine that such warn-ings were entirely thrown away upon him. As a bachelor, he does not seem to have known much about the usual period of gestation with women, or the practice has been entirely altered since, for he says,—

"Ten monethes women with theyr chyldren go,
And of theyr bodyes that tyme be they nouryashed."

Perhaps he fancied that, if he married, a family would not be formed quite so soon as by the modern practice. Amator is left to his fate, and the author apologizes for his ill opinion of and attacks upon women, while Robert Coplande adds an envoy, quoted by Dibdin, and converted into nonsense by misprinting "Endever thy selfe" **And ever** thy selfe. (Typ. Ant II. 337). Ritson makes a strange blunder (**Bibl. Poet.** 108,) when he splits this single small poem into two separate works, calling one "A lytell contravers," &c., and the other "The spectacle of louers." We need scarcely wonder that Lowndes (B. M. edit 1864, p. 2826) took his word for it, but he made the blunder more obvious by placing "The spectacle of lovers" at the commencement of W. Walter's works, and the "Lytill contravers" at the end of it. We ought to have mentioned (this Vol. p. 86,) that the translation of "Guistard and Sismond" by William Walter, was originally printed by Wynkyn de Worde.

WARNER, WILLIAM.—The first and second parts of Albions England. The former revised and corrected, and the latter newly continued and added. Contain-ing an Historicall Map of the same Island: prosecuted from the lives Actes and La-bors of Saturne, Jupiter, Hercules and Æneas, &c. With historicall Intermixtures, Invention and Varietie: profitably, briefly and pleasantly performed in Verse and Prose by William Warner.—Imprinted at London by Thomas Orwin, for Thomas

Cadman, dwelling at the great North-doore of Sainct Paules Church at the signe of the Bible. 1589. 4to. B. L. 90 *leaves.*

The first edition of this important and amusing historical work was published in 1586, when it was printed by R. Robinson for Thomas Cadman. This is the second impression by a different printer for the same bookseller. With regard to the first edition, we meet with the following remarkable, and, we think, unquoted entry in the Registers of the Stationers' Company, dated 1586:—

"Whereas the Wardens on Monday, the 17th day of October 1586, upon serche of Roger Warde's house, dyd fynd there in printinge a booke in verse intytled Englandes albion, being in English and not aucthorised to be printed, which he had been forbidden to prynte, as well by the L. Archb. of Canterbury, as well as by the Wardens at his owne house. Item, they found there In printinge the grammar in 8vo. belonginge to the priviledge of Mr. F. Flower &c. And for as much as all this he hath done contrarye to the late decrees of the honorable court of Starre chamber, the said Wardens seised three heapes of the said Englandes albyon, and the first leafe of the grammar In 8vo. and three presses and diverse other parcelles of printinge stuffe, by vertue of the said decrees, and accordingly brought them to the Stationers' halle. Whereupon it is now concluded and ordered, accordinge to the said decrees, that the said presses and pryntynge stuffe shalbe made unservyceable, defaced, and used in all pointes accordinge to the tenor of the decrees aforesaid."

It does not appear here precisely whether the fault was in Warner's book, or in Warde's printing of it, unless we are to conclude (as is by no means impossible) that the Archbishop of Canterbury had forbidden "Albion's England," on account of the questionable or objectionable nature of some part of its contents. What the cause might be we are without information, but we can readily imagine that offence may have been taken at various portions of the somewhat eccentric production. The edition before us, of 1589, concludes with "Chap. XXXIII.," ending with the following harsh and obscure lines, where Queen Elizabeth is called Pandora, and where "an ocean" of matter seems proposed to be entered upon in a subsequent impression of the work:—

"Then luckiest of the Planets were predominant, say we,
When this bed-match either heire that bloud-mart did agree,
When Seventh begot the Eight, and Eight the first and last for like
Our now Pandora, ere whose raigne our humbled sayles we strike.
For at her Grandsier reare we up our Colome plaine and poore,
Not writing as did Hercules on his—Beyond no more:
For he lackt search, our Muse lackes skill; an Ocean is in store.
It onelie rests we borrow leave in brevitie to say
Somewhat fore-said, not fullie said, and then is holiday."

Even in 1592, the date of the third edition of Warner's "Albion's England," there must have been some hitch as to the continuation of the subject. It there professes to be in forty-four chapters, divided into nine books, but, singularly enough, Book contains no more than the following enigmatical lines, under the heading of Chap. XLIIII.:—

"Elizabeth by Peace by Warre, for Majestic for Milde
Inriched, Feared, Honor'd, Lov'd, But (loe) unreconcilde,
The Muses Check my sawsie Pen for enterprising her
In duly praising whom themselves, even Artes themselves might err.
Phœbus, I am not Phaeton, presumptuously to aske
What, shuldst thou give I could not gide: gide, give not me thy Task:
For, as thou art Apollo too, our mightie Subject threats
A *non plus* to thy double Power.

Vel volo, vel vellem."

This is succeeded immediately by the word *Finis,* and why the writer had arrived at a *non plus* is not explained. In 1602 (there was an intermediate impression in 1597) the bulk of the work had been swelled to seventy-nine chapters, contained in thirteen books, and the last lines of "Book XIII." are these:—

"Nor perpetuitie my Muse can hope, unlesse in this,
That thy great name, Elizabeth, herein remembred is.
May Muse, arte-graced more then mine, in numbers like supply
What in thine Highnes praise my pen, too poore, hath passed by:
A larger field, a subject more illustrious none can aske
Than with thy scepter and thy selfe his Poesie to taske.
Thy peoples Prolocutor be my prayer, and I pray
That us thy blessed life and raigne long blesse, as at this day."

It seems certain that, at no date, could offence have been taken for any deficiency in Warner's poem of flattery to the Queen. The main features of the production are historical, but into these we need not enter; and Warner makes frequent efforts to lighten his grave subject, and his ponderous style, by episodes, anecdotes, and allusions, sometimes not very well adapted to the place where they are found. For instance, we should not have looked here for the following concentrated versification of a tale, we apprehend, anterior even to Boccaccio:—

"It was at midnight when a Nonne, in travell of a childe,
Was checked of her fellow Nonnes for being so defilde:
The Lady Prioresse heard a stirre, and starting out of bed,
Did taunt the Novasse bitterly, who, lifting up her head,
Sayd, 'Madame, mend your hood;' for why so hastely she rose,
That on her head, mistooke for hood, she donde a Canon's hose.'

The author indulges also in freaks of versification. His triplets are unusually frequent, and in one place (B. VII. ch. 37) he has four-and-twenty successive lines with the same rhyme. This, we own, is rather wearisome, but on the whole his performance is both amusing and informing. The versification is fourteen-syllable lines throughout

"A Continuance of Albions England, by the first Author W. W." came out in 1606' "imprinted by Felix kyngston for George Potter." It is dedicated to Sir Edward Coke, while he was Chief Justice of the Common Pleas. It consists of a 14th, 15th, and 16th book, in the same measure and manner as the preceding portions. At the close Warner calls upon King James to complete his undertaking by worthily treating the reign of Queen Elizabeth, whose acts were "pen-work for a King." The most remarkable portion of this "Continuance" is a preliminary address "To the Reader." in short lines, where the author refers to Chaucer. Spenser, and Stow,—to the tomb built by Brigham in 1556 for the first, to the accidental interment of the second in 1599, and to the starvation of the last in 1605:—

"The Musists, though themselves they please,
Their dotage els finds meede nor ease:
Vouch't Spencer, in that rank preferd,
Per accidens only interrd
Nigh venerable Chaucer, lost
Had not kinde Brigham reard him cost;
Found next the doore, church-outed neere,
And yet a Knight, Arch-lauriat heere.
Adde Stows late antiquarious pen,
That annald for ungratefull men:
Next, Chronicler, omit it not
His licenc't basons little got;
Liv'd poorely where he trophies gave,
Lies poorely there in notelesse grave."

This is very just and highly interesting. The last six lines refer to the license given to old Stow to place basins in different streets, to collect alms from the city he had illustrated by his famous "Survey" seven or eight years before. Warner himself died suddenly in his bed at Amwell, and the event was commemorated in the Register by the vicar, under the date of 1608-9.

Considering the personal particulars to be gleaned from his "Albion's England," it would be singular to find so many blunders regarding his history, if we did not know how little critics generally read even of the works of an author whose biography they are writing. Anthony Wood supposes Warner to have been born in Warwickshire, (***Ath. Oxon.*** edit. Bliss, I. 765,) and A. Chalmers asserts (Biogr. Diet Vol. XXXI. p. 164) that he was a native of Oxfordshire; when Warner himself (whose word ought to be accepted) informs us in ch. 62 that he "first breathed the air in London": from ch. 66 we learn that he began to live in the same year that Elizabeth began to reign. This, too, is a point not hitherto ascertained, and he was therefore only fifty when he died. As to his family, among other matters, he informs us, several times over, that his father had travelled in Muscovy, and had made discoveries that ought to have been remembered and rewarded. Warner also mentions having seen a traitor executed in Essex, who had pretended to be Edward VI.

Warner was praised by Nash for his "Albion's England" in the year after it first appeared. And he himself mentions his "Pan his Syrinx," which originally came out about 1584 (although no such edition is now known,) and was reprinted, "newly perused and amended," in 1597. (Warton, H. E. P. IV. 303, edit 8vo.)

WARREN, ARTHUR.—The Poore Mans passions and Poverties Patience. Written by Arthur Warren. Anno. Dom. 1605.—At London, Printed by J. R. for R. B. and are to be sold in Paules Church-yard at the signe of the Sun. 4to. 40 ***leaves.***

The title truly tells the nature and character of what follows it. Arthur Warren was, at the time he wrote, a prisoner for debt, and he has composed 260 stanzas full of complaints against his poverty, and assertions of the patience with which he bears it. He dedicates the whole, in four six-line stanzas (the form he adopts throughout) "to his kindest favourer, Maister Robert Quarne," and divides the whole of his production into two portions, one called "The Poor man's Passions," and the other "Poverty's Patience." From the latter we select two stanzas, perhaps better than the general ran of the lines, which are some-times crabbed, and not unfrequently conceited:—

"A little Cottage, common cloth, short meales,
Is safest seate, best rayment, surest health,
Not chargeably impayring Publique weales,
And seldom damnify mans private wealth:

It's sumptnous lodge, rich vesture, daintie fare
That robbe the purse,and make Bavenues bare.

"Double and troble chimneis mounting faire
Observe the single Hospitality;
All spent to build and buildings to repayre,
Which should support oppressed misery.
Great halls, large tables, gold plate, little meate
Feed but the eye, while month hath nought to eats."

In this way "the poor man" goes on grumbling and grudging that he is not as rich as some "rascals" whom he could, but does not, name. The piece is singularly deficient in any illustration of manners, and not an incident is employed to vary the monotony. At the same time, it is impossible not to feel some compassion for the sufferer, who seems at one time of his life to have been in much better circumstances. There are five or six known copies of his work.

WARREN, WILLIAM.—A pleasant new Fancie of a fondlings device, Intitled and cald The Nurcerie of names. Wherein is presented (to the order of our Alphabet) the brandishing brightnes of our English Gentlewomen. Contrived and written in this last time of vacation, and now first published and committed to printing, this present month of mery May. By Guillam de Warrino.—Imprinted at London by Richard Jhones, dwelling over against the signe of the Faulcon, neere Holburne Bridge. 1581. 4to. B. L.

Only two copies of this singular production are known, and one of them went successively through the hands of Steevens, the Duke of Roxburgbe, and Perry: the second is in a private collection. The first was that used by Ritson (*Bibl poet.* 386.) who, in merely giving the tide, makes several noticeable variation from the original. Of the second we have availed ourselves, and find the first two pages occupied by Latin and Greek verses, which are followed by "The prœeme to the Gentlemen Readers," subscribed "W. Warren, Gent." Here he claims that the present is his first effort; so that, if it be true, he can hardly have been the same W. Warren for whom Richard Jones, on November 7th, 1579, entered at Stationers' Hall "A pithie and pleasant discourse, dialogue wise, between a wealthy citizen and a miserable soldier, briefly touching the commodyties and discommodyties both of warre and peace." If they were distinct writers, Richard Jones was the publisher for both, and with an interval of only two years. Of the "A pithie and pleasaunt discourse" we know no more than the Register informs us (Extracts II. 73); and William Warren's "Nursery of Names" seems to have been written mainly to pay some extravagant compliments to Queen Elizabeth.

He takes the names of ladies alphabetically, from Anne to Ursula; and when he arrives at Elizabeth he falls into the subsequent rapture, printing the name in capitals:—

"ELIZABETH a noble dame,
a damsell faire and bright;
A dearlyng in our yearthly eyes
bereaves their honour quight!
A jewell rare, a gemme of golde,
a goddesse made of newe;
A Sydus, or celestiall starre,
that boastes of heavenly hewe!
A comete cleare, a Phœnix faire,
extracte of Venus race,
Descended from the line of love
to match Lucinas face!"

When, however, he speaks of the beauty of her figure, which he does at some length, he falls rather into an indecorous bathos:—

"Her waste have nothing waste or vaine,
or wantes that might prevaile,
But, fit and rounde on every side,
agrees from toppe to taile."

Afterwards he partially recovers his former extravagant flight, and continues thus:—

"If all the floating seat were incke,
if paper all the lande;
If trees were pennes, and Muses myne
would take the taske in hande,
The seas would ebbe their incke awaie,
the land be woarne out,
The trees be turned into stubbes,
and pennes obtrite their smowte;
The Muses braines would breake their wittes
before they could descrie
The grace that in her comely corps
and seemely shape doe lye."

Here for "Muses myne" we ought probably to read "Muses **nine**" and Warren's mythological allusions are, in the fashion of the time, pedantically numerous. The names upon which he dwells, besides that of the Queen, are not always among the most poetical: they are Anne, Bridget, Clare, Doritha, Francisca, Grace, Honour, Jane, Catherine, Luce, Margaret, Olyffe, Phrisewit, Rose, Susanna, Thomasin, and Ursula. His motive for choosing some of them was doubtless personal. We ought to mention that he inserts a special address "To the Gentlewomen of England," which he subscribes "your poore poet, and your old friend," as if he were not a young man, or a young author at the time he wrote.

WATSON, THOMAS.—The Tears of Francie, or Love Disdained. Ætna gravius Amor.—Printed at London for William Barley dwelling in Gratius streete over against Leaden Hall. 1593. 4 to. 32 *leaves.*

Only a single copy of the above work is known, and that is deficient of two leaves, containing sonnets numbered 9, 10, 11, 12, 13, 14, 15, 16: all the rest, consisting of 52 sonnets, remain, and the last is subscribed T. W., the only mark of authorship. We may, perhaps, take it for granted that T. W. meant Thomas Watson; for there then existed no other writer, with those initials, at all capable of producing such poems. Nothing is said in it to lead us to the belief that Watson was dead at the time this collection of Sonnets was published; but we know from a stanza in Richard Barnfield's "Affectionate Shepherd" 1594, that at that date he was no more. He thus addresses Watson by a name he had assumed in one of his works—Amyntas:—

"And thou, my sweete Amyntas, vertuous minde,
Should I forget thy learning and thy love,
Well might I be accounted but unkinde,
Whose pure affection I so oft did prove:
Might my poore plaints hard stones to pitty move,
His loss should be lamented of each creature,
So great his name, so gentle was his nature."

Thomas and Watson could not be uncommon names; but in the register of St. Bartholomew the Less, in which parish various literary men resided, we meet with the following entry of a burial, the date of which accords with the period when it is likely that our poet expired:—

"26 Sept 1592. Thomas Watson, gent, was buried."

It has never been anywhere cited, but we have little doubt that it applies to our poet.

In his "Pierce's Supererogation," 1593, Gabriel Harvey twice mentions Watson, once as "a learned and gallant gentleman, a notable poet"; and Nash, in his reply, called "Have with you to Saffron Waldon," 1596, says, "A man he was that I dearely lov'd and honor'd, and for all things hath left few his equalls in England: he it was that, in company of divers gentlemen, one night, at the Nags head in Cheape, first told me of his [Harvey's] vanitie, and those hexameters made of him,—

"But, o! what news of that goodly Gabriell Harvey,
Knowne to all the world for a foole, and clapt in the Fleet for a Rimer?"

Taken literally, the last line affords a new point in the history of Spenser's friend. Watson's **Amynta Gaudia** was printed with the date of 1592, and CM. [*forsan* Christopher Marlowe] in the dedication of it to the Countless of Pembroke, states that the work was posthumous. Watson's "Amyntas" had come out in 1585; but his "passionate Centurie of Lore," a collection of poems in eighteen-line stanzas, was published as early as 1582. Another production by Watson, entitled Compendium Memoriœ localis, *was in the possession of Mr. Heber, bat, at it was imperfect at the end, the date and printer are unknown. In 1581 Watson had published* "Sophoclis Antigone: *Interprete Thoma Watson L V. studioso." He also called himself* Londinensis I V. Studiosus, before bis "Amyntas" in 1585. He was educated at Oxford, (Wood's **Ath. Oxon.** I 601,) and studied the law, and perhaps love, in the metropolis.

"Fancy," as everybody is aware, was an old synonyme for *love,* and the fifty-two sonnets, under the title of "The Tears of Fancie," are all devoted to an unrequited attachment; therefore it is, in allusion particularly to the work before us, that Barnfield, in another part of his "Affectionate Shepheard," speaking of Spenser, Sydney, and Watson as **Amyntas,** tells Cupid,—

"By thee great Colin lost his libertie;
By thee sweet Astrophel forwent his joy;
By thee Amyntas wept incessantly," &c.

"The Tears of Fancy" are printed in Roman type, with the exception of this introductory sonnet, which immediately follows the title-page, but has no signature:—

"Goe, idle lines, unpolisht, rude, and base,
Unworthy words to blason beauties glory,

(Beauty that hath my restless hart in chase,
Beauty the subject of my ruefull story)
I warne thee shunne the bower of her abiding;
Be not so bold, ne hardy as to view her,
Least she inraged with thee fall a chiding,
And so her anger prove thy woes renewer.
Yet, if she daigne to rew thy dreadfull smart,
And reading laugh, and laughing so mislike thee,
Bid her desist, and looke within my hart,
Where shee may see how ruthles shee did strike mee.
If shee be pleasde, though she reward thee not,
What others say of me regard it not."

This address occupies the whole page, but in the rest of the volume there are two sonnets on every page. Sonnet-writing was much in fashion from about 1585 to 1595, and, after the example of Sydney and Daniel, many were produced that never found their way into print, or at all events until some time after they were composed. Most of these by Watson, we may presume, were scattered about in loose papers among his acquaintances. Sometimes they are separate, yet connected in subject, the last line of one forming the first line of another. The following is numbered "Sonnet XXVI.":—

"It pleas'd my Mistres once to take the aire
Amid the value of Love for her disporting.
The birds perceaving one so heavenly faire,
With other Ladies to the grove resorting,
Gan dolefully report my sorrowes endles;
But shee nill listen to my woes repeating,
Bat did protest that I should sorrow friendles:
So live I now and looke for joyes defeating.
But joyfull birds melodious harmonie,
Whose silver tuned songs might well have mooved her,
Inforst the rest to rewe my miserie,

Though she denyd to pittie him that lou'd her.
For shee had vowd her faire should never please me,
Yet nothing but her love can once appease me."

This is gracefully and elegantly worded, but none of Watson's thoughts are new or striking. Throughout he labors to employ double rhymes, and his efforts now and then give a comic effect to what he meant to be serious; as where he says:—

"Here end my sorrowes, here my salt teares stint I,
For she's obdurate, sterne, remorseles, flintie."

The subsequent (Sonnet XLVII.) is, perhaps, the best in the small volume, and it will be observed that the poet only uses one double rhyme in it:—

"Behold, deare Mistres, how each pleasant greene
Will now renew his summers liverie.
The fragrant flowers, which have not long beene seene
Will flourish now ere long in braverie:
But I, alas! within whose mourning mind
The grafts of griefe are onelie given to grow,
Cannot enjoy the spring which others find,
But still my will must wither all in woe.

The lustie ver, that whilome might exchange
My griefe to joy, and my delight increase,
Springs now else where, and showes to me but strange:
My winters woe, therefore, can never cease.
In other coastes his sunne doth clearly shine,
And comfort lend to every mould but mine."

Here we do not see the artificial involution of rhymes observed in the regular Italian sonnet, Watson being content with three ordinary quatrains, closing with a couplet The last sonnet, LX., is peculiar, and we know of no similar example, for every line, but the last two, asks a question, which is answered in the margin thus:—

"Who taught thee first to sigh, Alasse sweet hart?   love.
Who taught thy tongue to marshall words of plaint? love."

After the closing couplet of this sonnet we read "FINIS. T. W.," and the work abruptly ends. A few of the pieces consist of eighteen lines, as is the case with all in the body of the same author's printed probably in 1582: he has there, however, an introductory sonnet, headed "A Quatoryain of the Authour unto his book of Love Passions," which is strictly according to the Italian model. Another, which has never been remarked upon, possesses the singularity of being a mixture of rhyme and blank verse.

WATSON, THOMAS.—Melibæus Thomæ Watsoni, sivè Egloga in Obitum Honoratissimi Viri Domini Francisci Walsinghami, Equitis Aurati, Divæ Eliza-bethæ a secretis & sanctioribus consiliis.—Londini, Excudebat Robertus Robinson us. 1590. 4to. 11 *leaves.*

Thomas Watson, one of the most elegant Latin as well as English versifiers of his day, printed this piece in both languages in the same year. They came out sepa-rately, and probably the translation into English, under the title of "An Eclogue upon the Death of the Right Hon. Sir Francis Walsingham," appeared just subse-quently to the tract before us. It is a dialogue between Corydon and Tityrus, and in the dedication to Thomas Walsingham, son of Sir Francis, Watson says:—

"Dumque ego sum Corydon, Tityrus esse voli:
Ereptum nobis Melibæum flebimus ambo;
Flebimus, at raptum flevit amicus Hylam.
Dignitatis tuæ studiosus,
THOMAS WATSONUS."

Watson's translation of his "Melibæus" is in ten-syllable alternate rhyme. In it he thus mentions Spenser, confessing his own unfitness for the task of praising

Queen Elizabeth:—

"yet lest my homespun verse obscure hir worth,
Sweete Spencer, let me leave this task to thee,
Whose neverstooping quill can best set forth
Such things of state as passe my Muse and me," &c.

Watson is the poet whom Steevens (on the strength of his Passionate Centurie of Love," reviewed at great length in Vol. IV. of the Brit. Bibl.) pronounced "a more elegant Sonneteer than Shakespeare," and perhaps, if mere elegance be considered, the critic was not so far mistaken as many have hitherto supposed. [Note 1: In "the British Bibliographer," IV. 1, it is stated that Watson's Passionate Centurie of Love," was "entered on the Stationers' Books in 1581." This is a mistake from non-observance of the fact, that 31st March, 1581." according to our present mode of reckoning the year, was 1582. Hence we may safely infer that the volume did not make its appearance in the market until the year 1582 was advanced at least three months. See the entry in "Extr. from the Stat. Reg." II. 162. Bitson also (***Bibl. Poet.*** 387) fell into the error of stating that the was "licensed to Cawood in 1581"; and in both editions of Lowndes's Bibl. Man. the date assigned is 1581, but the figures are in parenthesis, to indicate correctly that they are not on the old title-page.] Steevens, however, was not acquainted with Watson's most "elegant" production, which has since been discovered, and forms the subject of the last Article.

WATSON, THOMAS.—The first set of Italian Madrigalls Englished, not to the sense of the originall dittie, but after the affection of the Noate. By Thomas Watson, Gentleman. There are also here inserted two excellent Madrigalls of Master William Byrds, composed after the Italian vaine at the request of the sayd Thomas Watson.—Imprinted at London by Thomas Este, &c 1590. 4to.

This production has always been mentioned in connection with the name of Watson, but we have never seen any extract made from it to enable the reader to judge of its character and quality. It seems to prove, what has not been before noticed, that Watson was a musician as well as a poet, and that he himself composed these Madrigals, after the Italian method, adapting to them hit own words. [Note 1: If the music be not by Watson it is clear that it was not by Byrd, or the "two excellent madrigals" by the latter would not have been separately mentioned.] The title cannot mean that he rendered the Italian verses into English, for it is distinctly stated that he did not English them "to the sense of the original ditty," but "after the affection of the note." MS. Rawlinson 148, Poetry, contains Watson's "gratification" to Dr. Case, for his book in Praise of Music, which was published in English in 1586. The two Madrigals by Byrd, were, like those of Watson, "composed after the Italian vein." We have only here to do with Watson's words, which are mainly in laudation of Sir Philip Sidney, Lady Rich, and Queen Elizabeth. There is not much merit in any of them, as may be judged by the two quotations we are about to make. The first relates to Astrophel and Stella, but really has "small meaning":—

> "When first my heedles eyes beheld with pleasure
> In Astrophell both of nature and beauty the treasure,
> In Astrophell whose worth exceeds all measure,
> My fauning Muse with hot desier surprized
> Wyl'd me entreat I might not be dispysed:
> But gentle Astrophill, with looks unfained,
> Before I spake said, Unles Stella dissembleth,
> Her look so passionate my love resembleth."

The second line certainly halts a little, but probably the music required that irregularity. The next lyric, addressed to Queen Elizabeth, is merely an octave stanza, but sprightly:—

> "This sweet and merry month of May
> While nature wantons in her pryme,
> And birds do sing, and beasts do play
> For pleasure of the joyfull time,
> I chase the first for holly daie
> And greet Eliza with a ryme.
> O! beauteous Qneene of second Troy,

Take well in worth a simple toy."

It almost seems as if nobody could write on the subject of May without pastoral grace and vivacity. In the 19th Madrigal Watson again returns to Sidney, and laments his death, but without any novelty, and omitting all mention of Stella. He also refers to Sir Francis Walsingham, then recently dead; but the author was so fond of the eight lines he had addressed to the Queen on May, that he repeated them at the close of his work. The words throughout are not separately printed, but under the music to which they belong. After all, Watson may not have composed the airs.

WEEVER, JOHN.—Epigrammes in the oldest cut and newest fashion. A twise seven houres (in so many weekes) studie. No longer (like the fashion) not vnlike to continue. The first seuen. John Weever. *Sit voluisse, Sat voluisse.*—At London, Printed by V. S. for Thomas Bushell, and are to be sold at his shop at the great north doore of Paules. 1599. 8vo. 54 *leaves.*

Beloe (Anecdotes, VI. 156) was the first to call attention to the contents of this book, which Ritson only speaks of as "a little book of epigrams, 1599." Beloe used a copy belonging to Combe of Henley, which he supposed to be unique; but there are, at least, two other exemplars of it. The additional notes in Warton (H. E. P. IV. 102, 401, edit. 8vo.) were taken from Beloe, and with Beloe's misprints. The Epigrams have little merit in themselves; bat when we add. that they relate by name to Shakspeare, Spenser, Daniel, Drayton, Warner, Ben Jonson, Marston, &c the volume cannot be looked at without great interest. The author was, perhaps, a friend of Ben Jonson, who in Epigram XVIII (p. 773. edit. 1616) couples him with a much greater poet in the same department. Sir John Davys.

In his dedication to Sir Richard Houghton, of Houghton Tower, the anthor deprecates severity towards his "young Muse"; and it appears elsewhere that he was not twenty when his epigram were written, and that he was only in his twenty-second year when they were published. We may pass over the commendatory verses in English, Latin, and Greek, only distinguished by initials or by unrecorded names; but eight six-line preliminary stanzas by Weever inform us that he was of Cambridge, and especially praise Daniel and Drayton, with a sly hit at Marston, whom, however, he applauds in a subsequent part of his book. From the body of it we select a few pieces on celebrated contemporaries, beginning with Shakspeare. It is Epigram 22 of "the fourth week."

"Ad Gulielmum Shakespeare.

"Honie-tong'd Shakespeare, when I saw thine issue,
I swore Apollo pot them and none other,
Their rosie-tainted features cloth'd in tissue,
Some heaven born goddesse said to be their mother:
Rose-cheekt Adonis with his amber tresses,
Faire fire-hot Venus charming him to love her,
Chaste Lucretia virgine-like her dresses,
Proud lust-stung Tarquine seeking still to prove her.
Romea, Richard, more whose names I know not,
Their sugred tongues and power attractive beuty
Say they are Saints, althogh that Sts. they shew not
For thousands vowes to them subjective dutie:
They burn in love, thy children Shakespear het the,
Go, wo thy Muse, more Nymphish brood beget them."

Here it is to be remarked that Beloe, quoting the above, besides other errors, arbitrarily altered "het," i. e. *heated, to let,* which quite changes the meaning of the writer.[Note 1: Chaucer, in his "Assemble of Foules," uses the same past tense of to *heat:*?"That one me *hette.* that other dyd me colde."] "Romea," for Romeo, was probably a mere misprint, however ignorant Weever professes himself to be of the names of Shakspeare's heroes. The following is important, not merely because it confirms the story of Spenser's extreme poverty at the time of his death, but because it may be said to establish that one of that great poet's minor works, his "Ruins of Time," had actually been called in:—

"In obitum Ed. Spencer, Poetœ prestanties.

"Colins gone home, the glorie of his clime,
The Muses Mirrour, and the Shepheard's Saint.
Spencer is rained, of our later time
The fairest ruine, Faeries foulest want:
Then his **Time ruines** did our ruine show,
Which by his ruine we untimely know:
Spencer therfore thy **Ruines** were cal'd in,
Too soone to sorrow least we should begin."

We must bear in mind, that Spenser's "Ruins of Time" had been written (under the title of **Stemmata Dudleiana**) as early as 1580, that they were devoted to the celebration of Lord Leicester and his family, and that, when printed in 1591, they contained a most severe attack upon Lord Burghley. For these reasons, in all probability, they had been "called in." The subsequent lines to Daniel are also worthy of extraction, relating as they do to the death of Ferdinando, Earl of Derby, who had died in 1594, "not without suspicion of poison, or witchcraft":—

"Ad Samuelem Daniel.
"Daniel, thou in tragicke note excells,
As Rosamond and Cleopatra tells:
Why dost thou not in a drawne bloudy line
Offer up teares at Ferdinandoes shrine?
But those, that e're he di'de bewitcht him then,
Belike bewitcheth now each Poets pen."

In his "Pierce Pennyless," 1592, Thomas Nash, as we know, had blamed Spenser for not having addressed a sonnet to the Earl of Derby, when he printed his "Fairy Queen," in 1590. Weaver's tribute to Drayton also refers to the death of Sidney:—

"Ad Michaelem Drayton.

"The Peeres of heav'n kept a parliament,
And for Wittes-mirrour Philip Sidney sent:

To keeps another when they doe intend,
Twentie to one for Drayton they will send,
yet bade him leave his learning; to it fled
And vow'd to live with thee since he was dead."

We wish we could make room for all the interesting personal matter in this little volume, more particularly, as it has never yet been adverted to in any detail; but we moat be satisfied with the two epigrams which apply to marston, Ben Jonaon, R. allot, the editor of "England's Parnassus," and Christopher Middleton, the writer of the "Legend of Humphrey Duke of Gloucester," which, however, was not published until the year after the date of the appearance of Weever's "Epigrammes."

"Ad Jo. Merston et Ben Johnson.

"Marston, thy Muse enharbours Horace vaine,
Then, some Augustus giro thee Horace merit;
And thine, embuskin'd Johnson, doth retaine
So rich a stile and wondrous gallant spirit,
That if to praise your Muses I desired,
My Muse would muse. Such wittes must be admired."

"Ad Ro. Allol et Chr. Middleton.

"Quicke are your wits, sharp your conceits,
Short and more sweete your layes:
Quicke, but no wit, sharps no conceit,
Short and lesse sweete my praise."

These have very little merit of their own, but they show the estimate of the men in their day. The same may be said of six lines addressed to the founder of

Dulwich College, in which Rome and Roscius are called upon to yield the palm to London and Alleyn. We ought to add that the Epigrams are divided into "weeks," and that each "week" is dedicated to a different patron.

WEEVER, JOHN.—The Mirror of Martyrs, or The life and death of that thrice valiant Capitaine, and most godly Martyre, Sir John Old-castle knight Lord Cobham.—Printed by V. S. for William Wood. 1601. 8vo. 41 *leaves.*

This very uncommon volume (of which we have never seen more than two exemplars) requires attention, not only for its own sake, but because it illustrates both Shakspeare and Spenser. These illustrations appear never to have been suspected; for although various poetical antiquaries have mentioned the book, and one of them quoted several passages from it, (**Restituta,** IV. 476,) nobody has alluded to these sources of increased value. Spenser is applauded by name, and Shakspeare borrowed from without name. The subsequent stanza thus speaks of the death of the former, and of his well-remembered episode of the Marriage of the Thames and Medway:—

"But how he courted, how himselfe he carri'd,
And how the favour of this Nimph he wonne,
And with what pompe Thames was with Medway marri'd
Sweete Spenser shewes (O greefe, that Spensers gone!)
With whose life heavens a while enricht ns more,
That by his death we might be ever pore."

The obligation of Weever to Shakspeare is certainly not great, but it has reference to the battle of Shrewsbury, and to the killing of Hotspur by Prince Henry, in the ensuing stanza:—

"And followed Percie to these civill broiles,
Who made do doubt of Henries victorie,
Emboldened by Scotlands late-won spoiles,
Yet left him slaine behind at Shrewsbury;

And all the armie, ventrous, valorous, bold,
Hote on the spur, now in the spur lie cold."

The lines by Travers, in Henry IV. Part 2, Act I sc. 1, (printed in 1600, and written before 1598,) need hardly be quoted:—

"He told me that rebellion had ill luck,
And that young Harry Percy's spur was cold:"

nor old Northumberland's reply:—

"Said he young Harry Percy's spur was cold?
Of Hotspur coldspur?"

Another illustration of Shakspeare is of a different kind, and relates to the character of Falstaff, who, when the two parts of "Henry IV." were first brought out, was called Oldcastle, though the name was afterwards changed. Weever, in the dedication of his "Mirror of Martyrs," speaks of his hero as "this *first true* Oldcastle," clearly alluding to the *second false* Oldcastle, in Shakspeare's two plays, to whom, however, the name of Falstaff had been given, instead of Oldcastle, before 1598. (See "Shakspeare," publ. by Whittaker and Co., 1858, Vol. III. p. 317 and p. 423.)

WELBY, HENRY.—The Phœnix of these late times: or the Life of Mr. Henry Welby, Esq. who lived at his house in Grub-street forty foure yeares, and in that space was never seene by any, aged 84 &c. With Epitaphs and Elegies &c.—London: Printed by N. Okes and are to be sold by Richard Clotterbuck &c 1637. 4to. 25 *leaves.*

We are informed in the body of this tract, that the subject of it was a man of considerable fortune, who had travelled much, and was of eccentric habits. His reason for retiring from the world is stated to have been a quarrel with a younger brother, who directed a loaded pistol at his head, which missed fire. He withdrew to his house in Grub Street, in 1592, and lived unseen by anybody but an old female servant, until the 29th of October, 1636.

An engraving of the unshaven recluse faces the title-page, which is followed by "the Description of this Gentleman," and two copies of verses upon him, one signed J. B., and the other by Shackerly Marmion. Then comes an account of Welby, and of his mode of life, to which are added Epitaphs and Elegies in verse by Tho. Brewer, J. T., John Taylor, and Tho. Heywood. From the nature of the tract, it is most likely that the prose portion of it was also written by Heywood. His verses are only such as, most likely, his poverty extracted from his pen, and they are not worth quoting. Welby, it seems, had been married, and left behind him a daughter, wife to Sir Christopher Hilliard of Yorkshire.

WELDON, JOHN.—A true Report of the incitement, arraignment, conviction, condemnation and execution of John Weldon, William Hartley, and Robert Sutton: who sufferd for high Treason in severall places about the Citie of London on Saturday the fifth of October. Anno 1588. With the Speaches which passed between a learned Preacher and them: Faithfullie collected, even in the same wordes, as neere as might be remembred. By one of credit that was present at the same.—Imprinted at London by Richard Jones. 1588. 4to. B.L. 12 *leaves.*

The main object of this tract seems to have been to show with what mercy and consideration the criminals were treated. The first two were Roman Catholic priests, who, after having been ordained in Paris, came to this country and resided in London contrary to law. The third man, Sutton, after becoming a Protestant, had been reconciled to Rome, and, though a layman, was executed with the others. The narrative seems to have been drawn up by the "learned Preacher" who had attended the prisoners in their last moments, and had endeavored to convince them of their errors. Their lives were offered to them if they would recant, but they preferred death. It is added, that at one time Sutton's courage nearly failed, but he afterwards recovered his resolution, and died avowing himself a Roman Catholic. All the texts of Scripture quoted against them by the Protestant divine are given in full detail. The men were hanged at different places: Weldon at Mile-end, Hartley at Holywell, "nigh the Theater," (at that date a usual place of execution, on account of the badness of the neighborhood,) and Sutton at Clerken well On the 26th August preceding, a person of the name of Gunter had been hanged "at the Theater," convicted of the same crime at Sutton.

WELL-SPRING.—The Welspring of wittie Conceites: containing a Methode, aswel to speake, as to endight (aptly and eloquently) of sundrie Matters: as (also) see great varietie of pithy Sentences, vertuous sayings and right Moral Instructions: No lesse pleasant to be read, then profitable to be practised, either in familiar speech or by writing, in Epistles and Letters. Out of Italian by W. Phist Student Wisdome is like a thing fallen into the water, which no man can finde, except it be searched to the bottome.—At London, Printed by Richard Jones: dwelling at the Signe of the Rose and the Crowne, neere Holburne Bridge. 1584. 4to. B. L. 51 *leaves.*

It is very likely that the name on the title-page, "W. Phist," may only be an abbreviation for William Phiston, but we have no right so to conclude, as is done in both editions of Lowndes's Bibl. Man.; and on this account we have placed our notice of this highly curious book under the first substantive of its title. It is supposed that W. Phist, or Phiston, was also the writer of a "Lamentation" on the death of Bishop Jewell, 1571, because it is said to have been composed "by W. Ph." (Brit. Bibl. I. 569.) Elderton wrote and subscribed a production of a similar character, and upon the same lamentable event, altogether unknown until it was reprinted in "Roxburghe Ballads," 4to, 1847, p. 139.

Of the work in our hands only two copies are supposed to exist; and it is dedicated, not by the translator, but by the printer, to "Maister David Lewes, Doctor of the Civill Lawes, &c. High Judge of the Admiraltie." Jones states in it that it was the first book that had come from his press since the entrance of the new year, 1584. Then we have"the Author's Preface," from which we learn that it was not merely a version into English of an Italian original, but that he had added other matter, "partly the invention of late writers, and partly mine owne." He claims to have "noted" in the margin where he had been indebted to "auncient and famous" writers, but he unluckily left the remainder without any information as to the modern sources to which he had been indebted.

The great body of the work is prose, and in the form of supposed letters with appropriate headings. At the end of all is a table of contents, but introduced by a few axioms in verse, thus headed, and thus irregularly printed:—

"Certaine worthie sentences, very meete to be written about a Bedchamber, or to be set up in any convenient place in a house.

1. The good Son grafteth goodnes, wherof salvation is the fruit. But the evill planteth vices, the fruit wherof is damnation.

2. Therfore at night call unto minde How thou the day hast spent Praise God if naught amisse thou finde, If aught, betimes repent.

3. Thy bed is like the grave so cold, and sleepe that shuts thine eyes Resembleth death, the clothes the mowlde in grave when as thy body dyes.

4. Therfore let not thy sluggish sleepe close up thy waking eye, Till with advice and judgement deepe thy dayly deedes thou trye.

5. Who any stone in conscience keepes when he quiet goes, More vertuous is then he that sleepes with twenty mortal foes."

There must be some misprint in the first axiom, because "fruit" and "damnation" do not rhyme; but the correction is easily made, as we may feel pretty sure that the word corresponding with "fruit" was *root,* although the old printer became confused, and misplaced, as well as corrupted, the true text.

We should not have said even thus much of this "Well-spring of witty Conceits," had not Ritson at one time, in the course of his distempered attacks upon T. Warton, expressed doubt at to the existence of the book. The contents of the various letters are the mere commonplaces of ethics and morals; and it is singular that, from the first page to the last, there is not one original remark, or one temporary, local, or personal allusion. On this account the work is, in our day, comparatively valueless.

WEST, RICHABD.—The Court of Conscience, or Dick Whippers Sessions. With the order of his arraigning and punishing of many notorious, dissembling, wicked and vitious Livers in this age. By Richard West—Imprinted at London by G. Eld for John Wright, and are to be sold at his shop adjoyning to Christ Church gate. 1607. 4to. 24 *leaves.*

An amusing, but apparently highly colored, work upon manners at the commencement of the seventeenth century, dedicated by Richard West "to his very loving friends" William Durdant and Francis Moore. Thirteen stanzas, of six lines each, commence the proceedings against the criminals before twelve jurymen; and as the author makes the "Upright Judge" and "good Counsel" two of the twelve, it seems as if he were not well versed in the proceedings of courts of criminal judicature. The rest of the jury are poetical impersonations, such as Zealous Patron, Faithful Minister, Godly Magistrate, &c; and after they have been impannelled comes an address "to all and singular Back-byters, Slothful Teachers, Graceless Truants, Cockering Parents, Cheating Thieves, Punkes, Bawds, Witches," &c. Some of the writer's knowledge appears to have been derived from earlier sources, but on the whole there is originality, not only in the accusations, but in the manner in which the arraignments are drawn and the proceedings conducted. There is clearly a good deal of personal allusion, now lost to us; and the following reads as if, in the minuteness of its information, there was an intention to single out some individual. It is headed,—

> *"Backbiter.*
> "You, Mai. Silke-strings, baudy embleme maker,
> Rimer and Ridler, come into the Court;
> Maker of songs by every channel raker,
> You are indited here what, all a-mort?
> Hold up your hand: heare your inditement read:
> Twill cost y'a whipping, ells Ile loose my head.

"And wherefore ist? because you spend your time
All the whole day among your baudy queanes
In ribauld talke and loathsome filthy rymes;
Superfluously it floweth out in streames,
Backbiting all men in a hidden sort.
Come, come, untrusse. O, here is gallaunt sport!

"And more then that; for still yon doe invent,
Sedicious like, gainst all men to exclame
In baudie ballads, being wholly bent,
In sort undecent, men unknowne to blame;
Thinking to excuse your selfe by giving quipps
Gainst those that never deservd your railing nips.

"What should I stand to tell you all your tricks?
I should backbite men, then, as well as you;
Nor yet your rabbles altogether mixe:
It were an endles work, I tell you trew.
A Jail delivyry further I must make
Of other knaves with you that share a stake."

This was too early a date for Martin Parker; and Thomas Deloney, as far as we can judge from what he has left behind him, does not merit any such injurious character: Guy, Climsell, and Price were then either not in existence, or hardly known; and, after all, West may have meant, as in the case of his jury, an abstract impersonation of a ballad-writing and traducing "backbiter."

In Vol. I. p. 63, we have favorably introduced the name of Richard West, as the author of an interesting humorous and poetical production, entitled "News from Bartholomew Fair," of the same date as the chap-book now before us. He was also the writer or collector of the poems inserted in a work called "The School of Ver-tue," 8vo, 1619, one of which, under the title of "The Book of Demeanor," was reprinted in 1817. The R W., who in 1608 published "a Centurie of Epigrams," was a different man, who terms himself on his title-page "Bachelor of Arts of Oxon," and affords evidence that he was a scholar. He may have been the translator of "Merry Jests concerning Popes, Monks and Friars," of which there is a copy in the library of Worcester College, Oxford. It was printed in 1617, (see *post,*) and several times afterwards. R. W., there described as "Bachelor of Arts of H. H. Oxford," gives his name at length.

WHETSTONE, GEORGE.—The Rocke of Regard, divided into foure parts. The first, the Castle of delight: Wherein is reported, the wretched end of wanton and dissolute tiring. The second, the Garden of Unthriftinesse: Wherein are many sweet flowers, (or rather fancies) of honest love. The third, the Arbour of Vertue: Wherein slaunder is highly punished, and vertuous Ladies and Gentlewomen worthily commended. The Fourth, the Ortchard of Repentance: Wherein are discoursed the miseries that follow dicing, the mischiefes of quareling, the fall of prodigalitie &c All the invention, collection and translation of George Whetstons Gent Formæ nulla fides. *4to. B. L. 132* leaves.

This work introduces to us a new name in our poetical annals—that of Robert Cudden of Gray's Inn, who was a friend of Whetstone, and contributed two or three pieces to the collection before us. He is not mentioned by Ritson, Wood, or Warton.

Whetstone speaks of the "Rocke of Regarde" as if it were his earliest work—"the first increase of his barren braine;"—and he promises more and better hereafter, if it were favorably accepted. The date is ascertained from the colophon on sign. R vi., where we read "Imprinted at London for Robert Waley. 1576." We thus learn that Whetstone's second essay in poetry was his "Remembraunce" of Gascoigne, which came out very soon after the demise of that poet in the autumn of 1577. This generally but erroneously, stands first in the list of Whetstone's many publications. As far as we know, he had printed nothing anterior to his "Rocke of Regard," and in it he included many youthful productions. He thus speaks to "the young Gentlemen of England" of himself and of his courses, before he became an author:—

"Some there be that, having eyed my former unthriftinesse, doe gape (per case) to view in this book a number of vaine, wanton and worthless Sonets: in some respectes I have satisfied their expectation, moved to suffer the imprinting of them, not of vaine glorie but of two good considerations: the one to make the rest of the booke more profitable, and (perhaps) lesse regarded the better saileable. The other, and chiefest, in plucking off the vizard of self conceit, under which I sometimes proudly masked with vaine desires."

As there is a long list of the contents of the volume in our hands in **Cens.** Lit. VI. 10, we shall not go in detail over the many productions, divided, as the title-page correctly informs us, into four separate portions, with four several dedications, and "epilogues" to each. Many love-poems are interspersed, and some of them relate personally to Whetstone, who there only gives his initials, G. W. It seems that he fell in love with a lady while she was "bathing at the Bathe," but like others he forbore to declare his passion, and therefore, as he never offered himself, could not well be accepted:—

"The silent man still suffers wrong, the proverbe olde doth say;
And where adventure wants, the wishing wight ne thrives:
Faint heart hath ben a common phrase, faire Lady never wives."

Some of the tales, which he tells at considerable length, were the same as are found in earlier translations. Thus we have the Countess of Celant as in G. Fenton's "Tragical Discourses," and in Painter's "Palace of Pleasure"; and "the Lady of Boheme" as in the latter, which again made its appearance, in a dramatic form, in Massinger's "Picture" [Note 1: In reference to Massinger, it may not be out of place here to notice again his father, Arthur Massinger, who was one of the confidential servants of the Earl of Pembroke, and who, in 1587, (three years after the birth of his son, the poet,) was a solicitor for the reversion of the office of Examiner in the Court of the Marches towards Wales. This is, we believe, a new point in the history of the dramatist's family, and we derive it from an original letter of Lord Pembroke, from which we quote the following paragraph:—

My servant Massinger hathe besought me to ayde him in obteyning a Revercion from tor Majestic of the Examiners office in this Courte, whereunto as I willingly hare yelded, soe I resolved to leave the craving of your Lordships furtherance therein to his owne humble sute; but because I heare a sonne of Mr. Fox (her Majestics Secretory here) doth make sute for the same, and for that Mr. Sherar,whoe noire enjoyethe it, is sicklie, I am boulde to dealer your Lordships honorable favour to my servaunte, which I shall most kindlie accepte, and he for the same ever rest bounde to pray for your Lordship. And thus leaving further to trouble you, &c. 28 Marche 1587."

It is worthy of remark that the whole body of the letter is in the handwriting of the candidate for the place, the signature only being that of Lord Pembroke. It does not appear what was the result as regards the father, but the poverty of the son would indicate that Arthur Massinger] Upon these we need not

The tenor and spirit of the piece may be judged from this speci¬men, and in the end Whetstone gives what he calls "A Larges to the World." It is in this portion of the work that the unknown versemaker, "Robert Cudden of Graves Inn," flourishes. He adopts a lyrical form, and thus addresses his friend. It is part of an "Answer to G. W. opinion of Trades."

"I thought (my George) thy Muse would fully fit
My troubled minde with least of settled doome,
And tell the Trade wherein I sure might sit
From nipping neede in wealthy walled roome;
But, out alas, in tedious tale
She telles the toyles of all,
And forgeth fates t' attend estates,
That seeld or never fall."

This address fills thirteen such stanzas; the last but one being this:—

"The Lawyer he, the man that measures right,
By reason, rule and lawe conjoyned in one,
Thy roving Muse squares much with his delight,
Whose only toyle all states depend upon:
For Lawyer gone, good right adieu;
Dicke Swash must rule the roaste,
And madding might would banish quite
Tom Troth from English coast."

The above does not much whet the appetite for more, but we find Cudden mentioned nowhere else, and perhaps he died early. "Whetstones Invective against Dice," by which he had clearly been a sufferer, fills eighteen pages, and the rest of the volume is apparently made up of his own mishaps and adventures, and of the exposure of four sharpers and cozeners, whom he calls Lyros, Frenno, Caphos, and Pimos, while he himself figures, as well as we can judge, under the name of Plasmos. The last lines of his fourth "Epilogus" are these:—

"All this and more my Muse at large reports
All this my Muse (for your availe) did hit:
In lue whereof she friendly you exhorts
To take in worth what of good will is writ.
Quod cavere possis stultum est admittere."

The whole volume tends to show rather the versatility than the vivacity of Whetstone's Muse.

WHETSTONE, GEORGE.—The English Myrror. A Regard wherein al estates may behold the Conquests of Envy: Containing mine of common weales, murther of Princes, cause of heresies, and in all ages, spoile of devine and humane blessings, unto which is adjoyned, Envy conquered by vertues. Publishing the peaceable victories obtained by the Queenes most excellent Majesty against this mortall enimie of publike peace and prosperitie, and lastly A Fortris against Envy, builded upon the counsels of sacred Scripture, Lawes of sage Philosophers, and pollicies of well governed common weales, &c. By George Whetstone Gent *Malgre.* Seene and allowed.—At London. Printed by I. Windet for G. Seton, and are to be sold at his shop under Aldersgate. 1586. 4to. B. L. 129 *leaves.*

This elaborate work, which is not of very uncommon occurrence, is divided into three books, the second and third having distinct title-pages. The second is called "Envy conquered by Vertue," and has upon it, besides, "A Sonnet of triumph to England" in eleven lines: the third is called "A fortresse against Envy," with the name of the author repeated as George Whetstone. Each book, like his "Rock of Regard," has its separate dedication. The first (after an acrostic to "Elizabeth Regina," at the back of the title-page) has a dedication to the Queen, followed by an address to the Nobility of England, and by commendatory verses by R. B., who asserts that "the Muses have always blessed the author's pen." A note, preceding a list of *errata,* shows that the volume was printed in the absence of Whetstone, who was at that date in Flanders. The second book is dedicated to "the Bishops and other devines of England"; and the third book to "the temporall majestrates of England."

The earliest division of the work contains a great many, then novel and interesting, details of foreign history, including the wars between the Guelphs and Ghibelines, the battle of Alcazar and the death of King Sebastian, with the calamities of France, Flanders, and Scotland. The second division relates more particularly to domestic affairs, and commences with a poem on "the blessings of peace." It treats of the immediate predecessors of Elizabeth, of the Tudor family, and of the accession of the Queen, with all its ceremonies. It afterwards notices her "peaceable victories" in Scotland, over the rebels in the North of England, &c., together with her preservation from various attempts at assassination, especially that of Dr. Parry, which was then recent. Campion and Throckmorton come in for a large share of abuse, and the book ends with an exhortation to English fugitives. The third division applies chiefly to internal government, to the duties of good kings and the ends of tyrants, to the "high calling of the nobility," to the "reverend calling of the clergy," to the "honourable calling" of judges, justisers, the reputation of lawyers, &c. In the course of this chapter Whetstone tells a short anecdote in verse, which may be quoted as not a bad specimen of his skill, although the jest itself is very venerable:—

"A poore man once a Judge besought
to judge aright his cause,
And with a glasse of Oyle salutes
this judger of the lawes.

"My friend, quoth he, thy cause is good:
he glad away did trudge.
Anon his wealthy foe did come
before this partiall judge.

"A hog well fedde the churle presents,
and craves a straine of law:
The hog received, the poor mans right
was judg'd not worth a straw.

"Therewith he cri'de, O partiall judge,
thy dome hath me vndone!
When Oyle I gave my cause was good,
but now to ruine runne.

"Poore man, quoth he, I thee forgot;
and see thy cause of foile;
A hog came since into my house
and broke thy glasse of Oyle.

"Learne, friends, by this, this reade of me:—
Smal helpes a vertuous cause,
When giftes do catch both Gods and men,
and friendship endeth lawes."

There are other pieces of verification in this third book, and the last chapter consists entirely of moral and didactic couplets, the last being the following:-

"As I began, so I conclude; let all men fear the Lord,
And Preachers see that godly workes with holy words accord."

As a whole, this production, by a man of considerable learning and ability, in its different parts is both instructive and amusing. At the close is a renewed address "to the Reader" in which Whetstone introduces a sort of puff of his "Mirror for Magistrates of Cities," which had been printed in 1584, bat never became popular.

WHETSTONE, GEORGE.—The Honorable Reputation of a Souldier: With a Morall Report of the Vertues. Offices, and (by abuse) the Disgrace of his profession. Drawn out of the lives, documents, and disciplines of the most renowned Romaine, Grecian, and other famous Martialistes. By George Whetstone, Gent *Malgre de Fortune.*—Imprinted at London by Richard Jones: dwelling neere Holburne Bridge. 1585. 4to. B. L. 22 *leaves.*

On the title-page is a woodcut, half-length, of a man in armor, merely the representative of a soldier, not unfrequently found in other places, appropriate and inappropriate. It has been, however, sometimes considered a portrait of Whetstone, and in our day we have seen it reëngraved for that purpose. No portrait of Whetstone is extant, that we are aware of.

The tract before us was hastily printed by its author,. in order, not so much to vindicate the reputation of soldiers, as to encourage persons to join that profession, the Queen being at that particular time in want of men to assist the United Provinces in their straggle against Spain. It was in July, 1585, that a large body of men, clothed and furnished at the expense of the City, was transported to the Low Countries (Stow's *Ann.,* 1605, p. 1187). It appears that Whetstone had already prepared his larger work, "The English Mirror," for publication; but as its bulk delayed its appearance at this juncture, he put forth the portion of it, here called "The honourable Reputation of a Soldier," before the rest, with a view to the effect it might produce in procuring volunteers for the public service. The rest of the work was deferred until the following year, when, however, it came out from the hop of a different stationer.

The small performance in our hands consists merely of a dry collection of examples from Plutarch, Aulus Gellius, &c, of ancient military services, all tending to the exaltation of the military character; but as there is no single instance obtained from modern history, we need not dwell upon its contents. It is dedicated to Sir William Russell, and there Whetstone admits that he was only forestalling his "English Mirror." He says nothing of his motive for hastening the publication of a part of it, but the circumstances of the time called for it, and he doubtless anticipated for it a good sale. Whether he was disappointed or not, copies of it are now very rare—more so than of his extended work, "The English Mirror." He does not here profess to be a soldier, capable of giving instruction in the military art, observing, "I myselfe have been brought up among the Muses."

As some proof of his qualifications in this respect, he prefixes a poem addressed "To the right valiant Gentlemen and Souldiers that are, or shalbe armed under the Ensigne of Sainct George." It begins,—

"God with S. George! Allon[s], brave Gentlemen,
Set speares in rest," &c.

And afterwards proceeds,—

"Thou art at fierce as is an Englishman,
The French still say, and proofe the same did teach:
Turne you the French into Castillian;
It hath a grace in such a loftie speach.
Your cause is good, and Englishmen you are:
Your foes be men, even as the Frenchmen were."

It consists of only five such stanzas, and in the last Whetstone that refers to his own want of good fortune:—

"I say no more, bat God be your good speede,
And send you hap, which I did never taste;
And if this booke yoa do witsafe to reade,
you cannot thinke your labour spent in waste,
Which doth containe the morall rules of those
That followed Mars in thickest preace of foes."

The only passage in the prose portion, at all of a modern complexion, has reference to excess in apparel, which, we are told, often induced young people to become soldiers, forgetting the hardships and perils they would have to endure. Whetstone admits, however, that he had never himself experienced the sufferings his pen depicts; and after passing allusions to the victories of Edward III. and Henry V. he ends with the subsequent exhortation to the troops, then on their way to Flanders: "And therefore, you worthy Gentlemen, which are armed in Gods and her Majesties service, for that your quarrell is grounded upon compassion and justice, and polliticke judgement for the safetie of your owne countrey, I hope (which thousands desire) you shall returne attired with your enimies overthrowe."

WHETSTONE, GEORGE.—A Remembraunce of the wel imployed life and godly end of George Gaskoigne Esquire, who deceassed at Stalmford in Lincolne Shire, the 7 of October 1577. The reporte of Geor. Whetstons, Gent an eye witnes of his Godly and charitable end in this world. Formœ nulla Fides.—Imprinted at London, for Edward Aggas, dwelling in Paules Churchyard, and are there to be solde. 4to. B. L. 8 *leaves.*

Only a single copy of this brief and valuable piece of biography is extant; but, as it has been twice reprinted in modern times, last at Bristol in 1815, we are not about to give any quotations from it, but merely to establish how very imperfectly the work of reprinting was done, even by the editor in 1815, who pointed out nine serious blunders committed by Chalmers five years earlier. We have gone over the whole piece, and are in a condition to show that the corrector of Chalmers, whoever he may have been, either from carelessness or incompetence, himself committed quite as many and as gross errors as he had detected in his predecessor.

Thus on p. 4, we have **garbe** misprinted for "garde": on p. 5, **set free** for "scot free": on p. 6, **lungs** for "tungs," *i. e.* tongues: on p. 9, **stinted** for "flirted," and **heard alone** for "wounds alone": on p. 11, **many** for "manly," and **loothsome** for "toothsome": on p. 15, **fear** for "force," while "for" is entirely omitted in one place, and misprinted **from** in another: on p. 17, **payre** is put for "payze," *i e.* weigh; and on p. 19 the sense and measure are destroyed by the omission of the preposition "of." These are only verbal defects; but the edition of 1815 also left out nearly all the marginal notes, stating the services of Gascoigne in the army, his imprisonment, and the unpublished productions he left behind him. To these are to be added other marginal notes, in which the dying poet is made to speak by name of his "Glasse of Government," of his "Steele Glasse," of his "Diet for Drunkards," and of his book on "Hunting." These had been printed.

Upon these matters Whetstone received information from Gascoigne himself; and therefore avoided such a strange blunder as he was guilty of, ten years afterwards, when he attributed Spenser's "Shepherd's Calendar" to Sir Philip Sidney. (See "Life of Spenser," 1862, Vol. I. p. xxxvii.") This blunder is the more inexcusable, because in his address "to the Reader" Whetstone severely called to acccount persons who had been guilty of error "for lacke of true instruction, and to the injurie that they did unto so worthy a gentleman." Whetstone's "injury," it is true, was to Spenser, not to Sidney. (See also Poet. Decam. 1820, Vol. I. p.64.)

WHETSTONE, THE.—The Whettstone. A Pake of Knaves. 4to. 20 **leaves.**

This is a series of twenty copperplates of foreign execution, probably Dutch or Flemish, without date, place, publisher's or engravers's name. The first plate forms the title-page, and represents a young man, dressed in the fashion of the time, throwing a whetstone, whim the words "The Whettstone" and "A Pake of Knaves." are placed above and behind the figure. "Hurting the Whetstone" was a phrase apparently equivalent to "throwing the hatchet"; and, with reference to it, on page 21 of our first volume, a tract is noticed, with the title, "Four great liars striving who shall win the Silver Whetstone." "Throwing the hatchet" is derived from the tale of a man who was so incredibly skilful, that he was able to throw a hatchet at a distant tree and sever it: "harling the whetstone" was an exaggeration of a similar kind, in which another man asserted that, but for his "hurling the whetstone," and sharpening the hatchet on its way, the achievement could never have been accomplished. Underneath the earliest engraving are the following lines:—

"The Whettstone is a knave that all men know,
Yet many on him doe much cost bestowe:
Hee's us'd almost in every shoppe, but whye?
An edge must needs be set on every lye."

Each plate is accompanied by four lines descriptive of, or applicable to, the subject of it The following is a list of the engravings, accompanied by some of the best of the verses:—

"The Busye.
The Sleepelove.
The Flye.
Sweetlipps.
The Damee."

"Dammees a rouing knavve that weares good clothes,
If his credit serve: his prayer are his oathes.
Hee's stout where sure he cannot be out brav'd,
And swears by God, but hardly will be sav'd."

"The Graceless.
The Sawce box.
Surley.
The nere be good.
The Overdoo."

"The double dilligent, or one that will

More then's comanded offer to fullfill,
Is a right Overdoe: who'ld care for such?
Tis better to doe little then to[o] much."

"Flatterall.
Noethrift
Much-craft.
A Prater."

"The prating knavve, whether tis right or wrong,
Is one that spight of all will use his tongue.
Whose talking humour never will admitt
Of silence, though his life depends one it."

"Swillbottle.
The Nastye.
A Cokes."

"A Servant by his Master sent a broad,
Or with a message, or some usefull load,
And stayes to gaze on strangers differing clokes,
Sightes, parrots, novvelties, is a right Cokes."

"A mere Scullion.
All-hidd."

The peculiar spelling of some of the words in the inscriptions shows that they were engraved by a person who did not understand English. The date of publication (if the plates were ever published) was, perhaps, the early part of the reign of Charles I.

WHIP FOR AN APE.—A Whip for an Ape: or Martin displaied.

Ordo Sacerdotum fatuo turbatur ab omni,
Labitur et passim Religionis honos.

4to. B. L. 4 *leaves.*

John Laneham, the famous actor, who was a leading member of the Earl of Leicester's Players in 1574, and was, in all probability, nearly related to Robert Laneham, or Langham (see Vol. II. p. 227), seems to have been the author of the singular and amusing tract before us; and although he does not place his name on the title-page, nor subscribe the verses at the close, he mentions himself near the end as the writer of the rhymes before us:—

"Leave Apes to doggs to baite, their skins to crowes,
And let old Lanam lashe him with his rimes."

He was an elderly man in 1592, and he had outlived Tarlton four years, whose death is thus by him commemorated:—

"Now Tarlton's dead, the Consort lackes a Vice,"

which of itself shows the connection, or rather identity, of the Vice of the ancient moralities with the Clown of the then popular drama. The whole piece may be said to establish that Laneham, to a certain extent, had taken Tarlton's place as an extempore rhymer. To present Laneham as an author, whose work was printed, is to give him a new character; for although we know that his popular rival, Robert Wilson, left behind him at least one comedy, and assisted in many others, it has not been supposed that Laneham was more than a comic performer. It now appears that his celebrity in that department led the enemies of the Puritans to avail themselves also of his literary services. It will be observed, however, that no printer nor stationer ventured to put a name at the bottom of the title-page, and the first stanza affords a curious proof that corresponding caution was sometimes used upon the stage:—

"A Dizard late skipt out upon our stage,
Bui in a sacke, that no man might him see;
And though we knowe not yet the paltrie page,
Himselfe hath Martin made his name to bee:
A proper name, and for his feates most fit,
The only thing wherein he hath shewd wit."

Thus we learn the manner in which Martin Marprelate, in one instance at least, had, as the Puritans often and loudly complained, been "brought upon the boards of a public theatre." The subsequent stanza mentions two persons whom Nash had made famous in one or more of his prose satires:—

"Now out he runnes, with Cuckow, king of May;
Then in he leapes with a wild Morrice daunce;
Then strikes he up Dame Lawsens lustie lay,
Then comes Sir Jeffries ale tub, tapde by chaunce:
Which makes me gesse (and I can shrewdly smell)
He loves both t' one and t' other passing well."

Here "lay" is misprinted, in the hastily published original, *lap,* but the rhyme detects the blunder. Laneham's last stanza is this:—

"And this I warne thee, Martin Monckies face;
Take heed of me: my rime doth charme thee bad.
I am a rimer of the Irish race,
And have already rimde thee staring mad:
But if thou ceaseat not thy bald jests to spread,
Ile never leave till I have rimde thee dead."

The above, if it were wanted, would form an apposite note to "As You Like It," Act III. sc. 2, where Shakspeare speaks of the fetal effects of rhymes upon Irish rats. Laneham is here clearly referring to Irish rhymes, which may have been the origin of the proverb. His penultimate unmusical line was, possibly, meant to be characteristic.

WHIPPING OF RUNAWAYS.—Londoners Entertainment in the Countrie. Or the Whipping of Runnawayes. Wherein is described Londons Miserie. The Countries Crueltie. And Mans Inhumanitie.—At London Printed by H. L. for C. B. 1604. 4to. B. L. 16 *leaves.*

A tract directed against those who ran away from the mortality of the plague, which had been raging in London;[Note 1: For another brief notice of this pamphlet see Vol II., p. 274, under LONDONERS.] and after the title-page we read the following heading of a page:—

"London to thy Citizens, especially to such right Honourable, right Worshipfull, and others, as were thy true-borne, ministring comfort to thee in time of visitation. Health, peace and plentie."

This is a brief and laudatory address to those who had remained in the afflicted capital to discharge their charitable duties; but, with some inconsistency, in the commencement of the body of his work, the writer cites "the Physicians advice, *Cito fugere, longe abesse, tarde redire,*" as the only safeguard from infection. Of course, the malady is attributed to the vioes of the kingdom, in spite of the redeeming virtues of the new King. The production is made up of verse and prose—the latter of the ordinary kind and of the usual import, and the former very little better. The following is called "an Ælegie", but it is more properly an Ecologue, by a shepherd "on the downs of Bucking-hamshire," lamenting over his flock:—

"No wonder though I waile,
my sheepe are poore;
Yet sorrowes naught availe,
for all my store.

The Sommers prime is winter unto mee,
My flocks are gaunt: no wonder though they be.

"My joy and comfort dies,
drown'd up in woe:
My Lambes by my moist eies
my sorrowes know:

They scorne to lire, since they my living feare,
And pine to see their masters pining cheere.

"Hust, silence I leave thy cave,
thy cave obscur'd,
And deigne my woes a grave,
woes long endur'd.
Though thou leave me, yet take my sorrows to thee,
Or leaving them, alas! thou doo'st undoe me.

"Silence, mov'd to pitty,
Sy. Wherefore undon?
Shep. Wayling for a City,
woeful London!

Whilst Loudon smyl'd my flocks did feede them ful
Skipping for joy that London had their wull.

"Woe is mee! they die now,
cause they feede not:
Shepheard Swaynes must flie now,
cause they speede not:

Yet when I pipe and sing that London smileth,
My sheepe revive againe, and death beguileth.
"Wherefore, silence, pittie
my Lambes mourning,

Joine in our sad dittie
till woes turning.

Sy. Mourne, Swaynes, mourne sheep, and silence wil weepe by you, And as you weepe, for mercie, Shepheards, cry you."

This is poor stuff, and' afterwards what is really an elegy, but is miscalled "an Æglogue," is no better, excepting that it is shorter. The tract was a performance merely for the day; but, as we never saw more than one copy of it, we have thought it worth a brief notice.

WHIPPING OF THE SATIRE.—The Whipping of the Satyre.—Imprinted at London for John Flasket 1601. 12mo. 48 *leaves.*

This production is directed principally against three celebrated authors,—John Marston, Ben Jonson, and Nicholas Breton. A long prose and prosing address, with which it opens, "To the vayne-glorious, the Satyrist, Epigrammatist, and Humorist," is subscribed W. J., and these letters also follow eight hexameter and pentameter verses, "Ad Lectorem." It is possible that they are the initials reversed of John Weever, who, as we have just seen, on page 227, himself published a collection of Epigrams in 1599, but who might nevertheless subsequently have "changed his copy," by attacking the species of writing he had practised. We know that this course was adopted by more than one dramatist. None of the three poets whom W. J. assails are mentioned by name, but they are sufficiently indicated by pointed allusions, and by the mention of their productions. Thus, on sign. D 2, we meet with these lines:—

"But harke, I heare the Cynicke Satyre crie,
A man, a man, a Kingdome for a man!"

This exclamation is from Marston's "Scourge of Villany," 1598, Sat. VII., where he parodies a well-known passage in Shakespeare's "Richard III" Again, in reference to the title of Marston's volume, W. J. says:—

"He ***scourgeth villanies*** in young and old,
As boys scourge tops for sport on Lenten day."

The allusions to Ben Jonson and Nicholas Breton are rendered even more distinct by marginal notes, and are contained in the division of W. J.'s work headed, "***In Epigrammatistam et Humoristam,***" where we meet with the following stanzas, a form of writing that is observed throughout:—

"It seemes your brother ***Salyre,*** and ye twayne,
Plotted three wayes to put the Divell downe:
One should outrayle him by invective vaine:
One all to flout him like a countrey clowne;
And one in action on a stage out-face,
And play upon him to his great disgrace.

"You ***Humorist,*** if it be true I heare,
An action thus against the Divell brought,
Sending your humours to each Theater,
To serve the writ that ye had gotten out,
That Mad-cap yet superiour praise doth win,
Who, out of hope, even casts his cap at sin."

At the bottom of the page, with marks of reference, are two notes "Against the booke of Humours," and "Pasquils Mad-cap." But for the assertion, that the "book of Humours" had been represented at "each theatre," it might have been supposed that the attack was levelled against Samuel Rowland's "Humor's Ordinarie," a collection of satires and epigrams, (see ROWLANDS, Vol. III. p. 346.) "A book" was not, at this period, an uncommon designation for a play. Five years after W. J. wrote, Barnabe Rich in his "Faults, and Nothing but Faults," tells us, "As for the humorous, they have beene alredie brought to the stage, where they have plaide their partes, ***Everie man in his humour.***"

"Pasquil's Mad-cap and his Message" is one of Nicholas Breton's acknowledged productions, and it was printed in 1600. (See Vol. I. p. 107.) This notice ought not to be concluded without quoting the subsequent stanza, containing a very early mention of Falstaff and John of Gaunt:—

"I dare here speake it, and my speach mayntayne,
That Sir John Falstaffe was not any way
More grosse in body then you are in brayne:
But whether should I (helpe me nowe, I pray)
For your grosse brayne you like J. Falstaffe graunt,
Or for small wit suppose you John of Gaunt."

The allusion no doubt is to Shakspeare's Falstaff; but probably not to **his** John of Gaunt, to whom "small wit" can in no sense properly apply.[Note 1: Perhaps the writer, when he speaks of the "small wit" of John of Gaunt, had in his mind what Richard II. (Act II. sc. 1) says of him, when ha calls Gaunt "lean-witted."] Possibly, W. J. refers to the John of Gaunt of an old play of "Richard II.," which preceded Shakspeare's, and where the Duke of Lancaster might be represented as a man of "small wit," or weak understanding. ("See New Particulars regarding the Works of Shakespeare," p. 68.)

"The Whipping of the Satyre" produced an anonymous reply in the same year, called "The Whipper of the Satyre, his Pennance in a White Sheete," &c, which was followed by "No Whipping nor Tripping, but a kind of Snipping," also printed in 1601.

WHITE, T.—A Sermon Preached at Pawles Crosse on Sunday the ninth of December, 1576, by T. W.—Imprinted at London by Francis Coldock. 1578. 8vo. B. L. 49 *leaves.*

The particular day of publication in 1578, namely, "February 10," is given in the colophon, but the Sermon of course relates to the year 1576, when it was delivered at Paul's Cross. It is curious in a dramatic point of view, because it contains the earliest notice of regular theatres in London constructed for the purpose of representing plays. "Look," exclaims the vehement author, "but uppon the common playes in London, and see the multitude that flocketh to them, and followeth them: behold the sumptuous Theatre houses, a continuall monument of London's prodigalitie and folly. But I understand they are now forbidden bycause of the plague: I like the pollicye well, if it holde still, for a disease if but bodged, or patched up, that is not cured in the cause; and the cause of plagues is sinne, if you looke to it well: and the cause of sinne are playes: therefore the cause of plagues are playes." In the same strain he inveighs against "the horrible enormities and swelling sins are set out by those stages," and loudly calls upon the authorities to put them down. White's arguments happily did not prevail.

The whole sermon affords an amusing, but probably not a very faithful picture of the manners of London at that date, and especially of the mode in which Sunday was spent by all ranks. It is to be borne in mind that the "sumptuous Theatre houses," built for the performance of plays, were then open on the Sabbath day; and in 1575-76 the Theatre and Curtain had been erected in Shoreditch, and about the same date a third "play house" was constructed in Blackfriars.

Of Sunday amusements generally, the preacher says: "Assuredly we come nothing neere the Jewes in this pointe; for on our Sabbothes all manner of games and playes, bankittings and surfettings are very rife. If any manne haue any businesse in the world, Sonday is counted an idle day. . . . Every man followeth his owne fansie. And the wealthiest Citizens have houses for the nonce: they that have none make shift with Alehouses, Tavernes and Inns, some rowying on the water, some roving in the field, some idle at home, some worse occupied. Thus what you gette evelly all the weeke is worst spent on the Sabboth day."

In Vol. III. p. 213, we have given a succinct list of the various productions between 1577 and 1587, for and against theatres and dramatic performances. Perhaps we ought to have commenced with the sermon before us, delivered in 1576, although not printed until 1578; but its general object was different, and it only touches upon the construction and employment of playhouses incidentally. It is, however, as we have said, curious as being the earliest known mention in our language of public theatres, erected in or near London for the purpose of dramatic representation.

WHITE, TRISTRAM.—The Martyrdome of Saint George of Cappadocia: Titular Patron of England, and of the most Noble Order of the Garter.—Printed at London for William Barley, dwelling in Bishopsgatestreete. 1614. 4to. 16 **leaves.**

Nobody has given the name of the author of this curious tract, although it stands at the end of one of the two dedications. The first is by the publisher to "his worshipfull good friend Mr. George Shilliton, Justice of Peace," &c, and the last by Tristram White, "to all the noble honourable and worthy in Great Brittaine, bearing the name of George." White merits notice, if only because he has the good sense and good taste to quote Spenser (the earliest illustration ever drawn from our great romantic poet) in reference to St George and his history. He does not give Spenser's name, but speaks of him as the author of "the Faerie Queene," and cites Lib. I. Cant. 10, st. 60, but it is really stanza 66 of that Canto.

"Thence she thee brought into this Faery lond," &c.

He adduces four other lines on the supposed birth of St George in England, and adds in his margin: "In S. George's English birth the Poet followes the vulgar errour, of purpose to fit his fabulous morall argument the rather." White's position, of course, is that St George was really born in Cappadocia. Near his commencement he thus describes his hero:—

"Saint George was all which Knight-hood can require:
His noble birth he much more noble made
By worthy deedes; the riches which he had
(And store he had) were but his vertues foiles.
Christ had the honour of his gotten spoyles.
Youth, Beautie, Grace in Court, Health, Vigor, Fame,
Or what else this fraile elemented frame
Of humane nature may support, he had;

And (which is more then mortall power can adde)
A spirit, Maister of his earthly parts,
Blest with high vertues, deckt with goodly Arts."

No particular fault can be found with this passage; but, we apprehend, that it is the best in the whole poem, which is desultory, and gives as no new information about St. George, not even regarding his victory over the dragon. White thus speaks of St, George's Chapel, Windsor, founded by Edward III:—

—"that brave chappell which doth lift the head
With pinacles and turrets garnished,
Above the wals of that triumphant seat
Whose rockie foote Thames overflowne doth beate,
By that victorious monarch reared was
To George's name, that none in sight can passe
Of windsors Towers (our England's best-built pride)
To whom this honor is not testifide."

Most of White's effusion is weak and unimpressive, and when he now and then breaks out with more fire and energy, he cannot sustain his fight, and drops down into the feeble and the familiar. Thut after such lines as the following,—

"Come you that languish in obscure retreats,
Whose bloud by fits true love of glory heates,
Shake off weake thoughts, and in this glasse behold,
What ods betweene the rash and rightly bolde;"

we might expect that he would continue at the same elevation; but what immediately succeeds is tame and prosaic.

In truth the most interesting portion of the work, with reference to the progress of our language, comes at the end. The main subject not entirely filling the last sheet, the author added a page of what he calls "Sapphicks" in English, and another page which he heads, "A soveraigne sure Remedie against the Seaven chiefe Sinnes." The last consists of fourteen lines, not worth extraction, but more in the form of an Italian sonnet than was usual with our poets of that day. The Sapphics we take to be rather a novel experiment, but it is not a happy one, and the measure is not sapphic, or anything like it, excepting by giving weight to syllables, which they were never meant to sustain. It thus opens:—

> "O my deare-bought soule! to thy God Creator
> No rebell be thou; for alas too feeble
> Is thy fraile temper set against his wils force:
> Thunder obeyes him."

This reads like mere prose, unless we give unwarrantable emphasis to the word "wils" in the third line, and the two preceding lines are a hobbling sort of measure. The same remark will apply to the conclusion, and especially to the pronoun "him" in the third line:—

> "O my deare bought soule! to thy God Redeemer
> Simply be subject, for alas without him
> Devels nothing hopefull: then O Soule! to him still
> Simply be subject."

The above might be meritorious as a first attempt of the kind, but it is anything but satisfactory, even to a moderately correct ear. The title-page contains, in a circle, an extremely good woodcut of St. George's great achievement, of which, singularly enough, White says little or nothing.

WILKINS, GEORGE.—The Painfull Adventures of Pericles Prince of Tyre. Being the true History of the Play of Pericles, as it was lately presented by the worthy and ancient Poet John Gower.—At London Printed by T. P. for Nat Butter, 1608. 4to. B. L.

We were the first, about thirty years ago, to direct attention to this volume, as a peculiar and especial literary curiosity. In fact, it is the only known early relic of the kind in our language. It is a novel constructed out of a play, and that play by Shakspeare. We have various novels upon which dramas were founded, but this is the single specimen of a narrative founded upon a drama.

But two copies of it are in existence,—the one, unfortunately imperfect, in the British Museum; the other quite complete, and preserved in the Public Library of Zurich. It was reprinted at Oldenburg, under the care of Professor Mommsen, in 1857, and so many copies of that reprint have been circulated in England that it is unnecessary for us here to dwell upon it. Our principal reason for noticing it at all is to supply from the Zurich copy what is wanting in our English one, namely, the dedication of it to a private individual. We transcribe it exactly, not from a manuscript, but from a photograph of the original, so that mistake is impossible. It is of the more value because it ascertains, what was not before known, the name of the author, George Wilkins, regarding whom we have already said nearly all that is necessary. (See Vol. I. p. 248.) His dedication of "The Painfull Adventures of Pericles "runs precisely as follows:—[Note 1: The copy in the British Museum is deficient of the dedication, and so far imperfect; we are, therefore, the more glad to be able to furnish it from a photograph of the original, kindly forwarded to us by Professor Tycho Mommsen.]

"To the Right Worshipfull and most woorthy Gentleman Maister Henry Fermor, one of his Maiesties Iustices of Peace for the Countie of Middle sex, health and eternall happinesse.

"Right woorthy Sir, Opinion, that in these daies wil make wise men fooles, and the most fooles (with a little helpe of their owne arrogaucie) seeme wise, hath made me euer feare to throw my selfe vpon the racke of Censure, the which euerie man in this latter Age doth, who is so oner hardie to put his witte in print. I see Sir, that a good coate with rich trappings gets a guy Asse entraunce in at a great Gate (and within a may stalke freely) when a ragged philosopher with more witte shall be shutte foorth of doores: notwithstanding this I know Sir, that Vertue wants no bases to vpholdo her, but her owne kinne. In which certaine assuraunce, and knowing that your woorthie Selfe are of that neere alliaunce to the noble house of Goodnesse, that you growe out of one stalke, A poore infant of my braine comes naked vnto you, without other clothing than my loue, and craues your hospitalitie. If you take this to refuge, her father dooth promise, that with more labored houres he can inheighten your Name and Memorie, and therein shall appeere he will not die ingratefull. Yet thus much hee dares say, in the behalfe of this, somewhat it containeth that may inuite the choicest eie to reade, nothing heere is sure may breede displeasure to anie. So leauing your spare houres to the recreation thereof, and my boldnesse now submitting it selfe to your censure, not willing to make a great waie to a little house, I rest

> "Most desirous to be held all yours,
> "GEORGE WILKINS."

The above reads, in one place, as if it had been the writer's first work,—as if he had not before "thrown himself upon the rack of censure,"—but we are sure that if he had not written the play called "The Miseries of Inforst Marriage," (which we impute to the elder George Wilkins, who died in 1603,) nor the tract of the "Three Miseries of Barbary," which came out, with out date, early in the reign of James I., yet that he must have aided Thomas Dekker in the tract entitled "Jests to make you Merry," which was published in 1607. (Vol. I. p. 247.) An author's averments of insufficiency are to be received with caution, because he is always anxious to make out the best case he can for the considerate judgment of his readers.

It will be observed that Wilkins makes no avowal of the source of the incidents he narrates, leaving that point to the statement on his title-page, namely, that his tract contained "the true history of the Play of Pericles," which had been "lately presented" at the Globe Theatre, by "the worthy and ancient Poet John Gower," who, we all know, had been "the presenter" of Shakspeare's drama. The resemblances between the two, and how far the narrative by Wilkins, obtained from recitation on the stage, supplies deficiencies in the printed play, as it has come down to us, are illustrated in the prefaces to, as well as in the body of the reprint which has reached us from Germany, where such genuine interest is felt in anything and everything that relates to Shakspeare and his productions. There is much in the novel that does not appear in the play, and we will dwell upon this point only for the purpose of making a single quotation. Act III. sc. 1, as it has come down to us, is occupied chiefly by the birth of Marina during a fearful storm, and Pericles, taking the infant in his arms, exclaims:—

"For thou'rt the rudeliest welcome to this world
That e'er was princes child. Happy what follows!
Thou hast as chiding a nativity,
As fire, air, water, earth and heaven can make."

In the prose of Wilkins (founded upon the drama as it was acted in the very year when the tract bears date) the passage commences with an apostrophe to the babe, which is in the true manner of Shakspeare, but which has no place in the printed copy of "Pericles":—

"*Poor inch of nature!* . . . thou art as rudely welcome to the world as ever princes babe was, and hast as chiding a nativity as fire, air earth and water can afford thee."

Here, excepting the words "Poor inch of nature!" all is in the printed play; and we may be very confident that that expression was omitted by the printer, became in his prosaic understanding he could not perceive why upon the stage a baby should have been called a "poor inch of nature": he had never in his life heard of a living child that was only an inch long; but Wilkins, as a poet, was sensible of the beauty of the figure, and therefore inserted it This treatment of the subject may afford some sort of clew to the manner in which our great poet's other dramas suffered in the press. We take it for granted that Wilkins took notes at the theatre, and afterwards transcribed them in the form of a narrative for sale, before any copy of the drama could be procured. "Pericles" may have been printed, as indeed it was, in 1609, (the year following the appearance of Wilkins's tract,) for the purpose of superseding less authentic representations of the conduct of the story.

WILKINS, GEORGE.—Three Miseries of Barbary: Plague, Famine, Civill Warre. With a relation of the death of Mahamet the late Emperour: and a briefe report of the now present Wars betweene the three Brothers.—Printed by W. J. for Henry Gosson, and are to be sold in Paternoster rowe at the signe of the Sunne. 4to. B. L. 15 *leaves.*

The dedication of this tract is "To the Bight Worshbipfull the whole Company of the Barbary Merchants," and it is signed Geo. Wilkins. It contains no information.

It has no date, but from internal evidence it must have been printed during the Plague in London of 1602-3.

WILLET, ANDREW.—Sacrorum Emblematum Centuria una, quæ tam ad exemplum aptè expressa sunt, et ad aspectum pulchrè depingi possunt, quam quæ aut à veteribus accepta, aut inventa ab aliis hactenus extant. In tres classes distribute quarum prima emblemata Typica, sive Allegorica: Altera historica, sivè re gesta: Tertia Physica à rerum natura sumpta continet Omnia à purissimis Scripturæ fontibus derivata, et Anglolatinis versibus reddita. Ezechielis cap. iiij. vers. j. ij.—Ex officina Johannis Legate florentissimæ Academiæ Cantabrigiensis Typographi. 4to. 32 *leaves.*

This work has been often mentioned, but never criticised, nor any specimens of the author's English versification afforded. There is no date on the title-page, nor at the end, and the nearest point at which we can arrive is, that it was published between 1590, when Sir Francis Walsingham died, and 1598, when Francis Meres, in his *Palladis Tamia,* published in the latter year, speaks of Willet, with Whitney and Combe, as distinguished English Emblematists (fo. 285 b.). Elsewhere (fo. 280) Meres introduces him (misprinting his name *Willey*) as having "attained good report and honorable advancement in the Latin empire." Besides other poems on Sir Francis Walsingham, Willet, in the work in our hands, has a Dialogue between two sisters, the Church and the Country, (*Ecclesiam et Rempublicam,*) on the death of that statesman. It opens thus:—

"Respub. ***Quid tam masta sedes soror atro cincta colore,*** &c."

We quote a small portion of the English translation appended:—

"***Country.*** My sister, why beest thou so sad
With mourning weede in black thus clad?
Church. The same cause we have both to mourne:
Mine eyes drop teares, thy garments torne.
Country. Then let us both in mourning strive.
Our friend is gone, and yet alive.
Church. Alive to God, yet sorrowe make,
As bankes and mountaines we may shake.
Country. Nay, that the heavens may give a sound
My mournfull voyce shall move the ground.
Church. From fountaine mine the teares that fall
With water shall fill every dale.
Country. Yet mourne I more as widowe left,
As childe by parent deere bereft.
church. As mother I whose some is gone,
Or fatherlesse childe so left alone.
country. Ah, woe is me! to death he's thrall,
Who husband, keeper was end all."

And so they proceed, one after the other, to mourn their common loss; but Willet's Latin verse, as may be imagined, is much superior to his English, or he would hardly hare acquired reputation as a classical writer. "The conclusion," as it is called, is this:—
"Y' have wept ynough, ye seems to me
Both overcome, or neither to be.
I can not say who hath lost more,

The dolefull Church, or euntrey poore.
But cease your teares; end now rejoyes
Of heavenly myrth he hath made choice."

Willet has several poems addressed to other individuals—to the Earls of Bedford and Rutland; to Dr. Bell, Dean of Ely; to Dr. Whitaker; to the Bishops of London and Lincoln; to Sir John Cutts; to his brother R. Willet, &c. We will extract seven couplets by Andrew Willet upon his father, beaded ***Senis Descriptio. M. T. W. charissime patri seni:***—

"Of olde mens state what may be thought
By figure present we are taught:
As Sunne is hid, and day is gone,
So pleasure now remaineth none.
The hand that kept the house doeth fayle;
The strong men bowe them selves and vayle:
The teeth the grist doe cease to grinde:
The watchman in the tower is blinde.
The bird which chirps doth him awake:
The harpe doth now no musicke make.
At cisterne as when wheele is broke,
So olde men in no worke beare stroke.
In blacke his neighbours present be,
His corps to grave to accompany."

We quote the Latin of which the above purports to be a translation, as a specimen of Latinity, but without any real originality of thought or expression:—

"Qualis decrepiti senis sit ætas
Præsens hæc loquitur figure nobis.
Umbra sol tægitur, dies fugatur,
Sic nusquam superest seni voluptas.
Custos ædis et imbecilla dextra est,

Curvans robore se pedes valentes.
Cessat mandere pabulum molens dens:
Cæcus prospiciens fit è fenestris
Si cantillat avis, senex quietem
Amittit, cytharæ silens canoræ:
Cisternæ rota frangitur rotunda,
Sic ad munus is imparatus omne est;
Tandem in limine vaste stant atrati
Vicini, et tumulo inditur cadaver."

Willet deals in various forms of Latin and English verse, bat he utterly fails in his attempts to assimilate the English to the Latin measures. We ought not to omit to mention that the whole collection is dedicated in four pages of Latin prose to the Earl of Essex. Willet was Rector of Barley, Herts, and after his death in 1621 his son-in-law published a character of him which may be seen extracted in *Censura Literaria,* IV. 287.

WILLET, ROWLAND.—Merry Jests concerning Popes, Monkes, and Friers. Whereby is discovered their abuses and Errors &c. Written first in Italian by N. S. and thence translated into French by G. I. and now out of French into English by R. W. Bac. of Arts of H. H. in Oxon. *Omme tulit punctum qui miscuit utile dulci.*—Printed by G. Eld. 1617. 8vo. B. L. 68 *leaves.*

The title-page sufficiently explains the character and object of this book of jests and tales against the Roman Catholic clergy. The prose address to the reader is subscribed Rowland Willet, and it is followed by six lines to him, with three copies of commendatory verses, two of them by W. R and H. I., and the third without initials. Some lines "to the Papist Reader" have J. H. at the end of them, and R W. closes an address from "the Translator to the Reader."

It is not necessary to transcribe any of the often coarse and not always humorous stories, of which the body of the book consists. They are all in prose, and are ended by the subsequent "Epigramme Englished," as it is headed;—

"A curate old within the towns of Breses
Did on a time to Masse address;
He was an honest man, esteemed of all,
And yet a great mishap did him befall;
For's sight being bad, and also being in hast,
I' th' Alter cloths he wrapt his God of paste:
So, when he minded was on him to food,
He could not find him out to serve his need;
Wherfore he turnd and gropt and lookt and cried,
Ho, ho! thou divell, where dost thou now abide?"

It seems likely that this work in 1617 was a reprint of some earlier edition, bat we are not aware of the existence of any such, nor indeed of a second copy, excepting, as mentioned on page 237, in the library of Worcester College. The exemplar we have used has been well thumbed and worn, but no part of it is wanting.

WILLIAMSON, THOMAS.—The Sword of the spirit to smite in peeces that Antichristian Goliah, who daily defieth the Lords people the host of Israel. Drawen forth by Tho. Williamson, Gentleman. 2 Cor. 10. 4. 5.—London Printed by Edw. Griffin 1613. 8vo. 72 *leaves.*

This is a rare book, though not intrinsically valuable or interesting. The author was a zealous Protestant, and held some office, not specified, under the Lord Mayor and Corporation of London. Although he was 70 when he wrote, having been born as he states in 1543, it was his first, and probably his last work. It has eleven not ill-executed woodcuts, the first representing Williamson in his study at a table with an hour-glass, death's head, standish, and book upon it; behind is a long shelf containing many books arranged in sizes. We apprehend that the work was never published (no bookseller's name is on the title-page), bat printed by Edw. Griffin for the author, who most likely presented it to his friends and patrons, the dignitaries of the city. Most of the other woodcuts are emblematical, like that where the Bible in a scale weighs down all popish trumpery; but one or two others deserve especial notice, such as that on page 79, where King James is trampling the Pope under foot. The most curious is the view of a printing-office, with press, pressmen, and a compositor, at work exactly as in our day, with a case of letter before him. Under it are these verses:—

"Loe! here the forme and figure of a presse,
Most livelily objected to thine eye;
The worth whereof no tongue can well expresse,
So much it doth, and workes so readily:
For which let's give unto the Lord all praise,
That thus hath bless'd us in these latter daies."

The author maintains, not quite so newly as truly, that the discovery of the art of printing (the date of which he fixes in 1458) was a great engine in forwarding the Reformation. The body of the work is divided into ten "tractates," all of a very similar character, and headed "The Religion of Rome idolatrous"—"The life of Rome detestable," &c. Many pieces of translated verse, not badly rendered, are dispersed through the volume; and if we are to believe Williamson, the famous Dr. John Reynolds, who wrote and printed his Romanœ Ecclesiœ Idolatria in 1596, was also author of an English poem on the same theme, from which the writer before us quotes the following lines:—

"A place of haunt for hellish sprites
Is Babylon, saith John:
Art thou desirous to bee sav'd,
From Babylon bee gone.
The names and trickes of Babylon
Rome on itselfe doth take;
Then, if yee seeke eternall life,
See that yee Rome forsake.
This hath the noble Germans done,
Bidding the Pope-adue:
England hath follow'd Germany,

Romes thraldome to eschew.
Behold! the Lord hath called on
The Flemish, French end Dane;
And Scotland hath escaped eke
The papall deadly bane.
O! that the remnant of the world
By faith to Christ were knit,
And princes to the Prince of all
Their scepters would submit"

When Williamson translates, he almost invariably quotes the Latin, as in the case of Thomas Drant on page 118, a well-known English poet; but both above and elsewhere, when he cites Reynolds's English lines, he only pat the name (without any mention of the work) in the margin. Of Williamson's prose we will only extract a brief specimen, where, in his usual style and spirit, be refers to a play acted by the Jesuits at Lyons. We quote it for the information it supplies, the author placing this reference opposite: ***"Lomed. Jesuit. Art 3 and 4,*** Novemb. Ann. ***1607,"*** so that the incident was of sufficiently recent occurrence. "The cursed Jesuites," he exclaims, "or rather Jebusites, make vauntes and boasts of their wicked and hellish trecherie: they have already acted publikely, in their comedy at Lyons in Fraunce, the condemnation of our Sovereigne King, and other christian princes professing the gospel, (my hart trembleth to rehearse the manner thereof) and the exaltation of their Jesuiticall traytors to the highest heaven." He concludes his little work by a long list of authors whom he cites, and the dates when they flourished, followed by twelve Latin hexameters and pentameters subscribed T. W. Among his authors are John Bradford the martyr, John Fox the historian of the martyrs, Richard Hackluit, (whom be styles ***armiger histor.*** and places in 1574,) Raphæl Holinshed, Isaac Casaubon, and Matthew Sutcliffe.

WILSON, GEORGE.—The Commendation of Cockes, and Cock-fighting. Wherein is shewed, that Cock-fighting was before the coming of Christ.—London, Printed for Henrie Tomes &c. 1607. B. L. 4to. 15 ***leaves.***

We gather from what the author, George Wilson, says of himself, that he was a celebrated Cock-fighter, and he dedicates his "Commendation" to Sir Henry Bedingfield, "both in regard of the good will you beare to Cocke-fighting (wherein I know you take exceeding great delight), and also to manifest my love and dutie unto your worship." He dates an address "to the Reader whosoever," from Wretton in Norfolk, and divides his work into six chapters, but without much method. He enters in some detail into the antiquity of this amusement, among other authorities quoting Drayton's Heroical Epistles; and he particularly mentions the building of a Cockpit at Whitehall by Henry VIII., which was subsequently used as a theatre for court-plays. A cockpit in Drury Lane, early in the reign of James I. was converted into a play-house, and at that date cock-fighting appears to have declined. Wilson's object was, in part, to revive the taste for it. In his last chapter, after relating the exploits of various cocks of the game, he speaks of one called Tarlton, "who was so entituled, because he alwayes came to the fight like a drummer, making a thundering noise with his wings." This passage alludes to Tarlton the celebrated actor, who, as we have seen, generally appeared on the stage with a drum or tabor. Wilson's tract was several times reprinted.

WILSON, THOMAS.—The Arte of Rhetorique, for the use of all suche as are studious of Eloquence, sette forth in English by Thomas Wilson. Anno Domini M.D.LIII. Mense Januarij. 4to. B. L. 130 *leaves.*

This is the first edition of Wilson's "Rhetoric," but two years earlier the same distinguished scholar, who was at one time Secretary to Queen Elizabeth, had put forth his "Arte of Logicke." Both of them were works of considerable importance, but the "Logic" is especially noticeable, because, as pointed out nearly forty years ago (Hist. Engl. Dram. Poetry, II. 445), it enables us to ascertain that Nicholas Udall's "Ralph Roister Doister" is the oldest original comedy in our language, taking precedence, by several years, of Bishop Still's "Gammer Gurton's Needle." [Note 1: It is not to be conclusively taken that Still was the author of "Gam¬mer Gurton's Needle," although there is good reason to believe it We have already seen, that it had been imputed to Dr. Bridges.] See also D. O. P. 1825, Vol. II. p.3.

Wilson's "Rhetoric," though it contains no such novel and valuable fact, is a work of great literary internet, including nearly all the information that, at that early date, could be introduced in illustration of the subject. The author wrote it at the instance of John Dudley, Earl of Warwick, to whom he dedicates it, and it is ushered by Latin Term by Walter Haddon, "the best Latin-man" in England, Nicholas Udall, Robert Hillermius, and Wilson himself. The Rev. H. J. Todd considered the "Rhetorie" "the first system of regular criticism in our language," but of course it has been little read during the last two centuries. To illustrate the success with which Wilson intermixes mere fun and humor with graver and more instructive matter, we may quote what he says under the head of the advantage to be gained sometimes by the "alteryng parte of a worde," which contains also a new and clever anecdote of Henry the VIIIth's jester, William Sommer, or Sommers, not then dead:—

"Alteryng part of a word is when we take a letter or sillable from some word, or els adde a letter or sillable to a worde, as thus. William Somer, seying muche a do for accomptes makyng, and that the Kynges Majestie of most worthie memorie, Henry theight, wanted mony suche as was due vnto hym, And please your grace (quoth he) you have so many franditors, so many conveiers, and so many deceivers to get up your money, that they get al to themselves. Whether he said true or no, let God judge that: it was unhappely spoken of a foole, and I thinke he had some Scholemaister: he should have saied Auditours, Surveyours and Receavours."

When Wilson wrote this, Will Sommer or Sommers was still alive, as is proved by the following entry, which we found in the Register of St. Leonard, Shoreditch, a parish then and afterwards much inhabited by persons of his class and character:—

"1560. Willm. Somers was buried the xv day of June."

It is a great merit in the work before us, that the author so often assists his argument by reference to familiar subjects, and to events and persons of his time: thus we meet with several notices of Sir Thomas More, Bishop Latimer, John Heywood, &c, to say nothing of Robin Hood and Garagantua. On folio 103 b, he speaks of Minstrels, not only as musicians and singers, but as reciters, "***talkyng*** matters altogether in rime." At the end is an alphabetical "Table" of contents, as we apprehend, one of the earliest of the kind.

WINTER, THOMAS.—The Second Day of the First Weeke of the most excellent, learned, and divine Poet, William, Lord Bartas. Done out of French into English Heroicall verse by Thomas Winter, Maister of Artes &c.—London, Printed for James Shaw. 1603. 4to. 24 ***leaves.***

At the back of this title is an address by the author "to his Translation," in two six-line stanzas, followed by a dedication to Sir Walter Raleigh: we have then Latin hexameters by to. Sandford, and by Ed. Lapworth, and English verses by Douglas Castillion and John Davies of Hereford, in praise of the author and of his performance. The latter gives Winter great credit for the literalness of his version, which commences after two pages of Argument.

Attention had been especially directed to Du Bartas by the admiration expressed of him by King James, who in 1591 printed a translation of "The Furies," and who in his, 1599, recommended him to his son Henry, as "most worthy to be read by any Prince." It seems that Prince Henry had encouraged Winter to proceed with his version, and, accordingly, in the next year, 1604, he produced "The Third Dayes Creation, and done verse for verse out of the Originall," with a dedication to the Prince of Wales. This was introduced by commendatory poems in French and Latin, by John Sandford, John Dunster, Thomas Mason, Nathaniel Tomkins, and Henry Ashwood. At the close are sonnets by Winter to Sir Thomas Chaloner, Sir George Somers, Sir Thomas Lucy, the younger, and Dr. James. Sylvester printed his version of the whole in 1605.

WIT.—Bought Wit is best. Or Tom Longs Journey to London to buy Wit.

Many men learn after-wit
By errors which they doe commit.

—London Printed by E. A. for Francis Smith, and are to be sold at his Shop on Snow-hill, over against the Sarazens head. 1634. B. L. 12 **leaves.**

Tom Long continued a sort of hero in popular literature for nearly two centuries. We first obtain information regarding him from a ballad entitled "Tom Long the Caryer," entered on the books of the Stationers' Company in the year 1561-62; and so profitable was it, that having been first licensed to William Shepparde, his right was very soon afterwards invaded by Thomas Hackett, who printed it in his own name, and was fined 2*s.* 6*d.* for so doing. The next we hear of Tom Long is in 1608, when was published "The merry Conceits of Tom Long," which show that he was "the Carrier of Gotham," and that he went through a series of adventures very consistent with the grotesque folly imputed to the "wise men" of that famous town. He was afterwards celebrated by Taylor the Water-poet as "Tom Long the Carrier," in one of his pleasant productions of 1630; and in 1634 came out the little performance, in prose and verse, in our hands. When "Tom Long's Lessons" first appeared we do not know, but it was a favorite chap-book, and copies of it exist as late as 1750. Thus we are able, in a manner, to trace his history from 1561 to the middle of the eighteenth century.

In the tract before us, of 1634, Tom Long is sent to London by the corporation of Gotham to purchase wit for them, under the promise that if he bring back "a whole horse-load" of that commodity, they will elect him Alderman. The address "to the Reader, gentle or ungentle," is subscribed W. S., which letters, we may speculate, were meant for Wentworth Smith, a dramatist whose initials have sometimes been mistaken for those of Shakspeare. However, W. S. does not profess to speak for himself, but for a friend who has just commenced authorship. He says:—

"Encourage his beginning, and he will
Entreate his friend to climbe the Muses hill,
Who, having tasted of their Spring, shall write
Some fresh conceits to yeeld you free delight.
In the meane time, you wisely may learne here
What some with sad repentance buy too deare,

Since 'tis an ancient truth, which is confest
By every one, that ***Bought Wit is the best.***"

The above is followed by sixteen other lines, enumerating many things that are to be bought in London, among them this book, which furnishes wit and merriment at a very cheap rate.

The body of the work informs us that when Tom Long arrived in London from Gotham in the spring, he put up at an inn, and then sallied forth "to seeke for his penniworths" of wit, which he had been commissioned to buy. He soon meets with one Musario, apparently a disappointed poet, "walking with crossed armes, his hat puld over his eyes, as if he scorned to looke upon the vanitie of the world." Tom inquires of him where wit is to be bought, and is answered that it can only be had second-hand, through woeful experience. Tom is delighted with his new acquaintance, and takes him to his inn, where Musario describes a number of persons and classes who have paid very dearly for their wit Among them are "drunken Barnaby" (from whom Brathwaite may have taken the name of his hero,) Phantastes, Mr. Young-age, Mistress Light-heels, Master Wilfull, Master Wildoats and many more. The last is thus described:—

"After this comes Master Wild-oates, and hee lookes as though he scorned to learne; bat yet at last out of Taverne reckonings, Taylors bills, Mercers bookes, false dice, horse-races and Taffety petticoats, he begins to learne these two letters B. O.; and that O bringes him to woe, and that woe brings him to have wit, when all is done."

There are several scraps of verse as we proceed through the different characters who are the purchasers of costly wit, and near the end we have in rhyme the description of the "School of Repentance" and its scholars. It opens:—

"Repentance keepes a Schoole where men do learne
To know their faults, when they, at last, discerne;
And though abroad like Trewants they doe runne,

Yet, at the length, unto this Schoole they come;
Where many formes and severall places bee
To fit all sorts, of high and low degree;
And hare they an some rules of wisedoms taught,
And to the knowledge of themselves are brought."

The verses occupy several pages, and are presented to Tom Long by Musario. The former promises to make due return, if the latter happen to come to Gotham; but we are told, quite at the end, that Tom Long remained in London until he had procured the account of his Journey to be printed, for the information of others who might wish to purchase Wit. The tract contains much various amusement, and some local information.

WITHER, GEORGE.—Abuses stript and whipt Or Satirical Essayes. By George Wyther. Divided into two Bookes, &c.

Despise not this what ere I seeme in showe,
A foole to purpose speaks sometime you know.

—At London, Printed by G. Eld for Francis Burton &c. 1613. 8vo. 160 *leaves.*

There are at least two editions of these celebrated Satires, &c. dated 1613. This is the first, and, although the text is substantially the same in both, they differ in several particulars. In the first edition (besides literal variations) "The Scourge" and "Epigrams" are not mentioned on the title-page; and after "The Contents" is inserted a long list of Errata, which are corrected in the second impression. The separate satires are also called "Chapters" in the first edition, and differently numbered, as "The Occasion," "An Introduction," and a poem "Of Man," are included. It has been said (*British Bibliogr.* I. 180,) that there was an impression in 1611; and, although no copy of that date has been discovered, circumstances, which it is not necessary to detail, seem to render it probable. The work was again published in 1614, 1615, 1617, 1622, 1626, and 1633, and no one of those reimpressions was exactly like any other that preceded it. The copy of 1617 has an additional poem, with a woodcut of a Satire prefixed to "the Scourge."

George Wither was born in 1590, so that in 1613 he was in his twenty-third year. He died in 1667, the latest of his many productions having been printed in the year preceding. Whenever he had not the sword in his hand he wielded the pen, and sometimes used both at once. He was a much better poet at the commencement than at the conclusion of his career, and had he ceased to write after he published his "Shepherds Hunting," in 1615, or, at all events, after his "Fair Virtue, the Mistress of Philarete," came out in 1622, he would have been handed down as one of the ornaments of our language. His "Shepherds Hunting" had been written when he was only twenty, for, in the fourth Eclogue, it is said of him:—

"But it will appeare ere long,
I'me abus'd, and thou hast wrong,
Who at ***twice ten*** hast sung more,
Then some will doe at fourscore."

"Fair Virtue, or the Mistress of Philarete," was written prior to "Abuses Stript and Whipt," where it is mentioned. Some lines by Taylor (this Vol. p. 145) contain a libel upon Wither's honesty.

WITHER, GEORGE.—Britain's Remembrancer. Containing a Narrative of the Plague lately past; a Declaration of the Mischiefs present; and a Prediction of Judgments to come (if Repentance prevent not). It is dedicated (for the glory of God) to Posteritie; and to these Times (if they please) by George Wither &c.—Imprinted for Great Britaine and are to be sold by John Grismond &c. 1628. 12mo. 289 ***leaves.***

This work relates principally to the great plague of 1625, during the whole period of which the author remained in London; and in the third of the eight cantos of which his poem consists, he states his reasons for hazarding the infection. An engraved title-page precedes the printed one, representing every species of pestilence overhanging England in the form of a dense cloud, while Justice and Mercy are seated above in the sky. Facing it are Tenet giving "die meaning of the title-page."

It is dedicated in twenty-two pages of closely printed verses to die King, and they are followed by "a Premonition" in prose, the most curious part of which relates to another work by Wither, called his "*Motto,*" which he had published in 1618. After the eighth canto is a "conclusion" in verse, filling twelve pages; for, when Wither took up the pen, his thoughts seem to have flowed so rapidly and readily, that he did not know how to lay it down again.

It has no printer's name, and no doubt was worked off at some private press; and in a note at the end respecting errors, it is said, "The faults escaped in the printing we had not such meanes to prevent as we desired, nor could we conveniently collect them by reason of our haste or hazard, and other interruptions." There are some noble verses by Wither in his "Preparation to the Psalter," folio, 1619.

WITHER, GEORGE.—Campo-Musæ or the Field-Musings of Captain George Wither, touching his Military Ingagement for the King and Parliament, the Justnesse of the same, and the present distractions of these Islands. ***Deus dabit his quoque finem.***—London Printed by R. Austin and A. Coe. 1643. 8vo. 40 ***leaves.***

At this period the author professed to be determined to "employ every faculty which God had given him for the King and Parliament," and in this spirit he dedicated his tract to the Earl of Essex, under whom he was still serving, although at the moment engaged in recruiting his "disabled troop." At the back of the title is an address in verse "to the English," the object of which is to rouse them from their supineness. The general scope of the poem is to justify the author in the course he has pursued, and at the end he promises his "Vox Pacifica," which came out soon afterwards. The whole is written in Wither's usual strain of puritanical patriotism.

WITHER, GEORGE.—Prosopopœia Britannica: Britans Genius, or Good-Angel personated; reasoning and advising touching the Games now playing, and the Adventures now at hazard in these Islands &c Discovered by Terrœ-Filius (a well knowne Lover of the Publike-Peace) when the begetting of the Nationall Quarrell was first feared &c.—London Printed by Robert Austin. 1648. 8vo. 59 ***leaves.***

This tract was published without the name of the author, but Wither had called himself Terræ Filius in 1643, and his style could not be mistaken. He tells "the scornfully censorious" (whom he addresses after "the meek ingenuous Reader") that the work had been seen in MS. eight months before, but that he had met with difficulties in getting it licensed. The poem, which is of a politico-religious cast, is divided into two "Lections," followed by brief epistles to the Parliament and to the King, and they contain an unusual number of happy separate passages.

WODHOUSE, W.

The XV fearfull tokens
preceding, I say,
The generall judgement
called Domes day.

Watch and pray for no man knoweth the hower.—Imprinted at London by William How for William Pickeryng. 8vo. 6 *leaves.*

Such is the title of this little tract, which serves to introduce a new name into our poetical bibliography. Whether W. Wodhouse was the ancestor of Peter Woodhouse, the author of "The Flea," published in 1605, we cannot determine. It would seem that it was originally intended to print these "XV fearfull tokens" as a broadside, and they were entered at Stationers' Hall to W. Pickering as "a ballad" in 1565-66 (Extr. I. 125); but as the piece consisted of thirty stanzas, like the following, they were probably found too much for the space, and were therefore brought out as a small separate tract:—

"Ther shal not help the Eloquence
Of Lawyers at the Barre,
Nor yet their crafty sapience;
Their owne deedes wil them marre.
Ther shal no bribes be take that day,
No man for to prevent:

Faire wordes nothing prevaile they may,
But he will geve judgement."

Two such stanzas are devoted to each of the fifteen signs, and the whole is subscribed "Finis. W. Wodhouse." This tract, if we mistake not, is no where mentioned.

WONDERS.—The History of Strange Wonders.—Imprynted at London by Roulande Hall, dwellynge in Goldynge Lane at the signe of the three arrows. 1561. 8vo. 26 *leaves.*

This book was entered for publication in the Stationers' Register by Rowland Hall, in 1561, but no other copy of it than the present is known, which, unfortunately, wants the title-page. The colophon is as above given. It is recorded by bibliographers only by the title as it stands in the books of the Stationers' Company (Dibdin's Typ. Ant. IV. 420). The whole is prose, although, from one of the heads of the divisions, "Certayn Eglogs taken out of divers Epistles," we might be led to expect verse. It consists of extracts from various printed works, and manuscript accounts, of miraculous appearances, foretelling future events, the application, or misapplication, being also usually given.

WOODHOUSE, PETER.—The Flea: *Sic parva componere magnis.*—London Printed for John Smethwick and are to be solde at his shop in Saint Dunstanes Churchyard in Fleet street, under the Diall. 1605. 4to. 18 *leaves.*

The fault of this piece lies more in its design than in its execution, for it is by no means deficient in cleverness. "The Epistle Dedicatorie," "to the giddie multitude," is subscribed P. W., and "The Epistle to the Reader," signed "Thy poore friend Peter Woodhouse."

It is in the form of a dream, by Democritus, of a contest for superiority between an Elephant and a Flea, and the strife is to be judged by a Bull and a Weazel. As far as the moral of the apologue shows the advantages of activity over strength, it is good; but we do not exactly see why the Bull and the Weazel were chosen as umpires, or rather as sticklers and arbitrators. "R. P. Gent" has three good introductory stanzas, justifying the design by the examples of Homer, Virgil, Apuleius, and Erasmus. When Heraclitus afterwards calls it "an idle dream," Democritus maintains its excellence, and laughs at those who would give personal application to so slight and unpretending an invention, observing,—

"Such fooles as these would descant on my dreame
And it interpret, as it best shall seeme
To their weake wit and blunt capacitye,
Censure each word, each sentence misapplye:
If I should light on such a giddie Asse,
I'd scorne to answer him, but let him passe."

The little attempt ends with the following sort of apology:—

"Many many things have written,
When th' ad better still have sitten;
Peradventure so had I,
Yet I know no reason why.
It's a foolish toy I write
And in folly most delight:
Then (I hope) it will please many,
And not be dislikte of any.
Even from tales of Robin Hood
Wise men alway picke some good.
None (I trust) offend I shall;
So, I take my leave of all.

"PETER WOODHOUSE."

If he wrote anything besides "The Flea," it is not known, and we are without any other information regarding him.

WOOD-STREET COUNTER.—Wonderfull Strange Newes from Woodstreet Counter. Yet not so strange as true. Being proved by lamentable Experience. The Relation of which

Will make you laugh, 'twill make you cry,
'Twill make you mad, 'twill make you try

many more wonderfull effects, as Tom-Tell-troth can witnesse.

It will convert a Whore, enrich the Poore,
And make a Sergeant kind,
Then buy it now, for I doe know,
That it will please your mind.

—London, Printed by T. Fawcet 1642. 4 to. 4 *leaves.*

The most curious part of this tract, written for the obvious purpose of being sold for two-pence, is the enumeration of those parts of London remarkable for unlicensed living. It is a dialogue between Plain-dealing and Tom Tell-truth. The latter has been confined for debt in Wood-street Counter, and maintains that it is worse than "Pickhatch, Covent Garden, Groaping Lane, Tower Hill, St Giles in the fields, Bloomesbury, Drewry Lane, Westminster, or the Bankside." White-friars is not included.

There is some spirit in the composition, and when Plain-dealing asks what associates Tom Tell-truth had had in the Counter, the latter answers: "Many of all sorts, from the gentile gallant with his perriwig and Spanish block, to the lowzy rascall without a shirt, or a shoe to his foot, the long haire gallant which sweares Damy, and the zealous Brother with never a hayre amisse. Indeed, there are all sorts; Lords without lands, Ladies without lackeys, Gentlemen without money, Captains without command, Citizens without credit, pittifull Poets which write their owne Tragedyes, undone Heyres, Pick-pockets with hanging lookes, taffaty

Whores falling to decay, Prentizes with pennilesse pockets, Journeymen that are at their journey's end."

It concludes with twelve lines, in couplets, to prove that the Counter is far worse than a Bawdy-house. We never met with any other copy of the tract than that we have used, but there may be several Its local character is its chief merit

WORCESTER.—Worcester's Elegie and Eulogie. By J. T. Mr. of Arts.—London, Printed by Tho. Cotes for Humphry Blunden, at his shop, at the Castle in Cornehill. 1638. 4to. 26 *leaves.*

We notice this work as a singular provincial poetical production, called forth by the prevalence of the plague and famine in Worcester, in 1637. The author's name is given at length to a preliminary address, and is punned upon by one of his eulogists:

"How'd the Muses joy
Were every child o' th' braine no worse a *Toy!*"

Nevertheless, there is very little in the tract to have gratified the Muses, or even worse judges of verse. No doubt the piece was very satisfactory to the Wigornian readers of that day, who were grateful for the disappearance of the fatal fever, and for the assistance the suffering city had received from her neighbors. Besides thankful poems addressed to the Bishop and Clergy, as well as to private individuals, there are tributes to Bristol, Tewksbury, Droitwich, &c.; but we are not disposed to extract more than a testimonial to Sir Walter Devereux, and that chiefly for his name's sake:—

"To Sr. Walter Devereaux, Knight and Baronet.
"Thou gav'st us corne (great Devereaux) and we
Presented unto heaven thy charity
In sacred vowes and prayers: heaven againe,
Hath promis'd for our faith on thee to raine

Full showers of better gifts; the trunk shall grow;
Thy branches with felicity shall blow.
Like fish thy flocks shall yield, thy corne-fields sing,
Thy pastures imitate perpetuall spring.
Who this event contemplates well may say
Thy graine was lent to heaven, not given away;
Yes, that our poore have given to thee, for thus
Thy gift hath made thee debtor unto us."

We do not suppose that our readers will feel themselves aggrieved by the non-insertion of any further specimen.

WORLD'S' FOLLY.—This World's Folly. Or a Warning Piece discharged vpon the Wickednesse thereof. Hor. Sat 3. lib. I. By I. H.—London, Printed by William Jaggard for Nicholas Bourne, &c. 1615. 4to. 19 **leaves.**

This is a prose attack upon prevailing vices, and parts of it are especially directed against the Stage, Plays, Actors, and Poets, with a direct reference to the comedy called "Green's Tu Quoque," (which had been printed in 1614,) and to a jig, or clown's merriment, known by the name of "Garlick." "Tu Quoque" was written by John Cooke, but it was subsequently called "Green's Tu Quoque," from the laughable acting of a performer of the name of Green in the part of Bubble. "Garlick" has not found its way into any of our earlier or later theatrical records; [Note 1: Haddit, a supposed dramatic author, mentions the extreme popularity of "Garlick" in the introductory scene to "the Hog hath lost his Pearl," 1614. 4to.] but that it and "Green's Tu Quoque" were very popular, about the same date, we know from H. Parrot's **Laquei Ridiculosi,** 1613, where

"Greene's Tn Quoque and those Garlick Jigs"

are celebrated in the same line. In his "Cast over the Water," Taylor gives it a second title, which serves to show its character—"The Jig of Garlick, or the Punks Delight" Of both I. H. in "The World's Folly" speaks in these terms:—

"I will not particularize those ***blitea dramata*** (as Liberius tearmes another sort) those Fortune-fatted fooles and Times idiots, whose garbe is the tooth-ache of witte, the plague-sore of judgement, the common-sewer of obscenities, and the very traine-powder that dischargeth the roaring Meg (not Mol) of all scurrile villanies upon the Cities face: who are faine to produce blinde Impudence to personate himselfe upon their Stage, behung with chaynes of Garlicke, as an antidote against their owne infectious breaths, lest it should kill their oyster-crying Audience. Vos quoque, and you also who with Scylla-barking Stentor-throated bellowing, flash choaking squibbes of absurd vanities into the nosthrils of your spectators, barbarously diverting nature, and defacing God's owne image by metamorphising humane shape into their bestiall forme."

The author, as if afraid of not being understood, adds marginal notes to make his readers quite sure that by "Fortune-fatted fooles," he alludes to the actors at the Fortune Theatre; that "roaring Meg" means "Long Meg of Westminister," a play then in course of daily performance; that by Impudence "behung with chaynes of Garlicke," he refers to the jig of "Garlick or the Punk's Delight," and by ***Vos Quoque,*** to the Comedy of "Tu Quoque." Of poets he speaks as follows:—

"The ***primum mobile,*** which gives motion to the under-turning wheeles of wickednesse are those mercenary squitter-wits miscalled Poets, whose illiterate and pick-pocket inventions can ***emungere plebes argento,*** slily nip the bunges of the baser troopes, and cut the reputations throat of the more eminent rank of cittizens with corroding scandals: these are they who, by dipping their goose-quills in the puddle of mischiefs with wilde and uncollected spirites, make them desperately drunke to strike at the head of Nobility, Authority and high-seated Greatness. And all this they doe but onely to purchase the fee-simple of a Long-lane suite, to entaile a Punke in some new-stript peticoate, and to cancell the tavern-bill for two bacchanalian suppers."

Of course, we are not to take such representations by puritanical assailants without many deductions; but there is no doubt, on this and better authority, that the lives of players and poets about this date were liable to much strong censure; and we are not to forget that the period, when they appear to have allowed themselves most license, was shortly after the retirement of Shakspeare to his native town.

WORTLEY, SIR FRANCIS.—Characters and Elegies, By Francis Wortley, Knight and Baronet Printed in the Yeere 1646. 4to. 38 *leaves.*

It has been supposed, from the absence of any printer's or bookseller's name, that this work was not published, bat intended for private distribution: the remark would, however, apply to much prose and poetry issued about the disturbed period of the Civil Wars.

The dedication is generally "to the Lovers of Honour and Poesie," followed by fourteen very loyal and gallant characters of the King, Queen, and various courtiers, male and female, in prose. These are succeeded by nineteen Elegies, (the last of them upon Francis Quarles the poet,) by some translated Epigrams, &c, and "a paraphrase upon the verses which Famianus Strada made upon the Lutanist and Philomel in contestation," the whole being wound up by the following pleasant and ingenious parallel:—

"Coblert are call'd Translators; so are we
(And may be well call'd so) we to agree.
They rip the soale first from the upper leather,
Then steepe, then stretch, then patch up all together:
We rip, we steep, we stretch, and take great paines.
They with their fingers work, we with our braines.
They trade in old shoes, as we doe in feet,
To make the fancy and the language meete.
We make all smooth (as they doe) and take care
What is too short to patch, too large to pare.
When they have done, then to the Club they goe
And spend their gettings: do not we doe so?
Coblers are often poore, yet merrie blades;

Translators rarely rich, yet cheereful lads.
Who thinkes he wants he is in plentie poore:
Give me the Coblers wealth, Ile aske no more."

The lines on page 55, "upon a true contented Prisoner," were, doubtless, written when Sir F. Wortley was imprisoned in the Tower for his loyalty, and they contain the following happy illustration of the effects of confinement in directing the eyes of the mind toward heaven:—

"Men in the deepest pits see best by farre
The sunne's eclipses, and flnde every starre,
When sight's contracted and is more intent:
(So is men's soules in close imprisonment)
We then can upwards look on things above,
Worthy our contemplation and our love."

WOTTON, HENRY.—A Courtlie Controversie of Cupid's Cautels: Conteyning five Tragicall Histories, very pithie, pleasant, pitifull and profitable: discoursed uppon with Argumentes of Love by three Gentlemen and two Gentlewomen, entermedled with divers delicate Sonets and Rithmes, exceeding delightfull to refresh the yrksomnesse of tedious Tyme. Translated out of French as neare as our Englishe Phrase will permit, by H. W. Gentleman.—At London, Imprinted by Francis Coldocke and Henry Bynneman. 1578. 4to. B. L. 176 *leaves.*

This work, which, though professing to be only a translation, we are convinced was in many parts original, was by Henry Wotton, whose initials only appear upon the title-page. Whether he were any, and what, relation to Sir Henry Wotton, the Provost of Eton, who was born in 1568, we have no means of knowing: Henry Wotton was, perhaps, brother to Edward Wotton, whom Sir P. Sidney mentions in the opening of his "Defence of Poesie," as having been with him at the Emperor's Court. Whether this conjecture be or be not unfounded, it is quite certain that Henry Wotton, whether as translator of the work in our hands, or as an original poet, is by no means a contemptible versifier. It is to be borne in mind that this "Courtly Controversy of Cupid's Cautels" was written some years before the work of Sidney; and the poetry it contains much more resembles the ease and grace of his school, than the formality, and even rigidity, of that in which Whetstone and Turbervile, some ten years earlier, were masters. Of his own qualifications Henry Wotton speaks thus diffidently, but sharply, in the commencement:—

"Yet I must needes confesse (notwithstanding the greate good will which urgeth me forward) that the mistrust of my disabilitie to finishe this enterprise (the whiche giveth me perfects knowledge of my selfe without flatterie) at the first encounter hath for feare frozen the yuke in my penne, knowing the carping wittes of our age, to be so cloyed with the sower taste of loathsome disdayne, as there is no sauce sufficient (howe delicate so ever it be) to restore againe their appetite, or at the leaste, to give them knowledge that the unsavory fault they finde in their meate resteth in their unseasoned mouths."

There is not much invention in the incidents which bring the five young people—three gentlemen And two ladies—together. France at the time was torn by civil wars, and the party retire lo the castle of a prudent matron to escape from the consequences of the hostilities, and there they amuse themselves by conversation not always very lively, and by tales not always very original. The two longest poems in the volume, of more than twenty stanzas, are entitled "The Complaint of the Civil Warres in Fraunce," and "A Welcome of Peace unto Fraunce." These are clearly translations, and it is in the shorter songs, ditties, and lyrics that we seem to trace the freedom and spirit of originality. We copy, in proof, three stanzas of a poem in dispraise of Cupid:—

"All such as love in loyall sort,
and hope reliefe to finde,
With them the Elfe doth make his sport;
he smiles to see them pinde:
He seekes to reave them of delight,
and breedes them all annoy;
It is of all the most despight

to trust the lying boy.

"Make love who list an angell then,
who list to like his wayes,
For neyther I, my tongue or pen,
will ever yeelde him prayse;
And who so doth shall live at ease,
devoyde of care and strife,
Unlesse that libertie displease,
to leade a quiet life.

"This Love, whom Poets call a God,
is but a fury fell,
Sent from above, a scourging rod,
out of the pit of hell,
To martyre and to put to payne
all poore afflicted wights;
But wise are they that can refrayne
this helhoundes hellish slights."

This may be rather plain-spoken, but it does not read like translation, and the same may be said of various other lively lyrics, in some of which, however, we are bound to say, we detect a French word or two: in the following *femme* is used, partly in the distress of rhyme:—

"Behold the guerdon due to love
Bestowed on a fickle femme:
As good of rotten wood to prove
The forging of some precious gemme.
Repentance last doth pinch the hart
That love consumes with bitter smart."

In the opening of what is headed "The fourth day's Delight," is a poem of considerable power and variety in praise of the vine, which we do not place among the original pieces, contributed, as we suppose, by the translator; and we say the same of the two subsequent stanzas: they are still on the subject of love, and, like much else in the volume, not very complimentary to the ladies of the party.

> "What moveth men abashed thus to stay,
> As tumbled from the cloudes in such a mase,
> Sith maidens mockes doe yeelde but mere delay,
> Whose cloking scarfes doth holds men at a gase,
> Whilst covered close in shape of masking showe
> By deepe deceyte our joyes they overthrowe?
>
> "Bereave them of their outwarde masking vayle,
> Yet inwardly disguised they remayne:
> Their thoughtes lye hidde, their tongues of truth do fayle,
> Till sugred wordes the harmlesse hart hath slayne:
> If in their chaunge they fast on men their hooke,
> Their smiling then convertes to louring looke."

The following, which alludes to the famous Dance of Death, is obscurely worded in the beginning, for the sake of brevity, but it ends with animation, and, if translated, runs without constraint:—

> "Why doo the Lillies fade away,
> and pleasant sentes resigne my grave?
> Let rather violets, freshe and gay,
> Bring heare to me my love so faire
> to quallifie my pining care,
> So as before the day when I
> must leads the daunce among the dead,
> All sorrowes from my sight may flye,
> and joy possesse my troubled bead."

Of the prose portion of the volume we cannot speak very highly: it is long drawn out, and somewhat dull; for even the ladies, who partake in the discussions arising out of the several stories, are not sprightly or animated, and, on the question of love and its abusers, they by no means stand their ground against the accusations of the ungallant gentlemen. There are some pretty descriptions of rural scenery, but here and there words are employed, which, if not French, are new in English, as where we are told "The young lambes frisking and leaping by the sides of their dams [were] nibling and brettyng the toppes of the preatye pagles in the greene pastures." Can "brettyng" be a misprint for *biting,* or is it a word derived from the French ***bretauder,*** which signifies to crop? Chaucer uses ***bretful*** but with him it merely means ***brimful.***

Among the five tales we meet with one that furnished the story of the old drama of "Soliman and Perseda," written about 1590, printed in 1599, and to which Shakspeare alludes in King John, Act I. sc. 1. The names of all the principal characters in "Soliman and Perseda," are derived from the novel translated by Henry Wotton in 1578, but the writer of the drama added some absurdities to the incidents and persons. Of another history William Rufus is made the hero, the scene being laid in England; and here we meet with one of the earliest echo-songs that we remember in our language, where the singer (in this case the King) puts a question, answered by echo according to the last word of the inquiry. A third tale of "contrarious love" relates to the adventures of two scholars, one named Claribel of Poictiers, and the other Floridan of Xaintes, in the conclusion of which an "Epithalame," as it is called, is divided between a Lover and his Lady. It is rather an enlargement of Horace's ***Donec gratus eram tibi*** than anything else, but it is easily and cheerfully written; what succeeds are the first two out of twelve or fifteen alternating stanzas:—

"***The Lover.***So long as I such favour founde
To flow from my faire Ladies face,
As by her to be vouched bounde
To serve as slave her noble grace,
My happy state and settled minde

Possessed more contented stay
Than any living prince may finde,
Though all the world should him obay.

"*The Lady.*So long as of a servaunt true,
The faithfull guage of loyal love
Posseste my hart; and I did view
His service sought his faith to prove,
I could not change this weale of mine,
Nor once reward him with despight,
To be partaker with a Queene
In worldly wealth and all delight."

It is not very clear at the end of the "Courtly Controversy" whether any more of it was really contemplated, but a continuation is hinted at. We never saw but a single complete copy of the book, though two fragments have, at long intervals, come under our notice; each had the colophon, "Imprinted at London by Francis Coldocke and Henry Bynneman. 1578."

WROTHE, SIR THOMAS.—Sir Thomas Wrothe his sad Encomion upon his Dearest Consort, Dame Margaret Wrothe. Who died of a Fever at Petherton Parke in the Countie of Somerset, about Midnight of the 14. day of October 1635, and was buried in the Parish Church of St. Stephen in Coleman Street, London, the 11. of November next ensuing &c.—London, Printed for Henry Seile. 1635. 4to. 6 *leaves.*

In 1620, Sir Thomas Wrothe printed "The Abortive of an idle Hour," consisting of "a Century of Epigrams," possibly for private distribution, and only two or three copies seem to remain. It is more than probable that he took the same course with this laudatory poem on his lady, which is unknown to bibliographers. It is written in six-line stanzas, and commences, without introduction, immediately after the title:—

"Can any sorrow be like mine, whose losse
Is more than toung may tell, or heart conceive?
Am I pickt out to beare this heavie Crosse,
And in obedience what is dearest leave?
With bleeding heart I must avow, that no man
Did ever lose more vertuous worthy Woman."

This is not exactly the style of elegiac verse. In the course of the poem, which consists of thirty-eight stanzas, he thus addresses the Fates, taking care to place their names in the margin, lest any mistake should be made from the terms he employs:—

"Discourteous Ladies who doe governe Life!
Can Ladies to a Lady be so cruell?
Ye might have taken me and spar'd my Wife;
In me there is no worth—she was a jewell."

What Sir Thomas Wrothe here says of himself may certainly be applied to his poetry. At the end are six couplets, called—

"*Consilium Amantis.*

"O, Man! who boasts of strength or wittie flashes,
Or ought beside, thou art but dust and ashes:
And sure thou shalt at Christs Tribunall give
A strict account how thou didst die and live.
Deferre no moment under vaine pretences:
Amend thy life, repent of thine offences."

The copy in the library at Bridgewater House is corrected in manuscript, probably by the author, before he presented it to the Earl.

Besides his "Abortive of an idle hour," Sir Thomas Wrothe printed in 1620 a fragment with the following imprint: "London. Printed by T. D. and are to be sold by Nicholas Bourne at the Royall Exchange, 1620." 4to. He called it "The Destruction of Troy, or the Acts of Æneas: Translated oat of the second Booke of the Æneads of Virgill &c. With the Latine verse on one side, and the English verse on the other." It is dedicated in two stanzas to Sir Robert Sidney, Viscount Lisle. and followed by "A Request to the Reader," in which Sir T. Wrothe informs him that, as translator, he had sometimes "purposely wandered from the original." Then comes "The Argument," and afterwards the translation begins thus:—

"Silence proclaim'd, and every tongue with mute attention tyde,
Ascending into some high place Æneas thus replide.
Too sad a tale, renowned Queene, you will me to relate,
How Trojan wealth, and Troy it selfe, the Greeks did ruinate;
Which I beheld, nor was the least who felt warr's heavy hand.
What Delops or what Myrmidon, or of Ulysses band
Who would not weepe to speake such things? But night draws on apace,
And starres descending summon rest; yet if so be your grace
Burne with desire to know the cause which all our woe procur'd,
And heare the story of those wars the Trojans long indur'd,
Although the thought dissolvs my heart, your all commanding charge,
I will obey, and of those broyles declare the truth at large."

As the work is of much greater rarity than value, we add only the Wrothovirgilian account of the death of Priam:—

"Nay then, qnoth Pyrrhus, thou shalt pack and to Pelides breake
Thy mind concerning this which I without remorse have done,
And let him know the cruelty of his degenerate sonne:
Thou shalt be soone dispatch't. This sayd, on his left hand he wounde
His hoary haire, and through the bloud effused on the ground
Of his slaine sonne, the trembling King doth to an Aultar draw,
And in his right hand over him his sword keepes him in aw:
Before that place where he so lute Polytes bloud had spilt

He thrust his sword into his sides up to the very hilt.
See heare King Priamus end of all the troubles he had knowne,
Behold the period of his dayes which fortune did impone!"

It shall be "the period" also of what we will "impone" upon the reader. We have called it "Wrothovirgilian," because it is so much more like Wrothe than Virgil that, but for the annexation of the original on each opposite page, the similarity, at all events of style, would hardly have been traced; the incidents arc of course the same. It is to be wondered that the Knight ventured in this bold way to challenge comparison.

WYRLEY, WILLIAM.—The true Use of Armorie, shewed by Historie and plainly proved by example: die necessitie therof also discovered with the maner of differings in ancient time, the lawfulnes of honorable funerals and moniments: with other matters of Antiquitie, incident to the advauncing of Banners, Ensignes, and markes of noblenesse and chevalrie. By William Wyrley.—Imprinted at London, by J. Jackson, for Gabriell Cawood. 1592. 4to. B. L. 82 *leaves.*

This very dull and wearisome performance, of more than 160 quarto pages, has been called "a very valuable tract," (***Cens. Lit*** V. 70,) bat it really possesses no merit but of a technical kind, and the two long poems, of which it mainly consists, are about the worst performances in verse that appeared at a date remarkable for the excellence of its poetry. How Wyrley could have deceived himself into the belief that what he wrote in rhyme was deserving of the press, at a time Spenser, Daniel, Constable, and Watson (to say nothing of Shakspeare, who did not step beyond the precincts of the stage until the next year) were publishing their beautiful poems, it is not easy to imagine. Wyrley writes somewhat in the strain of the old "Mirror for Magistrates," which he names and extravagantly applauds; but his attempts are much below the standard established, thirty or forty years earlier, by that memorable historical miscellany. Wyrley commences with a prose dissertation on "the true use of Armory," with woodcuts of shields and quarterings; but, avowedly taking his facts from Froissart, he proceeds to give in verse, and in tedious detail, the main incidents of the careers of Lord Chandos, and the person whom he calls "the Captall," or "Capital de Buz." Here, too, he renders his narrative still more unreadable by the insertion, on every possible occasion, of a minute description, in miserable measure, of the armorial bearings of nearly every person he mentions. Take, for instance, the following stanza:—

"Sir William Mesnile a chiff of burnisht gold,
Three gemels finely set in axurd shield:
Sir Simon Barley six bars equall told
Of black and yellow in his cliffe he held,
Of the mettaile two pales as first is speld;
In midst a scuchion of rubie fairly dight,
In it three bars of ermins plainly pight."

He is never tired of such knots in the thread of his narrative. As the work was reprinted a few years ago, we shall not enter into it farther than to give a specimen of Wyrley's manner, when he wishes only to be poetical, and does not interrupt himself by armorial blazonry. The following is the last stanza of the poem on Lord Chandos, who, like the heroes of the "Mirror for Magistrates," narrates his own story, and applauds his own achievements:—

"As silent night brings quiet pawse at last
To painfull travels of forepassed day,
So closing death doth rest to labors cast,
Making of our toilfull worke a stay;
Thoughts, griefes, sad cares are bandon then away:
In pomp and glory though brave daies we spend,
Yet happie none untill be knowen his end."

We do not scruple to say, that the above is one of the best stanzas in the whole poem, and we like it the better because it is the end of that long-lengthened production. Of the many pages devoted to "the Capital de Buz," we shall say no more than that it somewhat reconciles the reader to the briefer account of his English rival. At the close of the whole we come to "the Envoy," of which the last stanza runs thus:—

"Almightie God, that oft hast England blest
With glorious triumphs over enemie,
In thy puissance victorie doth rest,
And not in mans weake plotting policie;
Give to our Captains their true chevalrie,
Like constant vertue, truth and courage bold,
That Chandos and the Captall true did hold.

"FINIS.

"WILLIAM WYRLEY."

The above seems to be the only extant performance that its author left behind him, and it has been greatly over-estimated by those who are better judges of coat-armor than of poetry.

YATES, JAMES.—The Hould of Humilitie: Adjoyned to the Castle of Courtesie. Compiled by James Yates Servingman.

Captious Conceipts, good Reader, doe dismis,
And friendly weigh this willing minde of his,
Which more doth write for pleasure then for praise,
Whose worthlesse workes are simply pend alwaies.

—London Imprinted by John Wolfe, dwelling in Distaffe Lane neere the Signe of the Castle. 4 to. B. L.

The precise terms of the entry of this very rare work in the Stationers' Register have, as far as we know, nowhere been given, and they are important as showing that, when the work was brought to the Hall, it consisted, or was intended to consist, of three parts. They were these,—

"vii. Die Junij. [1182]. John Wolfe. Item recived of him, &c. to printe a book intituled the Castell of curtesy, the holde of humility, and the Chariot of Chastity . . . . . viijd"

The cost of the license was eightpence (instead of 4d., the price of a ballad, or 6d., the price of a single work), on account of the three-fold character of the book. But, though licensed together, the parts do not appear to have come out together. "The Castle of Courtesie" must have appeared first, and it was followed by "the Hould of Humilitie"; so that the meaning of the title-page at the head of our Article is that the "Hould of Humilitie" was a sort of supplement to "the Castle of Courtesie." The volume before us includes a production not mentioned in the title-page, though noticed in the entry, and which has a separate title-page of its own, in the following words:—

"The Chariot of Chastitie, drawne to publication by Dutiful Desire, Goodwill and Commendation. Also a Dialogue between Diana and Venus. With Ditties devised at sundrie idle times for Recreation sake: Set downe in such wise as insueth by James Yatis.—London, Imprinted by John Wolfe. 1582."

Here the name of the author is spelt *Yatis* and not Yates, as elsewhere, a trifling circumstance, which we only mention for the sake of identification. This portion is separately dedicated to Mrs. Elizabeth Reynowls, and hence we learn that "The Castle of Courtesie," had been inscribed to her husband. The numbers of the folios and the signatures begin with "The Hould of Humilitie," and there can be no doubt that "The Castle of Courtesie," had been previously published with its own signatures and pagination. Herbert mistook the date, and gave it as 1581 (Herbert's Ames, II. 1186), but the entry of the book at Stationers' Hall was not made until June, 1582.

Sufficient specimens will be found in *Cens. Lit.* II. 11, in Bibl. Anglo. Poet 1815, p. 423, in Extr. from Stat. Reg. II. 165, and in other places; but as we never saw more than the copy in our hands, and as it appears to differ in some important respects, we will describe it with some particularity.

Although there is no date on the title-page, "1582" precedes the first poem in "the Hould of Humilitie," which itself occupies seven leaves; then follow miscellaneous pieces, some of them dated 1578. Hence we learn that Yates, or Yatis, lived in the country and had friends at Cambridge and Ipswich. On fol. 22, are "Verses upon this Theame—Silence breaketh many Friendeshippes: written unto his friende G. P. (*forsan* George Peele)."[Note 1: It seems unlikely that Peele would be meant by Yates, when he speaks of his "friend G. P."] There are also lines in pious commemoration of the Earthquake "on Wednesday 6 of April, 1580, betwene 5 and 6 of the clocke at night" After fol. 30 begins "The Chariot of Chastitie," with a new title-page, as we have already inserted it On fol. 60 is "Yates his song, written presently after his coming from London." On fol. 63 we have "an Epitaph upon the death of the wife of Mr. Pooly, of Badley"; and in a marginal note we are informed that she was sister to Lady Wentworth. The "Dialogue betwene Diana and Venus, declaring what can be alleaged of eyther side for confutation" may be seen reprinted in Extr. from the Stat Reg. II. 166, and need not here be repeated. Another piece is quoted in **Cens. Lit.** II. 13, and a third called "A Sonnet of a slaunderous Tongue," in **Bibl. Anglo-Poet.** p. 424. In the middle of the volume Yates pronounces his own "Verdict of his Booke," in which the reader, however patient, is not likely to concur. The best specimen of this "Servingman's" versification is unquestionably the controversy between the Goddesses of Chastity and Beauty. They end, however, as they began, without producing conviction on either side, for Venus exclaims in her last stanza,

"To prove perswations now with me
You shall but lose your time.
Farewell! A dew! Be honest still:
To Riotte I will clime."

And so the ladies separate. All Yates's performances have a didactic and moral turn, bat as poetry they have little to recommend them.

YOUNG, BARTHOLOMEW.—Amorous Fiammetta. Wherein is set downe a catalogue of all and singuler passions of Love and jealosie, incident to an enamored young Gentlewoman &c. First wrytten in Italian by Master John Boccace &c. and now done into English by B. Giovano del M. Temp. &c.—At London Printed by J. C. for Thomas Newman, &c. B. L. 4to. 131 *leaves.*

The copy of this book at Bridgewater House wants the date at the bottom of the title-page, which has been torn off, but at the end it is inserted, namely 1587. The translator was Bartholemew Young of the Middle Temple, as the name is given at length in the dedication to Sir William Hatton, which is not subcribed by Young, but by Thomas Newman. In what way Newman became possessed of the MS. is not stated. The seven books are concluded by a table of Contents.

Bartholemew Young had translated from the Spanish the "Diana" of Montemayor, and its continuations by Perez and Gil Polo in 1583, that date being given at the end of the printed copy which appeared in 1508. He had spent two years in Spain, and had no doubt travelled in other parts of Europe, as, besides Italian, he must have been well acquainted with French. In the dedication of the "Diana" to Lady Rich, he refers to the time when "in a public show at the Middle Temple," it fell to his lot "unworthily to perform the part of a French Orator, by a deducted speech in the same tongue." Young also translated the fourth book of Guazzo's "Civil Conversation," 4to. 1586. The three first books of the same work had been rendered by G. Pettie, and separately printed in 1581. They had been licensed to R. Watkins in 1579; and three years earlier the same stationer had put forth the same translator's "Petite Palace of Pettie his Pleasure," which was popular enough to be reprinted in 1598, and has been repeatedly noticed by bibliographers. It contains no poetry, and the twelve histories, chiefly classical subjects, are not related with any attractive vivacity.

ZEPHERIA.—Ogni di viene la sera.

Mysus et Hœmonia juvenis qui cuspide vulnus
Senserat, hac ipsa cuspide sensit opem.

—At London, Printed by the Widdowe Orwin for N. L. and John Busbie. 1594. 4to. 22 **leaves.**

We apprehend that this could never have been a very common book, and the author probably printed it to gratify his own taste and ambition, rather than the demands of any numerous body of readers. At present only two or, at most, three copies are known of it; but the late Mr. Utterson caused twelve inpressions of a reprint to be struck off from a most careless transcript, in which sometimes the old spelling is used and sometimes the new, while particular words, on which the meaning (such as it is) much depends, are grievously misrepresented. Thus in the very first "Canzon," out of forty of which the volume consists, we have **attempt** for "attemper," and **Lass** for **"Lais."** We need go no further in an ungracious task.

There is no dedication or address to the reader, but at the back of the title-page is a short list of **errata,** followed by a sort of appeal to the poets of the author's day, under the heading **Alli veri figlioli delle Muse,** but he obviously limits himself to sonnet-writers, of whom, to no inconsiderable extent, he was a rather poor imitator. "Delian sonnetrie" [Note 1: This epithet may have no personal reference, and only a general application to the poetry of the time and to the isle of Delos, as the birth place of Apollo and Diana. Still, "our Western Isle" cau only mean England, in and before 1594, famous for its sonnets and short pieces of graceful miscellaneous poetry.] in the poem question (which we extract) refers to Samuel Daniel's sonnets entitled "Delia," published, and republished in 1592:—

"Ye modern Laureats famousd for your writ,
Who for your pregnance may in Delos dwell,
On your sweete lines eternitie doth alt,
Their browes enobling with applause and laurel,
Triumph and honour ay invest your wit!
Ye fett your penns from wing of singing swanne
When, sweetely warbling to her selfe, she flotes
Adowne Meander streames, and like to organ

Imparts into her quils melodious notes.
Ye from the father of delicious phrases
Borrow such hymns as make your mistresse live
When time is dead: nay, Hermes tunes the praises
Which ye in sonnets to your mistresse give,
Report throughout our westerne isle doth ring
The sweete tun'd accents of your Delian sonnetrie,
Which to Apollos violine ye sing:
Oh then your high straines drowne his melodie!
From forth dead sleepe of everlasting dark
Fame with her trumps shrill summon hath awakt
The Roman Naso and the Tuskan Petrarch,
Your spirit-ravishing lines to wonder at.
Oh theame befitting high-musd Astrophil!
He to your silverie songs lent sweetest touch,
Your songs th' immortall spirit of your quill.
Oh pardon! for my artlesse pen to[o] much
Doth dimme your glories through his infant skill.
Though may I not with you the spoyls devide
(Ye sacred of-spring of Mnemosyne)
Of endlesse praise which have your pens achiv'd,
(Your pens the trumps of immortallitie)
Yet be it leyfull that like mayines I bide,
Like brunts and scarres in your loves warfare,
And here, though in my home-spun verse, of them declare."

Here a meaning is only just discernible through a mist of bad measure and imperfect rhymes; and although now and then the unknown author (for no name has been hinted at) writes tolerably smoothly, yet in his best pieces his want of ear is constantly making itself apparent It seems that "Zepheria," was not his first poetical performance, for he speaks of others deserving commendation and acceptance, as in the following, where he mentions a Pastoral which he had sent to his mistress. We quote it with this preface,—that it is unquestionably, on all accounts, the best piece in the volume:—

"Canzon II.

"How wert thou pleased with my pastorall Ode
(Which late I sent thee) wherein I, thy Swayne,
In rurall tune on pipe did chaunt abroad
Thee for the loveliest lass that trac'd the playne!
There on thy head I Floras chaplet placed;
There did my pen proclayme thee Sommers Queene:
Each heard-groome with that honor held thee graced,
When lawnie white did checker with thy greene.
There did I bargayne all my kids to thee,
My spotted lambkins, choysest of my fold,
So wouldst thou sit and keepe thy flock by me;
So much I joy'd thy beautie to behold.
How many Cantons then I sent to thee,
Who though on two strings onely rays'd their strayne,
To wit my griefe and thy unmatched beautie,
Yet well their harmonie couth please thy vayne:
Well couth they please thee, and thou terme them wittie;
But now, as fortunes change so change my dittie."

Part of a single sonnet is quoted in **Cens. Lit.** II. 63, but the writer, as usual, does not express any opinion as to merit, but observes that the author "displays a good deal of mythological learning." It so happens, that the writer of Zepheria is more free from that sort of pedantry than most of his contemporaries. We do not find the production before us quoted, or even alluded to, by any of the poets, pamphleteers, or critics of the day. Like many bad, as well as good, poets, he fancied that his lines would give immortality to the object of his affections, and, anticipating her death, he says:—

"Yet then in these limn'd lines enobled more

Thou shalt survive richer accomplisht than before.

How he proposed to read the last line, so as to make it measure, we cannot pretend to determine. His best praise is that he was less of a plagiary than several sonnetteers who wrote better verses.

For instance, B. Griffin, whose "Fidessa," 1596, has been reprinted in modern times, and who stole a whole sonnet (with some variations) from Shakspeare. His thefts from Daniel and others have not been remarked upon, because they are not quite so barefaced, bat they are quite as certain: compare Griffin's

"Care-charmer sleepe, sweet case in resties raiserie,"

with Daniel's

"Care-charmer sleepe, sonne of the sable night;"

and Griffin's,

"I have not spent the Aprill of my time,"

with Daniel's

"The starre of my mishappe impos'd this payning,
To spend the Aprill of my yeers in wayling."

All the thoughts and images used by Griffin, in his sonnet beginning—

"My Ladies haire is threads of beaten gold,"

are borrowed from Daniel, and almost in the same words; thus, for

"Her blush Aurora or the morning skye"

of Griffin, we read in Daniel

"Restore thy blush onto Aurora bright;"

and for

"Her feete faire Thetis praiseth evermore"

of Griffin, Daniel has

"To Thetis give the honour of thy feete,"

and many more almost identical imitations, if we may so call them. However the most glaring plagiarism, after that from Shakspeare, is from an older poet, Gascoigne. In Griffin it begins with these lines:—

"Arraign'd, poore captive, at the barre I stand,
The barre of Beautie, barre of all my joyes,
And I hold up my ever-trembling hand."

Gascoigne commences thus, without Griffin's paltry pun:—

"At Beautyes barre as I did stand,
When false Suspect accused mee,
George, (quoth the Judge) holde up thy hande," &c.

Griffin, as he proceeds, spoils various points in Gascoigne's spirited lyric; and throughout "Fidessa" he lays other poets under contribution, whenever their thoughts or language suit his purpose. We do not wish to press this matter further, but when we see a man thus unconscientiously (certainly not unconsciously) begging, borrowing, and stealing from his contemporaries, in order to make up a small volume of poor sonnets, we need not hesitate long in deciding that Griffin was indebted to Shakspeare and not Shakspeare to Griffin, although the latter appeared in print in 1596, and Shakspeare's sonnet was, probably, not in print (though this is doubtful) until it came out in "The Passionate Pilgrim," in 1599.

We may add that the reprint of Griffin's "Fidessa," in 1815, is one of the most accurate that has fallen in our way; but it has this singular defect, that the list of "Faults escaped" of the old edition is omitted, while the blunders it was intended to set right are carefully preserved in the text Thus, the author is made to speak more nonsense than need be attributed to him, and his corrections are nowhere to be found.

Of B. Griffin, his occupation, birthplace or acquirements, nothing is known; and if (as some have conjectured) his "Fidessa," of 1596, followed an earlier impression of "The Passionate Pilgrim" than any that has come down to us, it is most likely that his sonnet—

"Venus and yong Adonis sitting by her," &c.,

was copied from that earlier impression; if not, Griffin must have seen it in manuscript Daniel's "Delia," from which, unquestionably, Griffin derived much assistance, had been twice published as early as 1592. (See Vol. I. p. 210.)

The Codes Of Hammurabi And Moses
W. W. Davies

QTY

The discovery of the Hammurabi Code is one of the greatest achievements of archaeology, and is of paramount interest, not only to the student of the Bible, but also to all those interested in ancient history...

Religion   **ISBN:** *1-59462-338-4*

Pages:132
MSRP $12.95

The Theory of Moral Sentiments
Adam Smith

QTY

This work from 1749. contains original theories of conscience amd moral judgment and it is the foundation for systemof morals.

Philosophy   **ISBN:** *1-59462-777-0*

Pages:536
MSRP $19.95

Jessica's First Prayer
Hesba Stretton

QTY

In a screened and secluded corner of one of the many railway-bridges which span the streets of London there could be seen a few years ago, from five o'clock every morning until half past eight, a tidily set-out coffee-stall, consisting of a trestle and board, upon which stood two large tin cans, with a small fire of charcoal burning under each so as to keep the coffee boiling during the early hours of the morning when the work-people were thronging into the city on their way to their daily toil...

Childrens   **ISBN:** *1-59462-373-2*

Pages:84
MSRP $9.95

My Life and Work
Henry Ford

QTY

Henry Ford revolutionized the world with his implementation of mass production for the Model T automobile. Gain valuable business insight into his life and work with his own auto-biography... "We have only started on our development of our country we have not as yet, with all our talk of wonderful progress, done more than scratch the surface. The progress has been wonderful enough but..."

Biographies/   **ISBN:** *1-59462-198-5*

Pages:300
MSRP $21.95

The Art of Cross-Examination
Francis Wellman

QTY

I presume it is the experience of every author, after his first book is published upon an important subject, to be almost overwhelmed with a wealth of ideas and illustrations which could readily have been included in his book, and which to his own mind, at least, seem to make a second edition inevitable. Such certainly was the case with me; and when the first edition had reached its sixth impression in five months, I rejoiced to learn that it seemed to my publishers that the book had met with a sufficiently favorable reception to justify a second and considerably enlarged edition. ..

Pages:412

Reference   **ISBN:** *1-59462-647-2*   *MSRP $19.95*

On the Duty of Civil Disobedience
Henry David Thoreau

QTY

Thoreau wrote his famous essay, On the Duty of Civil Disobedience, as a protest against an unjust but popular war and the immoral but popular institution of slave-owning. He did more than write—he declined to pay his taxes, and was hauled off to gaol in consequence. Who can say how much this refusal of his hastened the end of the war and of slavery ?

Law   **ISBN:** *1-59462-747-9*

Pages:48
MSRP $7.45

Dream Psychology Psychoanalysis for Beginners
Sigmund Freud

QTY

Sigmund Freud, born Sigismund Schlomo Freud (May 6, 1856 - September 23, 1939), was a Jewish-Austrian neurologist and psychiatrist who co-founded the psychoanalytic school of psychology. Freud is best known for his theories of the unconscious mind, especially involving the mechanism of repression; his redefinition of sexual desire as mobile and directed towards a wide variety of objects; and his therapeutic techniques, especially his understanding of transference in the therapeutic relationship and the presumed value of dreams as sources of insight into unconscious desires.

Pages:196

Psychology   **ISBN:** *1-59462-905-6*   *MSRP $15.45*

The Miracle of Right Thought
Orison Swett Marden

QTY

Believe with all of your heart that you will do what you were made to do. When the mind has once formed the habit of holding cheerful, happy, prosperous pictures, it will not be easy to form the opposite habit. It does not matter how improbable or how far away this realization may see, or how dark the prospects may be, if we visualize them as best we can, as vividly as possible, hold tenaciously to them and vigorously struggle to attain them, they will gradually become actualized, realized in the life. But a desire, a longing without endeavor, a yearning abandoned or held indifferently will vanish without realization.

Pages:360

Self Help   **ISBN:** *1-59462-644-8*   *MSRP $25.45*

☐ **The Rosicrucian Cosmo-Conception Mystic Christianity** *by Max Heindel*   ISBN: *1-59462-188-8* **$38.95**
The Rosicrucian Cosmo-conception is not dogmatic, neither does it appeal to any other authority than the reason of the student. It is: not controversial, but is: sent forth in the, hope that it may help to clear...   New Age/Religion Pages 646

☐ **Abandonment To Divine Providence** *by Jean-Pierre de Caussade*   ISBN: *1-59462-228-0* **$25.95**
"The Rev. Jean Pierre de Caussade was one of the most remarkable spiritual writers of the Society of Jesus in France in the 18th Century. His death took place at Toulouse in 1751. His works have gone through many editions and have been republished...   Inspirational/Religion Pages 400

☐ **Mental Chemistry** *by Charles Haanel*   ISBN: *1-59462-192-6* **$23.95**
Mental Chemistry allows the change of material conditions by combining and appropriately utilizing the power of the mind. Much like applied chemistry creates something new and unique out of careful combinations of chemicals the mastery of mental chemistry...   New Age Pages 354

☐ **The Letters of Robert Browning and Elizabeth Barret Barrett 1845-1846 vol II**   ISBN: *1-59462-193-4* **$35.95**
by Robert Browning and Elizabeth Barrett   Biographies Pages 596

☐ **Gleanings In Genesis (volume I)** *by Arthur W. Pink*   ISBN: *1-59462-130-6* **$27.45**
Appropriately has Genesis been termed "the seed plot of the Bible" for in it we have, in germ form, almost all of the great doctrines which are afterwards fully developed in the books of Scripture which follow...   Religion/Inspirational Pages 420

☐ **The Master Key** *by L. W. de Laurence*   ISBN: *1-59462-001-6* **$30.95**
In no branch of human knowledge has there been a more lively increase of the spirit of research during the past few years than in the study of Psychology, Concentration and Mental Discipline. The requests for authentic lessons in Thought Control, Mental Discipline and...   New Age/Business Pages 422

☐ **The Lesser Key Of Solomon Goetia** *by L. W. de Laurence*   ISBN: *1-59462-092-X* **$9.95**
This translation of the first book of the "Lernegton" which is now for the first time made accessible to students of Talismanic Magic was done, after careful collation and edition, from numerous Ancient Manuscripts in Hebrew, Latin, and French...   New Age/Occult Pages 92

☐ **Rubaiyat Of Omar Khayyam** *by Edward Fitzgerald*   ISBN: *1-59462-332-5* **$13.95**
Edward Fitzgerald, whom the world has already learned, in spite of his own efforts to remain within the shadow of anonymity, to look upon as one of the rarest poets of the century, was born at Bredfield, in Suffolk, on the 31st of March, 1809. He was the third son of John Purcell...   Music Pages 172

☐ **Ancient Law** *by Henry Maine*   ISBN: *1-59462-128-4* **$29.95**
The chief object of the following pages is to indicate some of the earliest ideas of mankind, as they are reflected in Ancient Law, and to point out the relation of those ideas to modern thought.   Religiom/History Pages 452

☐ **Far-Away Stories** *by William J. Locke*   ISBN: *1-59462-129-2* **$19.45**
"Good wine needs no bush, but a collection of mixed vintages does. And this book is just such a collection. Some of the stories I do not want to remain buried for ever in the museum files of dead magazine-numbers an author's not unpardonable vanity..."   Fiction Pages 272

☐ **Life of David Crockett** *by David Crockett*   ISBN: *1-59462-250-7* **$27.45**
"Colonel David Crockett was one of the most remarkable men of the times in which he lived. Born in humble life, but gifted with a strong will, an indomitable courage, and unremitting perseverance...   Biographies/New Age Pages 424

☐ **Lip-Reading** *by Edward Nitchie*   ISBN: *1-59462-206-X* **$25.95**
Edward B. Nitchie, founder of the New York School for the Hard of Hearing, now the Nitchie School of Lip-Reading, Inc, wrote "LIP-READING Principles and Practice". The development and perfecting of this meritorious work on lip-reading was an undertaking...   How-to Pages 400

☐ **A Handbook of Suggestive Therapeutics, Applied Hypnotism, Psychic Science**   ISBN: *1-59462-214-0* **$24.95**
by Henry Munro   Health/New Age/Health/Self-help Pages 376

☐ **A Doll's House: and Two Other Plays** *by Henrik Ibsen*   ISBN: *1-59462-112-8* **$19.95**
Henrik Ibsen created this classic when in revolutionary 1848 Rome. Introducing some striking concepts in playwriting for the realist genre, this play has been studied the world over.   Fiction/Classics/Plays 308

☐ **The Light of Asia** *by sir Edwin Arnold*   ISBN: *1-59462-204-3* **$13.95**
In this poetic masterpiece, Edwin Arnold describes the life and teachings of Buddha. The man who was to become known as Buddha to the world was born as Prince Gautama of India but he rejected the worldly riches and abandoned the reigns of power when...   Religion/History/Biographies Pages 170

☐ **The Complete Works of Guy de Maupassant** *by Guy de Maupassant*   ISBN: *1-59462-157-8* **$16.95**
"For days and days, nights and nights, I had dreamed of that first kiss which was to consecrate our engagement, and I knew not on what spot I should put my lips..."   Fiction/Classics Pages 240

☐ **The Art of Cross-Examination** *by Francis L. Wellman*   ISBN: *1-59462-309-0* **$26.95**
Written by a renowned trial lawyer, Wellman imparts his experience and uses case studies to explain how to use psychology to extract desired information through questioning.   How-to/Science/Reference Pages 408

☐ **Answered or Unanswered?** *by Louisa Vaughan*   ISBN: *1-59462-248-5* **$10.95**
Miracles of Faith in China   Religion Pages 112

☐ **The Edinburgh Lectures on Mental Science (1909)** *by Thomas*   ISBN: *1-59462-008-3* **$11.95**
This book contains the substance of a course of lectures recently given by the writer in the Queen Street Hail, Edinburgh. Its purpose is to indicate the Natural Principles governing the relation between Mental Action and Material Conditions...   New Age/Psychology Pages 148

☐ **Ayesha** *by H. Rider Haggard*   ISBN: *1-59462-301-5* **$24.95**
Verily and indeed it is the unexpected that happens! Probably if there was one person upon the earth from whom the Editor of this, and of a certain previous history, did not expect to hear again...   Classics Pages 380

☐ **Ayala's Angel** *by Anthony Trollope*   ISBN: *1-59462-352-X* **$29.95**
The two girls were both pretty, but Lucy who was twenty-one who supposed to be simple and comparatively unattractive, whereas Ayala was credited, as her Bombwhat romantic name might show, with poetic charm and a taste for romance. Ayala when her father died was nineteen...   Fiction Pages 484

☐ **The American Commonwealth** *by James Bryce*   ISBN: *1-59462-286-8* **$34.45**
An interpretation of American democratic political theory. It examines political mechanics and society from the perspective of Scotsman James Bryce   Politics Pages 572

☐ **Stories of the Pilgrims** *by Margaret P. Pumphrey*   ISBN: *1-59462-116-0* **$17.95**
This book explores pilgrims religious oppression in England as well as their escape to Holland and eventual crossing to America on the Mayflower, and their early days in New England...   History Pages 268

QTY

The Fasting Cure *by Sinclair Upton*   ISBN: *1-59462-222-1*   **$13.95**

In the Cosmopolitan Magazine for May, 1910, and in the Contemporary Review (London) for April, 1910, I published an article dealing with my experiences in fasting. I have written a great many magazine articles, but never one which attracted so much attention... New Age/Self Help/Health Pages 164

Hebrew Astrology *by Sepharial*   ISBN: *1-59462-308-2*   **$13.45**

In these days of advanced thinking it is a matter of common observation that we have left many of the old landmarks behind and that we are now pressing forward to greater heights and to a wider horizon than that which represented the mind-content of our progenitors... Astrology Pages 144

Thought Vibration or The Law of Attraction in the Thought World   ISBN: *1-59462-127-6*   **$12.95**

by William Walker Atkinson   *Psychology/Religion Pages 144*

Optimism *by Helen Keller*   ISBN: *1-59462-108-X*   **$15.95**

Helen Keller was blind, deaf, and mute since 19 months old, yet famously learned how to overcome these handicaps, communicate with the world, and spread her lectures promoting optimism. An inspiring read for everyone... Biographies/Inspirational Pages 84

Sara Crewe *by Frances Burnett*   ISBN: *1-59462-360-0*   **$9.45**

In the first place, Miss Minchin lived in London. Her home was a large, dull, tall one, in a large, dull square, where all the houses were alike, and all the sparrows were alike, and where all the door-knockers made the same heavy sound... Childrens/Classic Pages 88

The Autobiography of Benjamin Franklin *by Benjamin Franklin*   ISBN: *1-59462-135-7*   **$24.95**

The Autobiography of Benjamin Franklin has probably been more extensively read than any other American historical work, and no other book of its kind has had such ups and downs of fortune. Franklin lived for many years in England, where he was agent... Biographies/History Pages 332

Name	
Email	
Telephone	
Address	
City, State ZIP	

☐ **Credit Card**   ☐ **Check / Money Order**

Credit Card Number	
Expiration Date	
Signature	

Please Mail to: Book Jungle
PO Box 2226
Champaign, IL 61825
or Fax to: 630-214-0564

www.ingramcontent.com/pod-product-compliance
Lightning Source LLC
Chambersburg PA
CBHW081143020726
47504CB00009B/1981